Alien Innkeeper on Particle

by

Roxanne Barbour

Out of This World, Book 2

Alien Innkeeper on Particle

Cover Art by *Debbie Taylor*

The Wild Rose Press, Inc.
PO Box 708
Adams Basin, NY 14410-0708
Visit us at www.thewildrosepress.com

Publishing History
First Edition, 2021
Trade Paperback ISBN 978-1-5092-3637-4
Digital ISBN 978-1-5092-3638-1

Out of This World, Book 2
Published in the United States of America

"Causing trouble, I see," I commented.

"Syl, find culprits. On hotel grounds." Teeka's Irion skin color was a lighter beige than normal.

"How many were there? What were they doing? What did you uncover to upset them?" I blurted out.

"Good questions asked," said an unknown Particlan.

"Syl, Sain, this is Vara il Vast, in charge of Teeka's case," said Hart, pointing at me and Sain. So Vara would understand the additional players in this tragedy, he added, "Sylvestine Amera is the new General Manager of the Sath-Ooby Golden Hotel, and Sain Sath was in charge of security for Dedare Sath on Irion."

"Questions asked," said Sain.

"Since I'm in charge of the Sath-Ooby Golden Hotel, I need questions answered," I said.

Vara gave me a look I assumed was disbelief. I had no idea what he didn't believe, but I didn't care.

"For example, have you found anything on the hotel video footage to indicate the culprits who did this to Teeka?"

"Footage not watched."

Typical Particlan three words. "Well, I'm going to watch my copy of the footage, and I'm sure Sain will be beside me. If we find anything, we'll be sure to let you know."

Vara didn't respond, but Hart gave me a calm down, Syl glance. Hart knew me well, and I had no trouble reading his facial expressions.

"Investigation not yours," said Vara.

"I'll do anything I need to do to protect my friends, family, and employees. And I'll try not to get in your way."

Chapter One

"Sweety, why did the Particlans throw those cups of water on me?" I asked. I shivered in my cold, soaked clothes. "I assume it's water."

After a day of rest, during which we recovered from traveling from the planet Irion to our new home base on the planet Particle, our party now stood in the reception area of the *Sath-Ooby Golden Hotel*.

My limited experience of intergalactic hotels, on Mars and Irion, had led me to believe every hotel had a front desk. However, our new hotel had numerous small desks scattered about and no large area for check-ins or check-outs. This arrangement reminded me of a travel agency on my home planet of Mars.

On Mars, a travel agent helped each customer or group at a desk to provide privacy for their inquiries. At the Sath-Ooby Golden Hotel, our receptionists offered the same privacy at their individual desks to guests checking in or inquiring about room availability.

Sweety Finn, my best friend in the entire world— well, many worlds now—shook her head, and her red ringlets bounced about her face. "Syl, you must have missed this water greeting in your briefing booklet."

I knew she wanted to utter a tsk, tsk but had probably decided this stressful time wasn't appropriate. "So, just tell me," I commented, trying not to let an exasperated sigh escape my dripping body. I wondered what else I'd missed—although I'd had plenty of time to study the briefing booklet on the trip from Irion to Particle. After we'd discovered my allergy to the cryostasis drug, I hadn't joined my friends in sleeping through the two-week journey.

"Sylvestine Amera," said Sweety. "Particle is a water world. So get used to having water around. By the way, having water thrown at you is a sign of respect. Apparently, the Particlans look forward to having you run the Sath-Ooby Golden Hotel."

Sweety's comments made me grin. A new hotel on a new world charged my excitement.

The inhabitants of Particle were humanoid with two arms and two legs. The webbing between their three fingers on each hand and three toes on each unadorned foot made me glance at their whole body and notice the webbing between their shoulders and head. Pictures in a briefing booklet didn't do justice to an up-close view.

Mottled skin, with a tinge of blue and almost unrecognizable scales, dominated my view. One Particlan stood closer to me than the others, and her hands were clasped together. A shiny substance appeared on her facial scales. Her voluminous curly black hair floated about her face.

Sweety smirked. She knew how difficult, yet rewarding, our first posting for Sath Enterprises on the planet Irion had been. She'd found the love of her life, as had I.

Mind you, her fiancé Hart Adair, now husband, was as much a Martian human as Sweety and I were, but my husband-to-be, Dedare Sath, was from another race—Irion. Both males had stood in Reception, along with my mother and father, and watched me be drenched.

Back to reality, I admonished myself. What was I supposed to do now, dripping water all over Reception's floor?

Sweety spoke to the audience of Particlans and aliens and saved my day. "Hey, everyone, your new manager's going to change her clothes. Our clothing doesn't repel water like your outfits do."

She twirled and caught the eyes of everyone in the room.

"I suspect we're going to look into acquiring new waterproof clothes. In the meantime, Manager Syl needs dry clothing. We'll be back in a moment."

The universal translators hanging around our necks had apparently provided proper translations because the closest Particlan hotel employee came forward in a rush.

"Upset I am. Problems to foresee. Forgiveness to bestow."

"You can't foresee every problem. And forgiveness is not necessary. We all make mistakes from ignorance."

"What is your name?"

"Cara ast Hembole," answered the Particlan.

"Do you work in Reception?" I suspected her hand movements were a sign of nervousness.

"Yes, I do."

"Cara, I'll be right back, and then I'll introduce myself to everyone. Thank you for the wonderful reception I've had so far."

Mom, Hart, Dedare, and Charles remained in Reception while Sweety and I scrambled to my new

Particlan accommodations.

The Sath-Ooby Golden Hotel had numerous five-story guest structures. Hart and Sweety shared a suite, my parents shared another, and I cohabited with Dedare and my teenaged soon-to-be stepdaughter, Reena. My time on Irion had brought many changes in my personal life.

Of course, there were two major ones, and I wasn't sure which one had had the more major impact.

Finding out on Irion that Charles Clarke, an ambassador from Earth, was my genetic father had hit me like a sledgehammer.

My mother and Charles had been a couple, shall we tactfully say. And after he'd left Mars for a diplomatic assignment on Earth, Mom had discovered her pregnancy but had decided not to tell him.

Our sojourn on Irion had helped us become a family unit.

And then there was my relationship with my fiancé Dedare Sath that had developed on his home planet, Irion.

Back in my suite I asked, "Sweety, what else do you know about this water ceremony?"

"I actually don't know anything. I was teasing when I said the materials briefing had a description."

"I guess I'd better harass Dedare about insufficient information." I laughed as I thought out loud.

"Lighten up, Syl. Dedare could only learn so much on his previous trip to Particle. That's the reason he brought the rest of us along. You know our job is to understand Particle—society, culture, the whole big picture—for Dedare, and ourselves, of course. And your job is to get this new hotel in peak running order."

Sweety shook her head at me.

"And I'm really looking forward to learning all about Particle. And in particular the people. I think they might be more fascinating than Irions. We had Dedare to help us on his home planet, but now we're going to have to dig deeper. Should be fascinating."

We grinned at each other.

"Okay, let me finish changing so we can go back to the reception, and I can begin unraveling my new life."

After I'd removed my sodden clothes, I turned to Sweety. "Do you think this Particlan water smells funny?" I held my top out to her, and she took a sniff.

"I don't think it's the water, Syl, because I know Dedare had it checked before we left Irion. Along with foodstuffs, he had many items analyzed." She took a longer sniff. "I suspect it's the combination of the Particlan water with your human fabric, producing a perfume you don't recognize. Nothing to worry about."

"You're probably right. I'm just anxious." I needed to put the food poisoning I'd experienced on Irion behind me. Of course, that situation had been deliberate—engineered by a disgruntled employee.

"How about my hair? What has this water done to it?"

"Nothing. Your hair is still as blonde and fuzzy as ever."

I had hoped the water would give me a measure of control over my hair. Oh, well.

In no time, Sweety and I were back at the main entrance of the Sath-Ooby Golden Hotel. I wasn't a hundred percent sure how the new name of the hotel had come about but Sath was Dedare's last name, and he loved using the word Golden in his hotel names. His new hotel was situated in Ooby, the capital of Particle, so the title Sath-Ooby Golden Hotel made sense.

My previous desire to be the best innkeeper on Mars had translated to the best innkeeper on Irion after Dedare snatched me from my hotel manager job at the Mars Best—Tycho Basin Hotel and transferred me to Irion. Learning about his home planet had not been an easy task, but it hadn't gone too badly—as long as we ignored my kidnapping and potential death. Now I was on another new planet, and I needed to focus so I could become the best innkeeper in Known Space—a lofty challenge.

Why had I focused on this goal? A topic I needed to consider.

I had to laugh. What challenges would confront me on Particle?

Mom approached after we returned to the lobby. "I've got everyone figured out, so your introductions should go smoothly," she said.

"Mama A, you're the best," said Sweety, giving her a squeeze.

My friends had gotten into the habit of calling Mom by the *Mama A* handle as our names were too similar—Sylvestine Amera for me, and Sylvia Amera for my mother.

Charles, my father, the ambassador to Particle for all humans, had apparently resumed his research on Particle during our day of rest and discovered Particlans had no objections to the shaking of hands.

So Mom had taught the motion of a handshake and the notion of it being a greeting to the Particlans while I'd changed.

The introductions overloaded my poor brain. Not

only were all the employees of Reception present, but personnel from other hotel departments were also in attendance.

"Sylvestine, I'd like you to meet Tarin et Tong, Dedare's co-owner of the Sath-Ooby Golden Hotel," said my mother.

Dedare had a co-owner? How would this Particlan affect my management of the hotel? I glanced at Dedare and gave him a look indicating *we'd talk later*.

When we traveled, I got older and my friends didn't because they were in the stasis pods. Although the captain and first officer were awake—not in stasis—during every trip, for the most part I had only myself with which to converse. Dedare's officers had little to say. Thankfully, our space excursions were of relatively short duration, the last being two weeks. Dedare's ships had little accommodation space, and since he spent a good portion of his life travelling from planet to planet, cryostasis had become the obvious solution to prolong Dedare's life. However, spending two weeks quizzing Dedare about Particle would have immensely helped my preparations.

I glanced at the people milling about Reception.

"Thanks for the greetings, everyone. Your very first action today was unusual to me, but I managed to survive." I smiled and hoped they understood my words.

The Particlans each produced a faint whistle, quite pleasant, and Mom whispered, "That's how they laugh."

I stared at her, and I wondered what else I didn't know. A new world? Most likely a mountain of details.

"I'll speak with each of you individually over the

next few days. Now, enjoy the party." I waved and hoped the gesture didn't trigger any taboos.

Most of the Particlans moved toward the food tables. The humans and Irions mingled with the Particlans, and we were thankful for the translators hanging around our necks. We'd had universal translators injected in our bodies on Irion but, for some reason, we had to go back to wearing pendants on Particle.

I suspected we'd have an in-depth debriefing tonight to share our insights from the reception.

The reception wound to its end as Particlans returned to their duties or left for their off time.

Before I had a chance to take a deep breath and decide on an action, Dedare and his co-owner escorted me and the other off-worlders to my new office.

"Sweety, Hart, Mama A, Charles, talk outside," said my terse Irion fiancé as he ushered them out. and joined them.

I assumed Dedare wanted to discuss their new duties.

So that left me in my new office with Tarin et Tong. I studied my new workplace, and a surreptitious glance discovered Tarin studying me.

"Settling in hard. Midday meal together. Tomorrow here room."

If my great deductive reasoning worked on the Particlan three-three-three speech pattern, I thought Tarin wanted to have lunch with me tomorrow here in my office. Or perhaps Tarin had a room in the hotel.

"At what time shall we meet here in my office?"

We came to an agreement after a bit of a fumble on my part understanding Particlan time.

After Tarin left, I studied my office. At first glance, the objects seemed typical of any office on any planet. I had a large desk with the top filled with an electronic object indicative of a computer. A three-legged stool, like those in Reception, sat in front of the computer device.

The color tones ranged from dark-brown to light-beige. A glaring shiny blue conference table, taking up half the office space, was the exception.

The color scheme struck me as odd, so I decided to take the time to analyze the color schemes in other areas as I learned about my new hotel.

The Particlan day had grown late, and since no food for off-worlders had been available at the reception, my stomach informed me dinner time was near.

However, my priority needed to be making arrangements for the next day. Accordingly, I left my new office and walked to Reception.

"Hello, Cara ast Hembole." I remembered a good portion of the names of my staff, and Mom had made a list of their three-part names.

"Greetings, Ms. Amera. Working together excellent. Much to learn."

I decided Dedare's translator worked extremely well. I remembered Cara had been the Particlan upset after my water greeting, so I decided she needed reassurance.

"Cara, I need to learn how Reservations runs. Are you the Manager?"

"Agreed Manager status."

I suddenly realized three words were the new mantra.

More analysis would be required, but I suspected Particlans spoke in three-word bites. Or perhaps three bites of three words each. An interesting concept.

"May I follow you around tomorrow morning while you're doing your normal day's work?"

She twirled her right hand.

"Cara, does that motion of your hand indicate agreement?"

She glanced at her hand, and then at me.

"Physical reactions unique. Impossible to understand. This occasion, yes."

I decided I'd correctly interpreted her Particlan physical action.

"Good. Then, in the afternoon I'd like to see a few parts of the hotel. I need to get an overview of how the departments fit together."

She took a few moments to understand my words.

"Morning my work? Afternoon the hotel? This evening curious?"

"You've understood my words very well. This evening I'll relax in my room and think about all I experienced today. Particle is all so new to me—Particlans, the hotel, and the world itself."

Her blue skin darkened, which made her faint scales stand out, but I was sure I'd noticed pleasure in her dark eyes. I hoped her enthusiasm continued.

****

The next morning, I arrived early to my office and spent an enjoyable hour acquainting myself with all its attributes. With the help of Hart, I added a healthy dose of computer learning.

Hart left to pursue his own activities.

Cara appeared in my office doorway. "Time

Reception orientation."

That's right. I'd asked for a review of her management.

I spent a pleasant morning greeting and chatting with employees and understanding how Reception operated. The time also gave me a glimpse into other facets of the Sath-Ooby Golden Hotel, including a glimmer of how the departments fit together.

The structure of the Reception area appeared pretty straightforward—everyone reported to Cara. She arranged work schedules, applied for salary increases, and other management duties. I needed to look into the hotel's complete structure before I could even fathom if changes were needed.

I settled in my office and readied myself to tackle my computer—without Hart's help—when I noticed Tarin et Tong standing in my office doorway along with a hovering Cara.

Oh crap! I'd been so busy I'd forgotten about my lunch date with Tarin.

Chapter Two

"Tarin, please come in. Have a seat." I gestured to my conference table.

I gave Cara a glance of entreaty. "Is the food we ordered on its way?" I hoped she understood the importance of my question and didn't let out I'd forgotten about the lunch meeting.

"I will inquire." Cara scurried out.

I walked over and seated myself across from the co-owner of the Sath-Ooby Golden Hotel. "I hope you don't mind, but I had Cara order food."

Tarin didn't speak. We sat in silence.

Upon her return, Cara said, "Food soon arrive. Checked on quality. Understand food requirements."

Good. Cara had grasped my entreaty and backed up my memory lapse.

The food arrived within seconds of her comments, and the items were placed on my conference table.

After Cara disappeared, Tarin helped himself to sustenance.

"How shall I address you? Is Tarin appropriate?" I'd be feeling my way through Particlan culture for months to come.

"Tarin appellation correct."

"Do you have any questions?" I asked while I grabbed my own lunch. Cara had ordered interesting dishes, and Particlan and human food items were clearly separated.

"Background history required."

I decided not to take offense from his words. On first analysis I'd heard an order, but then I remembered Tarin was co-owner of the hotel.

"I'm from a planet called Mars. Although I call myself a Martian, I'm basically a human from our home planet, Earth."

"Home planet confusing," said Tarin.

I explained our species had sprung forth on Earth and then explored and settled other locations in our solar system. I went on to describe my previous position as the manager of the Mars Best—Tycho Basin hotel.

"Then Dedare came to visit Mars, and at the end of his stay talked me into moving to Irion to run his hotel, the Sath-Satre Golden Hotel. And now I'm here to run the Sath-Ooby Golden Hotel."

I decided not to reveal any information about the other Martians and Irions in our group—he could find out for himself.

"Any other information you require, Tarin?"

"Not this time."

When he didn't continue, I said, "I have an inquiry, Tarin."

He made a circle with his right hand, a gesture I assumed meant proceed.

"Cara told me this office," I said, waving my own right hand around the room, "was used by the previous general manager. Is General Manager my new title?" And I wondered what information, erroneous or not, my waving hand had imparted.

Tarin paused and then said, "Discuss with Dedare."

Much to my surprise, he abruptly stood and stomped out.

Had I offended my new Particlan boss? Time would tell. After all, I'd upset Dedare many a time in our recent past and lived to tell the story.

Most of the offenses had involved me trying to run the Sath-Satre Golden Hotel in a more efficient manner.

Of course, my human notions had run into resistance, and not only from Dedare. Everything had worked out well in the end. Hart and Sweety were married. My mother and father had found each other again. And Dedare and I had formed a romantic relationship.

I hoped Dedare and I would have time tonight to discuss issues that had emerged during my brief time on Particle. And I really wanted some private together time. My Irion fiancé and I needed to strengthen our bond before we took our relationship to a new level.

I took a breather at my desk and reflected on what I'd learned so far on Particle. Then Cara joined me.

"Where are we going this afternoon?" I needed a break from hotel owners.

"Recording studio room. Flying roof landings. Organic growth elevator."

I only understood a portion of her words, so I decided to let the tour clear up any confusion rather than inundate Cara with questions before we had even started.

At the start of my tour, Cara led me to a door resembling a human elevator. The inside walls, which appeared to be made of a glass-like material, shone with a green tinge. An unfamiliar spicy aroma greeted me.

"Are we going up or down?"

"Up to highest," replied Cara.

I waited for two more segments of three words from Cara, but they weren't forthcoming. Apparently, only three words also satisfied the Particlan speech patterns and their inherent world structure.

Thankfully, the elevator walls darkened as we ascended. "Do the walls also darken as the elevator descends?" Heights bothered me.

"Always they do." I received a glance I thought implied *why wouldn't they?*

We ended up in a room giving the appearance of a human high-tech studio.

Shiny equipment equipped with blinking lights lined the walls—although one wall was blank and had a table with stools positioned in front. Most of the equipment eluded my understanding, but I certainly recognized technicians moving about the large room and enjoying their work.

"What does the hotel record here?" I asked Cara.

"Room information packet. Sent to displays. Guests to watch."

Hmm, so a commercial about the hotel was available in each room, if I'd understood her words. Not bad.

"What else do we record?" I saw a huge messy tangle of equipment which seemed a bit overkill for a simple information packet for hotel guests.

"General public information. Sales to access. Public and worldview."

I took a few moments to understand her words. "Do you mean you make commercials so other broadcasting facilities can spread the word about the Sath-Ooby Golden Hotel?"

"Yes, the word," said Cara, giving me a wide smile.

I'd correctly figured out her interpretation, but I wasn't too enthralled with *spreading the word.* Almost sounded evangelical.

Cara introduced me to the studio staff, and after a quick examination of the equipment we moved on.

While we journeyed to our next destination, I pondered other uses for the room. Perhaps Hart could produce a variety of scientific videos or Sweety could create cultural videos about Mars to educate the Particlans, and Mom, the writer, could indulge in teaching the inhabitants her take on the history of Sath Enterprises.

However, I suspected the studio would be primarily Hart's domain. We'd need further discussions with Dedare about topics to be recorded since a few areas might be off limits. Perhaps tonight Dedare and I'd find a bit of discussion time. I had no idea what topics had occupied his energy today.

"Where are we going now?" I asked Cara. Her anxiety to get on with the schedule showed.

"Up to roof."

I remembered *flying roof landings* was next on the list Cara had earlier vocalized. Since we were on the top floor of our building, the roof should be close by.

After the elevator doors opened, we emerged onto the Sath-Ooby Golden Hotel's roof.

A spectacular view of the city of Ooby surrounded me. And the flying machine, or perhaps I should say helicopter, landing made a once-in-a-lifetime moment. If only I'd had a camera to record the image.

"Cara, what transpires on this roof? What is that wonderful machine landing?"

"Landings for food. Landings for equipment. Landings for guests."

Another glance at Ooby's airspace confirmed I hadn't recognized how much was occupied with flying machines. I tried to differentiate the numerous types and volumes. Cargo planes were evident, as were personal flying vehicles. Of course, there were odd types for which I had no inkling of their purpose. The bulb with wings particularly interested me. Did Particle lean toward being an aerial world?

"What about the ground? Do you have deliveries to the lowest floor of the hotel?" I suspected my questions confused Cara and perhaps also our universal translator.

"Deliveries on ground. Similar to roof. Why is question?"

Why indeed? I had no information regarding the cost of deliveries, the cost of staffing to accept the deliveries, and such. Did the hotel own the planes delivering to our roof? Did we own the ground vehicles? How could I tell if air deliveries were efficient?

"Do I have access to a helicopter to see Ooby and other areas?" My excitement began to grow—I had a new planet to discover and possibly a wonderful way of access.

"Yes, manager plane. Ready at once. Yours to command."

I grinned. Her words were clear, and a delight. "Tomorrow, would you take me on a tour of the surrounding areas? How much room is there? Can my friends join us?"

Cara uttered a faint whistle—a Particlan laugh.

"Plenty of room. Itinerary to ponder. Early start good."

I needed to speak with everyone tonight about my proposed adventure.

Then I realized what I'd arranged—a helicopter flight.

Would my fear of heights manifest itself? Would I lie on the floor of the passenger compartment and refuse to talk to anyone? Would I be so anxious I'd end up in the hospital?

Were there any hospitals on Particle? Would they know how to treat humans? Hart had better be on the helicopter tomorrow. He was the only one on this planet who knew how to treat me.

"Would you make up the itinerary for tomorrow's trip? Then I can let everyone know tonight what we're going to see." The tour would be a great introduction to Ooby and the surrounding areas for all of us.

"Send to you. After finish today. Changes be quick."

"We won't need changes—you'll plan the perfect introduction to Ooby." Her facial expression—a wide smile I could already recognize—told me she'd received my compliment. A great start to tomorrow's adventure.

"Will our plane hold all the Martians and Irions you saw today? My friends? How big is it?" I didn't want to leave anyone behind.

Had I already asked her that? I really needed to focus.

"Adequate for all. Any changes advise. Tonight is best."

"I'll talk to my friends after we gather for dinner. Are we going to your third topic now?" Much as today's tour had so far been enlightening, I wanted to get back and soak up non-Particlan conversation. My long day had led my energy level downwards toward zero.

"Organic growth elevator. Last on tour. Little travel needed."

I followed Cara to the elevator we'd used to access the roof. She ushered me inside and then entered instructions on the keypad. Cara hadn't done that before, so her action intrigued me.

"Why did you use the keypad?"

Her glance informed me my question imparted minimal information, so I resisted a second try. More words would only add to Cara's confusion. I took a couple of deep breaths and waited.

After a moment, she ushered me out of our current elevator and into another.

"Organic growth elevator," were her three words.

What did that mean? I had a feeling Cara wasn't being deliberately obtuse, but why didn't I understand?

I tried to stay calm. As the doors closed, I studied this new elevator and found no apparent difference from the elevators I'd previously encountered on Particle.

Then that changed and the windows popped clear. I slouched against the elevator door and saw greenery on the left and right sides and an expansive view before me.

"Cara?" I hoped she'd understand my one-worded question, and it turned out she did.

"Grow hotel sustenance. Elevator provides access. Employees to maintain."

Hotel sustenance? "Can we go outside? Outside the elevator, I mean?"

Cara pointed to a door hugging one wall, and then I noticed a similar door on the opposite side. Access to the greenery? The third side offered a spectacular view.

I laughed. What a comedown when the greenery outshone a fantastic view.

"Is this food for the hotel?" I assumed *grow hotel sustenance* meant they grew greenery for the kitchen. If true, hotels on Irion and Particle were further advanced in providing their own food than our Martian hotels.

"Most greenery grown. More to add. Independence is hard."

"I can only imagine. Do other hotels in Ooby grow food?" I wondered if the Sath-Ooby Golden Hotel had leaped ahead of its competitors.

"All lesser extent," said Cara. "Now to explore?"

"Sure." I grinned. "What should I do?"

Cara pointed to one of the doors and then opened it and stepped out onto a platform.

With small, timid steps I followed her outside. Safety relieved me as the platform I placed my feet onto had a high railing giving one hundred percent protection from any accidental fall. So I relaxed—at least somewhat.

The vegetation within my view had a slight hint of blue. Because Particlans also did? Hart, our science advisor, had numerous questions to research, and one of them was the genetic code of Particle.

"Do you think I'll be able to eat these greens?" I asked Cara.

"Head botanist, Slia est Parcet. Communicate with advisors. Hart to reveal."

So Hart already had a Particlan contact and project. Good for him. I'd really like to sample a few Particlan delicacies during our stay.

"What a great place, Cara. Are our hotel guests allowed to visit the organic growth?" I had no other way to describe the greenery before me.

"Only specific tours. Guest viewing area. Available level one."

"Would you mind showing me this guest viewing area? And then I think we're done for the day. I don't know about you, but I'm running out of energy."

"Past home time. Many times late. Part of job." Cara's face sported a huge smile.

I'd acquired an excellent employee. She'd certainly accommodated my every request during our travels today.

Cara and I traipsed to the guest area. Slowly because I tried to study everything as we traveled. I'd found a wonderful place!

The ground floor of the building was open to the Particlan environment. Abundant plants were strategically placed. A rectangular pool of water occupied the center of the guest area. And Cara told me parking spots on this level were also available.

"Is this a swimming pool?"

"A confusing word. Let me inquire. For other versions."

I watched Cara try to digest the translator's offerings for her inquiry. I listened and wondered at a few of the options offered. I heard a couple of strange interpretations from Dedare's translator. Then I believed I saw understanding on Cara's face.

"We have contests. Most water sports. Every two cycles."

I understood *water sports* but I'd have to research what she meant by *cycle*. I suspected cycle meant a year, or the equivalent. I had many questions for Hart.

The hotel guests in the pool area came forward and surrounded me.

What was going on? What should I do? I glanced at Cara, but the smile on her face wasn't particularly informative.

Once again, water drenched me.

Chapter Three

The Particlan hotel guests stood in a group and sported huge smiles.

I threw out my arms. "Thank you for your warm and wet welcome." I laughed. "If you have any questions regarding the aliens now in this hotel, please visit me. I'm the general manager of the hotel, and I'd love to talk with each of you."

The hotel guests strolled up and, one by one, patted my wet hair and then moved on without a word.

After the last guest left our vicinity, I spoke to Cara. "Have Particlans met aliens before?"

"Yes, one time."

"Who were they? What can you tell me about them?" Another race—how exciting.

"Talk to diplomats. Not to say, information from me."

Her words and demeanor appeared firm. Why would she not reveal anything?

"The pool must help the plants grow," I suggested to Cara, attempting to change the subject.

Her glance conveyed confusion.

"Growth unknown me. Not expert botany. Introduce to botanists."

"Hart may have already found out many of the answers to my questions, but I'll let you know if I need a follow up."

Cara still seemed to have a question in her eyes. "What's the problem?"

"What all know. What all want. Understanding or confusion?"

This time her words made me ponder my own. "I'm interested in many things. Is that what you're asking?"

She wiggled her head side to side—a movement I took as a yes.

"Small topic normal. Focus on details. Broad emphasis unusual."

"I like many topics. For one thing, information helps me understand the different types of people I meet. Many details also help me recognize what I might need to know about Particlans to make the hotel function well. Your tours are very useful. Please continue to introduce me to as many new ideas as you can."

Cara appeared pleased by my words, and a wide smile covered her face. We continued our tour of the open floor area. A number of guests were using the pool and others wandered about the greenery.

We received numerous glances as we toured. Perhaps some of them had welcomed me with the water ceremony, but I really couldn't tell. Perhaps this would be a suitable location where Martians and Irions mingle and educate Particlans.

As I stood and watched the swimmers, I was surprised by the lack of a chlorine smell. In fact, my nose indicated cinnamon. Probably not cinnamon as such, but certainly Hart could investigate their sterilization techniques.

The greenery around the pool varied from tiny blooms to large bushes. I suspected a pattern to their placement, but the gardener's design wasn't revealed.

I really needed to stop calling the vegetation greenery, but *blue-ery* didn't quite work.

Eventually we returned to our starting point and I said, "Thank you, Cara, for the tour. Have you thought about what we're going to see tomorrow?" I happily anticipated using my own helicopter.

"Surprises for everyone. List arrive soon. Advise if confused."

Her plan was manageable. "Would you take me back to Reception so I can meet my friends? We agreed to congregate there at the end of the day."

Cara laughed and pointed at the elevator. I suspected I could've found my own way back. I knew I already had a good understanding of the hotel layout, but Cara felt useful, I imagined.

Hart, Sweety, Mom, and Dedare were in Reception. "I hope no one's waited long."

"No, we all just arrived," answered my mother. "I had a wonderful time today researching in the hotel library. Time just flew."

I didn't know we had a hotel library. Hmm. I hoped Dedare had adjusted his Irion character reader to also translate Particlan written language.

"Hart, how was your day?" I asked.

"Questions asked, and many answered. I suggest we snuggle up in your rooms, order food, and discuss what we've all discovered today. Many hours should pleasantly pass."

I laughed. I loved Hart's suggestion. I glanced at Dedare.

He gave me a smile. "Food arranged, arrival shortly. Reconvene." Dedare made sure everyone understood his words. The Particlans were weird with their speech patterns, but the Irions used words economically, and that had led to past misunderstandings.

The group of us settled into the suite Dedare and I shared. Reena, Dedare's teenaged daughter, joined us. She occupied the second bedroom in our suite and had lived with us on Irion after Dedare and I'd gotten together.

"So, what've you been up to today?" I asked.

"Little. Unpacked and arranged."

Her face had an unsettled look, so I asked, "Did you go anywhere alone?" Our new home on Particle was too foreign to allow solo wanderings for a young, inexperienced person.

"No. Stayed here." Reena fidgeted on her stool.

Mom interrupted with a few words. "I acquired a little information about the Particlan school system today. I think I know where you'll fit in, Reena."

"Did you look into your schooling, Reena?" I asked after the young lady didn't respond to Mom's words.

"No." She avoided meeting anyone's eyes.

Guilt about doing nothing productive today was my first thought.

"Holiday from school?" Reena asked, a hopeful sound in her Irion voice.

"No, I don't think so," said my mother. "You and I'll see about your education tomorrow." Mom glance around. "If that's okay with you, Dedare?"

He smiled. "Perfect solution."

"Not fair. Too many mothers," protested Reena.

"Perfect solution," Dedare repeated. Reena didn't respond verbally, but her slumped back position on her stool indicated teenaged sulking, to my mind.

"Reena, have you ever been on a trip to a new world with your father?" I asked. She might have been too young for the experience, and she certainly hadn't been with Dedare when he'd come to Mars and recruited me for his Irion flagship hotel.

"No. Stay with uncle, Sain."

Another perfect solution—after the death of her mother. "Did you regularly go to school on Irion?" I knew she had been going to school during the Martians' recent stay on Irion.

"Yes. Proceeded through structure."

I assumed she meant she went through the Irion grades, or ranks.

"So now you get to decide what courses to take and where you fit in on a brand new world. I'd be excited. Actually, I think you and Mama A might have a difficult time deciding what's relevant, what you already know, and how you fit in with the Particlan age groups."

I glanced at my mother. "I don't envy you your task, Mom, but thanks for offering to help with Reena's schooling."

Grins appeared on everyone's faces, except for Reena and my mother.

I may have irritated the two of them. Nevertheless, Reena needed to go to school. She had an opportunity for excellent experiences on a new world, and she was old enough to enjoy the situation.

I caught Hart's eye, and he took my hint. "Today, while I focused on science, I learned many things about Particle."

"Do tell," said Sweety, his wife of a few months.

The newlyweds, Hart and Sweety, had individual attitudes to life that always made me smile. After they became a couple, their glow enhanced their enthusiasm. My two best friends.

"Give us something a little less vague," I directed. Hart's attention had drifted, and I wasn't sure whether the culprit was Sweety or his other love, science.

"Certainly. A good portion of Particlan science focuses on water. A water world has unique advantages, but also problems."

I spoke before Hart had a chance to continue. "But isn't Earth a water world? Wouldn't we have the same issues?"

"Not really. Earth has way more land mass than Particle, and Mars has little water and much more land mass, comparatively speaking. Mars and Earth are land-based worlds. Our understanding of Particlan problems may be skewed and lead to false conclusions."

"So give me a hint of one of their problems," I suggested, too tired for subtlety. "I need lots of detail. Your information may help decide my actions over the next few months." I also required a discussion with Dedare regarding his future plans because I needed to understand how long we'd stay on Particle.

"Okay. You've seen how all the buildings—at least most of them—are three stories of living space, one story of above ground parking space, with a bottom level that's open to the elements. Essentially their buildings are on stilts." Hart took a deep breath. "That's because of the planet's tectonics."

Hart stopped, then immediately started talking after I glared at him. "Tectonics create problems. Earthquakes, especially underwater, create waves, very tall and aggressive waves, especially in the right circumstances. Particle has a large number of underwater earthquakes every cycle, and they compensate by having the waves pass under the buildings." He sighed. "Don't get me wrong, but sometimes the upper levels of the buildings are also affected, but not often. Of course, any vehicles on the ground, and sometimes their vehicles on the first floor, may need servicing after an earthquake, but I believe they're making them more self-contained every year." Hart must have noticed my confusion because he added, "What I mean is they are trying to make them impermeable to earthquakes—like a submersible. Think submarine, but on land."

Hart had a way with words.

"I assume there are warnings when a tsunami is about to happen. How'll we know?" Mom worried about all of us.

"Outside sirens and also warning systems on their electronics. Of course, I haven't figured out all the electronics yet, but they assured me there'd be no conceivable way to miss notice of an imminent tsunami."

"How often do these waves appear?" I asked. For some reason, waves made me think of sports. Water sports were one of my favorites. After seeing the hotel pool, I decided we might be able to introduce an interesting activity or two to the Particlans.

"Approximately twelve times per Particlan cycle."

"You mean monthly?" I asked.

"Sort of. However, Particle doesn't have any moons, which I would consider the main reason for monthly cycles. One of my projects is to understand what produces the tsunamis."

Sweety and I glanced at each other. How would this affect our personal physical cycles? And, come to think of it, I had no idea what cycles Reena or any female Irion went through. Or even the males. And then there were the Particlans. Thank goodness, Hart had a science doctorate and was also an MD. These sorts of events were his babies, so to speak.

Before I had a chance to actually digest his words, our food arrived. Dedare proceeded to lay it out on the low table around which our stools had been placed.

"Dedare, what is this stuff?" I asked.

"Food edible by Martians and Irions."

"Well, I hope so. I'm really hungry, and some of this stuff isn't visually appealing."

Everyone laughed at my aversion to foreign food. There may have been an incident or two on Irion contributing to my opinions—being poisoned was one, and then there was the death of Chef Virem. Such sad memories. He had been such a good guy.

Despite my history, I loaded up my plate and sampled everything Dedare had provided, and the rest of the crew did also. So an unnatural silence filled our suite.

The metal cutlery we'd been given consisted of items similar to tongs and spoons. There were no forks to be seen. The food had been processed into small pieces, so using tongs to put items into our square-shaped bowls was easy. And for the most part spoons adequately conveyed the food to our mouths.

Finally, Sweety broke the silence. "Pretty good. I particularly love these purple, ah, eggs."

Sweety had the shape and color of the food right, but they weren't one of my favorites. "Well, I like the little green trees. Reminds me of broccoli, which is something I haven't had enough of since we left Mars. Frozen broccoli is adequate but doesn't add up to fresh produce. These little green trees, though, are fresh, and their flavor sparkles."

"How can a flavor sparkle?" asked my mother.

"Ah, like when you made lefse, that Scandinavian flat bread. When the mashed potatoes and salt were in the right amounts you could put any spread on the lefse and the combination would melt on your tongue."

"Maybe it was my exquisite cooking," commented Mom.

The Martians laughed, but Reena asked, "What is lefse?"

"It's a food we used to eat at home on Mars." I hoped my mother understood she'd let me down in recent years.

Mama A sighed. "Reena, it's a type of flat bread. It's rolled out into a round shape and cooked in a pan. When ready, you spread various condiments on the surface and then roll it up and eat it."

Reena glanced at Mom and then me. "I do not understand. Will you make lefse?"

"Of course. Once we're settled and I've investigated the cooking facilities and found the necessary ingredients, I'd love to make lefse. I'm not sure how authentic it will be here on Particle, but I hope you'll help me make them."

Reena grinned. Mom acted like a grandmother, and Reena lapped it up. I needed to remember to ask Dedare about grandparents. I hadn't even thought about his parents or his deceased wife's parents, and I certainly hadn't heard Reena or Sain, Dedare's brother, discuss them at any time.

"Sweety, what did you find on your wanderings today?" I asked.

We'd renamed my friend Sweety years ago because she called everyone Sweety.

For example, "Sweety, can you pass the salt? Sweety, I have a problem."

My friend really was a sweety, so she'd been adorned with a new first name, and she loved it, thank goodness.

"The strangest thing is that the hotel doesn't have a restaurant," Sweety answered in response regarding today's discoveries.

"We're going to starve to death," I replied.

Laughter erupted as my friends pointed at the food on my plate.

"Okay, maybe not starve to death. I may have exaggerated a little. Sweety, how do our guests get nourishment? How did we get this dinner?" A restaurant would be a reliable source of hotel revenue, I imagined.

"We have a tremendous kitchen taking up half the second floor of the main building. By the way, most guest accommodations are in the other attached buildings. The building where Reception resides contains the facilities necessary for running a hotel.

Thank goodness there's a quick transportation system connecting all structures."

Sweety looked at Dedare and continued. "You know, Sain could build an excellent restaurant. I'm not sure if there's room in the main building, but a large space could be easily attached. And I'm sure we'll be coming up with so many ideas you'll need a new five-story building to match all the others of this hotel."

Dedare laughed. "Will consider. Sain and Teeka arrive tomorrow. Discussion tomorrow night."

Sain was Dedare's brother, and Teeka was Dedare's friend, and a policeman I'd been attracted to on Irion. "Why is Teeka coming here? What about his job?" I asked. "And why Sain? Doesn't he have to look after the Sath-Satre Golden Hotel?"

"Under control," said Dedare. "Planned."

"Why didn't they come with us? I mean, on our spaceship?" I asked, stunned at Dedare's announcement.

"No room. Security and construction needed on Particle, so second spaceship required."

"What took up all the room on our spaceship?" Mom wondered.

"Food and supplies."

Which made sense. I had no idea how long we'd stay on Particle, and probably Dedare hadn't either when he'd arranged necessities for our stay.

"Ah, you have two spaceships?" asked Hart.

Dedare smiled. "More." Then he added, "One will always stay."

Why didn't I know these things? Then I admonished myself. To be fair, I'd never asked Dedare the relevant questions. We'd need a discussion, and soon.

Sweety interrupted my anxiety attack. "What did you experience today, Syl?"

"I had an excellent day. I found out I have my own air vehicle that's like a helicopter so I can go anywhere I want. By the way, Cara is taking us on a tour tomorrow. Don't ask me where. She said she had lots of ideas of what we'd want to see. She's supposed to send a list so we can change her itinerary, but I'm not going to. We'll go with the flow."

"Okay, okay, back up. Where did you find this helicopter of yours?" demanded Hart.

"On the top of the main building. Cara took me to three areas today, and the helicopter was in one of them. She said guests arrive by plane, as do supplies. Then, as I gazed around the sky, I noticed all sorts of flying objects filling the airspace over Ooby."

"What do you mean?" Hart sat on the edge of his seat.

"Air vehicles of different shapes and sizes, and even ones without windows or pilots. I don't know what they were, perhaps drones? You might find it fascinating to look into this, Hart. Anyway, the hotel owns many helicopters, and one of them is for my own use."

"What else did you experience during your enjoyable day?" asked Mama A. Being my mother, she knew I still internally bounced from today's experiences.

"Cara took me to the recording studio."

"Studio?" asked Sweety.

"Yes. Quite high tech. Apparently, the hotel records messages which are delivered to our guest rooms and also creates messages for commercial broadcast. I think the studio was somewhere on the second floor of the main building." I laughed. "Sweety, I can so see you broadcasting all sorts of interesting topics about Mars to the Particlans. What do you think?"

"I wouldn't turn down being a broadcasting star. Of course, Hart could also talk about science topics that would interest the Particlans, I imagine."

Sweety caught Hart's eye. "We'll discuss this later." Hart clearly focused on something else—a helicopter, I suspected.

I grinned at Sweety. "After our tour tomorrow, why don't you ask Cara about producing videos? She'll know who to talk to." I finished the food on my plate and sat back.

"What was today's third point of interest?" asked my mother.

"Oh, Cara took me to an organic growth elevator."

My words generated a momentary silence as my friends and relatives attempted to digest the words I'd put together.

"Something to do with gardens?" asked my mother.

"Yes. You get the prize! Today I discovered the hotel grows vegetables on the outside walls. Look around the next time you're outside. You should see greenery on many of the buildings. The special elevator I was in lets the hotel gardeners out onto platforms, and then they prune, water, harvest, fertilize, and such.

Pretty cool unless you're allergic to heights, but our buildings are not that tall."

I'd ignored my issue with heights as well as I could.

"So that was my day," I said. "An interesting one."

I turned to Dedare. "And how was your day?"

"Excellent. Investment areas studied."

Dedare must have enjoyed his day as he sported a huge smile. And he did love to make deals. Of course, the typical Irion terseness hadn't revealed a lot of information.

I waved at Hart—he chomped at the bit to know more.

"Dedare, what investment areas are you interested in?"

Hart leaned forward and practically fell off his stool as he waited for Dedare's response.

"Spaceship building, foodstuffs, and hotels."

"Spaceship manufacture and hotels I understand. But foodstuffs?" asked Hart.

"Exotic alien foods desired by all."

"I understand," commented Hart. "I would love to be able to say that I tasted that delicious Irion food, for example." Hart grabbed Sweety's hand. "Actually I can, but you want to market food to the rest of Mars, for example. Superior reasoning, Dedare."

Dedare had an amused look on his face, although Hart may not have picked up on it. I was a lot closer to Dedare than Hart would ever be.

I glanced around and found smiles. We'd all had new experiences and mostly pleasant ones.

Hart yawned and then said, "As much as this was a great meeting, I'm tired. I think I'll retire and rest up for Cara's tour."

His words reflected the general consensus, so our living room quickly emptied. Even Reena sped off to her bedroom.

Dedare and I cuddled on the couch. "Such a long day, but fascinating," I commented.

"More of them," responded Dedare, as he stroked my skin, particularly my cheeks. Irions found cheeks erotic.

"I imagine so, since we're on a new, unexplored planet. What're you up to in the next few days?" I asked, distracted by his intimate actions.

"Returning to Irion. Matters to arrange."

I stilled and then turned to Dedare. His face reflected uncertainty. He knew I wouldn't be happy about his disappearance so soon, but we hadn't been a couple for long enough for him to understand how I would be shocked at his announcement.

Being overly tired, the first words I uttered were not particularly endearing. "Why're you leaving me? I thought we'd have some time together to explore our relationship. We had so little time together on Irion."

Dedare pulled back. My words had wounded. "Business dealings."

"What business dealings? Couldn't you have arranged things before we left Irion?"

"Satre Council elections. Wish to be on council."

"You want to be on the Satre council? Couldn't you have someone you trust be an official? You're away from Irion so often, and you love traveling to new worlds, so being on Irion and interacting with council members might be hard to arrange."

Dedare studied my face. "Leave soon after Sain arrives. Decision made."

Our evening ended on an uneasy and unhappy note. I had no desire to argue with Dedare—but obviously his decision had been made without my input.

So to give myself some thinking time, I elected to sleep on the couch in the living room—not with Dedare this evening.

Chapter Four

Of course I couldn't sleep with so much on my mind, so I dressed and went for a walk.

The late evening had a pleasant temperature. I actually wasn't quite sure which season Ooby was in, or if seasons were relevant, but the current ambiance delighted me. The smell from flowers and other items in Ooby and the sea breeze created a wonderful aroma. And then I discovered the canals.

Radiating from the hotel were numerous waterways. And alongside the ones in my vision were paths and trees. Some of the trees were in flower, and some were not. The paths included sitting areas, so I'd found the perfect conditions for a walk.

As I strolled, I studied the boats on the waterway I'd chosen. Mostly small in size, they reminded me of personal conveyances. A mode of transportation to family homes, perhaps?

I started to relax from my hectic, emotional day. Perhaps the sound of water lapping against the bank drew me to the edge. Or perhaps the sunset caught my attention. Whatever caused my straying from the path, I welcomed.

My opinion changed after I landed in the water.

The cold made me gasp. And then I felt the current tug me away from shore. I started to panic. Although I was an excellent swimmer, the cold had frozen my limbs and I started to sink.

"Syl, Syl, pay attention," a voice said.

My frozen brain had enough energy left to ask, "Sweety?"

"Yes, dear. Now hold on to me."

The next thing I knew, Sweety and Hart had lifted me out of the waterway and deposited me on the grass.

"What happened?" My teeth chattered.

"You fell in the water, apparently. We didn't see it happen," Hart responded.

"Yes, and now we need to get you home to Dedare. What're you doing out here alone, anyway?" Sweety wrapped her jacket around me, and the two of them helped me limp home.

"Not talking. Dedare leaving," I answered with a tongue that barely worked.

"Ah. Well, let's get you back so you can have a nice, warm shower. It'll help you sleep," added Sweety.

So they brought me home to Dedare. Sweety bundled me into the shower while I imagine Hart had a few words with Dedare.

A few moments later, Dedare said, "Syl, Syl, join me."

I mumbled, "Annoyed, unhappy," sounding like an Irion. I was so tired.

"I understand. Topics for tomorrow. Now cuddle."

Dedare had all the right words.

****

The next morning we gathered on the roof of the main building for our tour. Cara already waited there, and after we arrived she ushered Dedare, Hart, Sweety,

Mom, Reena, and me into a spacious helicopter. Charles was occupied with ambassadorial duties.

My helicopter! Mama A and Reena had joined us as the tour was going to last only a half day. They'd pursue Reena's education in the afternoon. The second Irion spaceship carrying Sain and Teeka was due to arrive this evening, so we didn't have time for a whole day's tour.

"What do you have for us?" I asked. Cara settled us onto stools welded to the floor, and then she helped us don harnesses, strapping us to the inside dirty gray walls.

On one level, I was thankful there were few windows so my fear of heights could be easily contained. Yet the richness of a view of our travels would be missed.

"Many items morning. Surprises will develop. Enjoyment to behold."

A little vague. I did remember last night to ask her to hold her tour to only the morning. We needed to get back to the hotel and work on our various projects in the afternoon.

"So, what's first?" asked Mom.

"Government house reception."

After further discussion, her three-word description proved accurate. We were to meet with the representatives of the three-island country called Pistile, where the hotel was situated. The governing council of the world Particle was also located here in Ooby. So country representatives from the city of Ooby and its surrounding country, Pistile, and also Particlan world representatives were our mates for a small reception. Although the political structure confused me, I began to understand an inkling of my new world. Of course, having a country and a world governing from the same set of three islands likely contributed to my confusion.

We landed without incident on the roof of Particle's government house. It turned out the country and world representatives shared this three-story building, so the location provided a natural place for all parties to meet.

Cara led us from the roof down a circular flight of stairs, and we emerged into an elegant meeting room decorated in blues and greens. Food and drink filled tables along the walls, and various seating groups and an open space were situated in the middle of the room.

The reception fascinated me. On the surface, the activities were similar to any human counterpart. Food occupied tables, and there were groups of individuals discussing who knew what. And to top it off we were showered with gifts.

Food for Irions and Martians had been arranged on one particular table. Someone—probably Dedare—had provided signs for each item indicating the worlds suitable for feasting.

I found numerous items I'd consider vegetables. They were fresh, and I happily devoured broccoli trees and sticks resembling celery but with a slightly sweet taste. And my favorite item turned out to be something resembling yams.

The yams were purple and tasty. One of my favorites, though, was the blue broccoli trees. Perhaps an unusual color, but the taste was exquisite.

Out of the numerous gifts we received, I found the water-repellent material the most intriguing. I suspected waterproof clothing would become a necessity on

Particle, so I needed to find a seamstress. As for the most useful item amongst our gifts, my vote went to a shiny gold tote bag, large enough to hold all my gifts.

"Dedare, did you research possible food for Irions and humans for this reception—well, our stay on Particle, I guess I'm asking?" We'd found a moment alone.

"Prudent to issue lists for possible meetings," he said.

How had he done this when he'd only been here once? Or perhaps that was an incorrect assumption on my part and he'd been here many times. Perhaps he'd sent investigators? My fiancé had a lot of questions to answer. On the other hand, he'd done an amazing job.

Annoyed with Dedare for leaving fairly quickly, I still had to admit he was ahead of me on all sorts of issues in our lives. However, we hadn't discussed anything this morning over breakfast. Had he avoided our dispute of yesterday, or did he consider it unimportant?

So much to learn about Irion males, and I didn't think I was doing a particularly fantastic job. My problems seemed to stick around and not resolve.

I talked to the head of the planetary council, Axert al Tiste. He suggested a few departments located in this building might hold information to help with my assimilation into Particlan culture. Some of the offices he mentioned made no sense, but I nodded a lot. I hoped he understood my action. I knew Cara would field a million questions at the end of today's tour.

Then Cara introduced me to Saska et Tong, the high priest of their religion, or one of their religions, I wasn't quite sure. Tong wore a flowing gown of green and blue.

"Study religions here?" Saska asked.

"I haven't gotten that far. I'm still getting used to my position in the Sath-Ooby Golden Hotel."

"Participate church classes. Understand Particlan people. Join in church."

I wasn't sure I wanted to join a church on a foreign world, but the classes should be informative.

"I'd love to take some classes, Saska et Tong. Please have your representative contact me."

Saska bowed and then turned away.

I glanced at Cara, but she offered no words. I wondered what I'd gotten myself into.

Then I ran into Dedare's hotel partner. With Dedare not having total ownership, hotel operations could be tricky. Would I need to get approval from both Dedare and Tarin for any changes I wanted to make?

"Tarin et Tong, nice to see you here. Are you part of the world government or the country one?" I asked. And a question popped into my mind—is he related to Saska et Tong, the priest?

"Member world council. Owner of buildings. Maker of rulings."

If I'd deciphered them properly, his last three words sounded ominous.

What did he want to rule on? I really wasn't interested in politics, but I needed to be, I suspected. Did he want to rule on matters pertaining to aliens? Is this why Dedare was so interested in politics, at least on Irion? I sidled over to Dedare and isolated him from the crowd after Tarin was taken away by a Particlan.

"Tarin et Tong owns a portion of the Sath-Ooby Golden Hotel. Is your portion larger?"

"Yes."

Well, at least my decisions might have a little sway.

"So when I want to change something in the hotel, to whom do I talk?" I gave Dedare my biggest smile.

"Both. My opinion most." He smiled and rubbed my cheek.

I noticed our exchange had garnered a great deal of interest. I reminded myself to ask Cara about interspecies relationships. How tactful should I be?

"Okay, but you're going back to Irion. How're we going to handle this as I learn more about Particle? I know I'm going to want to make the hotel more efficient, and that'll mean change."

"Deal with Tarin et Tong," said Dedare.

Fun, fun, fun. I hadn't yet dealt much with Tarin, but he wasn't one of my favorite people. Did Dedare really understand the situation he'd dumped me in?

Cara caught my attention and said, "Time to continue. Gather up crew. Next stop close."

"Will do. This portion of our day has been quite illuminating. Where're we going now?" I asked.

Cara smiled. "Medical surprise visit."

Another one of her Particlan cryptic messages. However, I shouldn't complain. Her tour so far had revealed a multitude of topics I wanted to explore.

We trooped onto *my* helicopter *(what a concept!)* and then traveled for approximately fifteen minutes. We set down at a spacious landing pad filled with numerous helicopters, planes, and ground vehicles.

"Where are we, Cara?" I asked.

"Emergency services headquarters."

Oh, then this might be Hart's favorite place since he was both a scientist and a medical doctor. "Hart, Cara just told me where we've landed. I think you need to be lead for this stop."

"What do you mean?" His complexion contained a tinge of red, matching his red hair.

"This is Emergency Services Headquarters. We need you to be our liaison for anything affecting Martians and Irions, in a hurtful medical manner, I guess I mean." My words came out awkwardly.

"Your words are clear, Syl. And I agree Cara has brought us to a beautiful place. Sweety and I may disappear here occasionally, that is after I determine what kind of equipment they possess."

His words confused me for a long moment, then I had a revelation. "Sweety, are you pregnant?"

I noticed a slight blush. "Yes. A surprise for both of us, but we're looking forward to the little person." Sweety grinned and patted her stomach and then put her arm around Hart.

I grabbed both of them in a hug. "This is outstanding news." I couldn't help grinning—for the situation and for my relationship with both of them.

"Ah, we hadn't planned this happening so soon, but what can you do? At least I have the necessary experience in these matters," said Hart.

He might be a medical doctor, but I didn't think he was as blasé about the actual experience as he let on.

"But shouldn't you go back to Mars for the birth?" Children weren't part of my usual experiences.

"Well, we'll see how long we're actually on Particle. And how I feel in the next few months. At least the gravity on Particle is quite similar to Earth and our Martian cities after a higher gravity was installed. I don't want to be tired along with everything else going on. Well, more tired." Sweety smiled. "Perhaps Mama A can help me with my questions. After all, you turned out okay."

The Martians surrounding me had a good laugh. Harrumph.

"So, this Emergency Services Headquarters is also a hospital, Cara?" I asked.

"One of numerous. Many areas covered. Quick to respond."

Extensive coverage for medical emergencies was a bonus. "Hart, perhaps you can look into Particlan birthing procedures just in case."

Cara glanced at me. "Time for child?"

"Oh, not me." I pointed at Sweety, and then patted her stomach after a quick glance from Sweety gave me permission. Thankfully, Sweety wasn't one of those who found touching her belly a rude gesture.

Cara glanced up and down Sweety's body and appeared to be full of questions. How could Cara even imagine human birthing? For that matter, how did I imagine Particlans gave birth?

Since he had a vested interest, I decided to leave the research to Hart and also the explanations for the rest of us.

We were given a detailed tour of the health facility. And since Particlans with medical experience surrounded us, we received the most study.

"Hart, maybe you should give classes to the Particlan staff explaining the physiology of Martians." I added, "And Irions," after glancing at Dedare and his daughter Reena. "After all, there'll be a couple more Irions arriving tonight."

"Perhaps we'll exchange classes," enthused Hart. "If I have more information, I may be able to help a Particlan in the case of an emergency."

We stayed only a short while since our available time began to run out. "Cara, how many more stops do we have this morning?" I asked.

"One more visit. Time is limited. Many visits later."

I assumed Cara was telling us only one location remained for this morning's tour.

"Where're we going?" asked Sweety while we climbed into the helicopter.

"Location fish farm," responded Cara.

I deduced we headed for a facility built on the water for growing fish for Particlan consumption. I turned out to be mostly correct but with a twist I hadn't envisioned.

After our helicopter landed and we disembarked, I saw rows of shiny, blue pyramids running off into the distance, similar in color to the ocean surrounding them. At the lowest visible levels, bridges connected the pyramids. After Cara led us closer, I saw troughs filled with water circling each building from bottom to top.

"Cara, are the fish grown in those pools on the sides of the buildings? Do they contain water?" I pointed to the pyramid in front of us. I didn't want to say sea water, as I had no idea of the composition of the oceans and other bodies of water on Particle. Maybe these pools contained special ingredients.

"Yes, fish ponds. Grown vertically tall. When ready, fall."

An amused Cara smiled at me and our surrounding group.

"You mean the fish fall?" I asked.

Cara pointed under my feet. We stood on one of the bridges. The flooring of the structure consisted of a mesh-like material. Beneath the bridge, a trough filled with water and fish moved at a fast pace. The fish were being sent for processing, I assumed.

We walked up and down the pyramids, and Cara revealed more of the process. I noticed a tinge of green on Sweety's face, so I suggested we return to the hotel for lunch.

Back at the hotel, the off-worlders dispersed for lunch and their own various projects. I asked Cara into my office so I could elicit information about hotel staffing and positions.

"Cara, can you organize lunch for the two of us so we can continue working?"

She spoke into her brooch and then turned back to me.

"Cara, who had this office before?" I needed to find disgruntled employees before they found me—like on Irion.

"General manager hotel. Always general manager. Look after all."

Cara smiled and added, "You General Manager."

What did a general manager do? I'd been the manager of the Mars Best-Tycho Basin Hotel, not the general manager.

Then Dedare had lured me to Irion with the position of manager of the Sath-Satre Golden Hotel.

The GM of the Mars hotel had been a jerk, and Simon had followed us to Irion and caused trouble. Of course, all sorts of interesting and sometimes life-threatening problems had cropped up, but everything had worked out in the end.

I'd have to talk to the owners, Dedare and Tarin, to confirm what my actual duties were. Did being a general manager also involve other hotels or other facilities? The situation reminded me of my impetuous trip from Mars to Irion to manage the Sath-Satre Golden Hotel. I had little idea of my duties then, either.

We sat at my conference table with our lunches and continued our conversation.

"Cara, who was the previous general manager, and where is he or she now?" Was my terminology correct? I needed to get Mom to learn about the sexes on Particle or, at least, their physiological structure and mating habits.

"Another hotel beckoned."

Was the general manager let go? Would there be any resentment toward me from the previous GM?

At the moment, I needed to ignore the whole situation. I apologized to Cara about the lunch mishap with Tarin and had her send in the Reception staff, one by one, for short conversations.

I didn't learn a great deal, but they seemed content with me having the position of their manager.

After I'd spent time with the last one for today, I spoke to Cara. "Is there anything you want to discuss? Perhaps about what should be changed or left the same? I'm always open to suggestions. So don't worry about offending me. I'll listen to your comments."

"No suggestions yet. Must wear brooch. Contact with employees."

Cara handed me a shiny blue object. I studied the item but couldn't make much of it. "This is used so employees can contact me, if they need to?"

She pointed at her own brooch. Then I remembered seeing them on other Particlan hotel employees.

"This will be good. I can also contact the Martians and Irions?"

"Everyone is available." She showed me the functions of the brooch until I became comfortable with the process.

I hoped this brooch would solve a number of communications problems. Although I suspected my issues with Dedare wouldn't be among them.

"Cara, I'm comfortable with the brooch, so how about you take me around the hotel and show me new areas."

We first approached a pair of tinted glass doors which opened at our arrival. After I entered the room, a shower of water unexpectedly drenched me. Not again! Cara appeared amused which annoyed me, but perhaps I'd read her incorrectly.

"Cara, what is this place? Community showers?" I asked, wiping the water from my face.

"Place of worship."

"So what's with the shower?" Drenched two days in a row didn't improve my sense of humor.

"Cleansing of soul."

"Well, you could've warned me," I muttered.

"No cleansing Martians?"

"No. We don't have water to waste," I replied with little grace.

Cara's voice wavered.

"Unknown to Particlan. Hard to anticipate. Forgiveness to me."

Cara appeared ready to flee, so I regretted my previous words. "Don't worry. It's only water. How can you anticipate what an off-worlder would like or dislike? Water doesn't hurt me. However, I'll need to change."

She didn't move a muscle, so I needed to redeem my poor behavior. "How about explaining the chapel to me?" We were on the other side of the waterfall, so I expected to stay dry, or at least not wetter, for a little while.

While Cara prepared her words, I studied the room. I recognized benches, stools, tables with items, and a lectern. Pretty much the usual items found in chapels on the various worlds I'd visited so far. How many worlds would I visit in my lifetime? I had to laugh—not a question I'd ever expected to ask.

As Cara started to speak, I interrupted and asked, "Who is that Particlan sitting to the side of the dais?"

During the time I'd taken my first glance around the room, the Particlan had blended into the background so I hadn't noticed him.

"Saska et Tong."

Of course. I'd spoken to him this morning at the reception.

"Cara, why is the chief priest of one of your religions in our hotel chapel?"

"Regular chapel blessings."

Before I had a chance to ponder the reason for his presence, Saska approached.

"Happy meeting today. Research improve understanding. Religious classes soon?" Saska waited for my answer.

I had to laugh. "Cara has been quite helpful with my education so far. I've experienced many things today. We'll arrange the religious classes very soon."

Saska smiled and turned away. Before I'd had a chance to continue our conversation, he'd disappeared. No matter. I knew I'd see him soon.

Cara's explanation of the chapel included descriptions of a couple of religions, but the analysis went completely over my head—probably the universal translator's, too. Spiritual and mystical concepts could confuse both animate and inanimate objects.

"What's next on our tour?" I asked after we'd returned to the entrance of the chapel and the waterfall.

Cara moved to the wall, pressed a button, and the waterfall ceased.

"Oh, thank you, Cara. I'm almost dried out, and I didn't want to get wet again." Could she have done that on the other side before we entered? Possibly, but I suspected she hadn't even considered my situation in her excitement to show me the chapel.

Outside the chapel, Cara said, "Now to Mista."

I started to follow Cara, but she abruptly stopped. I peered around her to see what had caused her action. I noticed Saska et Tong walking toward us, accompanied by both a female Particlan carrying a baby and a male Particlan.

Cara turned to me and said, "Manager stay still."

I assumed she wanted me to stop walking, so I did. Probably wanted me to stop talking, too. I laughed to myself—that would take an effort on my part.

Cara moved forward and spoke with Saska and the female Particlan. They appeared to come to an agreement, and then Cara walked back to me.

"Religious ceremony follows. Beginnings of life. Manager wishes to view?"

A religious ceremony? This should be fascinating.

I conveyed my acceptance to Cara, so she led me back into the chapel after giving me an apologetic glance.

I recognized the apology for what it was after the second drenching, but I also realized the Particlans needed the religious aspect of *cleansing* to be followed.

Oh well, what was a little water?

The parents with their child and the chief priest walked up to the dais, while Cara stopped me and pointed at stools a few rows back.

Saska said a few words which my translator had trouble deciphering at our distance.

Then he picked up the child and plunked it face down in a pool of water.

I started to rise, but Cara put a hand on my shoulder to hold me down in my seat. She recognized my distress.

"Discuss later time."

As much as the situation confused and upset me, Cara was correct. Interference from an alien allowed to witness the religious ceremony would not be appropriate.

However, I desperately watched for movement from the Particlan child. After what seemed like forever, the child turned over and wailed. The sweetest sound I'd ever heard, especially after the mother and father picked up their offspring and then grabbed each other in obvious joy.

The chief priest said a few more words, and then the family had a few private words with Saska. The ceremony complete, the parents started to leave the chapel. As they passed Cara and me, the parents smiled and waved their hands.

Although anxious to ask questions of Cara, I kept quiet until we again found ourselves outside the chapel.

"Cara, why was the baby put into the water? It wouldn't be able to breathe face down. What if it died?"

"Ceremony to determine. Right to life. All Particlans partake."

I clearly understood the meaning of her words. Alien societies were certainly different, but that was what I was here to find out about. "How old is the child?"

"Age half cycle."

"So most babies would be able to turn over and breathe, and survive the ceremony?"

Cara smiled and indicated her agreement with a hand motion pointing outwards.

"And the ones that couldn't?"

"Ceremony of Death."

Depressed, I didn't want to continue this conversation.

I sighed. "What's next?"

"On to mista."

Oh right, our original destination.

"Mista? What's that?" Apparently another word to add to the translator.

"Guest game room."

An interesting concept. Games for guests to play. "What kind of games?"

Perhaps Cara didn't understand my question. She only said, "Show various items."

The game room was in the main hotel building. The bright color scheme included bookcases and shelving of various heights painted in oranges and reds. The décor overpowered my senses, for some reason. Thankfully the addition of numerous boxes and containers muted the blinding colors a trifle.

Cara pulled out boxes I recognized as board games. She didn't try to explain them—it was simply a show, not tell. Then she led me to a table full of items like pool cues, pusher sticks, and other unrecognizable small items.

"What kind of game is this?" The two thoughts that popped into my mind were battlefield, or a large building game.

"Battle for dominance."

Okay, so I wasn't far off, but I had no idea how to play.

I thought this would be a job for Mom or Sweety. Either one of them could sweet talk a guest into explaining the point of the game and how to play.

I didn't remember a game room in the Sath-Satre Golden Hotel on Irion. Perhaps an idea to be introduced. If guests liked gaming, they might spend more time at the hotel. The more reasons to stay at a hotel, the longer the stay.

Sweety would be the best person to talk to guests. She'd made a perfect hostess in our hotel in Satre, and the Irions had loved her. They had wanted her around for more time than she had available.

In the beginning stages of our time on Particle, we still had to decide how she could help us learn as many aspects of Particlan life as we needed. New worlds were a challenge.

I turned to Cara to ask about our next visit, but she listened to her brooch. Kind of freaky but I knew someone had called.

"Must go roof," Cara told me.

"Why? What's on the roof?" A confusing demand.

"Helicopter pick up off-worlders." A grin spread across her face.

"Oh, well. In that case, let's go." My excitement grew.

Cara grabbed my arm and led me to a nearby elevator. After she punched in *roof*—I was getting the hang of this—we sped upward.

On the roof, I ran toward the only helicopter. The call sign on the body matched the one on my helicopter. Then I noticed Teeka and Sain and a couple of others standing outside the helicopter and taking in the view of Ooby.

I ran up to them and received comforting hugs. Sweety had introduced hugging while we were on Irion.

"I'm so happy to see you guys. Most unexpected because Dedare didn't tell me until yesterday you were coming. How was your trip?"

"Chilly," said Sain, a humorist.

"Quiet," said Teeka, a realist.

I'd missed these guys. Only these two could describe traveling in stasis in quite these ways.

Although the love of my life was Dedare, Sain Sath, Dedare's brother, and Teeka Cole, a homicide detective and Dedare's friend, had eventually taken second and third place in my heart.

"Let's find the others and have a reunion." I glanced at Cara as she spoke into her brooch to obtain the locations of the other Martians and Irions.

A shiny discharge started to drip from Cara's eyes. "Manager, Reena lost."

Chapter Five

A distressed Cara momentarily shocked me. "So where is Mama A? She's supposed to be with Reena looking into her schooling," I asked.

Teeka and Sain watched our exchange and were concerned. Of course, they had no idea of the situation on Particle and what each of us had been up to.

Cara gave me her brooch. "Mom, what's going on? How could you lose Reena?" Not very tactful I realized, but my unease caused my momentary lapse in judgment.

Her emotion-filled voice mumbled, "She walked away with students we'd met at the school, so I thought she was in good hands. Then she never returned. I went to the school office, but they didn't understand the problem, so I called Cara. Will you help look for Reena?"

"Of course. Sain and Teeka have arrived, so I'll get them involved. What had you done, or what activities had you discussed before she disappeared?" I clutched at straws. Ooby was a large city, and I didn't have any clues as to where to look for a teenaged Irion.

"Well, first we went to the school office to get information about the curriculum so we could see where Reena fit in. I had a nice chat with the principal, and she appeared receptive to Reena attending her school while we were on Particle. We picked up a bunch of brochures and course descriptions, and then we were shown to the school library so we had a place to sit and study the paperwork. I had Dedare's reader so I could understand the Particlan characters. Although the reader worked, the descriptions were quite bizarre. Reena and I chatted about certain subjects, and then some students came in the library. Reena popped up and went over to talk to them. I thought she wanted to discuss teachers, course subjects, and such. Then, after she'd walked out the door with the Particlan students, I decided we'd made a good start with our trip to the school. I continued my study of the brochures. After she didn't return within a reasonable time, I went looking, and I can't find her. What should I do?"

I explained the details to Sain and Teeka and then I gave the brooch to Sain.

"Go to office and explain situation again. Ask for help. How far is school?" asked Sain.

I leaned close to Sain to hear my mother's words.

"We took transit this afternoon for the experience. So the school is a little way from the hotel. It's called the Heeght-Ooby Pre-school."

"We arrive quickly," said Sain. He gave the brooch back to Cara. "Do you know transit to the Heeght-Ooby Pre-school?"

"Yes, school near," answered Cara.

"Arrive soon as possible?" asked Teeka.

A question I could answer. "Let's take my helicopter. Cara, is the pilot still around?"

Sain and Teeka studied me as if I'd lost my mind. After Cara had us settled in my helicopter, they readily accepted I really had a helicopter at my disposal.

"Cara, have the pilot take us to the Heeght-Ooby Pre-school as quickly as possible."

After we took off, Sain asked, "Syl contacted Dedare?" He was concerned about both his niece and his brother.

"No, no, not yet. I'll call him right now. I wanted to get going immediately."

Dedare wasn't happy about the situation. Since he was off site, he said he'd meet us at the school.

I should've called him right away. What was I thinking? My immediate concern had been to find Reena, so that's what I'd gone with. I tried to convince myself I'd taken the right action.

After a short flight, we landed on the school's roof, and Cara helped us find our way to the school office. Mama A was talking to the staff when we arrived. After introductions, we quickly spread throughout the school. The Martians and Irions were paired up with Particlans so we could connect with each other and not get lost, I assumed. I accompanied the principal, who had a pretty good idea where Reena might be, if I'd understood her words. Meekly I followed her through the corridors of her school keeping an eye on her soft brown curls so I wouldn't get lost. The hair had a hint of blue, as did her two-piece beige outfit of top and trousers.

I tried to study my surroundings while we hurried down the hallways, but the images overwhelmed me. In many respects, this looked like a typical human high school, but I had no idea what subjects were taught. For example, I discovered a sign on one wall which Dedare's machine deciphered as "Particulates"—a word with no meaning for me.

The principal and I eventually arrived at a room with a large swimming pool, seating up the walls, and areas in front of the benches for swimmers and coaches—at least that physical description fit with my human experience. The area reminded me of a typical human Olympic-sized water facility.

"Is Reena here?" I asked, since the principal, Samilt et Tong, kept walking and not talking.

She pointed to the far end of the pool. Then I saw Reena climb out and then be thrown back in by one of the Particlans. She landed close to the pool's edge and climbed up the ladder to get out.

I rushed to Reena's side, but before I got there a different Particlan student threw her into the water.

Movement stopped after I arrived at Reena's side. "Are you okay? Why are you being thrown into the pool? Tell me you're fine. Wait a minute," I babbled.

I asked Cara to tell everyone Reena was okay and that we were at the pool and to meet there. I turned back to Reena.

"Ritual of acceptance," said Reena. "Happy I will go to school here."

"But why so many times?" Not a particularly intelligent question on my part, but Reena understood my underlying concerns.

"Each person wants to welcome me," explained Reena.

"Well…well…" I sighed. "Tell them you're tired and make them wait for another day when it gets too much for you," I instructed in a quiet voice. I couldn't tell Reena to refuse. First contact had become a tricky situation, or should I say a *wet* situation.

I heard a noise and turned around. Dedare stood behind me. "Did you hear everything?" His face remained stoic.

However, I expected nothing else. He'd lost his wife, and the mother of Reena, to an unfortunate laboratory accident, and I knew that had taken a tremendous toll on his emotions, but I'd managed to pierce his shell.

"Safe and happy," Dedare replied.

I assumed he referred to Reena.

"Dinner in rooms and welcome for Sain and Teeka," announced Dedare.

"Perfect. I'm hungry, and I'm sure everyone else is. Will you arrange the food?" I asked.

His head movement of agreement reassured me. I hadn't been to the hotel's cooking facilities yet, and I had no idea how to order food. I hoped our hotel guests were adequately informed.

"Meet in one hour in our rooms," said Dedare, and he passed the word to the others.

"Let's go back to the hotel via helicopter, and then we can all meet to discuss our day. We need to get Sain and Teeka settled in their rooms." I glanced at Dedare, and he motioned that appropriate rooms had been acquired. How much of the hotel were the Martians and Irions taking up? Oh well, not my problem.

Actually, I guess it was. Hmm.

After Dedare and I settled Sain and Teeka in their two-bedroom suite, we walked back to ours. I collapsed on a couch. My day had been long. "Dedare, just give me a half hour nap before the others arrive. I'm exhausted."

He pulled a blanket over me and rubbed my cheek. "Longer is appropriate."

"Oh, no. I need to be alert to greet our guests. Is the food ordered?"

"Yes. Just rest." He sat beside me and warmed me with his presence.

The next thing I knew, people began arriving and Mom and Sweety got me up and organized in the kitchen. Well, really, they got everything organized and I sat and tried to wake up.

Eventually, after my brain began working, I asked about Reena.

"She's very happy and talking with her new friends. I think this school will be good for Reena," answered Mom. "Particle is working out well for her. So far."

A perfect situation for Reena's first off-planet experience.

Reena wandered into the living room and joined the rest of us. She appeared rested and happy with her life.

"Reena, what did you learn today during your interaction with Particlan students?" I asked.

"Happy with school. Courses unusual but interesting. Made choices." A smile appeared on her face.

As we'd prepared to leave her home planet of Irion, Reena became apprehensive about our journey since she'd never taken a spaceflight, let alone one with her father to an unknown planet. After only a brief time on her first new home, Reena apparently had no regrets. I hoped our stay continued to delight her, and she'd have numerous adventurous journeys. I had to laugh—not too adventurous, though.

"What courses have you signed up for? What days will you need to be at school?" Actually, I didn't know the length of the Particlan week or what their name for week was. And I had made lots of assumptions about how various Particlan systems worked.

"Hart, or anybody for that matter, I have a question. What's the length of the week here on Particle? Do they have a week? How does their yearly cycle progress is what I'm really asking, I think?" I didn't remember reading anything about these details on my trip from Irion.

"In this respect, Particle is interesting," said Hart. "They sort of have monthly cycles for a total of twelve. Then they have six weeks, for want of a better word, within each month, and then they have six days within each week. All multiples of three you'll notice."

I hadn't noticed because my mind still dwelt on six weeks and six days. At least Particlans were consistent with their numbers.

"Reena, how many days do you have to be at school?" I wondered how busy she`d be and if she`d have any time to help in the hotel, as she had on Irion.

She shifted her gaze to Mama A.

"Okay, Mom, what've you planned for this teenager's life?" Laughter filled the room, and even Reena joined in.

"Reena will most likely have three school days a week. Three days out of each six. I only picked three courses because starting in a new school with new friends and teachers and, certainly, new and unusual topics will be a challenge. Reena has her three classes on each of those three days. Doesn't sound like much, but I think she will have her share of work. From my past experience, it would be for me."

"I'm sure Reena will handle it," I commented. "Now, how are you getting there? Taking transit?"

Mom interjected, "I think transit will be too slow. Could your helicopter take her to school and pick her up when she's done?"

"Barring emergencies, I would imagine so. I'll have to check with Cara. I suspect she'll know how often the helicopter is used. Reena, you'll need to take transit if the helicopter is unavailable. Any objections, Dedare?" We were taking over his daughter's schooling, so he needed to be involved.

"Correct decisions," he responded. "Reena, let know if problems."

"Even ones dealing with water." I rolled my eyes and added, "Of course, I had my own water experience again today."

Laughter erupted, and Sweety said, "Do tell, Syl. You never cease to amaze me with your alien experiences."

"Yes, well, Cara took me to the hotel chapel. Apparently, the first experience is walking through a wall of water to be cleansed spiritually."

"Makes sense," said Dad. "I'll be studying their literature—particularly pertaining to religion. It'll help me deal with the Particlan Ambassadors."

I thought for a moment about how Martian Ambassador Charles Clarke had become part of our group. Although neither he nor I had previously known about the situation he'd turned out to be my father. Mom had to do a lot of explaining after she'd announced this detail on Irion. And then Mom and Charles had rekindled their relationship and, much to my surprise, Charles proposed marriage and Mom accepted.

"Check out the hotel library," I suggested to Dad. "They should have numerous volumes pertaining to history and religion."

Dedare put a hand in one of his pockets and pulled out an Irion reader and passed it to Dad.

"Thanks. That'll be helpful."

"Sweety, maybe you and Mom could investigate the chapel and see if there's any way we can modify it to accommodate Martians and Irions," I said.

"I will help," spoke up Sain.

I nodded. I should've mentioned Sain in the first place. Sain had implemented all my wild ideas at the Sath-Satre Golden Hotel on Irion. So now he would get to do it here on Particle.

"That'll be perfect, Sain. You can keep Mom and Sweety's wild ideas under control."

My remarks created a lot of laughter, and on my account, I suspected.

I didn't want to introduce a somber mood, but I had a desperate need to discuss what I'd experienced today. I described the *right to life* ceremony I had witnessed.

"Oh, Syl, how upset are you?" asked my mother. Tears threatened to spill down her face.

"Quite a bit. I might have had to watch a child die." The image of the baby placed face down in the water would remain with me for a long time.

"So…no one was there to revive the child, if necessary? No medical personnel?" asked Hart.

"No." I shook my head. "Apparently not for a *right to life* ceremony." I had no idea how I would have reacted if the child had died.

Dad spoke. "Being upset at another race's ceremony is common. However, we cannot interfere. This is a Particlan custom, or tradition if you wish, that must be observed and accepted, whether we approve or not."

He had the diplomatic words, but they weren't to my liking.

"I believe I'll research this custom in the hotel library to understand its history."

No one argued with my words. In fact, no one spoke, so the time had come to change the subject.

"I really would like to understand what three subjects Reena will study. Would anyone, like Mom or Reena, care to enlighten us?"

"Not understand," said Reena.

Did she not understand the topics or my question?

"I have to admit the topics sound strange, but the principal assured me they'd be appropriate for Reena." Mom rummaged in her bag and pulled out a piece of paper. "Let's see. Hmm. Ah, *Water to Unfold*, *Particulates in Motion*, and *Olympic Studies*." She laughed. "That's all I can tell you. The descriptions in the brochures were not particularly illuminating. When I find out more, I'll enlighten everyone."

No wonder Reena hadn't understood what she'd be studying.

I needed to shift the focus away from Reena. "Hart, what did you learn today?"

"Mostly I spent time with the medical services. I explained Sweety's and my situation and what I needed. Then the Particlans and I tried to figure out if any of their machines would be useful."

"What situation is this?" asked Dad.

"Syl, you didn't tell everyone?" interrupted Sweety.

"No. It's not my business to inform the world." I tried to hide my smirk.

"Please, someone, tell me what's going on," said my father.

"Oh, Charles! Everyone! Hart and I are pregnant. Very early stages. I have lots of questions for Mama A," said Sweety, "since you raised such a lovely daughter."

More laughter on my account.

Mom jumped up and gave Hart and Sweety hugs. "Congratulations again. You're making our journey a wonderful adventure, and I wouldn't have it any other way." She grinned. "Sweety, we'll have lots of mommy talks. Let's plan to have our first one tomorrow."

Smiling people filled our living room. Sweety gave Mom another hug.

"Birth on Particle?" asked Dedare.

"We haven't decided," said Hart. "That's why I'm investigating the medical facilities in Ooby. Perhaps we should have the baby on Irion? On Mars? So many choices." Hart shook his head. "Dedare, you'll need to let us know how long we'll be staying on Particle so we can make plans."

"Unknown." Dedare's face had a serious expression.

"I know we've only just arrived on Particle, but this pregnancy was a surprise, and you certainly couldn't have planned it in your logistics," said Hart.

"Spaceship always available," Dedare replied.

"Of course. I'd forgotten you have more than one. You're leaving for Irion soon, and then the second spaceship will be here for us." I wasn't happy about his departure, but I felt more comfortable with Sweety and Hart's situation knowing a spaceship would be available for their use.

Dad, always the diplomat, rubbed his gray crew cut and changed the topic. "My office at the embassy headquarters is quite adequate. Apparently, the Particlans make office space available for all visiting diplomats, and in the same building, making easy access to other ambassadors. Unlike on Irion," he added.

Ambassador Dad had dealt with numerous issues on Irion.

And Dad's words made me think about my many adventures on Irion. However, I didn't want to dwell upon, or even remember, my abduction.

"My questions of the day include why are you guys here? Not that I'm not happy to see you," I said, after glancing at Sain and Teeka.

Before either had a chance to answer, Dedare said, "Teeka for security, Sain for security and construction. Syl will have many crazy ideas about changes."

I decided it was *pick on Syl* night.

"Syl's ideas are wonderful," said Sweety. "She always finds interesting things for me to do."

I put a big smile on my face. "Since you've brought the topic up, Dedare, my first crazy idea is a restaurant. This hotel doesn't have one, as Sweety pointed out, so our guests need to eat in their rooms if they want to partake of food onsite. Not a particularly friendly atmosphere. Actually, isolationist. Also, we need Particlans wandering in from outside and wondering about the excitement. One goal is to make more Particlans want to stay in the hotel, and a multi-species restaurant and menu would help."

My statements excited the Martians, but the Irions weren't quite so demonstrative.

"Syl, amenities shop?" asked Reena.

Reena had worked the gift shop at her father's flagship hotel on Irion. She'd quite enjoyed her position and had received excellent experiences for a young teenager.

"I don't think there's one. So maybe a gift shop should be attached to the restaurant."

"Discuss later," said Dedare.

I glanced at Dedare and also Sain, who would have to implement my approved ideas. What were their opinions about my suggestions? Knowing them, they would soon let me know.

"I think a restaurant is a great idea," said Sweety. "Hart and I'll need to make up menus focusing on each species. And Hart will get to sample lots of food as I give Martian and Irion recipes to the chefs to try. The populace will be excited."

Hart grinned. He loved to eat, but he couldn't cook. And Sweety had the perfect recipes for every race.

"I found another interesting place today," I said. "The hotel has a game room for guests."

"What's in there?" asked Hart.

"I saw what looked like board games. Then there was a table covered in pool cues, pusher sticks, and other items. I didn't quite understand their purposes. Cara called it Annihilation or something. Sweety, perhaps you could look into the game room, especially if you hostess the restaurant as you did before. You could direct our guests toward the game room, and it would help keep them in the hotel, and maybe they could order snacks after they'd played for a while. Then there's the guest pool area I saw yesterday. Almost an Olympic-sized pool, which makes sense on a water world. Especially since the pool at Reena's new school reminded me of the Olympics."

"Maybe that's what *Olympic Studies* is all about. One of Reena's classes, remember?" asked Mom.

"What an interesting planet," I commented. "I need to find out whether they have something like the Olympics. I might take up diving again."

"Did you dive in the Martian Olympics?" asked Dad.

"Almost." I grinned. "I'd almost qualified for our town, but then I got busy with managing the Mars Best –Tycho Basin hotel and ran out of time to practice. And now I'm starting to get excited about the idea of the Particlan Olympics, although I don't expect to have a lot of time to pursue physical activities, and I have no idea what their Olympics include."

"You need to live a balanced life," said my ever-practical mother.

"Hmm. Perhaps. Most importantly, I need to talk with my bosses about what my actual duties are. Cara had some interesting comments today, but we'll talk later," I added for Dedare's benefit.

Hart stood. "On that note, Sweety and I need to return to our rooms and unwind. Much to think about."

A baby would do that.

My dinner companions took their dishes to our little kitchen and then said their goodbyes. Reena disappeared to her room, and soon Dedare and I were alone.

"Did you have a good day, Dedare? Buying things?" I asked.

"No purchase. Much investigation."

"Well, we haven't been here long, so investigating is good." I paused. "I have an important question, though. Should I ask it now or wait until we've had a rest?"

"Now." Dedare tugged me closer.

"Cara told me my office was for the general manager. Does that mean I'm the general manager of the Sath-Ooby Golden Hotel?"

"Yes. Able to cope?" asked Dedare.

"I think so, but I don't really know what that entails." I gave him a kiss. "However, I do have another question. Am I also the general manager for other hotels or businesses? I need to understand the scope of my managing."

"Other hotels and businesses reason for trip," said Dedare. "Possibilities exist, but acquisitions unknown at present."

Okay, sensible, but I mentally sighed.

Now for the topic I desperately wanted to discuss. "Then shouldn't you stay here and concentrate on researching hotels and businesses, rather than returning to Irion?"

"Already arranged. Need to research politics potential on Irion. Decisions to be made. Will consider your proposal of representative." Dedare rubbed my cheek. His action made me feel better, but I had a tough time unwinding. For Dedare to be on Particle for such a short time made me anxious. For unknown and alien reasons, I might need his advice as the days progressed.

"I'm going to miss you, Dedare. Make sure you come back quickly." I really was going to miss my fiancé.

"Will try. Now, retire?" He leaned over to kiss me.

Ah, a little romantic time with my favorite Irion— what more could I ask for?

Chapter Six

I didn't know where to start this morning. Should I have Cara show me around parts of the hotel? Perhaps meet more of my employees?

Then there were a bunch of other topics about which I should inquire. For example, did the hotel have procedures manuals, what parts of the chain of command had I not been informed about, were there any special holidays the hotel observes…

Cara knocked on my office door, interrupting my mental ramblings.

"Human wishes stay. Unknown objects requested. Confusion in Reception."

Ah, my first fascinating problem of the day. I walked out of my office only to discover someone I knew—Richard Branson sat at a reception desk.

Richard Branson the Fourth, a direct descendant of Richard Branson, a futurist, sat in front of a bewildered Particlan.

"Richard, what an unexpected pleasure," I said. "I thought you'd gone back to Mars, or was it Earth?" Richard had stayed at the Sath-Satre Golden Hotel on Irion.

"For a fleeting time I returned to Earth, but I do like to explore. I asked Dedare to keep me up to date on your travels, and he did. I knew you wouldn't stay long on Irion and would take off on another adventure." He blushed. "Sorry. I'm not stalking you. I like to see the world, I mean worlds, and you seem to be leading the way." He stood and then grabbed my hand. Standing a few inches taller than my five foot, eight inches, I still noticed a few strands of gray in his brown hair and a few smile lines around his blue eyes.

"It's nice to see a familiar face," I commented. "Now, Richard, you seem to be confusing my staff, just like on Irion. What's missing in your room? That appears to be the question my Particlan staff think you're asking."

"Is it true there's no restaurant in this hotel?"

I nodded. Richard would understand my action. I hated that question, and I'd only been on Particle a brief time. Such a wrong way to run a hotel.

"Then where do I go for food?" Richard seemed stressed, and I understood. Food for a traveler was paramount.

"Food is obtained through the hotel's room service. There's a great kitchen for serving the entire hotel, and most guests order food to their room many times a day. I'm looking into adding a restaurant to the hotel, but it won't happen overnight. I'm sure there are restaurants outside the hotel you can visit, but try our room service and let me know what you think. In the meantime, have you seen your room?"

There were so many things I hadn't looked into yet. I had to laugh. I'd have to stick to the hotel and stop sightseeing.

I received a room key from the reception staff who'd tried to deal with Richard, and then Cara and I took him up.

Thank goodness there were vertical elevators in each building. I soon discovered there were also horizontal elevators, or people movers, I guess you would call them, between buildings, so access was easy.

Richard's room was on the top floor of his particular building, so he had a splendid view of downtown Ooby.

Cara explained the equipment in his room. The little kitchen had a microwave-type device for heating food and a small fridge for storing perishables.

"What's missing is a tea kettle," said Richard. "I know I can heat water in the microwave, but I like to brew a pot of tea. Tea bags steeped in perfectly boiled water are what I strive for. And I brought my favorite tea bags with me."

His British background waved a flag.

"Cara, do you know what a kettle is?" I asked. I knew tea was always available for me, but I only received the finished product—teacup and teapot full of tea.

"Heating water hot," she replied.

"Exactly. Does the hotel have one that Mr. Branson can use during his stay with us?" I didn't remember one in my own rooms. I was sure I'd also hear about that lack from my mother and, perhaps, Sweety. Especially since Sweety wouldn't be imbibing alcohol for the required amount of time. But early days.

"Available in housekeeping. Not always room. Little use Particlans."

So the Particlans didn't often heat water via kettle. Interesting. "Cara, please find one for Mr. Branson. Can we get it quickly? Is there a power supply in this room for its use?"

"Kettle available soon. Power always available," she replied and left briskly.

"So, one problem solved. Richard, do you see anything else missing that would add to your comfort?"

He turned and for a few moments surveyed his room. "No, nothing seems to be missing, but I'm sure if there is, it'll soon become apparent." Richard smiled and gave the impression of being in a relaxed and happy holiday mood.

"Well, if there's anything else you need, don't hesitate to let me know." There was that Mars Best motto returning to loom over me.

The Mars Best hotel chain had the motto *If we can't supply your needs, your stay is free*. Of course, there were limitations. And the motto was nice for the guests but had often given me a headache. Dedare became smitten with the motto during his stay on Mars and wanted me to implement it as best I could in his hotel on Irion.

I suspected the motto had followed me to Particle.

Richard and I chatted for a few moments until Cara returned with the tea kettle. She showed Richard how to plug it into a hotel circuit, and we left him happily putting together his pot of tea.

"Cara, I need to get to the roof. Dedare is leaving today, and I want to say goodbye." She escorted me up and then left to return to her duties to give us a little privacy, I suspected.

Dedare waited in the shade of my, actually ours, helicopter. I rushed over and ran into his arms. Our hug was full of grief and wanting, but I tried to give him a good sendoff.

"How long will you be away?" I asked. I knew what his answer would be, but my emotions were taking over my rational thoughts.

"As necessary. Will return soon," he replied.

We kissed and hugged and rubbed cheeks until Dedare said, "Must go. Spaceship awaits. Messages sent, if possible."

"Oh, thank you. I'll also send letters. Have a safe trip, Dedare, and please come back as soon as you can." I had trouble with my words.

The pilot opened the passenger door—a strong hint.

I gave Dedare one last hug and backed away so they could leave.

For several forlorn moments, I watched the helicopter and my fiancé recede in the distance.

Trudging back, I realized I hadn't expected to feel this level of emptiness at Dedare's absence. Our partnership was my most committed relationship, and it triggered feelings I needed to deal with. And, having been brought up by a single parent and no other family, I now had more attachments than I'd ever dreamed of. I needed to learn how to communicate.

However, I still had a job to do.

In my office, I came upon Sain sitting at the conference table.

"What's up?" I asked.

Before he had a chance to answer, Cara burst into my office. "Another human arrive."

More humans? How could this be?

An unknown human sat at a desk in Reception. The length of his limbs were slightly shorter in proportion to Martians, so perhaps he'd been born on Earth.

I hurried over, and Cara scurried behind me.

"Hello, I'm Sylvestine Amera from Mars, and I'm the general manager of this hotel, the Sath-Ooby Golden Hotel. How may I help you?"

Thank goodness, we'd equipped the Reception staff with translators. I needed to remember to talk to Hart about the rest of the hotel.

"We have some confusion. I'm sure it's my fault. However, could you help me regarding items in my room? I've asked if certain items are available, but I seem to be confusing everyone."

"Of course. Let's finish getting you checked in, and then we'll go up to your room and you can tell me what you need."

Thaddeus Trent was indeed from Earth and was thirty-five years of age. He gave the impression of an easy-going, inquisitive human. His brown hair and eyes, and light, white skin, average height, and relaxed manner, did nothing to refute my first impression.

"So, a kettle, big mugs, large platters, and a large pan for popping popcorn are your current requirements?"

After his nod, I glanced at Cara, and she promptly left his room to find Thaddeus' needs.

While we waited, I asked, "How did you get to Particle?"

"I was on Earth and actually met an Irion at a Reception at the Martian Embassy. He worked for a fellow called Dedare Sath, and they were willing to allow a few humans to travel on their spaceship. I chose a trip to Particle. And here I am."

Apparently cryostasis hadn't affected Thaddeus, or he would have mentioned the problem.

"When do you need to be back on Earth?" Not that it was any business of mine.

"Oh, whenever I like. I actually have enough resources I don't have to work, but I'm also associated with the diplomatic corps. So what I really do is travel around and gather information for whoever needs it."

Thaddeus sounded like a spy, but I didn't utter those words out loud.

"Well, I hope you enjoy your stay on Particle. This planet is almost as new to me as to you."

At that moment, Cara arrived with Thaddeus' requested items. We both admired her choices, and Thaddeus started to look around his room—to decide their placement, I assumed.

"If you have any other requests, please let Cara or me know."

Thaddeus smiled. "One last request for today. Manager Amera, do you have a human called Charles Clarke on Particle?"

"Yes, he's here. Why?"

"Just tell him I've arrived. I'm sure he'll want to contact me."

Extremely curious, I said, "I'll do so. Have a great day."

Cara and I left Thaddeus in his room organizing the new items. While we walked back to Reception, my mind churned with connections.

In my office, Sain still sat at the conference table.

Oh yeah. "So, back to my original question—what's up?"

Of course, my words didn't translate very well, as Sain looked at the ceiling after I asked my question. "I mean, why are you here? What did you want to discuss?" My words were abrupt, so I tempered them with, "I'm glad to see you on Particle. We really haven't had a chance to talk since you arrived."

Sain smiled. "Restaurant is up. Location found?"

"So you think a restaurant is a good idea?" You never knew with Sain.

"Stir the Particlans. You love." Amused at his own words, Sain relaxed on his stool.

I wasn't sure how to respond, so I said, "Why don't we look around the hotel—this level preferably—for appropriate locations. And let's take Cara. The advice of a Particlan should prove beneficial."

Cara hovered outside my office, so I asked her in. Sain and I described the idea of a restaurant in the hotel and watched her reaction.

"Unusual, but ideal. Restaurants usually detached. Hotel addition interesting."

Cara steered us around the entire first floor of the main building. I found a couple of locations I thought might prove suitable. I wondered what Sain thought, but we'd agreed not to voice opinions until we'd seen all possible areas. Eventually, we arrived back at my office, and Cara ordered lunch. Thankfully, Particlans were on approximately the same sustenance schedule as every alien I'd met so far.

"So, Sain, where do you think we should add a restaurant?" I asked.

"Close to kitchen. Make door into kitchen for access for servers." He pulled out a map he'd drawn during our tour, and I easily understood his references.

"Cara, what do you think?" I asked after she'd also taken a look at Sain's drawing.

"Excellent location choice. Close to Reception. Available for questions."

"Agreed." I laughed. "Now, where could we add an Amenities room, you know, a gift shop?"

Sain and I took a few moments to help Cara understand the notion of a shop catering to items a guest might have forgotten or, perhaps, a tourist item to add to the memories of their trip.

"Should be close. Reception could advise. Items of necessity."

A quick study, Cara understood our description of a Gift Shop. So, while Sain got underway designing the renovations necessary for a restaurant and gift shop, Reena could help Cara decide which items were necessary for stocking the shelves of the Amenities shop.

Too many projects for Cara? Something to keep in mind. In the meantime, I needed approval for these changes.

Chapter Seven

I thought about Reena. Quite a big step she'd taken coming to Particle, but I thought the end result would be excellent experience for the teenager.

A new restaurant would impact the kitchen staff schedules, and certainly the available new recipes for aliens. So I needed to learn about the facility and its employees. As of yet, I hadn't entered the kitchen, so I decided a house call would be better than a brooch call. I needed more practice reading Particlan facial expressions anyway.

Much to my surprise, I found a locked kitchen door. I hesitated, and then an employee, perhaps room server, popped up beside me and put his brooch on the door pad. Immediately, the door opened. So they did use electronic keys in this hotel. The employee pushed his cart through the open doors, and I followed along. The kitchen clatter hushed immediately after the occupants caught sight of an alien.

"Hello, everyone. I'm the new general manager of this hotel. I may look a little strange, as I'm from a planet called Mars, but don't hold that against me." I heard the Particlan laughter of faint whistles, so I was off to a good start.

"I'd like to talk to everyone individually, so that needs to be set up. In the meantime, is the head chef here? I'd like a conversation with him or her. Please come forward and identify yourself."

I waited. However no one moved. Then Cara, who I hadn't noticed popping up beside me, said, "Chef Petra advance."

A bulky Particlan moved forward at a slow pace. After he reached our location, I said, "It's nice to meet you, Chef Petra. I'm Sylvestine Amera, the new general manager of the Sath-Ooby Golden Hotel. Do you have any questions?"

He didn't utter a word.

Now what was I going to do? I really needed to be able to communicate with the head chef of the hotel.

"Chef Petra, I'm back." Sweety's voice was welcome. "I've brought Hart, so we can start sampling your dishes, and so I can tell you about the dishes the Martians and Irions would like. Hart has his camera so he can take pictures and show off your marvelous cooking."

I stared at Sweety. Once again she'd charmed the chief chef at a hotel I managed. And, by the look on his face, this fellow was the usual smitten alien chef.

Sweety to the rescue, so Cara and I slipped out.

Back at my office, I asked, "Cara, would you please start arranging interviews with the kitchen staff. Make it a comfortable number a day because I'd like to have time to continue with my hotel research."

Eventually, I settled down to attack the paperwork on my desk. Before I had a chance to get a good start, Teeka strolled into my office and sat at the conference table. Happy to see this Irion, I joined him.

Before I spoke, Teeka leaned over and rubbed my cheek.

"Teeka, I don't think you should be doing that," I said.

"Yes. Know where *frindes are merged*," he said. "Happy to see friend."

On Irion, *frindes are merged* meant the two people involved were a romantic couple, and Teeka referred to Dedare and me.

I wouldn't argue with Teeka about his gesture. Kissing between friends was allowed, at least on Mars. "So, why are you here? What about your detective work on Irion?"

"Leave of absence. Dedare wished me to help Sain with security. New world for everyone."

Dedare's logic made sense. Dedare had enticed me to Irion and his hotel, and even on Dedare's home world security had been an issue. Teeka was Dedare's close friend, so I suspected this friendship had been the clincher in Teeka getting his leave and traveling to Particle.

"So what're you going to do first? I mean, how do you oversee and analyze the security of a hotel?" I had no idea where he'd start, and no idea what questions to ask him.

"Walk around grounds looking for problems. Study hotel security and personnel, investigate new concepts and related security for off-worlders. Much to ponder."

"Will you keep me updated with what you find? Maybe at dinner every evening?" His information would prove invaluable to our whole gang.

"Agreed." He smiled and stood.

"I'll call you if I need security help," I said, glancing at my brooch and the one on his tunic.

"Good." Without another word Teeka strode out of my office. Terse Irions were the bane of my existence.

I called Cara and asked her to start the employee interviews.

After I finished with the interviews Cara had arranged for today, I suggested she accompany me to the roof. I needed a good study of the city of Ooby, and she'd be able to answer any questions that came up.

I walked along the perimeter of the rooftop, holding onto the railing. The metal bar steadied my discomfort with heights. I first noticed acres of green with a tinge of blue. "Cara, are those fields for growing edibles?"

"Supplement for greens. Vertical not sufficient. Horizontal growth necessary."

My interpretation of her words suggested combining the vertical growth on walls of buildings such as hotels with the horizontal fields gave sufficient food stuffs for the Particlan population. I wondered how they could, or would, accommodate new alien species arriving on their planet.

Cara and I continued our walk around the rooftop. Most buildings in my view were five-story with the open ground floor pattern. However, I did notice one building of at least thirty stories.

"Cara, why's that building so tall? What's it used for? All your other buildings are much shorter." I pointed at the building I'd discovered.

"Library of Particle. Keeper of documents. Ancient to now."

A library? The information contained in the tall building would be more than I could assimilate in a lifetime.

"Everything you've ever written? I mean every book that's ever been written on Particle?"

Cara smiled and said, "Newer to electronic. Older to physical. Saver of history."

Her particular trio of word groupings proved difficult to understand. Eventually, I decided she meant newer volumes were digital, and ancient ones were printed. I thought for a moment. Were they printed on paper or something else, perhaps plastic? Although plastic didn't seem appropriate for older works. They were probably printed on something I couldn't imagine—a substance unique to Particle.

"Do Particlans also want the newer books as physical copies?"

"Trend is true. New building arises. Storage of physical."

Cara pointed to a hole in the ground located next to the existing Library of Particle filled with machinery.

Libraries were on my list of happy places.

"Fantastic." I took a long look at the old library and the new hole in the ground. "Cara, after I've settled in a bit more, please take me to the Library of Particle." A library tour would make a wonderful afternoon excursion.

I continued my roof circuit. The amount of air traffic astounded me, and most buildings had helipads on their roofs. I also noticed canals, like the one I'd fallen into. They were everywhere.

Then I noticed a group of domed buildings nestled together surrounded by what looked like a two-story parking lot. The upper floor had markings reminding me of helipads.

"Cara, see all those domed buildings?" I pointed them out.

"So many questions," commented Cara, trying to hold back a smile.

"Sorry, sorry. The view's so interesting." And I hadn't even completed my travel around the roof top.

"Olympic stadium area. Every bi-cycle competition. Water sports preeminent."

"What kinds of water sports?" I hoped I'd understood her words.

"Swimming, diving, dancing."

"Is this an important competition on Particle?" I asked.

"Worldwide competitive fun."

"Where are the world championships held?" More and more this sounded like human Olympics, and our universal translator seemed to think so, too.

"Here in Ooby. Held every bi-cycle. Important to commerce."

Commerce caught my attention. How could we make the Sath-Ooby Golden Hotel an integral function of the Olympic competition?

Competitive room rates? All-inclusive bookings perhaps—especially if we had a new restaurant to fascinate the Olympians?

I wanted to ask the Martians and Irions what they thought about an Olympics and how it might affect the hotel. Did the Irions have any notions about an Olympics? I certainly hadn't heard any discussion about physical competitions when I'd been on Irion.

My study of Ooby continued as Cara and I strolled along the rooftop railing. The next objects of interest to me were six deep holes in the ground circling a green open area.

"Cara, are those the basements of new buildings?" They didn't really remind me of what I imagined the beginning of construction would look like, but this was an alien world, and I was no expert on building.

"Construction of gardens. Botanical history museum. Newest world exhibition."

I laughed and made a wild guess. "Are you making Ooby into the museum capital of Particle?"

"Yes, I believe."

Okay, perhaps I shouldn't have laughed at the concept. After all, Ooby was the political capital of Particle. Museum capital would be the natural next step.

When I noticed we were back at the beginning of our wandering path, I suggested we retire to my office. I wanted all these new visions to sit in my brain and percolate while I continued my day-to-day routines.

I settled in my office, and Cara ordered lunch. Before I had a chance to partake, Tarin et Tong, Dedare's co-owner showed up.

"Sylvestine, consult time." His three words sounded ominous.

Chapter Eight

Tarin dropped onto a stool at the conference table, so I joined him and left lunch on my work desk. His clothing today was dark brown and drab, but his eyes flashed. Cara disappeared.

"Presence of Sain. Indication eating establishment. Attachment to hotel?"

Apparently Sain had already released my idea of a hotel restaurant.

"Yes. It's a wonderful way to get potential new guests into the hotel. They can see how the hotel is run and how wonderful it would be to stay here. And current guests wouldn't have to stay in their rooms for every meal. I assume you have restaurants in the city, so this way our guests might stay longer in the hotel. What do you think?" What a loaded question, and one of the ones that always popped out of my mouth. I never learned.

"Cost constraints consider. Dedare's opinion approval. Many details study."

"Dedare already likes my idea." I hoped I wasn't lying. He'd been here when I mentioned the problems with having no restaurant in the hotel, and he also knew how I'd improved the Sath-Satre Golden Hotel in Satre, the capital city of Irion.

"Do you like the notion of a restaurant in this hotel?" I held my breath.

"Excellent new beginning. Update with ideas. Discuss before implementation."

I think I understood his words' implications. "I'm glad you like my idea. I'll certainly consult about other suggestions I have."

Tarin smiled at my words, and then he stood and pointed at my desk. "Lunch. Must eat." Before I had a chance to reply, he'd left my office.

After a moment, Cara slid into view. "Keeping an eye on me, are you?" I asked, adding a grin.

"Happy to help." I suspected the look on Cara's face implied mischievousness.

"Do I have anything planned for this afternoon?" I'd started to treat Cara as my aide.

"Nothing I know."

"Cara, I'm giving you extra duties, and I'm treating you like my assistant. Do you mind?"

"Interesting days arrived."

"Good. In that case, I'm going to make you Manager of Reservations and Planning.

I'm adding Planning to your duties. Of course, we'll adjust your salary to reflect your new responsibilities, and you'll probably need to pick someone in Reservations to help you with your duties there. You're certainly doing a great job helping me adjust to this new world."

"Happiness with plans." Then Cara pointed to her brooch. "Brooch updates necessary."

Three-word Particlan statements sometimes confused me and made me uncomfortable. I certainly didn't want to misunderstand. "What needs updating?"

"Jewels along perimeter." She took her brooch off her uniform and pointed to the stones along the rim, so I took mine off to compare.

Gems filled my brooch's whole rim, while Cara had four. "Cara, what do the stones signify?"

"Rank in organization."

I suspected I had the highest rank. Well, I knew I did, except for the owners. However, I needed a better understanding of the hotel management structure. That should have been one of my first projects upon arrival.

"Cara, do you have a brochure, or pamphlet, explaining the different levels of stones on brooches?"

"Yes, will find."

"Excellent. So, assistant, what do you think I should do this afternoon?" I amused myself and also Cara, as she tried to hide a smile.

"Meet more employees. Create new clothes. Discover other areas."

She'd just confirmed my opinion she was an excellent assistant. "So what does *create new clothes* mean?

"Make waterproof clothes."

I could go along with that concept considering my past experiences. Who knew what other situations on Particle would drench me with water?

"Do we have a tailor in the hotel?"

"Yes, for staff. And for guests. Emergencies and uniforms."

"Okay, let's start with the tailor. I love your idea of waterproof clothes."

Cara led me to a small room nestled at the back of Reception. Guests could inquire, and one of our staff would usher them the short distance.

I was introduced to Baria tas Confit, the seamstress. "I'm looking for waterproof clothes. I keep getting drenched because our alien clothes are not impervious to water. The Particlan clothes I've seen all shed water nicely and quickly. Could you make me a couple of outfits with waterproof material? I'd like the outfits in a design like this Martian outfit because I want to look suitably off-world but be comfortable and dry. Oh, and I have some material I was given at our recent reception."

Baria gave my clothes a quick study. My tunic and trousers were comfortable for a workday but suitably alien to the uniforms my staff wore.

The seamstress motioned to Cara and me and took us into a medium sized room lined with shelving. Bolts of cloth were stuffed into every available corner.

"Many designs available. Pick out five. Wardrobe ready in three days." Baria's brown eyes sparkled.

"Can you really sew five outfits in three days?" Her announcement astonished me.

Baria gave me a Particlan smile.

"You're amazing." A grin covered my face. "Cara, will you help me choose the fabrics?"

"Happy to help."

Her own garment complemented her voluminous, slightly curly, black hair, and I knew her choices would be appropriate.

The two of us rummaged through the bolts of cloth, and the variety stunned me. "Okay, I've chosen three. Cara, would you pick out the other two. I'm overwhelmed."

Cara laughed and immediately showed me two fabric designs.

One had what I thought of as geometric designs in a red and gold color pattern, and the other bolt had interlocking circles in the hotel's blue and gold color scheme.

"Good color choices. Skin tone different. But Martian suitable," said Baria, after we brought the bolts of cloth to her.

I agreed with Baria about my skin tones being different from Particlans. I was the typical white human with fair skin that burned easily, while most Particlans were impervious to the effects of the sun, I'd been told.

"Baria, I can't wait to wear my new clothes, and in only three days. Thank you so much."

The hotel seamstress appeared pleased with my comments and took a few more measurements before Cara and I said our goodbyes and returned the short distance to my office.

"What's next?" I asked after I'd settled behind my desk.

"Interviews with staff. Must accomplish soon. Employee reassurance necessary."

"Until now, have my employees been reassured?" I asked. I'd received the vague impression they were, but I wanted a Particlan perspective.

"Yes. Excellent accomplishment."

Cara's approval strengthened my spirit. "Please start sending staff in. After we're finished today's interviews, will there be time to see another part of the hotel?"

Cara smiled. "Appropriate area chosen."

Apparently, Cara had a good handle on the number of employee interviews reasonable for one sitting because she came into my office and said, "Last one today. New location chosen. Interest Manager Syl."

"Where're we going?" I asked. As much as I loved my employees, interviewing caused a heavy emotional strain.

Cara smiled and led me to the top floor of our building. We exited the elevator into a room holding an Olympic-sized swimming pool. The required areas for a swimming venue surrounded the pool, and a diving board had been secured. A small spectator stand rounded out the facility.

"Cara, why do we have another pool as part of the Sath-Ooby Golden Hotel?"

"Employee training facility," she replied.

"Training for what?" Lifeguards, maybe?

"Particle Olympics presence."

I needed a much better explanation, but I didn't know where to start. "The employees train for the Olympics? Only the ones that want to?" I said.

"On own time," said Cara.

"Are the employees part of a country contingent?"

"No, hotel contingent."

"So you have business teams, as well as country teams."

"Many kinds teams. Business, country, city. Family, and others."

"Surely, not everyone can compete in the Olympics?"

"Elimination rounds qualify."

Okay, qualifications rounds would be necessary with that many teams wanting to proceed. "Does the Sath-Ooby Golden Hotel always send a team to qualify?"

"Every year try. Not successful, elimination. Always try again."

"So, let's make this year successful." My thoughts churned. "Cara, do the Olympics have diving competitions?"

She pointed at the diving board.

"Would you send me as much information as you have about the Particlan Olympics? They sound fascinating. Oh, and do you have any videos I could watch?"

Cara gave me a curious glance. "I want to learn everything about Particle. Your world is intriguing."

I hadn't let it be known to the Particlans or Irions, and only a few Martians, that I used to be quite the diver. Diving had been one of my passions as I grew up on Mars.

Mom had allowed me to search out my own interests as a teenager, with only a little guidance whenever I started to go astray...numerous times.

I'd let my interest go after I'd taken over management of the Mars Best—Tycho Basin Hotel.

A knock interrupted my thoughts. Cara answered the door.

"Oh, hi, Cara. Nice to see you again." Sweety gave me a glance.

"Cara, I think we've both done enough for today. And a good day it was. Go home and relax. I'm sure tomorrow will be terribly busy, especially for my new assistant Manager of Reception and Planning."

Cara glowed as she left my office.

"What's up, Sweety?" She didn't look unhappy, so I had no idea why she wanted to talk to me.

"Are you ordering tonight's dinner?"

"I really don't want to. I have only a slight idea of what Dedare previously arranged."

"Good. Because I want you guys to try some of the Martian dishes I helped Chef prepare. I haven't gotten to Irion dishes yet.

That'll take another day." She laughed. "I'll order tonight's feast. Shall we say an hour?"

"Sounds good to me. I might try a little catnap before dinner." At the moment, my days were particularly tiring.

I tidied up my office and left for my rooms.

On my way home I took a short detour and decided to snoop around the second floor of our building. Most of our investigations so far had taken place on the first above-ground floor of the main building and on the roof above.

According to Dedare's character reader, the first door I came to had a name plate indicating I'd found the hotel laundry. I didn't know what I'd do without his little machine.

After I opened the door, high humidity and heat assaulted me. Not unexpected in a laundry area.

No one greeted me, so I cautiously investigated the area. Numerous machines whirred in the background, and tables piled with sheets, towels, and other linens were situated in front.

The whole area appeared organized and worthy of a deeper look, so I decided to return when there was someone with whom to converse.

After deciding to leave, I turned the door handle, but nothing happened. So I added my shoulder. The door ignored me. It seemed like the door was locked from the outside.

I found a stool and sat down to wait. I didn't imagine the laundry had closed for the day.

After thirty minutes, I began to rethink my assumptions. I'd looked for water and found none. I'd tried the door numerous times, with no luck. And I'd tried my brooch, but no reception was found.

I had no idea what to do.

The worst part continued to be dehydration. I started to fade physically and mentally.

The next thing I knew, someone burst through the door. I barely recognized Teeka and Sain with Sweety and Hart right behind.

Hart did a quick exam. "Take her to the hospital. Her major condition is dehydration, and we can treat that quickly there. I also want to run additional tests."

Teeka easily carried me to the roof. The helicopter had blankets, so Hart insisted I lie on the floor. Didn't seem very safe, however I didn't argue with him.

Hart arranged for an empty two-bed room for the night and hooked me to an IV to help with my hydration.

"Is it necessary for me to stay overnight?"

"Yes. And if you complain, I'll arrange for two nights. I'm in charge." Hart grinned.

This would be a losing battle, so I didn't bother. "Fine. Now go away so I can get some rest. Tell everyone what happened, and that I'll see them tomorrow."

"We'll all have breakfast together," announced Sweety. "Since you've missed dinner tonight, everyone will want to talk to you."

"Good plan. I'm sure I won't want to partake of hospital food for breakfast."

Hart, Sweety, and Sain made their goodbyes and left my room.

I glanced at Teeka. "Why are you still here?"

"Stay night." He bounced on the second bed.

What was going on? "Why?"

"Security."

"I need security?" Our conversation was going nowhere.

"Heard about canal incident. Now, second happening. Protection needed."

I hadn't expressed my concern about falling in the water, but obviously Teeka had put two and two together.

I spent a restless night in the Particlan hospital. At one point, Teeka taught me an

Irion card game since we both couldn't sleep. Well I couldn't, but I wasn't quite sure about Teeka. Looking after me, I suspected.

The next morning, Hart arrived and bundled me up for the trip to the hotel after he examined my test results.

"Everything's good, Syl. Your fluids are topped up, and the blood tests reveal no abnormalities. Let's go have breakfast."

Hart did love to eat.

"I want to hear about everybody's day. We have a lot to catch up on. By the way, Sweety, this version of spaghetti and meatballs is to die for." For some unknown reason, they were the best I'd tasted in years.

"The rest of us are having more normal breakfast items, but I kept your dinner from last night." She laughed.

"Particle has the best spaghetti, or pasta I guess I should say. It doesn't get mushy or fall apart. That's probably why it tastes so good. As everyone should assume, I spent yesterday in the kitchen teaching Chef Petra numerous Martian recipes. Don't worry, Irion dishes are next."

"Again, we have a chef smitten with Sweety. What's with you and guys who love food?" I asked, sending a grin Hart's way.

Sweety didn't reply but did give her husband a hug.

"By the way, how did you guys find me yesterday?" I thought of the question this morning, but the excitement of leaving the hospital threw it out of my mind.

"When you didn't show up for dinner, we broke up into groups and went looking for you throughout the hotel," answered Mom.

"My group found a Particlan who had seen you go in the laundry," said Hart. "And the rest is history."

"Why did somebody lock me in the laundry room?" When only silence greeted my question, I changed the subject.

"Sain, how did yesterday go for you?" I asked.

"Many measurements taken. Addition of restaurant planned. Also, Amenities room. Curiosity from hotel employees and guests."

"Excellent. Curiosity is contagious. Listen up, everyone, I have excellent news. Tarin et Tong, Dedare's co-owner, has agreed to our expansion. So, Sain, you can start with the restaurant construction immediately."

I knew how to read Irions, and Sain was shocked by my announcement. I also suspected the others in my living room were surprised at the quickness of my negotiations.

"Dedare agree?" asked Sain.

"Dedare knows about the restaurant," I said, not exactly answering his question. I hadn't directly asked for Dedare's permission, but in my opinion our discussions had indicated consent.

Although I suspected Sain understood the underlying meaning of my words, he didn't raise any audible objections.

"Teeka, what did you find out yesterday before you were stuck babysitting me all night?" I asked.

"Hotel security minimal. Must be updated for well-being of guests. Unknown hazards on Particle." He threw his hands outward.

And I knew he referred to my recent incidents.

"Hmm. I agree we don't know about hazards on Particle, and especially the ones relating to Martians and Irions. Perhaps you could put a report together outlining what you think should be done in regard to security for the hotel. I'll take the report to Tarin et Tong for approval, if Dedare's not back when your report's completed."

There were no arguments from Teeka, or anyone else in the room, for that matter.

Mom remarked, "I see you had a busy day yesterday. Of course, not counting your excitement in the laundry room."

"You have no idea." I laughed. "Now, Mom, what's excited you recently?"

"I spent a lot of time in the hotel's library. They have many fascinating books. I focused on Particle's history. I thought it would be an effective way to understand the underpinnings of their society, and I learned a lot."

"Have you written up anything yet?"

Mom shook her head.

"When you have something composed, please send it to me. I'm sure it'll help me put bits and pieces of Particlan society together." Mom immediately received requests from everyone present for copies of her writing. Judging by her face, our reactions pleased her.

"Hart, other than fussing over me, thank you by the way, how have you spent your time?" He always dug out interesting tidbits.

"I spent time at the hospital examining their equipment and getting to know the medical staff—our equivalent of nurses, doctors, and paramedics. This is important for all of us, but especially for Sweety, of course." He grinned at his pregnant wife.

"Since I'm also the only expert on Irion and human physiologies, the Particlans welcome my experience." Hart grinned.

"I imagine they do. They must be overwhelmed with two new species landing in their midst," I commented. "Our stay is an excellent learning experience for everyone. Did your medical activities last all day yesterday? I know how your day ended, of course." Laughter followed my words.

"No. I managed to find time to help Sweety with her kitchen exploits."

Kitchen exploits, indeed. 'Eating exploits' would be more appropriate.

"Dad, what's happening on the diplomatic front? Are there other alien races we should know about?" I sighed. "Sooner rather than later?" I hated being surprised with requests from a race I didn't even know existed.

"I had a number of meetings with one of the Particlan ambassadors. Aliens are a relatively new concept for them, and two at once, humans and Irions, have overwhelmed them. However, I'm finding my way as are they."

"Good, because I have an idea that may cause problems."

"What're you proposing, Sylvestine?" asked Dad.

"Particlans have their version of an Olympics. Country teams are naturally created, but teams can also be from businesses, families, however you want to put together a team of athletes. Now the Sath-Ooby Golden Hotel has had a team every year, and I want to be part of the diving contingent. So somehow we need to get approval for non-Particlans to be allowed to take part." I sighed. "Dad?"

"A challenging task, Sylvestine, but certainly one I expected from you. I'll start making discreet inquiries. A basic question, though, dear. Surely not all teams created can actually be in the Olympics?"

"No, no." I shook my head. "They have qualifying rounds. The teams need to meet specific requirements in each area. That's all I know. I only found out about the Particlan Olympics yesterday."

"Do you think you'll have time to practice your diving and also manage your duties at the hotel?" asked my astute mother.

"It's going to be a challenge," I answered, "but I'm going to enjoy the exercise. The hotel has a second pool and diving platform on the top floor of the main building for employees only, so they take the Olympics seriously. It'll also help me get to know a portion of my employees better."

I rubbed my head. "However, if I feel the diving time interferes with my hotel duties, I'll stop. And if anyone feels I'm neglecting them or my duties, give me a smack."

Reena's eyes widened.

"Just a mental smack, Reena. Don't worry, we don't go around hitting each other."

Reena processed my translated words, and then she asked, "Teach diving?"

"You want to learn how to dive?" Reena surprised me. I hadn't really seen much in the way of pools on Irion, but I knew I'd missed a lot of their culture during our relatively short stay.

"Can you swim?" If she couldn't swim, diving was definitely out of the question for the immediate future.

"Yes. Learned in school." She laughed. "Found out Particlan students very interested in pool."

Her school indoctrination had proved that simple fact. And this would be a perfect way to help her get acclimatized to diving. "Let me do some research, and then we can discuss the details."

With a huge smile, Reena sat back in her chair.

A thought popped into my mind. "Oh, Sweety, I found a hotel employee yesterday you should meet. She'll help you in the future."

"Out with the details, Syl. Stop being so cryptic."

I laughed. "The hotel has a seamstress. I'm getting her to make me Martian-designed clothes out of water-resistant Particlan fabrics. I think you should talk to her about your needs." I held my hand a few inches out from my stomach.

Laughter rang in my living room. "Oh, clever idea. I hadn't even thought that far ahead. Mama A and I did have a little talk, though. Very informative." Sweety beamed at my mother.

Our discussions eventually lost energy, so I said, "The only other item I should mention is that two other humans have registered at the hotel. Not a problem, but I was surprised. The one I know is Richard Branson. The other came here on one of Dedare's ships, so I need to get Dedare to forward me personnel manifests so I can be prepared."

"But this is a human?" asked Mom.

"Yes. His name is Thaddeus Trent. Anyone know him?"

Charles cleared his throat. "I do."

"I suspected you might, Dad. He asked for you by name."

"How do you know him, Charles?" asked my mother. "Part of the embassy staff on Earth?"

"No, but his mother is, or at least she was on staff when I was there. Thad's my son."

Chapter Nine

Charles has a son. I have a half-brother. I stared at my mother. Her facial expression told me she knew no more than I did about this Thaddeus Trent, although I had actually met him.

"I need to rest. Having a baby is demanding work." Sweety obviously wanted to avoid stressful situations. Then she realized what she'd said and sent Mom an apologetic look. Perhaps not such a tactful issue to bring up. Then I noticed Sweety mentioned having a rest in the morning. She really was upset.

Sweety grabbed Hart's hand as he appeared reluctant to leave my drama-filled living room.

Then Mom announced, "I also need to get some work done. Syl, I'll see you later." She didn't even glance at Charles as she sailed out.

"Dad …" I didn't know what to say or ask. Why hadn't he told anyone? Didn't he trust us?

"I need to talk to your mother."

Reading my mother had proven easy for me, however I could only imagine Dad's problem.

Secrets broke relationships. Although Mom and Dad had recently gotten back together after years apart, I didn't imagine their relationship was currently always on an even keel. How would Mom handle the idea of a stepson?

Of course, there were questions about legitimacy, donated sperm, and "accident"—the list went on in my poor overloaded brain.

And how would I handle the idea of a half-brother? Time would tell, I guessed. First a father I never knew, and now a brother I didn't realize I had.

As for Reena, she gave me a wide-eyed look and then disappeared. I presumed she left for her room to think about what had just happened.

Time for work. The rest would sort itself out...or not.

Cara joined me in my office, and we sipped tea. "Any problems with Reservations, new assistant manager?"

We laughed. I suspected she still rode high on her promotion, and rightly so. Cara had so far proven to be an excellent assistant.

"No, running smoothly. Any hotel problems? New General Manager?"

Cara's sense of humor apparently matched mine, which would work out well for our future interactions.

"No. No problems. Much to understand, but exciting times are upon us." And also uncomfortable ones. I really didn't want to dwell on the old Chinese curse *may you live in interesting times*.

While Cara and I were deep into planning our day, Mom rushed into my office. Her shaking hands and blanched face alarmed me.

"Teeka's been hurt. He's over at the medical facility—that one we were at the other day. Can we use your helicopter to go there?"

I glanced at Cara. Mom had spoken so fast, I'd wondered if the universal translator had kept up.

"Check on availability," she responded, and then talked into her brooch. "Yes, available now." Cara motioned toward the elevator, and Sweety and Hart joined us. They'd waited outside while Mom relayed the news.

We rushed to the medical facility. The Particlans didn't need explanations as to why we were there. Aliens wanting to see aliens was obvious to everyone.

Hart used his connections from previous trips to the medical facility to talk to Teeka's doctor while Cara settled the rest of us in a waiting room.

"Mom, what happened? What do you know?" I asked. "How badly is Teeka hurt?"

"I don't know anything. Someone from the hospital called Hart, so we rushed over to your office. We wanted to tell you the news and get to the hospital as soon as possible. We hoped your helicopter was available but if not we knew Cara would find a way to get us here quickly." Mom gave Cara a big smile as Cara passed out cups of tea.

The tea reassured my nerves, but I really wanted news of Teeka.

After a short time, Hart returned and settled amongst us. "Teeka's condition is precarious. It appears he was beaten, and quite badly. The incident happened early this morning, and someone found him lying on the hotel grounds and called the medics."

"Who found him? A hotel employee?" I asked.

"I imagine so, but I'm not really sure. Teeka needs an operation on one of his internal organs. Something like a knife was used on him in addition to the beating. His chances are fifty-fifty."

Sweety grabbed Hart in a hug.

"I'm going to stay here and assist with the operation. The Particlans are happy to have me on their team. They think I know all about Irion internal organs. I don't, but I do know more than they do." Hart sighed. "Anyway, I'm going to be here for a long time. I want the rest of you to return to the hotel and go about your regular duties. I'll call as soon as I have any news. Don't worry. I've been most impressed with the medical staff and equipment at this facility."

I wouldn't argue with his logic because I knew we couldn't help by sitting in a waiting room. "Cara, organize our return to the hotel please and then keep my helicopter available. We want to be able to return to the hospital when necessary, or Hart may want to join us at the hotel."

Cara left to find the helicopter pilot. She returned within a moment and ushered us out. We had a quiet ride back, with everyone immersed in their own thoughts.

In my office, I said, "Cara, I don't think I'm up to interviewing employees right now. I wouldn't be a happy camper."

"Not happy person?" she asked.

"Yes, sorry. I know my expression confused you. It's from my human past." I hugged myself. "Cara, I'm upset about Teeka, as I imagine you realize. What should we do to help me understand the hotel and Particlans more? I need to find out why this happened to Teeka."

"First, call Sain."

Of course. Why hadn't I thought of that? Sain probably hadn't even heard about Teeka's situation.

So Sain and I had an abrupt conversation, and then he asked to use the helicopter. "Yes, of course. I'm having it left on standby for us until further notice."

Sain soon popped into my office, and Cara ushered him to the helicopter.

After she returned, I said, "Cara, that was a thoughtful gesture to remind me to tell Sain. Sain and Teeka are friends, and I should've told him. I'm so upset I'm not thinking straight."

"Medical situation understood. Distress for friends. Waiting causes anxiety."

Apparently Particlans and aliens were not unalike in this situation, and Cara understood. "Okay, what should we do while we wait to hear about Teeka? I need to keep busy."

"Olympic practice current. Top level busy. Wish to watch?"

Watching my employees conduct an Olympic practice would certainly occupy my mind. After a time, we were on the top floor and Cara had settled me in the bleachers.

I noticed I'd already met a number of the employees practicing their swimming and diving. The unknown others studied me closely, as I did them.

"Manager Syl, alert. Employee wishes words. Like to communicate?"

Did I want to talk to one of my employees? Is that what Cara asked? I took a guess. "Of course, Cara. Please bring the employee up here." I paused. "Or should I go to them?" I had no notion of the current Particlan protocol.

Cara didn't answer but simply went down the bleachers and brought the employee up to where I sat.

How did she know he'd wanted to talk? I certainly hadn't seen any indication.

"General Manager Syl. Takka et Tong. Wishes few questions."

"Certainly, Cara. Takka, please ask your questions. I'll endeavor to answer." What urgent topics were on his mind? My consciousness noticed there were a lot of *et Tongs* I had come in contact with.

"Choose Olympics team?" He stood a step below me, grasped his hands behind his back, and shuffled his feet.

My knowledge of his question shocked me. "Takka, are you asking if I'm going to choose the Olympic team for the Sath-Ooby Golden hotel? Cara, is that what Takka means?"

"Knowledge is correct."

At least, Cara's three words reassured me of my conclusion.

"No, Takka, I'm not choosing the team. How do you usually handle it? Do you have judges you can call on, or do other hotel employees handle the task?" The magnitude of choosing Olympic-class athletes was certainly beyond my capabilities, particularly on an alien world.

"General Manager chooses," said Takka.

I couldn't believe what I'd heard. "Well, this General Manager is not going to judge our employees as Olympic athletes. I have no information about judging or even the specific Olympic categories. And Particle is a new planet for me. What other options would you suggest, Takka?"

He didn't answer, so I glanced at Cara.

"Many options available," she replied.

"Please elaborate." I wondered who made the final decision on judging options. "What do other teams on Particle do?"

"Common option decision. Of all applicants. For Olympic team."

"Do you mean all athletes trying to get on the team mutually decide who should advance?"

Cara took a moment to understand the translator's words. "Competitors understand judging."

Of course the athletes understood the criteria. How else would they be able to improve their performance? The Olympics would be a clever way to increase my understanding of Particlan behavior.

"That would be an outstanding way for us to choose our team. Cara, can you get all the employees who want to qualify for our Olympic team together so I can have a chat with them? I also want to understand the criteria for each competition." I made some notes. "Let me know when you've arranged a meeting. In the meantime, do you have any information about the Olympics I can study?"

Had I already asked her that?

I took a moment to catch my breath, and then Cara led me back to the elevator. As I left the pool area, I waved at the participants. Hopefully, my action wouldn't be considered rude.

Back at my office, Cara left after she told me she'd find Olympic materials and arrange a meeting.

I needed to formulate a plan before I announced to my employees, and everyone else, I'd also like to try out for the Sath-Ooby Golden Hotel Olympic team.

Finally alone in my office, I called Hart. "Any news on Teeka?" My mind had been directed to the Olympics for a time and now needed to refocus.

"No news is good news, Syl. We're still operating, but we're taking a short rest break for fuel. So far, Teeka's holding up well, but he has severe damage to various body parts. I'm working with the Particlans to ensure quick healing after the operation. They have quite fascinating procedures, and I'm learning a lot."

"Well, keep me updated. I'll let everyone know Teeka's status. How long will it be before another update from you?"

"Ah, I'm not sure what the next procedure will be, or when. Besides fuel, this current break is to plan our surgical attack. When I have any information, I'll contact you."

I let Hart return to his meeting and monitoring. I suspected he was both excited and anxious about Particlan procedures and how they affected an alien.

The day wore on, and then Martians and Irions started to collect in my office. "Sweety, have you heard from Hart?" I asked.

"All he ever says is that Teeka's doing well. I have no idea what that means." Sweety wiped her eyes.

"I think Hart means Teeka's not doing badly. Hart's pretty busy, you know, and he'll call when he has a chance," I said. "The Particlan procedures must be fascinating, especially if they're significantly different from Martian ones, so Hart needs to be totally involved to help the Particlans treat Teeka. Of course, I have no idea what I'm talking about. I've never even been in an operating room." Thank goodness.

"Manager Syl, what is happening? Danger to Teeka?" asked Reena.

Oh dear, no one had updated her. I went over and enveloped her in a hug. "Reena, Teeka's been hurt. Hart's at the hospital, and Teeka's having an operation to fix his injuries. I'll update you when I know more," I said. "Now, why don't we retire for the day? Will you order dinner, Sweety? I'd like to see what you managed today."

She nodded and tried to control her tears. Sporting a weak smile, Sweety added, "Not a great deal, but a few new dishes. So be surprised."

"Why don't we all meet in my space in an hour? If anyone hears anything before then, be sure to pass it along, but let's have a break, and then we can all discuss how our day went."

I heard no arguments. As we dispersed few words were spoken.

Instead of a nap, I had a glass of wine. Dedare, my sweetheart, had provided my favorite Martian wine for our trip to Particle. My friends would probably also need a glass or two with dinner. Today had been stressful.

Mom and Dad were the first to show. Mom's eyes gleamed, but I didn't ask why. I suspected I didn't want to know at this point. Mom and Dad—that notion still required time, since I'd grown up without a father—and the idea of Charles, Dad, having a son had been a surprise to all, except Dad, I assumed.

I poured wine and then greeted the remainder of my guests as they trickled in.

"Sweety, you've outdone yourself again. Thank you," I said, after I'd sampled my choices. "How's

Chef Petra handling your requests? Does he mind you suggesting food items?"

"He loves me. Well, I mean he's enamored with my Martian alien characteristics, so he's easy to charm. And I've found a lot of our Martian dishes are similar to Particlan ones—which surprised me. The spices are different, but the dish structure is essentially the same. I have no idea how that could happen on different worlds. Anyway, progress has been made. Hart and I've been printing new menus each day, and I think your employees put one in each room. Distribution is something for you to look into, Syl."

Sweety sighed. "Of course, my emotions are on a roller coaster, and it's not because of my pregnancy," said Sweety, patting her stomach and giving me a quizzical look.

"No, I haven't heard recently from Hart about Teeka's condition. I do wish someone would contact us."

I needed to change the subject. "Reena, how did your classes go?"

"More information about classes acquired. Strange, interesting curriculum. As I acquire subject structures, I will know more."

I'd certainly expected an alien experience for Reena from the details Mom had been able to provide. Thankfully Reena appeared to be coping happily. I hoped she'd let me know if she became overwhelmed or distressed.

Before I had a chance to bring up another subject, Hart popped in. Sweety jumped up and hugged him and then pulled him down onto a stool beside hers.

"Sweety, how are you? How's Teeka? Do you need food?"

True to form, Sweety continued to call everyone *Sweety*. No wonder we'd all started calling her Sweety on Mars, rather than her given name, and her new name had stuck. She could overdo it at times, however in this instance she talked to her husband so I gave her leeway.

"Sure, I'll take food. I'm really hungry. It's been a long day, and I knew you guys would be here." He paused and gave Sweety a kiss. "And, Syl, having a helicopter at my disposal is certainly an advantage."

"Hart, you need to tell us about Teeka. How's he doing?" I asked. My stomach hurt from worrying all day.

"Teeka's doing very well, actually. We've repaired his injuries. He's still in critical care, but he attempted to sit up and talk to me while I was at his bedside."

"Has he told you what happened?"

"All he's been able to say so far is *hotel security bad*. I have no idea what that means. However, he really is doing well."

"Can I visit Teeka?"

"At the moment, that's a bit iffy. Since he received numerous serious injuries, he needs rest and quiet for a considerable length of time. If he's coherent enough to ask for you, we'll let you visit of course, Syl," said Hart, "but he's really not well enough yet. Give him time."

"Thanks for the information, Hart." My investigative thoughts wouldn't shut up. I needed details of the attack from Teeka himself.

The subdued atmosphere in my living room upset me so I asked, "Who'd like to play a game? Anybody have any they brought along to Particle? I packed a Martian deck of cards, and I also have a couple of board games."

Mom perked up and organized our group into one big game of cards. The rules weren't entirely clear to me, but Mom was there to keep us in line. Her rules certainly kept our minds off Teeka.

Reena was fascinated by the flow of cards. I wondered what types of games they played on Irion. We hadn't had time to delve into games before we'd been shuttled off to Particle.

We laughed and teased each other while we played Mom's game. She and I succeeded in our intent for a distraction. However, before we'd finished the game alarms began screeching, and I had no idea why.

Chapter Ten

Cara rushed in and motioned for everyone to follow. We scurried to the main building and up to the top floor. In addition to the employee pool area, the floor held a large conference room.

"Large waves arriving. Safe on top. Remain until alarm."

I interpreted her words to mean we needed to remain here until the next alarm sounded. An all-clear alarm, I assumed.

Our situation confused me. Cara had our safety in hand, but what was really happening?

"Syl, everyone, just relax. This is perfectly normal for Particle," said Hart. "We're experiencing our first tsunami. They happen on a regular basis, and procedures are in place to minimize any damage to buildings and people." Hart smiled. "In fact, I was told that no one had died as a result of a tsunami for hundreds of cycles. Some minimal structural damage happens each occurrence, but that's about all. Particlans have the situation under control. Cara?"

"Regular normal occurrence."

Although everyone appeared calm, I knew a diversion was required to help us relax during our first tsunami.

"Did anyone bring the cards?"

My mother held up her pack.

"Mom, you're the best. How about setting up another game? Now that I know what's going on I might win."

"Not likely," said Sweety. "You're so bad at cards."

"Is that why you like to play with me?" I asked.

Our banter covered up the fact Sweety was stressed. She'd grabbed one of Hart's hands with both of hers.

While Mom and the others set up the game, I pulled Cara aside for a discussion. "Is everyone at the hotel safe? By the way, thank you for rescuing us. I had no idea what was happening."

"Hotel guests safe. Confusion with aliens. All settled now."

"But where is everyone? I know we're here, but what about the hotel guests?"

"Safe room exists. Top each building. Employees help secure."

"Why did you bring us to this building and not the top of our own?" I asked. According to her words, shouldn't there be a safe room above our residences?

"Safe room employees."

"So this room is for hotel employees only?" Sometimes only three words confused me with their lack of detail.

Cara smiled her agreement.

"Well, where are the other employees? Shouldn't they be here?"

"Help each building. Soon return here. Wait for signal."

So my employees made sure our guests found shelter. Nicely organized. Then I had a thought. "Cara, should I visit the other hotel buildings and make sure everyone's okay? After all, I'm the general manager." After I uttered my words, horror appeared on Mom's face.

"Waves hit soon. Best to stay. All buildings secure." Cara patted her brooch.

So Cara received updates on the hotel guests. I suspected she'd received them, as I'd appointed her my assistant. Should I get them also?

"Cara, you're doing a fantastic job." I reached over and gave her a hug. Her acceptance of my embrace indicated to me her understanding of human actions.

"Hart, have you heard from the hospital?" My mind wouldn't settle.

"All patients are located on upper floors, so no relocation was necessary. I'm checking on Teeka's condition as we speak."

In other words, *leave me alone, Syl.*

I glanced around the room and noticed a bunch of monitors with an employee each seated in front.

"Cara, what're those screens for?" I pointed in their general direction.

Before she had a chance to answer, the room began to fill. The new arrivals found places to sit. A couple of the new Particlans rummaged in the cupboards attached to one wall and began handing out snacks and bottles of water. I passed on the snack, but I welcomed the water.

After the interruption, Cara answered my question.

"Monitors survey hotel. Check wayward guests. All in shelters."

"An excellent idea," I said. "So we have surveillance on every part of the hotel grounds?"

"Yes, always monitoring."

I thought for a moment. "Do we keep copies of the surveillance? I mean copies of each day's activities?"

"Yes, able to view."

"I need the surveillance for yesterday." Maybe I could find out what, or who, happened to Teeka.

"Police take copy."

"Do we only have one copy?" That would be unfortunate.

Cara smiled. "Kept copy Syl."

"You're the best, sweetheart. Send it to my computer. I'll take a look after I get back to my office." Happily, the Particlans had computer software I understood, so I didn't have to bother Hart every five minutes. Certainty not as I had to when we were all on Irion.

I thought for a moment. "Cara, who's in charge of the police investigation surrounding Teeka?"

"I can answer that, Syl. Vara il Vast has already been at the hospital. He wanted to interview Teeka, but Teeka was sedated," interrupted Hart.

"I need to talk to this Vara il Vast. I want to know about his investigation and what he's found out. Cara, can you make arrangements?"

"I will organize."

"In the meantime, we'd better get back to the card game. Cara, how long does our isolation last?" I sighed. "I guess I'm asking how long is a typical tsunami incident?"

"Not long time. Regular tidal happening. Much prediction possible."

"So you can predict the tsunamis? Is this always the case?" Her words gave me pause. Did they minimize the damage to their world?

"Not always possible. Rogue wave happens. Seldom but devastating."

"Devastating if not prepared, I imagine you're saying," I commented. "Is this a regular tsunami then?"

Cara agreed. Why didn't the Particlans react to tsunamis in a different way? For example, would retaining walls around the edges of their inhabited areas, or even around their short buildings, solve the current problem? I needed a talk with Hart when we found a less stressed moment.

A siren sounded, so I glanced at Cara.

"End of danger," she said.

"So everyone goes back to their regular duties?"

"After checking damage."

"The hotel is well organized. I'm impressed. Where would we find damage?" I asked.

"Open area pools. Routine damage likely. Easy to fix."

"Are there any other places we could possibly check for destruction?"

"When high waves." Cara put her hand over her head. "Locations vary considerably."

Nothing we could predict I suspected.

I watched my employees gradually exit the safe room and return to their duties. I still had much to learn about the hotel structure and employee duties, but that would come. Today had been a welcome exercise.

Hart broke up our various conversations by announcing, "Teeka is now fully awake and able to receive visitors. The police are on their way to the hospital. Syl, can I use the helicopter?"

"Sure, but Sain and I are accompanying you." I'd caught Sain's eye a few seconds ago. I knew he wanted to start his own investigations. In addition to renovations he'd managed security for Dedare's holdings on Irion.

After a short wait at the hospital, we were ushered into Teeka's room.

"Causing trouble, I see," I commented.

"Syl, find culprits. On hotel grounds." Teeka's Irion skin color was a lighter beige than normal.

"How many were there? What were they doing? What did you uncover to upset them?" I blurted out.

"Good questions asked," said an unknown Particlan.

"Syl, Sain, this is Vara il Vast, in charge of Teeka's case," said Hart, pointing at me and Sain. So Vara would understand the additional players in this tragedy, he added, "Sylvestine Amera is the new General Manager of the Sath-Ooby Golden Hotel, and Sain Sath was in charge of security for Dedare Sath on Irion."

"Questions asked," said Sain.

"Since I'm in charge of the Sath-Ooby Golden Hotel, I need questions answered," I said.

Vara gave me a look I assumed was disbelief. I had no idea what he didn't believe, but I didn't care.

"For example, have you found anything on the hotel video footage to indicate the culprits who did this to Teeka?"

"Footage not watched."

Typical Particlan three words. "Well, I'm going to watch my copy of the footage, and I'm sure Sain will be beside me. If we find anything, we'll be sure to let you know."

Vara didn't respond, but Hart gave me a *calm down, Syl* glance. Hart knew me well, and I had no trouble reading his facial expressions.

"Investigation not yours," said Vara.

"I'll do anything I need to do to protect my friends, family, and employees. And I'll try not to get in your way."

Sain laughed and said, "Control our general manager."

I gave Sain a dirty look. We'd discuss his words at a later time.

Then I turned to Teeka and asked, "Do you remember what happened? What were you doing out on the hotel grounds?"

"Security checking." Teeka sipped from his glass.

"See anyone?" asked Sain.

"No. And not heard. Surprised when attacked." Teeka tried to move but groaned from the effort. His recovery would not be short, I suspected.

"Did you see any people, any faces? Any clues at all?" I asked.

Vara laughed. I didn't think we were the detective's favorite people, but our sleuthing attempts held his attention, if not his disdain.

"No details," said Teeka. "Happened too fast."

"Okay. Well, I'm going back to the hotel and watch the security tapes. Do you need anything?"

"Stay at hotel," he responded.

I tried not to laugh. "That's not going to happen in the near future. When you're allowed to leave, we'll take the helicopter back, and there will be a nurse to look after you night and day. Hart will let me know when you're allowed to leave." Even I understood

Teeka needed to stay in the hospital for at least a few days to speed his recovery. Home would be more comfortable—even if his current one was so new.

Teeka turned to Hart but said nothing after Hart shook his head.

"Do you need anything?" I asked again.

Teeka didn't answer. Actually, I thought he'd fallen asleep. I glanced at Hart, and he motioned us outside.

"You may as well go back to the hotel, guys. Teeka won't be up for conversation or anything else for quite some time. I'll join you, but I'll return early tomorrow."

"Good plan. I want to study the security tapes. Maybe I'll see something." I'd actually gotten my second wind thinking about the tapes and what I might find.

"No action possible," said a voice behind me.

Startled, I turned around and found Vara. "What do you mean?"

"If clues obvious. Present to me. I will deal."

Sain grabbed my arm to forestall any outburst. "Agreed, Vara. Call you tomorrow if details emerge."

"I—" was as much as I uttered before Sain grabbed my arm again. I suspected he really wanted to put a hand over my mouth.

Hart interrupted the staring match between Sain and me to say, "Let's go back to the hotel. I need food. I really haven't eaten enough today."

"Sure, we'll order a snack from the kitchen," I said. On our trip back, my mind only half focused on what we talked about. My thoughts jumped from topic to topic.

At the hotel, Sain, Hart, and I relaxed and chatted in my rooms until food arrived from the kitchen. Then Hart projected the videos from my brooch through my room's television-like device.

The three of us sat for hours watching the hotel security tapes. We sped up each of the various cameras' footage, since we had a time frame within which to work.

Eventually we found a tape containing Teeka's attack. However, the images were dark and blurry. We did observe two assailants surrounding Teeka. They first punched him numerous times, and then one pulled out a knife.

"Hart, can you blow up that image and print it? Or at least store it so I can print it on my office printer. I don't think I have a printer anywhere here at home."

"Of course. I'll send you an image file. I also want to blow it up and print copies of Teeka's assailants. The photos may help Vara see particular Particlan characteristics we know nothing about."

Hart understood we needed to work with Vara. Since Teeka was a detective on leave from his job on Irion, I suspected he'd be the one. "Hart, we need to give copies of the pictures to Teeka. They may help him remember, and his job is being a detective. We'd better make five copies. One each for the three of us and also for Teeka and Vara."

"For once, Sylvestine, you're being quite logical," said Hart. "What're you up to?"

"Hart, I'm insulted." I hadn't yet revealed I thought I recognized one of the muggers.

Chapter Eleven

I didn't know how to handle my possible recognition of one of Teeka's muggers. If I told either Sain or Hart, they'd insist I back off. At least, I should probably tell Vara. "Who's in charge of hotel security?"

"I have no idea, Syl. Isn't that under your supervision? Talk to Cara and get an employee chart. I know you're overwhelmed with information from the Particlans you've already talked to, but you haven't been logical about the entire hotel." Hart rolled his eyes at me.

Hart loved to call me illogical, and I certainly could be. And occasionally Hart used the notion as an excuse to tease me. However, in this case I suspected he'd correctly deduced my problem. I had no idea who was in charge of security and I should have. I'd left that aspect up to Teeka after I knew that was his reason for joining us on Particle.

"You're right. Sain, let's meet with whoever's in charge of security tomorrow. I know you're not here for only security, but perhaps we can help Teeka while he's invalided."

"Agreed," said Sain. "Renovations wait."

"Well I wouldn't say wait, but they won't be our top priority." I sighed. "Okay, guys, I'm tired and I want an early start tomorrow. Sain, let's meet in my office in the morning." We agreed upon a time, and then Hart and Sain retired.

I reflected upon my day. Lots of stress and anxiety had led to a profound tiredness. I had to decide between painting or going directly to bed. In the end, I gathered a glass of wine and a novel and read my book in bed for a whole ten minutes.

****

The morning dawned clear, and I noticed little evidence of the previous day's tsunami. My hotel employees had excellent cleanup routines. What had Particlan history developed in regard to this unfortunate physical phenomenon?

Hart popped into my office while I sipped my first cup of tea. "Syl, I need the helicopter to get to the hospital." He noticed the alarm on my face. "Nothing's wrong, but I want to check up on Teeka as soon as possible. He may have remembered something from the attack but mostly I need to check on his physical well-being. And friends at the hospital have been contacting me with all sorts of questions about Irion physiology." He sighed. "I'm very popular at the moment."

"Of course. Just coordinate with Cara. She'll arrange pilot and helicopter." Hart ran out, and that was the last I saw of him for quite some time.

My next visitor was my mother. "Is there anything I can do to help, Syl? You must be overwhelmed."

She read me too well. "Actually, there is something. It was pointed out to me yesterday that I hadn't even met the Particlan who's been in charge of hotel security. Could you get together with Cara and produce a flowchart of the hotel employees and their duties. You know, departments and all, who they report to, and highlight who I've already spoken with. I haven't acted logically since I arrived on Particle, at least according to Hart."

"I will certainly be the assistant to your assistant," said my mother. "I suspect it's quite an important job, especially since you've been keeping Cara busy with all the crises we've been having."

"Mom, you're the best. Of course, I'll try and raise your salary." We both burst out laughing. Remuneration wasn't something either one of us had focused on.

"No problem. This is the kind of project I like, darling daughter, and it'll help me with my history of Sath Enterprises. Now don't get stressed. You're doing a superb job. However, I'll run and harass Cara. You may need her help during the rest of today, so I want to get this project started."

She started toward my door.

"Mom, wait. Don't run away so fast." I didn't quite know how to approach my next topic, so I just jumped in. "Have you and Dad discussed Thaddeus Trent?" How would my new half-brother affect our innumerable relationships?

"Ah, no, not really. Actually, I'm not currently talking to Charles. I'm too upset." Her stiff posture should have given me that clue.

Very unlike my mother. She'd normally discuss any topic to death.

"What did Dad do?" Just a little spat, I hoped.

"He didn't tell me about Thaddeus. How many other offspring does he have running around the galaxy?"

I bit back a laugh because I knew it wouldn't go over well. And I certainly didn't dare retaliate and ask how many offspring she had running around the galaxy.

Of course, I knew the answer, but I didn't want to stir the pot so to speak.

"Hmm, Mom. You didn't tell Dad about me for many years. How is this any different?"

Tears glistened in Mom's eyes. "Now that we're back together again and supposedly engaged to be married, I thought we'd be open with each other."

What else is he hiding was on both our minds, I suspected.

"You have an excellent point. However, give Dad some slack. None of us have had an easy time lately. Thaddeus probably hadn't even entered his mind after we'd landed on Particle."

Mom sighed. "You're right. Where did you get such wisdom?"

"Oh, probably from Dad." I laughed. "Or perhaps from you." My comment elicited a small smile.

"Okay, I'll go interfere with Cara and get that organization list for you," said Mom.

A brief time after my mother left Sain entered. He held out a sheaf of photos, and I pounced. I pulled one out. "Sain, I think I know this person. I believe he's part of the hotel's security team."

"Agreed. Talk with him today." Sain started to pace in the confined area of my office.

"With Vara present?" I asked.

Sain sighed. "Of course. Message sent."

I knew how much he wanted to confront the character we both recognized, but he needed to include the Particlan police. "Let me know when the interview happens. I want to be there," I added.

Uttering no further words, Sain strode out of my office.

Then I realized what a general manager should do this morning. Outside my office, I found Mom thanking Cara for her help. "All organized, Mom?"

"Yes. Cara's been most helpful. She's sent me her files on staffing and the interviews you've had so far. Now I need to integrate the information into one big flowchart. Easy."

"Good. Will you be occupied for a long time?"

"Probably. If I finish early, I want to take another look at certain parts of the hotel. In particular, the library. The more I learn about Particle, the better I can do my historian job and the more information I'll be able to impart to the rest of you." Mom grinned. I knew she loved research. "What about you? A big day planned?"

"I haven't quite figured it out yet, and that's why I need to talk to Cara. So I'll see you for dinner?"

"Well, of course. I know Sweety has recipes to teach the kitchen staff, even if Hart can't be around much to record the experience." After her statement, Mom grabbed her overstuffed bag and took off.

I turned to Cara. "Please take me on a tour of the hotel because I need to check on the areas the tsunami affected." I wasn't sure about the expression on her face, so I asked, "Do you understand my request?"

"General Manager duties." Cara gestured to the elevator.

Our first stop turned out to be the guest pool area. Hotel employees were washing down the entire ground floor and walls because a coating of mud smeared every available surface.

"Only short time. Remains for opening. Pool to guests."

"So you'll be filling the pool with clean water. Is this a popular area for our guests?"

"Guests love hotel. Pool area available. Not in others."

"Let me get this straight. Our guests love this hotel because there's a pool for the guests, and other hotels don't offer this luxury." I gave Cara a questioning look.

She pointed to the guests checking out the pool area.

"They're waiting to see when the pool will be available?"

"Very popular spot."

"Then we should make other spots popular. The restaurant will be our first priority, and then we'll keep on the lookout for other opportunities to keep guests on the premises."

"Revenue from guests."

"Yes." I grinned. "We'll attract new Particlans and aliens, and that'll keep the owners happy."

We traveled over the hotel grounds and through the lowest floor of each building. Minor damage was evident, and what particular bits I did notice were being cleaned up or fixed. Even the landscaping had been designed to survive most tsunamis.

"Cara, I think …" My brooch rang.

"Syl, you'd better get over here to the hospital," said Hart.

What could be wrong? Had Teeka taken a turn for the worse?

"Teeka's anxious to talk to you, Syl. I'm not sure why, but I sent the helicopter back. Would you bring Sweety along? She can calm anyone, and Teeka's twitching. He really needs to relax and heal."

Cara and I found Sweety and flew over to the hospital.

"What's up, Teeka? You need rest," I said.

"Remember one assailant. Works hotel security. Recognition from photos. Sain find him."

"No problem. Don't worry. Sain's already working on finding your assailants, and we're communicating with the police. We'll get to the bottom of this. Is this person the one who used the knife?"

"No. Other was culprit." Teeka sipped his drink and appeared unbearably tired.

I suspected Sweety also noticed his fatigue because she said, "Teeka, I'm busy teaching the kitchen Irion recipes. By the time you're back at the hotel you'll have a range of dishes to choose from. We'll fatten you up, don't worry."

While appearing alarmed at being fattened up, Teeka still gave Sweety a wan smile.

"Now, I want you to sleep, and later today I'll bring you dinner from the hotel. Won't that be fantastic? Hospital food is usually so terrible."

We left Teeka dozing in his bed and took the helicopter back to the hotel. Hart joined us for the trip.

"I need food. So I think it's best if Sweety and I slink around food services. Under the guise of adding options to the menu, of course," Hart said.

Sweety laughed and pulled Hart toward the kitchen.

Before I had a chance to consider lunch, I contacted Sain. "Have you tried to call? I've been at the hospital with Teeka. He recognized the same Particlan we did."

"Meeting this afternoon with Vara." Sain and I agreed upon a time to run over to police headquarters for the appointment.

After a few additional planning moments, I asked, "Cara, how about ordering lunch? I have to go over to police headquarters with Sain a little later, and I haven't had much to eat today. Then we can discuss what we need to do next."

After Cara left my office, I sat back and reflected on my day. Teeka's appearance had improved over yesterday, but he still had a long healing road ahead.

My mind diverted to another subject. The hotel employees knew how to recover from a tsunami, but I wanted to think of ways to minimize the actual damage during future events. Perhaps Hart could help. And Sain would have ideas about possible renovations to minimize devastation. Of course, I knew I was arrogant to assume our ideas would be better than the Particlans', but I still wanted to look into it.

Before I realized, time had flown, and it was time to visit Vara at police headquarters.

Vara retrieved us from his reception area. His office consisted of a typical government box—small, spare, and overflowing with cabinets. Why had I expected anything different on Particle? Particlans were remarkably similar to humans. Some of their thoughts were downright strange, but their activities mostly mirrored ours.

To my surprise, Vara's walls were painted a bright red, and his ceiling sparkled with gold flecks. His shiny blue filing cabinets were similar in shape to human ones.

"Interview room available. Vara does talking. Aliens observe only."

Vara il Vast, the detective, made himself quite clear regarding our possible actions. Of course, the situation was ultimately better than being excluded completely, which I'd been afraid might happen.

So Vara ensconced us in the drab viewing room—no bright red, pink, or blue this time—and then he left to confront Takka.

"What's his name? Recognition?" asked Sain, using typically terse Irions words.

"I was up in the employee training area when he asked me a question about who would make the decisions on the hotel's Olympic team. His name is Takka et Tong."

"Employee training area? Olympic team?" asked Sain. "Lots of questions."

"I'll explain later. Vara's started his questioning," I said, pointing at the window. I assumed we had the typical one-way view screen in a sound-proofed room because Takka, the suspect, hadn't glanced our way while we spoke, and I'd heard Vara's voice being piped in.

"Why assault alien?" asked Vara. Takka sat at the table while Vara hovered.

"Action not performed," replied Takka.

Interesting. He didn't say he hadn't encountered any aliens. Takka hadn't even asked which alien Vara referred to.

"Activity action caught," said Vara, placing a photograph on the table. "Your image obvious."

Takka clasped his hands together. His two thumbs showed a tinge of darker blue. I'd seen his action before, so I recognized anxiety. Another datum to add to my notebook on Particlans.

"Not my image."

"Analysis says yes," Vara insisted.

"Forced to comply," replied Takka, after a long, silent moment.

Just a minion, as I'd suspected. He had a boss in the background.

"Leader to reveal," said Vara.

Takka's slightly scaly skin began to shine in the harsh light, and I couldn't blame his reactions. He wouldn't win with his controller by answering Vara's demand.

Vara and Takka went around the subject for a few long moments. Finally, Vara asked, "Did you knife?"

"No. Only punch. Alien to retreat. Not wish killing."

Vara gave Takka a stare. "Name required knifing."

Takka stared at the tabletop.

"Answer name required," Vara repeated.

Again no response.

Vara left Takka and entered the observation lounge. "Any questions ask?"

I glanced at Sain before I spoke. I thought perhaps he'd have better questions than I would, having been involved in security for many years, but he deferred to me.

"Is Takka a relative of Tarin et Tong?" I asked. Their names were too similar for my comfort.

"Nephew of Tarin," responded Vara. "Why ask relative?"

"Tarin et Tong is the co-owner of the Sath-Ooby Golden Hotel. Why would his nephew, who works at the hotel, try to kill an alien? Who's Takka working for? Would it be Tarin? And why would that be? His hotel wants to cater to aliens."

"Too many questions," said Vara. "However, good ones."

"So what're you going to do with Takka?" I asked. During our exchange, a quiet Sain surprised me.

"Hold in jail. Assault charges pending. Visit to court."

"That's all fine and dandy, but we need the name of the other assailant and the name of whoever arranged for them to assault Teeka." I started pacing.

"Understand criminal nuances," replied Vara.

Now I'd upset him. "Yes, I know you do. I'm just upset because Teeka's been hurt. Please forgive me."

"Understand personal relationship," said Vara.

What did he mean by that? I glanced at Sain. I knew I'd been interested in both Teeka and Sain, along with Dedare, on Irion, but how did Vara know this? I'd probably misinterpreted his words.

"Yes, Teeka's a friend of mine. What should we do to help him?" I asked.

"Leave Takka me. Hotel investigations yours. Gather to consult."

Vara was being exceeding generous allowing us to investigate the details of Teeka's assault at the hotel and then meet with him to compare information.

"Thank you, Vara. If Sain or I uncover any details, we'll be sure to let you know right away. By the way,

Teeka seems to be healing well. After he's allowed to leave the hospital he'll rest at the hotel, of course. I'd like Teeka to take sufficient time to recuperate, but I expect he won't. I hope he'll come up with new clues while he rests. Anyway, thank you. We really appreciate your time and effort. If you have anything to share with us, that would be wonderful."

With a currently cooperative Vara, I gathered up Sain and we made our exit before I changed Vara's mood.

In the lobby of the police headquarters I asked, "Sain, do you have anything else you want to do, or shall we return to the hotel?"

"Wish to pummel, but restrained self."

"Pummel whom?" I hadn't noticed Sain's anger, but his quietness at police headquarters had probably been indicative.

"Takka. Juvenile male needs instruction in better ways."

I had to laugh at Sain's behavior. I just learned humans weren't the only ones to have this reaction to criminals. In my mind, Takka was too young to be considered a criminal. He was really only a delinquent. On the other hand, I had no idea about the justice system on Particle and whether justice depended on your age.

How should I handle the hotel's Olympic team? Who would be upset Takka was in jail and couldn't compete? I needed to find out when the Olympic trials began or when we needed to present our team to be included in the trials. Cara should know the answers to my questions, though.

Sain and I took the quick trip from police headquarters to the hospital. We met Hart in the lobby. On our way to Teeka's room, I asked, "How's he doing, Hart?"

"Very well. Of course, Teeka wants to return to the hotel, but we need to dissuade him. The hospital is his best bet for a couple more days."

Under protest from the staff, we entered Teeka's room. Apparently, patients were usually only allowed one visitor at a time. And much to my surprise we found Cara sitting by Teeka's bedside.

"Cara, how nice of you to visit and see to Teeka's needs. You've been such a jewel the past few days," I said. Her skin color seemed a darker blue than normal. However, I hadn't been here long enough to make any complete analysis of Particlan skin colors and their meanings.

Cara stood and then backed away from Teeka's bed. I noticed his eyes followed her movements. A budding relationship? Wonders never ceased.

"Meeting with Vara?" asked Teeka.

Back to topic. "We had a most productive get together. Takka admitted to assaulting you but said he didn't use a knife. However, he wouldn't offer the name of his cohort. Vara'll be looking into the identity of your second assailant and who could possibly be Takka's controller. We did find out Takka is the nephew of Tarin et Tong, the co-owner of our hotel. I hope that won't be relevant."

"Need to leave hospital. Feeling well," said Teeka. He glanced around the room. I suspected he hoped for a miracle—someone to agree with him.

Silence enveloped the hospital room.

Finally, Cara broke the quiet. "Need another day. Own room nurse. Available tomorrow hotel."

Teeka glared but finally said, "One more day convenient. Make sure I leave tomorrow, Cara."

She reached for his hand. "Promise to keep. If general manager. Agreement to bestow."

Okay, so she put the decision on my shoulders. Sigh. "Sain, please find Hart and talk to the Particlan doctors. I'm not agreeing to Teeka leaving if they're adamant he should stay."

"My decision," said Teeka.

"I don't think so. I'm the general manager; you have to listen to me." I laughed, and Teeka gave me a little smile. I hoped he'd backed off, at least for a moment. After we had a few moments of general conversation, Sain and Hart returned.

"Syl, the doctors say it's okay for Teeka to move to the hotel tomorrow, as long as he takes pretty much complete bed rest for a couple of days. They'll meet with him on the third day to evaluate how he's doing." Hart said, "Their advice sounds good to me."

"Excellent. Teeka, you have no opinion in this matter." Laughter erupted, and even Teeka sported a little grin. Then he slumped back in his bed, so I knew it was time for us to leave.

"Okay, guys, our chariot awaits. Teeka, I'm sure some of us will be back to visit. We won't leave you lonely." I glanced at Cara, but she studied the floor.

Cara joined Sain, Hart, and me, and we flew back to the hotel.

I found Tarin et Tong outside my office, pacing back and forth.

Oh, oh, he wanted to talk about his nephew. "Tarin, how are you today? Cara, would you order tea, please."

"No tea, talk." Tarin glared at me.

Chapter Twelve

I shook my head at Cara to indicate *no tea*, and then I gestured Tarin inside. I sat at my conference table, and Tarin joined me.

"What can I do for you?"

"Nephew in jail."

"Yes, he violently attacked one of my employees, who is also my friend. And his buddy used a knife and hurt my friend, Teeka. In fact, Teeka was in the hospital in serious condition and still is. We have video evidence of Takka's involvement, and he admitted to punching the Irion. Realistically, he has to go to jail and suffer the legal consequences of his actions."

"Release from jail," demanded Tarin.

"I can't do that, and no Particlan would listen to me anyway. He's now in the hands of your police." Although concerned about my position as general manager of the hotel, I still thought Tarin's demands were unreasonable.

"Release to me." His stress level seemed to have risen as his skin started to shine.

"You'll have to talk to the police," I said. "I have no idea how your legal system works, and I am not a citizen."

Tarin stood and glared at me for a long moment and then stomped out of my office.

Cara peeked into my office. "Now for tea?"

"I'd love a cup, thanks. Bring some for yourself, and we'll have a chat."

After Cara returned, we settled at the conference table. "When should I meet with the employees who want to be on the hotel's Olympic team?"

"Meeting already arranged. Tomorrow morning early. Send documents tonight."

"That's excellent. Do your documents include what the Olympics are all about, the various competitions and such?" I had so much to learn. Cara had already sent a lot of information but obviously had more to relay.

"Also judging data." Cara smiled.

"Well, I don't imagine I'll understand the judging, but I do want to understand the various categories. That should be my first step." I laughed. "That's fabulous, Cara. Thanks for arranging the meeting." My mood had improved. "How many employees do you expect tomorrow morning?"

"All employees interested. Schedules arranged appropriately. Much excitement indicated."

Cara didn't exactly answer my question about the number of interested employees, but I'd find out at the meeting. Excited employees were a benefit. I needed an upper after the downer of Teeka's medical problems.

"Inquiry regarding Tarin?" asked Cara.

I heard the question in her voice—why had he been here? What could I tell her? The truth was probably best, although she might be Takka's friend. "One of the two assailants who attacked Teeka was Takka et Tong. Tarin is Takka's uncle, so he wanted me to set Takka free. However, I said no. Takka needs to be held accountable for the injuries he inflicted. Tarin wasn't happy with my decision. Although I don't imagine I have any say with your authorities, anyway."

After she understood my explanation for Tarin being here, Cara announced, "Justice for Teeka."

"I agree. Now we need to find the Particlan who put the knife in Teeka. Maybe you could look at the photos. You might recognize the culprit." An awful duty to put on Cara I realized after I'd uttered my words. In this case, however, my feelings favored Cara leaning toward Teeka's rights rather than a Particlan's.

"Wish to view," she replied.

I walked over and rummaged through the documents on the desk and handed her copies of the photos we'd printed.

She processed the images.

"Possibility, however unclear. Will pass around. Report with answers."

"Please be careful, Cara. Only talk to people you trust. We don't want this second person to attack you, as they did Teeka. I need you as my assistant. You're doing such an excellent job."

What had I done? I couldn't believe I'd possibly put another employee in danger. My heart pounded with remorse.

"Help for Teeka," were her only words.

I changed the subject. "You've been working too hard, Cara. Before you go home, can you settle me in the hotel library? I want to see what's offered and do some research."

She led me to the library and settled me at a table. The library was otherwise empty. "Tea soon arrive."

"That's lovely, Cara. Go home and relax. You've done a lot of work for me today, and I appreciate your help. I'll see you early tomorrow morning in my office, and then we can go together to the employee training facility."

After Cara retired, I sipped tea and studied the library. Their bookshelves were the same as bookshelves everywhere. The Particlan books were more of a square shape than I was used to. The color scheme of the walls and shelves were a warm dark blue. I might spend quite a few hours in this comforting room.

I pulled out my character reader, and then I walked over to the shelving and examined a few books. The titles and cover pages gave me an idea of what we had, and the shelving labels would narrow down any search.

Cara had sent me a pile of material referring to the Olympics, but I wanted to find out a bit more about the beginnings of the competition. Why had it started? Which outstanding athletes had been discovered over the years? Were there any particular rivalries I should pay attention to? Really, I had no idea what questions to ask.

I eventually found a couple of relevant books and settled down to read. The character reader was a bit awkward to use, but I got the hang of it after a while.

My brooch buzzed.

"Where are you, Syl? We're waiting at the front desk. It's time for dinner," said Mom.

I glanced at my watch. Oops. "I'm in the library. Why don't you bring everyone here so they can see what's available, and then we can have dinner?"

Our group arrived and exclaimed over the selection of books. I handed my reader to Sweety, and she disappeared into a corner.

After a bit of conversation with the others about their day, I spoke. "Sweety, it's time for dinner. Apparently, I've kept everyone waiting long enough."

She caught my humor and laughed. "Here's your reader, but I need to have one of my own. Hart?"

"I do have an extra. I'll give it to you later. Perhaps you could you order food? I'm starving."

"Of course, you are. You haven't had a lot to sample today." Sweety laughed. "Everyone, gather at Syl's. I'll pop into the kitchen and order up a storm."

Over dinner, we caught up with our day's activities, and I related my conversation with Tarin. "He wasn't happy with me, but I didn't think letting his nephew get off without any repercussions would be a great precedent to set."

"Inhabitants must abide by their planet's rules. So you made the correct decision, Sylvestine. You may not have been able to do otherwise. I will study the Particlan Justice system," commented my father. As an ambassador, what else could he say?

"Now, I did ask Cara to study the photos to see if she could figure out who the other assailant was, but I told her to be careful. I don't want her assaulted. So I'm a little worried because the other guy was the one who used the knife. What else could I do, though? I don't know all my employees."

"Natural one to study the photos, knows the hotel employees," said Sain. "However, should not be alone."

"From the looks she and Teeka were exchanging, I don't think she'll be alone very often. She's arranging a nurse for his hotel convalescence." I laughed. "Hart, are the doctors really allowing Teeka to return tomorrow?"

"They had no problem with only one more day in the hospital. Apparently, they understood his anxiety and knew we wouldn't let him do anything strenuous."

"I don't think he'll be doing anything at all for a couple of days. He's not very strong."

"You're right. However, he'll be much happier being here in the hotel with us," added Hart.

"And Cara so happens to spend a lot of time in the hotel. Don't get me wrong, she's been an immense help," I said. My living room echoed with laughter. "Of course, I may be totally misinterpreting the situation."

No one argued with my gossip. "So what's the news from everyone else?"

"I walked around and took pictures of the hotel and its surroundings. This is quite a pretty area, and the employees had the tsunami damage cleared in no time," said my mother. "Then I spent the rest of the day riding the transit system to understand how it works and where it runs. Pretty efficient and with good coverage."

I glanced at Sain. "I'm not sure I like you wandering around the city on your own. Teeka's had an incident, and I don't want anything to happen to anyone else."

Dad cleared his throat. "I agree, Sylvestine. I suggest no one goes out alone. Join up. At least two people at all times when not in the hotel. We need to understand this society. After we do, perhaps we can relax."

Mom wasn't terribly happy with our suggestions, but she didn't argue.

"Reena, were you at school today?" I knew she had classes three days a week.

"Full day."

"Anything interesting?" Mom asked.

"Classes confusing. Students helpful, but little understanding between races. I need more time observing this culture."

"No doubt you do, as do the rest of us. Have you been using the helicopter?" I asked.

"Yes, helpful."

"Continue to do so. It's safer for the time being. If there's an issue, let me know." I sighed. Bringing up a teenager on a foreign world was not for the lighthearted. I had little experience with children or young adults.

"Sweety, what were you up to today?" I asked my best friend.

"I introduced new recipes to the chef and his cooks. Mostly Irion, but I added a couple of Martian ones. I may back off for a couple of days—Chef's getting overwhelmed."

"There are lots of other areas in this hotel you should explore." Let alone plan for the impending birth of their child, I thought.

"I've barely touched the surface of Particlan science and technology, and that's why I'm really here on Particle. So, yes, a couple of days to catch up on those topics and Particlan medical techniques would put my mind at ease," commented Hart.

"My question of the day is how am I going to contact Dedare to tell him what's been going on? You know, Teeka and all the other little bits." I wanted to keep him updated, even if he didn't do the same.

"Ah, make yourself a video talking about whatever you want. Then send it to the orbiting spaceship, and they'll forward it to Dedare," said Hart.

"Good idea. I'll work on that tonight." Why hadn't I thought of that or asked before now?

And that's how my evening with friends and family ended.

Being alone and preparing a video for Dedare used more of my mental capacity than I'd expected. I managed to produce a message and send it off. Trying not to whine, I suggested Dedare send regular updates to all of us—meaning me, of course.

The time had come to pull out my paint supplies and daub. I'd used my hobbies as a way to pass time on the trip to Particle, and I had numerous paintings to show for my effort. My novel writing hadn't been quite so productive.

Tonight's endeavor appeared to focus on blues and greens—not surprising given the major color schemes of Particle. What most interested me were a few thoughts emerging from the painting. As an abstract artist, I was always coming up with interpretations, and I knew my mood could usually be determined from recent paintings. Today, the colors depicted loneliness with books floating freely. Interesting.

Chapter Thirteen

The kitchen delivered breakfast to my office. I wanted an early start to my day so I could focus on the Olympian documents I'd received from Cara. I also had the packet containing the hotel's employee organization Mom and Cara had worked on. The document I'd received from Mom turned out to be complicated and mentioned departments I knew nothing about.

Mom popped into my office. "Reena and I are going to take the Ooby transit system today and wander about the city. Who knows what wonders we'll find, and I want to continue my previous explorations."

I recognized the determination on her face, so I needed to be careful with my words. "Perhaps you should take someone along. This world is still strange to all of us."

"We'll be fine. We'll stick to public transit and have it drop us off at tourist attractions. I've done my research, and I have an itinerary."

Mom and I glared at each other.

"Excuse me. I'm sorry, but I overheard your conversation." Thaddeus Trent stood in my doorway. "Ms. Amera, I'd like to join your expedition, if I may. Safety in numbers, you know."

My half-brother gave Mom a dilemma.

Mom and I knew about Thad, and I'm sure he knew about us. I hadn't yet spent any time with him, but I didn't know about Mom. So I decided this situation was in her court and gave her the appropriate signal.

"Ah, sure. That would be great."

"I will attend," said a voice. I glanced around and found Sain standing in my office doorway. What was it about that doorway?

"Reena and I'll have no problem with Thad as a companion and security guard." Mom sighed. "Syl and Sain, let me send you my itinerary," said Mom. "That way you'll know where we'll be all day. I hope to be back early afternoon. I don't want to overdo Reena's first excursion. New experiences can be tiring. Sain, thank you for your offer, but the three of us will be fine."

Sain and I exchanged glances but didn't comment. Naturally, Teeka was on our minds. "Well, be very, very careful. If you so much as stub a toe, this'll be the last time you go out without a significant escort," I said.

Oops. Hopefully Thad wasn't irritated by my not-so-tactful words.

Mom decided not to argue. "See you guys later." She hurried out, hoping to avoid further restrictions. Thaddeus scrambled to keep up.

"Sain, have you found anything out about Teeka's other attacker?" I asked.

"No. Images too fuzzy. Need more details. Taking photos to hotel security employees. If one suspect was in Security, the other may also."

I loved Irion terse language—sometimes. "Good thinking. Let me give you a list of the employees that fit your criteria." Mom's research had already come in handy.

Sain took my list and disappeared.

Cara was my next visitor. Harrumph. I'd hoped to eat breakfast before it was time for lunch.

"Cara, how're you today?" Her face carried a flush. "Are you all right? Do you feel well?" I thought her face suggested tiredness or, perhaps, some Particlan disease.

"Everything Particlan normal. Foreign affairs confused. Handling nursing concerns."

Hart told me Teeka was healing nicely, so what concerns did she have?

"You're working on finding nurses for Teeka?" I didn't know what else her words meant. *Foreign affairs confused* caused even greater confusion.

"Yes, hotel soon."

Nurses would be arranged soon, or Teeka would arrive soon? Or did her words imply a topic completely different? I had no idea what she meant. Nonetheless she didn't look well, so I decided not to ask for elaboration but simply inquired, "When's our meeting with the hotel's Olympic team hopefuls?"

"After lunch now. Organization schedule complex. Time everyone available."

Yes, getting interested parties together would be a nightmare. And keeping the hotel running smoothly at the same time would add to the challenge.

"That's great, Cara. You've done a tremendous job dealing with another complex detail." I thought for an additional moment. "Considering Teeka. I agree he'll be here soon, if he has anything to say about it. Why don't you go to the hospital? You can arrange for Teeka's release with the doctors much better than I could. Go as soon as Teeka's nurses are organized. You'll need one to be here for his settling in."

A wan smile appeared on Cara's face—a very tired, almost exhausted smile.

I took a wild guess and asked, "Cara, when are your days off? I haven't figured out anyone's schedule yet."

"Rest days past. Wish to learn. Necessary new duties."

My random question turned out to be relevant. "Cara, I'm going to need my assistant available to run the hotel when I want to take a rest day. And we all need rest days."

How to proceed? "Now, I know we have things planned for today, but let's try and squeeze in time to make a schedule of rest days for both of us. What do you think?"

"Excellent plan emerges. Feel energetic already. Scheduling later today."

Another plan of mine coming to fruition—what a wonderful feeling. "Sounds good. Now you need to be off and get Teeka released. He'll love you dearly."

"Any questions, Syl?" Cara asked before she disappeared.

"No, I think I should be able to handle a few hours alone. If I have any problems, I'll call."

Cara didn't argue. I suspected Teeka would be back to the Sath-Ooby Golden Hotel before I had a chance to finish my current cup of tea.

I laughed. Now, world, leave me alone while I finish breakfast.

I actually managed fifteen minutes of solitude before Dad knocked on my door. "Please come in. Can

I get you a cup of tea? I'm going to call for more as mine's grown cold."

"That'd be wonderful," he said. "I have a few topics to discuss."

We sat at the conference table, and I waited for my father to start.

"Sylvestine, I'm meeting a great deal of resistance about your idea of aliens being allowed in the Particlan Olympics. Most Particlans I've met believe the Olympics are only for them. I'm not sure what to do. The Particlans I spoke with were quite adamant. They talked about the different gravities, oxygen levels, physiques, and so on. On one level I had to agree with their objections."

"And on the other levels?" His response was not the one I'd sought.

"I think they are afraid one of us might be successful at trying out and then participating in their Olympics. However, since none of us have observed the Particlan Olympics I expect we wouldn't be able to compete at their level. In fact, I have no idea who'd even want to."

I laughed. "There we have a problem. I've studied the diving contests, and I think I'd have a chance. You probably don't know I did a lot of diving on Mars. What can we do? I'd really like to compete. Of course, my first hurdle would be becoming a member of the hotel team."

"The hotel team? Oh my goodness. There's so much I need to learn. There are many sides to consider, and not only the diplomatic one. Subtlety can sometimes work, but this situation involves many people and species. In the meantime, try and become a member of your hotel's team. If you do, that might make a difference in my negotiations."

I understood Dad's concerns, and I agreed with his analysis of the first step I needed to take.

"I'll do my best to qualify. Perhaps my acceptance may sway a few votes when the decision time arrives." I gave Dad a big smile. His position as ambassador must often come into conflict with his personal connections.

"I'll work on the big picture, so to speak, Sylvestine. What a wonderful time we live in!"

I agreed with the wonderful time, to a certain extent. My personal life with Dedare had wonderful highlights but also had issues. However, now was not the time to speak of them. I'm sure Mom and Dad had plenty of topics to discuss, including my well-being, and now my half-brother's. In particular, they had their own personal relationship to unravel, especially now with the presence of Thad.

"I'll see you at dinner, Dad. Who knows what the afternoon will bring?"

He kissed my cheek before he left. I'm glad I'd discovered my father after all these decades, but a modicum of shock still resonated in my nervous system.

Cara popped into my office. "Teeka settled room."

"That's great. I think I'll go along and have a chat," I said. "Join me if you'd like. And then it should be time for our meeting with the hotel's Olympic hopefuls."

Cara's face appeared a bit shiny. Perhaps she'd raced over here.

Using the hotel's transportation system, we arrived at Teeka's and Sain's suite. A Particlan hovered over Teeka.

"You are here, Syl. Nurse not needed," announced a disgruntled Teeka.

His color had improved considerably since yesterday. "Can you run around the hotel?"

"No, but..."

"When you think you can take a walk around the hotel, let me know. I'll go with you. I need exercise, and that will let me determine how fit you are. Someone in charge of security needs to be quite fit, don't you think?"

Teeka glared at everyone.

"Look, Teeka. You need rest. Your wounds need to heal. Cara has arranged medical help for you. In a couple of days we'll have a doctor visit. Hopefully he'll decide you require less attention. For now, you need to have your bandages changed and accept help with other activities. Be a good boy, Teeka."

"Annoying person."

I didn't know whether he meant me or the nurse, so I grinned at the nurse and said, "Aren't patients wonderful? If Teeka gives you too much trouble, let me know. I'm the hotel's general manager and Teeka's friend."

Teeka closed his eyes and ignored the three of us—Cara, the nurse, and me.

"I need a minute alone with Teeka because I have security questions. I won't take long," I announced.

Cara and the nurse removed themselves to the living area and shut Teeka's bedroom door behind them.

"Teeka, look at me. Do you remember anything else from the night of the incident? Any little thing? Anything?"

"One wearing necklace."

"What kind of necklace? What color? What shape?" A good start, but I'd hoped he'd have significant details. A necklace could be easily discarded and we'd never find it.

"Around neck. Perhaps black stones," replied Teeka. "No other information. Perhaps later. Sleep now."

If stubborn Teeka wanted to sleep, apparently he needed to. I'd let him recuperate according to his own schedule. I tiptoed out of the room after his eyes closed. According to the reports I'd received, his health was more precarious than he realized.

I entered the living room. "Teeka's fallen asleep. I suspect his waking hours will be very rare for the next little while. However, he's out of the hospital and where he wants to be. Thank you for your help," I said to the nurse. "Cara, it's time we met with the Olympic hopefuls."

I soon found myself on the top floor of the main building. There were many Particlans swimming in the pool and even more waiting for our arrival in the seating area.

How should I handle this? I hadn't even met all my employees.

Cara started the session off by introducing me. Her words lasted about three seconds, and then my turn arrived.

"Hello, everyone. Thank you for coming to this meeting regarding our Olympic team. If you know of

162

anyone who'd be interested and couldn't make it, please update them later."

I mentally sighed. Public speaking wasn't my favorite activity. "The first thing we need to discuss is the choosing of our team. In the past, the hotel general manager chose the team. However, since I'm new to the planet and your Olympics, I don't think that's a good idea."

A few of the Particlans laughed.

"What I would like to do is form an Olympic Hotel qualifying committee. We need people to judge each event and choose hopefuls. Would anyone like to be part of this committee?" After I recognized confusion, I added, "If so, please raise a hand."

Quite a few hands lifted, which pleased me.

"Now, this committee will determine the rules regarding judging for the hotel team. For example, can someone who wants to be eligible for a particular category also judge in that category?"

I glanced at my audience. The majority appeared to follow my words.

"Should there be one committee judging everything?" I laughed. "Other questions will no doubt arise, so you can understand how important this committee will be in choosing our team." At the end of my speech, I added, "Anyone who wants to join this committee, please give your name to Cara, as we wish to commence soon."

A lot of talk started amongst the attendees.

"Does anyone have questions?" I asked in a loud voice.

"On committee yourself?" asked a Particlan I hadn't met.

"No. I don't know enough about your Olympics to be able to judge—at least not yet." As I studied my audience, a young female Particlan stood. "Please ask your question," I said.

"Will you join?"

I hoped she meant join their team hopefuls because that was going to color my answer. "I'll be practicing my diving. I'm not sure if it'll be up to your standards or performances, but I do enjoy swimming and diving."

The murmurs in the audience grew.

"I may be only diving for my own pleasure. There are questions about whether an alien will be allowed in the Particlan Olympics."

Silence enveloped the room, and I saw no one with a hand raised, so I said, "Remember to give Cara your name if you wish to be part of the Hotel Olympic judging committee so she can make arrangements."

Cara and I backed up and leaned against a wall.

The hotel staff soon returned to their practice. I'd wanted to study their diving, but no one ventured to the diving board.

Back at my office, Cara and I worked studiously for the rest of the afternoon. Martians and Irions started appearing, so I knew dinner time was near. "Cara, why don't you join us this evening, unless you have other commitments?"

"Glad to comply."

"Good. Since I think Teeka will need a break from his bed, why don't you and the nurse wheel him over to my place and he can join us, too."

Sweety spoke for a moment with Cara, and then Cara left.

"Syl, what're you up to?" Sweety asked.

"What do you mean?" I responded as sweetly as possible.

"Why're you throwing Teeka and Cara together?" Sweety added a sigh at the end of her question.

"You're imagining things," I said. The rest of our party, particularly the males, appeared bewildered. "Sweety, did you order lots of good stuff for dinner?"

"Of course. I even added items for Cara after I spoke with her about her favorites."

"You're the best, Sweety."

After Teeka settled in my living room and the rest of our friends and relatives arrived, I started our discourse. "Who has anything to report about their day? Mom?"

"Reena and I visited a bunch of interesting cultural buildings. I don't pretend to understand everything we encountered, but I'll continue my research in the hotel's library. I quite enjoyed Ooby's main library. And the new addition will rescue them—the old building is bulging with books."

"I hear they're going into something like eBooks," I said.

"Yes, they are. However, that won't take up much space. The new addition is meant for the overflow of printed books. You know how that goes."

"I never have enough bookcases," I complained.

"The workers are busy installing the new floors since they've completed the foundation. I kind of sweet-talked them into giving us a tour when the walls are all up and it's safe to wander through. I wonder how different this building will be from the main. I didn't quite understand the explanation I received, so I'll have to see the results for myself."

"Let me know what you find out. I have so much to learn about this society." I reflected for a moment and then continued, "And how did your excursion go with Thaddeus along as support for you and Reena?"

"He's a pleasant young man, although he really didn't talk about himself. He had Reena and me doing most of the talking. I need to spend time with him to get to know him better."

Didn't we all.

Our food arrived, so we sat around my coffee table and filled our plates. I started to lift a mouthful when I noticed Cara staring. What could she be thinking?

"Cara, do Particlans have a ritual before each meal?" I asked, grasping at straws.

The rest of my friends and relatives, the aliens, immediately stopped their actions and concentrated their attention on Cara. And Dad had a horrified expression. As the ambassador to Particle, he should know about Particlan rituals. However, since it was early days for all of us I expected we'd forgive him for not knowing everything.

"Must give thanks," said Cara.

"How do we do that?" I asked. And I had no idea what we were giving thanks for.

"Everyone water glass." Cara went into my kitchen and came out with a pitcher of water and numerous blue glasses. She went around the living room and gave everyone a glass filled with water and then she sat on her stool.

"Water is life," she said, and then took a sip. We followed suit.

"Life is water," she added, taking another sip. Again we mimicked her action and words.

"All done now." A big grin covered her face. Teaching aliens apparently delighted her.

"Also at end. Blessing continues then. Only when final."

Cara studied our faces and seemed to decide we understood her actions.

We dug into our meals. "Thank you, Cara, for sharing your ritual with us. We haven't had an evening meal with Particlans. At least, I haven't," I said. Although, come to think of it, Cara hadn't mentioned this ritual when we had lunch, so I suspected *only when final* meant the last main meal of the day.

A change of subject seemed like a realistic diversion. "Cara, does a necklace of black stones mean anything? Is it significant in your society?" I asked. I needed to delve into Teeka's recently revealed detail.

"Member of church. Black stones monument. On city edge."

Our translator was all fine and good, but the words it uttered could be cryptic. "I'll need more detail. Can you explain this church and what the necklace means?"

Cara's mouth hung open. Apparently, she'd explained the situation as well as she could and had no idea what other words to use. So I added, "Cara, why don't you take Mama A to visit this church with the black stones monument sometime. Then she can see the monument and the church itself, and she'll be able to understand how that church works." I glanced at Mom, and she nodded agreement.

"Sweety, Hart, anything interesting to report?" I asked after a few bites.

Hart blushed, and Sweety said, "We went to the medical center and I had an ultrasound. We're having a baby boy, and a baby girl!"

My mind boggled. Two babies?

"Twins? That's wonderful," said Mom. "I suspect you're overwhelmed, especially since it's your first pregnancy."

"Oh, Mama A, I have so many questions," replied Sweety. Her tears threatened to spill.

I glanced at Hart. His eyes had glazed over, and his hands trembled. We wouldn't be getting any coherent words out of him tonight. As he was a medical doctor, I suspected he'd bounce back fairly quickly. However, being a new father put a wrinkle in his brain.

"You'll both be fine," said Mom. "Just go with your instincts. In the meantime, I have a few books on childbirth and the early years of child rearing on my electronic reader, so I'll send them to you." She smiled. "Hart, although I suspect you know most of the information it wouldn't hurt to skim them," said Mom. "And then, after you've both collected your questions, I'll have a get together with the two of you."

"Of course," they said in unison, and we all laughed. I suspected we wouldn't get much interaction from the two of them for the rest of the evening. Stunned would be the operative word for Hart and Sweety. To be honest, so was I, and I wasn't a parent.

I turned to Dad. "Anything interesting on the diplomatic front?"

"Reluctantly, I'm finding out information about other alien races the Particlans have contacted."

"Why are you reluctant?" I asked.

"Sorry. I meant the Particlans are uneasy giving out information. Don't get me wrong. I'm not reluctant, although I suspect the Particlan ambassadorial staff want me to focus on Particle. Unfortunately, I need to keep any alien information to myself until I've gathered sufficient details."

Again, I was kept in the dark. "Dad, if you know of an alien race visiting Particle in the near future, you'd best let me know. I may need to update the hotel to satisfy their needs." I hated being surprised. I hoped he understood my message—I wanted to minimize disruptions.

"News to share," interrupted Sain.

Our attention focused on Sain. "Checked all hotel security personnel. Teeka's second assailant not member of security. Tomorrow, check all hotel employees."

"That's a big job, Sain. Thanks for doing it," I said.

I had a random thought. "Hey, Mom. How did you get around today without local currency? You know, entrance fees to the facilities and such. Are they free?" I should've thought of this before.

"Oh, Dedare gave us lots of local currency before he left. He also gave each of us a credit card, I guess you could call it, to pay for larger expenses," said Sweety, giving me a confused glance.

"Well, I didn't get anything," I said, fuming. How could he forget me?

Chapter Fourteen

"Cara, it looks like everyone's finished eating. Please lead us through the final blessing." My mind churned, but I didn't want to upset anyone, and Particlan traditions should be observed.

She did so, and then my mates stood and prepared to return to their own accommodations. "Sweety, would you mind staying to help me look for whatever Dedare gave you guys? Maybe he left something for me and I didn't realize."

"Of course." Sweety glanced at her husband. "Hart, shoo. I'll be along shortly. Syl and I need girl time."

After we were alone, Sweety asked, "You really didn't get anything from Dedare?"

"No, nothing. Of course we weren't on the happiest of terms at the time of his leaving. I didn't want him to leave so soon, and he thought he needed to. We haven't had much time together, and I'd been hoping Particle would be different."

"Are you realistic, Syl? You know what he does for a living—he conquers worlds, more or less. You and he need to be more accommodating with each other. Relationships are all about compromise. Of course, I mean to a point. You can't give up everything, but you need to think about your partner's needs too. Your relationship is not going to be easy for either of you."

Sweety studied my face. "Did you give Dedare an ultimatum?"

I sighed. "No, not an ultimatum. I suggested he appoint someone to be on the Satre city council rather than himself. Dedare needs to gallop around the galaxy rather than stay in one place and govern. Perhaps I overdid my protests."

"Or maybe not," said Sweety. "Seems to me to be a reasonable activity to oppose. Anyway, let's take a look around and see if we can find any Particlan currency. Of course, you haven't had much chance to buy anything and thus need the currency, but hopefully that'll change."

"Ah, Manager Syl, I mean Syl," said Reena, standing in the doorway to Dedare's office. "Have a package. Father gave it to me for you. Sorry. Forgot until now." A teary teenager greeted Sweety and me.

"That's it," said Sweety. "That's the package Dedare gave all of us. Look inside and you'll find currency and the equivalent of a credit card."

I opened the envelope and discovered Sweety was correct. I'd maligned Dedare, so my mood turned to miserable. Of course, a hormone-infused teenager added to my plight. She was almost my stepdaughter, so I needed to tread carefully.

"Reena, I'm glad you remembered the package. I had some bad thoughts about your father, but now I'm happy." Not as happy as I let on, but she didn't need to know. Sweety, bless her soul, had no problem reading my feelings.

"Reena, I think we should let Syl relax for the evening. She needs private time," said Sweety after taking a good look at my face.

Sweety hugged me, and then Reena and I were alone.

"Sorry for problem," said Reena.

"That's fine. Give me a hug, and then I think I'm going to paint. I need to relax. By the way, do you still want to learn how to dive?"

"Yes." A wide, Irion smile emerged.

"Then be ready at seven tomorrow morning. I'll be going up to the employee pool to start my new daily practice. You may join me, and perhaps we can start your training."

"Excellent. I will be ready." She grabbed a hug and then left Dedare's office.

I hadn't wanted to push her away, but I needed time alone. I had much to think about, and my relationship with Dedare and my corresponding reactions topped the list.

****

The next morning, Reena appeared before I was ready. Eager to begin diving, I suspected she didn't want me to leave without her. Little did she know she probably wouldn't dive during her first session. I needed to assess her swimming ability and her physical agility. Deciding where I'd start her diving instructions would be my first task.

The employee area hopped this morning. Particlans were doing laps in the pool, and others were diving. I recognized timing of laps and discussions of techniques.

Reena and I took off our covers and revealed our garments. We certainly attracted attention. Ours were completely different from each other and also radically opposed to the Particlans. Our hosts had garments that covered them from head to toe, while Reena and I had suits that only covered our torsos. Our hair caps were another significant difference. The Particlans let their voluminous hair run free. "Reena, why don't you warm up by swimming a few laps? As you do, I'll keep an eye on your form."

I didn't know if Reena knew what form meant, but she readily jumped into a free lane in the pool. She did a few warm-up laps, and then a Particlan spoke to her after she'd climbed out of the pool.

The two of them walked over. "Manager Syl, cannot understand this Particlan. Why?"

I laughed. "Reena, you don't have your translator. I noticed you took it off before you went in the water. A good action, by the way. Water would probably damage it."

Reena glanced at the translator hanging around my neck. So I said to the Particlan, "Could you please repeat the words you spoke to Reena. She doesn't have her translator, so she couldn't understand you."

The Particlan grinned. I suspected she'd worried she'd done something very wrong.

"Asked to record. Time trials important. For Particlan Olympics." She glanced at us to gauge our understanding.

"What's your name?" I asked.

"Sara ild Tamark."

"You work in this hotel?" If so, I hadn't met her yet.

"Housekeeping and cleaning," Sara replied.

"I'm happy you'd like to help Reena with her swimming. Perhaps you can let us know how she's doing in regard to the Olympic trials. Reena will also be learning how to dive. She's never dived before, so she doesn't expect to compete in that discipline."

I glanced at Reena. Apparently she'd had other ideas. "Reena, perhaps you and Sara should go back to the pool so she can time your laps. I'll hold your translator and keep an eye on you, so if there're any questions, you can flag me down."

Apparently, the translator correctly interpreted *flag me down* as Reena nodded her acceptance of my plan and started off with Sara. I followed their path at a leisurely pace. I wanted to also study my many employees engaged in water sports.

I watched Sara time Reena's laps. After a few, Reena leaped out of the pool and gestured for Sara to join her.

"Manager Syl, please provide translation. Sara, how have my lap times been? Much too slow for Olympics?" asked Reena, beginning to grasp the complexities of her situation.

"Somewhat slow times. Possibility to improve. Sara will help."

Surprised by her positive comments, Reena grabbed Sara in a hug. "Thank you for saying that. How can you help me improve my times?"

Sara stood rigidly still.

I intervened. "Sara, Reena's action is called a hug. It shows appreciation for your words. If the physical nature of a hug is not to your liking, please let us know."

Reena's face showed confusion. Then she seemed to suddenly understand how a species might not understand a different species' actions. Amused, I watched Reena respond to Sara's reciprocal hug. Understanding had been reached.

"Action considered nice. Scores to improve. Sara to help."

"Thank you, Sara. Now you two go off and practice. Reena, perhaps you can time Sara on her laps. I'm sure Sara also needs practice and data about her own speed. I'm going to do a little swimming myself." The two dashed off. I suspected Reena had found her first Particlan friend. Since they were near in age, I accepted the friendship. I swam a good number of laps in our Olympic pool. Swimming needed to be included in my exercise routine before I started diving because I was woefully out of practice.

After I'd tired, I pulled myself out of the pool and sat on a bench and toweled off. My major activity at this point was watching the Particlans diving.

Their routines perplexed me. Different from what I'd been used to, they reinforced my need to study the Olympic materials I'd received from Cara.

Speaking of Cara, she suddenly appeared.

"Manager Syl, quick. Problem in Reservations. Alien, please attend."

My goodness. More aliens? "Cara, do I have time to change?"

"No. Great problem."

I threw a translator to Reena, draped my body wrap around me, and followed Cara at a gallop. Reena would understand my sudden disappearance.

At Reception, I found an unknown alien. To my consternation, green fluid covered the floor around him.

"Other than the mess on the floor, what's the problem?" I demanded. Hmm. Perhaps not a diplomatic way to phrase my question.

"Refusal, refusal," replied the new alien.

I hoped the translator's words were accurate. "What's been refused?" I asked. "Who's been refused?"

"Room, room," replied the alien, before any Particlan had a chance to respond.

"We can certainly offer you a room. Do you have any particular requirements? Food, bedding, bathroom facilities?" I had no idea what to ask, and I sure hoped the translator worked well with words like *bathroom facilities*."

"Room, room," the alien replied.

I gestured at my reception clerk. After receiving a key, I led the alien to the elevator. As we moved, he turned in circles and shook his head quite violently. He hovered close to me, and I suspected he wanted to pick me up so he could get to his room quicker.

Humanoid, with two stubby arms and legs, two eyes, his skin could only be described as slimy, chubby, and wrinkled gray. He seemed to ooze from every part of his exposed skin. Thus, the mess on Reception's floor.

If you ignored the nature of his skin, the alien had elegance. His six-foot height, combined with a glossy, black tunic and royal blue flowing cape contributed. For some reason, his naked feet make me shudder. Perhaps because of their association with his discharge.

Did he still ooze? Would I need to have Housekeeping follow our path?

I had no idea whether *he* was the appropriate word, and I didn't even know the name of his species.

The alien scurried in after I opened his room door. After his survey of the room, he said, "Adequate, adequate."

"Is there anything you need?" I asked. The leading question I'd always hated.

"Tomorrow, tomorrow," was his reply, and then he continued with, "Sleep, sleep."

"Of course, we'll leave you to sleep. Contact Reception if you have any requirements, and they'll get hold of me. Have a good rest."

After I left his key on a table, I moved Cara out. Hopefully he'd understand the key's purpose. "Cara, let's go back to Reception and get as many details as we can about this incident."

We traveled in silence. My mind churned with endless possibilities.

Before I started questioning the reception clerk, I called Hart and Charles and asked them to join me in Reception as soon as possible. I didn't enlighten them as to the purpose—just stressed my urgency. I was happy to see the alien's slime hadn't been cleaned up.

Cara spoke to the clerk with whom we'd previously dealt.

"Any information available. Species, requirements, allergies. Length of stay?"

After he'd gotten to his feet, my employee stood rigidly.

"Only ask room. Agitated and release. Fluid on floor."

The alien had certainly slimed the Reception area floor. I didn't want anyone touching his emanation until we'd determined its effect on Particlans, Irions, and humans.

"Cara, do you know anything about this alien? Have you heard of them before?"

"No reports yet. Alien new guest. Requirements be determined."

"You got that right. If you don't know anything about this alien, then we're going to have to wait until he's awake to get further information."

I noticed Hart doing a fast walk toward us.

"Syl, what's up? You sounded urgent." Hart took a moment to catch his breath.

"A new alien arrived. One we've never encountered. We have him resting in a guest room. He left this mess on the floor. I need to know if his fluid affects any of us—humans, Irions, Particlans. The floor needs to be cleaned, but I need information first. I'm worried about my staff and the rest of us."

"Syl, that's many more words than you'd normally use to explain a situation." Hart laughed. "I'll get on this. I'm going to take a sample and run it over to the hospital. Can I use your helicopter?"

"We'll find one. Cara?" I asked.

"Contacted helicopter pilot. Leave when needed. Move to roof."

"I'll go right up. Just let me take an adequate sample." Hart pulled a bag out of one pocket, and a scoop out of another. He took little time acquiring his sample.

"Syl, you might put barricades or something around the messy area until you hear from me. The tests shouldn't take long, but you never know. We do have three species for which to examine the residue."

Dad arrived while I watched Hart stow his samples. "What mess is this, Sylvestine?"

"A new alien. One I've never encountered. We have him sleeping in a hotel room. He doesn't wish to speak with anyone until he's rested, which is fine with me. Dad, what can you tell me about this new race? I know nothing about them. I don't even know what they call themselves."

I suspected Dad understood my frustration. "Can you help me?" I asked.

"So early in the morning. Sylvestine, you're not even properly dressed," said my father, glancing at my swimsuit and cover.

Harrumph. "I was practicing my swimming in the employee area when this situation popped up. I haven't had a moment to change. The hotel comes first."

"I'll be sure to tell Dedare of your dedication," said my clueless father.

I needed a talk with my mother. Dad's diplomacy occasionally sagged.

"That's nice, but who are these aliens? I need information in order to run the hotel." My disposition plummeted toward grouchy.

"I have no idea. I'll question the other ambassadors as soon as I can make contact. The timing is not bad, considering this is Particlan morning. Do you have a picture I can use?"

Dad had a good point. "Cara, do we have any cameras in Reception that would have captured images of this alien?" I asked.

Hart had decided on additional samples and was still in the lobby, so he answered my question before Cara had a chance. "Yes, you do. You know the studio where your employees record various videos? Well, they're also the ones who store the feed from all the hotel cameras. Just go there and ask for the camera in Reception on day blah, blah, blah, etc. That should do it." Hart went back and finished his evidence gathering.

"I'll be back as fast as I can, Syl. I really think you should cordon off the area until I get a definitive answer. From what I can see, no one is suffering from any goo emanations, so you should be all right in the meantime. Just don't clean it up until you hear from me," added Hart.

Hart grabbed his sample bag and left for his ride.

I turned around and noticed Dad and Cara had also disappeared. I suspected they'd taken a quick trip to the video lab. I hoped we'd have clear pictures to help Dad interview the other ambassadors, and I wanted to make sure I had copies. Who knew when I'd need the reference material?

While everyone was away, I took five minutes to shower and change.

Back at my office and before I eased into my uncertain daily routine, I decided to have another talk with the Reception clerk who'd made the initial encounter. A confused conversation ensued.

"Demand new room. Privacy needed immediately. No food issue."

"What happened to cause the alien to leak?" I tried not to laugh but *leak* was a clumsy word that worked.

"Asked for information. Answered with six. Confusion, fluid ensued." said my clerk, whose skin had gone a shade darker blue.

"Do you mean he uttered six words and you didn't know what they meant?" I suspected the alien's words had also strangled the translator.

"Agreement with manager." A measure of relief passed over his face, and his body visibly relaxed.

Okay, the new alien had uttered six words, probably in his unique two-word format. "Tell me exactly what he said."

"Aliens unusual. Molting excitement. Behold enjoyment." So the new alien had used a different format and delivered a mixed bag of topics. How could I untangle the alien's thoughts?

I noticed Cara had returned, and without Dad. I also recognized my Reception clerk had had enough emotional engagement for the time being.

"Cara, why don't you take Tamars to the employee lunchroom for a break. This encounter has exhausted all of us." I'd noticed Tamars ata Vilue's name tag on one of my visits to Reception, although I hadn't spoken to him before today.

"Employee lunchroom please?" Cara sounded confused.

"Do you have an area where employees can take breaks throughout the day?" I asked. What other words could I use?

"Room to relax," replied Cara.

"Yes, that's the room I mean. Take Tamars there and let him relax for a while. Meeting aliens would be stressful for anyone."

A smile lit Cara's face and slowly one appeared on Tamars' face after he'd deciphered my words. The two of them walked away.

I settled in my office and considered the new alien's words, *"Aliens unusual. Molting excitement. Behold enjoyment."*

The alien's words seemed positive, but how could I really judge?

"Manager Syl, why are you scowling?" asked Reena. After her morning pool exercise, she'd showered and dressed in her day clothes.

"Reena, we have a new alien in the hotel, and he left a residue on the floor. At the moment, I'm just trying to understand the words he said to the Reception clerk."

"Words?" Reena asked.

I repeated them.

Reena laughed. "Nothing unusual. His happiness at being amongst aliens resulted in molting. A positive happening in his culture."

If Reena was correct, I wondered how the new alien's culture dealt with cleanup.

"Well, we'll wait for Hart's assessment of hazards before we attempt to restore the floor. What's your schedule today?" I added.

"Stop where you are!" exclaimed Hart, dashing into my office. "Don't touch that goo. It's dangerous."

Chapter Fifteen

"The goo is hazardous to humans." Hart grimaced. "Irions and Particlans will have no problem, just humans. Syl, make sure you aren't involved in the cleanup—you'll get an awful rash. The slime isn't deadly, but it's a major irritant. Thankfully, there are no gaseous emissions to worry about. Make sure you let all the humans know," said Hart, huffing from his sprint from the helicopter.

"Have a seat. I'm glad you rushed to tell me this but catch your breath." I settled him at a stool at my office conference table. Particlan stools accommodated most life forms.

"Have you told Sweety?" I asked.

"Yes, I called her on my way back. I also spoke to Mama A and Charles. Have I covered everyone?" Hart continued to exhibit anxiety.

"Why didn't you call me?" I wasn't annoyed, just curious.

"I'd already told you not to touch the goo, and the rest of my short trip back to the hotel was filled with speaking to other humans. I knew I'd be here soon enough to confirm my earlier edict."

"I'm only teasing. Your panting indicates you've rushed to get back and let me know. You'd never abandon me," I said.

Then I noticed Cara hovering in my doorway. "Cara, I know Richard Branson, a human, is staying here, and also Thaddeus Trent. Are there any other humans also on our property?"

"I will check." Cara turned and scurried away.

"Hart, I think I've found a subject for your first round of videos. Aliens and their idiosyncrasies."

"What do you mean?"

The gleam in Hart's eyes led me to believe he had a good hunch about where my idea led. We knew each other so well.

"We need to educate the Particlans about the aliens they're starting to meet. That way we can forestall possible misunderstandings. Not all confusion, of course, but I think it's our job to educate. We're like emissaries to this world, coming in through a back door, so to speak. So if you created a science, or I guess in this case historical series of educational videos about the various races, they'd go a long way toward educating Particlans."

Then I remembered a question from yesterday. "Do we have something like a television in our quarters? I know there's a machine there, but I haven't had a chance to figure out what it's for or how to use it, but I know you used it to play videos. You know, the hotel tapes."

Hart laughed. "Yes, it's like a cable station. This evening remind me to show you how to set it up. And I do like your idea of educational videos. I'll have to figure out if our translators will work across that medium. If nothing else, we'll run a strip of Particlan words across the bottom."

Cara returned. "All humans found. Richard Branson informed. Thaddeus Trent notified."

I grinned. "Thanks a lot, Cara. You've saved me a lot of trouble."

"All staff notified," she added.

Hart rose from his stool.

"Where are you off to, Hart?"

He laughed. "I'm going to check out the media…"

The co-owner of the hotel stepped into my office. Perhaps he'd knocked, but I hadn't heard anything. Maybe Particlans didn't knock. Regardless, Tarin et Tong occupied my office space, and his face did not reflect pleasure.

"Incident with alien?" he asked.

"Yes, we had a situation today. Did you know a new species would visit the hotel?" I'd decided to go on the offensive. I wondered if he'd heard about the goo.

"Understood last day," replied Tarin.

I interpreted his words to mean he'd received an update the previous day about the presence of a new alien. "I should've been told. I need to prepare my staff for any unusual arrivals, and I need to understand any new requirements before I can do so. I need to be kept updated." I wanted to stomp my foot.

"Alien is Sarturn. Arrived Particle today. Present is new," Tarin replied and then turned away.

I bit my tongue and let him go. His words implied a bit of an apology, and I'd accept that. *The present situation is new* was my interpretation of *present is new*.

"Ah, Syl, perhaps you were a little blunt with your boss?" suggested Hart.

"Maybe, but I do need as much information as possible to run the hotel without drama, and I need it before any situations happen. Surprises are difficult to react to. Tarin somehow knew about this new alien before I did, and he also knew the Sarturn would stay at his hotel. By not telling anyone Tarin made our situation dangerous."

"You're right. I keep forgetting what you have to deal with. You have my sympathies." He glanced around my office. "Now, I'm off to scout the media room. I need information, too." Hart grinned and waved as he turned to leave.

However, I stopped his exit. "Hart, when you're wandering about, can you keep an eye open for paint canvases? I'm almost out."

"Of course. Sweety also has a shopping list, although I think most of the items are for the baby, I mean babies." Hart sighed.

"Letting her do the shopping would be best," I said.

"I know. My job is to find the stores." We both smiled.

"I'm sure I can find a longer list or even come with you."

Hope settled on Hart's face. "Ah, I'll give you a map, and then you and Sweety can have a shopping spree. I will most likely be busy on my projects."

Hart wasn't a shopper.

After he left, my stomach growled. "Cara, would you order food, please? I haven't had anything to eat today."

I relaxed with food and a cup of tea, then all hell broke loose. I heard enough commotion to make me run to the doorway. A horde of Particlans roamed throughout Reception while hotel security attempted to herd them outside. An excruciating level of noise hit my eardrums.

Cara approached. After we retreated into my office where the noise level was considerably less, I asked, "What's going on?" My sudden headache subsided a little.

"Particlans resisting aliens," replied an unhappy Cara.

"Are they hotel guests?" I really hope not.

"No, Ooby residents."

"Who's in charge of hotel security?" I asked. I knew theoretically Teeka was, but who was now that Teeka was invalided out?

"I am," said Teeka, after he stopped in my doorway. His nurse had pushed his wheelchair through the crowd. "Handle this. My line of expertise."

"But Teeka…"

He waved a hand at me to desist. Then he made his nurse turn him around so he faced Reception and he could gesture over one of the hotel security personnel. Their conversation was too quiet for me to hear.

The next thing I knew, Teeka wheeled into the midst of the crowd with the help of his security guard. His nurse moved over to me.

"Concerned about patient," she said.

"Agreed. However, your patient does whatever he pleases. Let's wait and see what happens." She wasn't happy, but then neither was I.

After a few anxious moments, Teeka wheeled out of the crowd and toward where I stood. His security assistant stood respectfully back after he'd maneuvered Teeka up close to us. I watched the crowd slowly disappear out the hotel's front door while our security staff kept a close watch.

"Okay, what happened, Teeka? I couldn't hear a thing," I said.

"Listened to concerns, but unrealistic. Crazy ideas about planet contamination with breathing, and terrible ideas kill people somehow." Teeka laughed. "After hearing complaints, I pointed out my Particlan scars."

"Your flesh probably did the trick." At least Teeka had recovered enough to join me in laughter.

"Perhaps. I convinced them ambassadors would be better, and they *mostly* agreed. More hotel security needed. General manager agree?"

"Yes. I should probably run the expense by Tarin, but I'm not happy with him right now. Apparently, he knew yesterday about the new alien who arrived this morning, and he didn't let me know."

"New alien?"

I laughed. "We have a member of a new species staying at the hotel. The aliens are called Sarturn, and they ooze. While the alien was in Reception, he left a pool of goo on the floor. Hart took samples to the medical complex, and they've determined there's a risk for humans—but not for Irions or Particlans. So I'm upset I hadn't heard about this potential guest before he showed up."

"Understand concerns. Tarin should also let security know." Teeka laughed. "Perhaps tell general manager about alien, and then general manager tell Security." Teeka massaged his scalp. "News channels broadcast hotel demonstration."

"Why didn't your security staff let anyone know? Surely they saw the newscast?"

"Similar situation, Syl. They should have spoken or been prepared. I am needed. Promise to rest because I need to get fit."

We conversed right outside my office. Teeka glanced around. "Desk in this area?"

His request surprised me.

"One in security, but too far. For the next while need to keep eye on new guests and hotel ambiance, so need to be out front."

"We need to talk to Sain, our master renovator, but I've been thinking about a small office over here." I pointed to an area right outside my office door. "Cara's now my assistant, and she needs a work area closer to me. What do you think?" My gentle way of interrogating Teeka about Cara.

"Here is Sain," said Teeka.

His words contained a measure of relief, I suspected. Either that, or I was making up a great story in my head.

We updated Sain with my masterful plan about a new office. He didn't immediately resist, so I was hopeful. On the dark side, I now had another item to discuss with Tarin.

"Will design office to fit in with restaurant scheme. Areas adjacent," said Sain.

"Don't forget about the Amenities shop," I said. "And this new office should also have access to my conference table. I'm not sure how to make that happen, though."

"Design no problem," said Sain. "Your future updates, maybe."

We all laughed. My propensity for continuously having new and better ideas—at least in my mind—had followed me to Particle.

"Design will continue. Work with Vara il Vast will continue. Consultation with Teeka will continue," said a grinning Sain. "Approval from Tarin, or Dedare?"

"Let that be my worry," I said. "You do your usual excellent work, and I'll arrange approvals." Of course, I had no idea how easy or difficult my job would be.

Then my best friend in the world—many worlds really—arrived. "Sweety, how nice to see you. I need female company. These two are driving me crazy."

Sweety and I laughed. The two of us loved males, and Sain and Teeka were amongst my favorites. In fact, on Irion they'd competed for my heart. And I continued to have feelings of friendship for both of them.

"What's up?" Sweety asked, flinging her red curls around. Would her children have a version of her hair? I hoped so. Considering Hart had long red hair, the odds were good.

"I assume Hart updated you about the new alien, the Sarturn?"

"Oh, yes, immediately. You know Hart. He's quite worried about our unborn children, as he should be," Sweety remarked.

"Yeah, and he's out looking for retail stores for you. What more could you ask for?" I asked.

We both laughed. "Don't forget to invite me along for some of your shopping parties. I need a break. Actually, we should try and have a touristy day, maybe all of us together. The ones we had on Irion were fun. Of course, they sometimes had issues, but we coped."

"Syl, our excursions definitely had issues, but we survived, as you say. I hope the ones here'll be calmer," said Sweety. "I need to maintain my levelness, for the sake of my children." Sweety patted her stomach. "Oh, Syl. How did this ever happen?"

I knew what she asked, but I decided to be funny. "Sweety, do you really need a lesson about human reproduction?"

She gave me a light, friendly smack on my arm. "You know what I mean."

"Yes, I do." I gave her a hug. "Sorry, I tried to be funny. Too much severity lately." I sighed. "Okay, here's the deal. You met the love of your life, and you're having his children. In my opinion, that's the best thing ever. You're making a new family and a new life together. I know you're on a strange world, but you actually love meeting new unknown aliens. They always respond to you in a positive way." Everywhere we went, Sweety became the star of the show.

"I don't know if Hart has told you, but I asked him to make videos about the new aliens Particlans may meet when they're out. We need to introduce them to different customs and societies. Why don't you help him? I think your twist on life and your, hmm, procreation might make for an unusual combination and fascinate the Particlans."

"An interesting idea, Syl," said Sweety. "What else could I talk about?"

"Recipes. They're turning out to be your forte on any planet. And I haven't had the heart to introduce the subject yet, but this new alien, the Sarturn, is going to need food. Just work with Hart; you'll come up with something. You always do."

"Interesting idea, Syl." Her attention drifted, and then she added, "I need to find Hart and throw ideas around. Do you know where he is?"

"I imagine he's still in the media lab. He left here a short while ago on his way there."

"I'll check. See you later." She bounced off. Only Sweety could make a bounce look elegant and natural while pregnant with twins.

Sain and Teeka had disappeared during our girl talk.

I sat at my desk to plan the rest of my day. Of course, I'd forgotten about the food I'd asked Cara to order, but my stomach reminded me of its needs. So I first focused on my tray. The cup of tea was particularly delicious. I needed to watch my fluid intake since I didn't want to get dehydrated having added swimming practice to my daily schedule.

Reena popped in and sat across from me. "Do you need food?" I asked.

"No. Ate at home. Anything to tell?"

So I told her about the new alien, the Sarturn, and how humans could be irritated by their bodily discharges.

"Reminder of mother," Reena said with a thoughtful facial expression.

Of course. I should have thought of Reena's mother before bringing up the Sarturn. Her mother had died after contracting a disease in her lab. At the time, Reena had been young. I knew the experience had deeply shaken the child and her father.

"What're you going to do today, Reena? No classes, I assume." I didn't know her schedule, but I wanted a better handle on where she'd be.

"Mama A and I are going shopping. Join us?"

"Oh, I'd like to, but I have too many things to do. Perhaps we can pick a day next week."

I added, "Reena, what do you know about the Particlan division of the days of the year? Do they have weeks and stuff?" Not a very scientific question, although I did know some of the details already.

"Six days similar to week. My classes three days per week." She shot me a questioning glance.

"I need to keep track of various things. Could you make a calendar?" I pointed to the wall facing my desk. "Then we can put your school days on it and other appointments I have or other people have. That way I can figure out when I can take a day off and go shopping with you and stuff like that. What do you think?" I knew the calendar was possible, but I wanted her response. Would she think I and Mama A were controlling her too much? A computer calendar would probably be more efficient, but this would be a visible event calendar for everyone to update. And a way to bring us all closer, I hoped.

"Excellent idea. Will work on this. See later." With those words she skipped out of my office.

I rummaged in my computer to-do list. Too many projects. My mind needed a plan. Before I had a chance to choose today's tasks, my mother popped in.

"Did you understand Hart's message, Mom?"

"That we've found an alien we're allergic to? Of course. I'm surprised it hasn't happened previously. There is no reason humans should be able to tolerate any other species. Good thing Irions are on our tolerable list." Mom laughed.

"Very funny. I'll be sure to share your joke with Dedare. Seriously, Mom, do you think we're jumping into these projects with insufficient research? I know today's alien was unexpected, but how many unusual happenings should we expect?" I wanted contingency plans; I wanted to be proactive, not reactive.

"I think today's alien surprised everyone. No one knew he was here or even existed, so how could we be proactive? Charles is not happy about the situation, although it gives added weight to his demands for updated species information. I suspect the Particlans have been holding back, but maybe that's Charles' influence on my thoughts."

At least Mom and Dad were communicating.

"Mom, someone did know the alien was around or about to appear. Tarin, Dedare's co-owner, told me about the alien after I asked. He even told me the species name—Sarturn."

"Well, that's annoying. I don't really like him, by the way." She focused on my face and my response to her words.

"More than annoying, Mom, dangerous. I suspect I upset him with my demands, but he didn't give me any grief, thank goodness. I just don't know how to be proactive rather than reactive. I wish Dedare was here. He can handle anything."

"Dedare has great faith in your abilities, and ours also, to handle any situation. Otherwise, he wouldn't have left us to pursue his own activities."

"Okay, I'm lonely. How's that?" Words I could only say to my mother.

"I know, dear. However, I also know Dedare's trying to return to Particle as fast as he can."

"What do you mean?" How does she know this?

"Dedare and I had a little talk before he left." Mom smiled.

"What did you talk about?" Our conversation began to annoy me.

"You, of course. And how much he loves you and wants to spend his life with you. You have nothing to fear, Syl. Dedare is wise and perfect for you."

Mom's words left me speechless. Dedare had told her more than he'd ever told me, although I imagine I exaggerated. "Mom, thanks for telling me about your dialogue with Dedare. I've been pretty lonely since Dedare left. I suspect I'll be composing a long message to him tonight."

"Of course you will, dear. Now, I need to be on my way. Reena and I are going shopping for a few hours. May we use the helicopter? I've found a market, and I think we'll spend our time in only that one area, so we won't need the helicopter for long. I'll send it back so someone else can use it."

"Perfect. Just talk to Cara. Now I've given Reena a project, so you might want to talk to her about it. It's simply a wall calendar for my office so I can keep track of appointments, Reena's days at school, and other activities. I don't want to keep track of everyone but items that are important and impact my actions. For example, I want to find a free day so I can go shopping too."

We laughed. I hadn't had much free time on Irion, and a good portion of it had proven stressful. So finding a free day on Particle would boost my spirits.

"A clever idea. I'll talk to Reena, and we'll come up with a gorgeous, big calendar."

"You're the best, Mom. Now, don't spend your money all in one place."

"Do you need anything from the mall?"

"I asked Hart to look for canvases, so perhaps keep your eyes peeled for them. And maybe paints? I don't really need much, just the actual shopping time!"

Then I brought up an awkward subject. "Ah, Mom. I talked to Dad today. You know, sometimes he seems a little clueless about how people react to various issues, and he's a diplomat, so I'm confused. For example, his reaction to me dealing with a new alien. He acted like he thought I handled the situation poorly." I shook my head. "It's hard to explain what I mean."

Mom laughed. "I think you're experiencing a father issue. Your father wasn't around when you grew up so you're confused, even though you accepted him. And Charles, now having a daughter, and an independent one to boot, confounds him. He's not sure how to treat you. Give him a little time, Syl. You know he wouldn't be the human ambassador if he didn't deserve the position."

"Okay, I'll try and look at the situation from your point of view. Perhaps I don't know how to react, either."

"I'll keep that in mind, and I'm so glad you reminded me. See you at dinner." Mom grinned and headed out the door.

Such a smart ass. Oh well, I loved her dearly, and she'd done a wonderful job raising me alone. However, I needed to work. What to do? What to do? What to do first?

Cara entered my office. "Interviewee has arrived."

"I'm interviewing staff?" Cara and I needed better communication. Perhaps a new calendar would bring all of us in line.

"Many this morning. Staff are interested. In dialogue exchange."

"And I'm interested in meeting them. Thank you, Cara, for arranging this." And I did want to meet every employee. I tried not to imagine I'd never reach the end.

The rest of my morning rushed by but in so many ways I had an excellent experience. The differences between Particlans and other races—humans included—astounded me.

From my experiences, each race focused on different areas, and I noticed in today's conversations water was the one in common. The staff of life for every species I'd so far encountered. Each different species' focus, though, came from a unique angle.

Irions were rather blasé toward water—even though they needed it to survive—while humans desperately looked for clean water wherever they were.

The Particlans' focus seemed almost spiritual.

Every Particlan I'd met today first said *water is life* as they greeted me, and *life is water* as they left. I'd need a talk with Cara. Perhaps we could have a dinner discussion so all non-Particlans would be updated with the results of my cultural examination.

Disrupting my reverie, Cara entered my office.

"Something different today. For noontime meal. Surprise for manager." Cara smiled.

Chapter Sixteen

"You have a surprise for me? I love surprises. Where're we going?" I had to admit I'd tired of eating in. Going to a restaurant once or twice a week would improve my mental health.

"Sain, Teeka, join?"

"Of course, I'd love them to have them as lunch companions. Go ahead and make the arrangements. I'll work here until it's time." I glanced at the pile of paperwork on my desk.

"Time to go," replied Cara.

No time for office work, then. I wasn't terribly disappointed. "Okay. Let me pack my bag, and then I'm ready." My day pack carried all the items I might need on any trip away from the office, such as water and nutrition bars. A few needed to be constantly replaced. Excited about going out for a meal, I told myself to have Cara arrange lunch out as a regular event.

Cara led Sain, Teeka, and me up to the roof. Using a helicopter as a taxi instead of a land vehicle still seemed strange, but I'd happily adjusted. From what I'd noticed, so had Sain and Teeka.

A restaurant situated on a portion of Ooby's shoreline turned out to be our destination. The facility overlooked a bay filled with fish farm pyramids.

The noonday sun glinting on the fish troughs which created the pyramid shape at first blinded me. However, once my eyes adjusted, the pyramids combined with the fishing boats anchored alongside created a wondrous texture contrasting with the villages visible on the nearest islands—an efficient use of available resources.

The four of us entered the eatery through a back door and then traversed the noisy kitchen to our table out front.

Apparently, Cara had previously spoken with the restaurant manager. Presented with special paper menus with a section for humans and one for Irions, I assumed Cara received the facility's regular menu. The texture of the menu appeared different from human paper. Particlan paper making, although a suitable topic for Hart, greatly interested me.

They were half a dozen items listed for humans and also for Irions, so the chef had been suitably educated. The human portion contained my favorite.

"Cara, how did the restaurant know what to put on the menu? I mean, here I am on Particle, and they offer me spaghetti and meat balls. How wonderful is that?" I had my suspicions.

She smiled and reluctantly offered, "Suggestions to chef. Table to reserve. Service to provide."

"Well, then how did the restaurant's chef know how to cook human and Irion food?"

A serious look plastered Cara's face. Then she smiled and waved her hand. Sweety rushed through the kitchen door and ran over and gave me a hug.

"Surprise!" Sweety gave everyone a big grin.

I always loved encountering a delighted Sweety. "Aren't you secretive? I'm so glad you found time to run over here and educate the chef. What about adding a cooking show to your media madness? Chefs all over

Ooby and Particle, for that matter, would then be prepared for off-world guests." I glanced at Sweety. "I think I'm giving you too much to do."

"No problem, Syl. When I need breaks, I'll take them. Your idea about media channels is such a great one. Hart and I talked to the techs, but they had no idea what we referred to. However, an understanding was eventually cemented. In the end we, Particlans and humans, decided our new channels would also be a great way to advertise the hotel." Sweety grinned. "Besides, I love to perform. Hart's going to have more of a challenge, but he's excited about the concepts we've discussed."

"We're going to wake up Particle. They won't know what happened to them." I laughed to myself. I still wasn't quite sure what'd happened to me, but I tried to enjoy the ride. "After we're finished, Particlans will be more receptive to meeting new species." I shook my head. "Do you remember the *Martians Go Home* incident on Irion?

"Of course you do. All species are timid when it comes to the new and strange." Although I thought I might have to rethink my conclusion after we came across a warlike species.

I turned to Cara. "You're the best assistant ever for making these lunch arrangements. Perhaps we could do this once a week so I develop a better feel for what's offered in Ooby. You've made me very happy today."

Cara glowed. Of course, I suspected her emotions were probably also amplified by Teeka's presence.

After ensuring we had everything we needed to enjoy our meal, Sweety joined us. Her own meal and our table conversation seemed to enhance her day, and it certainly did mine.

Sain and Teeka devoured their lunches and uttered good words for both the restaurant and Cara. Sweety soon disappeared and then returned with the restaurant's head chef.

"Opinions on food. Good or bad. Welcomed by me."

"Thank you for being so accommodating, Chef. The food I ate was perfect. Sain, Teeka?"

Teeka waved his hand towards Sain, so Sain said, "Choices for Irions were welcome. Flavors and inspiration inspired. The Sath-Satre Golden Hotel kitchen on Irion needs improvement."

Chef seemed to understand and appreciate Sain's compliments.

I wondered if I was allowed to offer Chef a position in our new restaurant, or would I upset numerous Particlans? Although, I imagined we'd need an extra chef to help cover both the hotel and the new restaurant.

"Please return soon," said Chef Mastis tel Ramand.

"We certainly will." I loved the ambiance, and I think Chef Matis had improved the flavor of the meal I'd eaten. I'd recognized the seasoning of my spaghetti and meatballs as being slightly different from what I'd expected but nonetheless exceptional.

After our desserts were finished, one of the servers approached and had a rapid conversation with Cara. The universal translator couldn't keep up.

We watched the server disappear, and then Cara said, "Fans desire prints. Wish to know. To your liking?"

"Prints? What do you mean, Cara?" I asked. Prints? I had no idea what she talked about.

The confusion on her face was obvious, especially after she looked at her thumb. Thumbs were one thing humans and Particlans, well everyone so far, had in common.

Teeka saved the day. "Particlans want record of thumbprint?"

Cara made an affirmative motion with her hand in response to Teeka's question. Apparently, Particlan fingerprints were also unique.

"It's fine with me. Sain, Teeka?" They both agreed. "How should we do this?"

"Print procedure known. By Particlans involved. Details unveiled shortly."

A lineup of Particlans began to form. Apparently, Particlans liked to have bottles of water fingerprinted. I suspected the bottles were special in some way, but I couldn't read the Particlan writing without my little reader, and I hadn't thought to bring it along. The character reader would become a new staple for my backpack.

Water is life was, indeed, appropriate.

The Particlans were polite as I tried to engage them in conversation. Our discussions were informative for the most part, but some Particlans were reluctant to speak. I exerted effort to put them at ease, and I put the situation down to shyness.

As we added to their fingerprint collections, we also signed our names on the water bottles in the designated spot.

I understood human collectibles, but I hadn't even considered them on Irion, and now we were on Particle.

Collectibles needed to be added to my list of topics to study on a new world.

On our way back to the hotel, I asked, "Cara, are fingerprints on water bottles a collector's item?" I knew they were after today's experience, but how important were they in their society?

"Water is life. Prints of interest. Collection very impressive."

We dropped Cara and Sweety back at the hotel, and then Sain, Teeka, and I continued to police headquarters. Vara had asked for a consult, so I hoped he had information to impart.

Sain and I walked into police headquarters while Teeka rolled his wheelchair. His coloring had improved, and the wheelchair didn't seem to hamper his mobility. I suspected his upper body strength had mostly returned, and as stubborn as he was we'd soon see him hobbling around the hotel using a cane.

Vara waved Sain and me to stools, and Teeka pulled up close. Vara glanced at Teeka but didn't comment.

"So what's your news?" I asked. "Do you know the name of the second culprit, the one that knifed Teeka?"

"Culprit is revealed. Relative of Takka. Also of Tarin."

Well, since Takka and Tarin were related part of his conclusion didn't surprise me. I glanced at Teeka, but his face revealed nothing.

"Has this suspect divulged any details? Like why he knifed Teeka?" My emotions were on the warpath.

"No words spoken," replied Vara.

"Name?" asked Teeka.

"Sakka et Tong." Vara appeared amused.

"In custody?" Teeka continued.

"Awaiting justice decision. Photo sufficient evidence. System takes time."

Interesting information from Vara. Legal systems everywhere seemed to have the same time lags.

"Access to criminal allowed?" asked Sain.

"Not to non-citizens. Questions to ask. Forward to me."

Vara's response was logical. As much as his words annoyed the security types in my midst, we were off-worlders.

"Anything else you can tell us?" I asked. So far, Vara had been most accommodating.

"Wish to involve. Tarin et Tong. As guilty mastermind."

Oh, my. How would this affect the hotel? Did Vara have an issue with Tarin? Nothing I'd seen so far had pointed specifically to Tarin except the fact the participants were related and the additional fact I didn't particularly like him.

"Vara, do you have information about Tarin you could share? After all, along with Dedare Sath he's the co-owner of the Sath-Ooby Golden Hotel, and we're all involved in the running of the hotel. I deal with Tarin all the time." Actually, more often than I liked, but I wasn't about to share that little detail with Vara.

"Political issues abound," Vara responded.

Back to those nasty political issues. And here was Dedare having the desire to join Satre city council on Irion. I really didn't understand political issues, and I had no urge to. Boring, boring.

Although I knew politics ran Earth, I'd hoped alien worlds would be different. Perhaps these worlds were.

However, I suspected I was naïve. Oh well, I needed to return to my primary motivation—making a hotel run smoothly.

"Vara, thanks for your information. We'll keep an eye on things at the hotel. Is there anything, or anyone, we should look for or watch out for? Do you have problems with drugs on Particle? Is Tarin a drug overlord?"

I suspected my words confused everyone. The three non-humans in my midst studied me like I'd come from another planet. I laughed—I actually amused myself.

"Drug mastermind perhaps. Not involved, possible. Somewhat involved, yes."

I didn't understand the words *somewhat involved*. From the information I'd gathered, Tarin was certainly involved in the political world of Particle but to what extent I had little information to draw a conclusion.

"Thanks for your updates, Vara," I said. "If we uncover any, ANY, information, we'll be sure to let you know."

On that note, we took our leave. Vara followed the three of us to the police headquarters' entrance. He put his hand on my arm to hold me back while Sain and Teeka continued to our transport.

"Swim together soon," said Vara.

"I don't know what that means." And I couldn't interpret the expression on his face.

"Wish dinner together."

Oh my, another complication. "Vara, you do know Dedare and I are engaged to be married, to make a family together?"

Were my words understandable? So far, Particlan family relationships had been the farthest from my mind.

"Yes, but friends."

This never worked, but I continued to be a sucker. Actually, I was friends with Sain and Teeka, but…. "Of course, Vara. When would you like to have dinner?"

"Call with arrangements," he said.

"That's fine. I'm pretty busy, but I'm sure we can find a mutual time."

Sain and Teeka watched us as they waited for me outside the helicopter.

"I must get along. The boys are waiting. Thank you for the dinner offer. I look forward to seeing you." What was I saying?

Trouble, Syl, trouble.

Chapter Seventeen

What had I agreed to? How could I be friends with Vara? Although he really was a nice guy.

I had to admit I'd been attracted to Sain and Teeka at the same time as Dedare and I were getting together, and Sain, Teeka, and I have managed to retain a friendship after Dedare and I formalized our engagement. Perhaps a benign relationship with Vara could work. Aliens were aliens, after all.

Sain and Teeka occupied themselves on our short trip back to the hotel. Were their actions deliberate? If so, I mentally thanked them for their kindness. I had too much to think about to engage in conversation.

Cara had filled my afternoon with hotel employee interviews. I really hoped we were getting to the end. Actually, I knew we were because I tracked the employees I met on my new hotel organization chart. As much as I loved talking to everyone in my employ, I also had other projects with which to invest my time.

Eventually today's interviews ended, and then Mom and Reena appeared. Apparently their shopping trip had gone well, and they spent a few moments setting up a calendar. I now had a huge calendar on my wall and sticky paper to add appointments and schedules.

"You guys are the best." This would help me immensely in keeping track of people.

"Wait until you see what else we found. Thanks will be coming our way for days." My mother grinned, and so did Reena.

"Let me see," I demanded. Mom knew how to push my buttons.

"We'll show you at dinner…or maybe afterward. After all, I did pick up underwear." Mom laughed her head off.

What a tease Mom was. She acted like I was her young child.

Well, actually I was her child, but not that young anymore at thirty-eight. I suspected her words were mostly for Reena's benefit. Mom possibly tried to point out to the young Irion that she treated everyone similarly and to not take her words too seriously.

No never mind, since I understood dinner time had arrived as Sweety and Hart strolled through my doorway.

"What a wonderful day I've had." Sweety glanced at my desk and, I assumed, the exasperated look on my face. "Syl, take your work home. After we get a little food in your stomach and you relax with your most favorite people, you'll feel much better and have energy to complete another project. I know downtime is hard for you to understand, but at least try with a friends and family dinner. Oh hell, let's just say family dinner. By this time we're all family. Cara, we'd really love to have you join us."

Sweety recognized Cara's positive expression, so she said, "You and I should order food. The rest of you start on your way to Syl's." Sweety made shooing motions, so we obeyed without complaint. My dear friend got away with everything.

Dinner turned out to be a lively affair and a relief from the day's challenges.

"Mom, if I keep eating like this I may need larger-sized clothing."

"No, you won't. I know how much energy you're using up with swimming and all. Are you sure you're not taking on too much?" Mom knew I had a penchant for overbooking.

"I quite love my projects, and I have Cara to keep me organized, so it's all good."

Cara beamed, and I noticed Teeka studied Cara with pleasure on his face.

"And in no time Teeka will be up on his feet, so I'll be able to find lots of projects for him," I added.

Teeka's smile dimmed, so I wasn't sure if he approved of *lots of projects.* Time to change the subject. "Sweety, how was your time in the tech lab?"

"Excellent. I've decided to focus on a cooking show. First, I'm going to show how to cook Martian dishes. Perhaps one per episode. At the end of the episode, I'm going to offer to attend a Martian dinner at a Particlan's house and help them with their cooking. I think we'll integrate better into Particlan society if we spend time in their homes. Don't worry. I'll take someone along. Certainly one of the studio techs because I think we might film part of my evening in the Particlan home, and probably Sain or Hart or Teeka as security. What do you think?"

Conversations erupted after Sweety's declaration. She received numerous suggestions regarding the format of her cooking show. Some were quite impractical, but a couple of them were to my liking and obviously to Sweety's by her response.

Mom had suggested the demonstration videos should also include at least one Irion and one Particlan on screen. One reason would be to show how the different races could get along and another to give a hint of other recipes to be taped. Much to my surprise, neither Sain nor Teeka wanted to be involved with the on-screen aspect—possibly a security issue.

On the other hand, Reena and Mom were practically jumping off their stools. Sweety would have her hands full keeping everyone happy. So many budding actors.

"Cara, would you help me out in the studio?" asked Sweety. "I'd like a Particlan involved on screen in each episode."

"Pleased to assist," said Cara.

I noticed Cara looked a bit uncomfortable during our current discussion, so I asked, "Do you think this series of cooking videos will be well received by Particlans?"

"Unknown until viewed. Never before experienced. New research needed."

"Cara does have a point," I said. "Sweety, you might want to study the other shows on Particlan television. Since your project is new, you might want to include ideas from their shows. You might find ways to make your show more accessible to Particlans. I know I'm babbling."

Cara didn't interrupt, so I suspected I'd grasped her earlier remarks. My understanding of Particlan English continued to improve.

"I know, Syl. My project is not trivial. However, keep spewing your ideas. You never know what may trigger an insight." Sweety blew me a kiss.

"Syl, I talked to the captain of Dedare's orbiting ship, and he told me you haven't accessed your mail. Apparently, you have a whole bunch from Dedare waiting for you," said Hart.

Mail for me…from Dedare?

My mood improved. "Hart, how do I access these letters?"

"Give me your handset," Hart demanded, holding out his hand.

We all had a small computer-like device for various activities, along with our brooches for communication. I noticed Mom and Sweety studying my facial expressions while trying not to let on they were doing so.

"Apparently, I have a lot of reading material for later this evening," I said after Hart had handed back my handset and I'd had a look at its contents.

Sain interrupted the awkward silence. "Extra office ready soon. Workers and materials arranged for tomorrow."

Oops, maybe I should inform Tarin of the goings-on. However, *easier to get forgiveness than consent* might be appropriate in this situation. Nonetheless, a particular someone needed to be updated.

"Cara, I'm having an office built beside mine. It'll have access to the conference table so both parties can use the area when needed by either. I assume Sain is having some kind of folding walls put in so as to give privacy to the other party." I smiled. "Cara, this new office will be yours as my assistant. In the meantime, though, you need to share it with Teeka. Until he's back on his feet, literally, he needs to be closer to the action in the hotel. What do you think?"

Cara flushed.

"Assistant is wonderful. Office is useful. Share Teeka possible."

Share Teeka, indeed, but I didn't dare go there.

Hart piped up. "Syl, I found and purchased canvases today, so we have a source when you need more."

"And Reena and I found paints. Now I didn't purchase a great quantity as I know nothing about whether these are the same type you use. I tried to talk to the shop keeper, but we had a bit of a communications problem. So I only bought a few of three different types. You're going to have to go to the store after you study my purchases and make your own decisions. They have lots of colors. Quite a well-stocked hobby store," said Mom.

"Thanks, guys. I'll check out the paints and canvases, tonight—after I write a long letter." I sighed and stared off into the distance.

Dad cleared his throat. "Sylvestine, I'd like to update everyone regarding the diplomatic front."

"Of course." He really didn't need to ask for my approval—we were all in this together.

"The Sarturn were a surprise to all diplomatic staff except the Particlan ambassador. Sorry, Cara, but the Particlan ideas regarding diplomacy are strange to my ears."

Cara glanced at Dad's head. Holding my amusement back proved difficult, however Dad caught her action all on his own.

"Your ambassadors perform diplomatic actions much differently than we humans do. However, after we had a discussion your ambassador has begun to understand the current problem. They'll now inform us if any new races are expected to appear or have appeared. We still don't know who first knew about the impending visit of the Sarturn—before your ambassador found out, I mean."

"Did you ask Tarin et Tong? He told me he knew about the Sarturn, but I didn't ask him how he found out." It'd be like Tarin to keep the information to himself so he could host the alien in the Sath-Ooby Golden Hotel.

"Interesting information, thank you, Sylvestine. I'll investigate this data tomorrow. I have other research this evening, so I shall take my leave. Sylvia?"

"I'll be along later. I have purchases for Syl, so that'll take a while," answered my mother, with a laughter-filled voice.

So Dad left, as did Hart and Sweety. I suspected our days were long and tiring for a pregnant woman.

"Anything else required?" asked Cara.

"Oh, no. You've done marvelously today. Get some rest. I'm sure we'll have a busy day tomorrow." I marveled at the skills of my assistant.

Reena, Mom, and I watched Cara wheel Teeka out of my suite.

"Stay for little time?" asked Sain with a mischievous look in his eyes.

Mom and I understood he wanted to give Cara and Teeka a bit of private space. I suspected Reena hadn't picked up on the maneuvering.

We left Sain attempting to understand a Particlan media station on the machine in my living room. Our translators were overworked these days.

Back in my bedroom, three females drooled over the shopping Mom had done for me. Lots of new clothes, and waterproof to boot. The canvases were usable, but I didn't know about the paints. I needed to try them and then have a discussion at the retail outlet with the results of my experiments.

Eventually, Mom made her goodbyes. After she left, Reena started toward her room.

"Reena, are you up to morning swimming practice?" I asked.

"Look forward. Particlans to meet."

"Good. Let's see how your practice goes, and then I'll show you a basic dive, if you're up to it." Reena's swimming was at a satisfactory level, so I'd start with the simplest dive to properly begin her training.

A delighted Reena popped off.

After I was alone, I spent a couple of hours reading Dedare's missives while drinking wine. Happy tears flowed, and then I wrote back. My mood had improved considerably by the time I'd relaxed enough to sleep.

****

The next morning, Reena was first to be ready for the day. Glad to see she had a healthy subject occupying her mind, I did nothing to discourage her interest.

"Looking forward to swimming, Reena?" I asked while I pulled on my cover-up and shoes.

"Yes. Practice needed."

A glance at her face told me all I needed to know. Diving fascinated her, but she didn't want to bring the subject up in case she became too pushy. It amazed me how similar our species were regarding certain aspects.

Of course, my interpretation may have been completely wrong.

After we arrived at the employee training area, Reena went in search of her new friend, Sara. They took off their cover-ups and started swimming. I watched as they warmed up and then started timing each other's laps. I decided I needed a few laps in before Reena became anxious regarding diving. Of course, I needed to limber up before doing any diving myself.

As I loosened up, I watched the Particlan divers perform. Their dives were certainly different from human ones but not radically so. I might need a lot of practice, though, in order to compete. I'd superficially studied the diving material Cara sent, but I expected to require deeper research on diving moves and the scoring thereof.

The diving board became free, so I made a few dives. As I climbed up for a fifth dive, I noticed every Particlan in the room had stopped their activities. Thankfully, spectator pressure didn't bother me.

Since I had an engrossed audience I tried one of my more complicated dives. A slight error crept in but not enough to trigger discouragement on my part. After all, I hadn't dived in quite some time.

Reena helped me out of the pool. "Reena, would you like to try a couple of simple dives?"

"Yes." She beamed.

"Now, these are basic diving moves. They're very simple, but you must learn them well as they form a part of complicated dives. Do you understand?"

"Will not be doing your last dive for a long while," she said, laughing.

"You got it." Thankfully, Reena was rarely a moody teenager.

I started with a simple form and showed her the sub-parts while we stood on the ground. Then I climbed the ladder and did the dive.

"Now, do you remember the steps of this dive? Your foot movements, your arm movements, and such."

She waved her hand in a gesture of agreement.

"So, go on and give it a try. Perhaps a few times."

Reena flubbed her first try, but she immediately got out of the pool and tried again. Her second try was much better, and by the delighted look on her face she understood.

So I left Reena with her new friend, Sara, and went off to talk to Cara, as I'd noticed Cara stood in the background.

"Cara, you're here early," I said as I draped my towel over my shoulders. The Particlan towels were an odd shape, actually a square, but they served the same function. The hotel provided a cabinet full of towels for its staff facility.

"Discuss many things. Not enough time. During busy day."

"You got that right. So what do you need to discuss?" I kept my eyes on Reena while Cara and I conversed.

"Olympic judging committee."

"Have we found enough Particlans willing to help out?" I hoped so. I certainly couldn't judge anything myself. I didn't even have a handle on the actual categories and rules for swimming and diving.

"Enough judges available. Rules being discussed. Questions about Takka."

Her comment regarding Takka confounded me. Takka resided quite properly in jail for his attack on Teeka. "Did Takka judge the hotel swimmers?"

"Always as judge."

Her comment now made sense. "Do the others know what Takka did?"

Cara indicated ignorance.

"Well, tell the others Takka cannot be a judge as he's in jail. He attacked Teeka and needs to pay for his sins, ah, crimes. I'm sure everyone will understand. If they don't, let me know. I'll talk with the hotel's new Olympic judging committee if you think that's wise."

"Time will tell," responded Cara.

Time solved everything—or maybe not. A discussion for another day. I waved Reena over, so she and her friend ran my way.

"What do you think about diving, Reena?" I asked—not that I had any doubts.

"Wonderful sport. Teaching Sara ild Tamark what you teach me." Reena and Sara beamed in their own species ways.

"You are already better, Reena. You learn well, and practice makes perfect. And Sara, Reena is a good teacher—you've already learned much. Do you both want to learn more?"

Two enthusiastic young females grinned. "Okay, we'll add new skills again tomorrow. If you get a chance, practice again today."

"Practice all day," chirped Reena.

"No. You need schooling and other activities. You may practice for a little while longer right now. And then this afternoon you may practice for two hours but no more. Don't overdo your physical activities. Do you understand, Reena?"

"Yes. Advice appreciated." Reena and Sara both turned and ran back to the diving board.

"Cara, it's time I changed and went to work. I'll see you shortly." I headed back to my suite for a shower and change of clothes.

After I arrived at the office, I found a breakfast tray on my conference table with Cara waiting. She'd ordered enough for both of us, so we had a quiet moment sipping tea and enjoying the other sustenance she'd ordered.

"This is lovely, Cara. Thank you. How did you know what I like for breakfast?"

"Chef had ideas. Sain had thoughts. Teeka had opinions."

Cara amused me. We ate our breakfast in a companionable silence. I suspected we wouldn't have many quiet periods for the remainder of the day.

A commotion started outside my office, so we jumped up to see what the fuss was about.

Our new alien, the Sarturn, stood in front of a hotel security personnel. Of course, the Sarturn didn't realize he talked to security not a reservations personnel.

"Excuse me. May I help you?" I asked.

The alien yelped, "Need many things."

So I had an irritated Sarturn on my hands. "Why don't you follow me into my office, and we'll discuss your needs. Just a moment, though, we need to make arrangements."

I whispered to Cara. "Can you put a cover on one of the chairs at the conference table? I don't want him poisoning the fabric."

She knew exactly what I needed, so she pulled a tablecloth out of a drawer of her Reception desk and ran into my office. The fabric reminded me of plastic, so it would do the job perfectly.

I guided the Sarturn and settled him at the covered chair at my conference table. As far as I could tell he wasn't particularly agitated. "Would you like something to eat or drink?" I asked. Had he even eaten today?

"Kitchen adequately supplied."

One good thing in our favor. I wondered what he'd actually eaten from the hotel kitchen. The list of items would be necessary for my database on Sarturn foods and would certainly help Sweety and her menus. I had much information to collect as the aliens mounted up. My words made me laugh and think of piles of dead aliens strewn about.

"What do you need?" I asked. "We'll do our best to help."

"Food adequate. New dishes welcomed. Tourist required." His skin glistened. I hoped he wasn't going to start spewing fluids all over my office. How could I tactfully ask him to refrain?

"First, I'd like to tell you your excretions are toxic to humans like me. Do you understand?" I pointed toward my chest.

He glanced at me. "Human?"

"Yes, I am. We've discovered the fluid you left outside Reception yesterday affects humans. Can you refrain from expelling that liquid?"

"Possible. Take much concentration."

"Please try. Now, I have someone who would be happy to help Chef with new Sarturn recipes. However, she is with child, so you must stay at a distance if you speak with her. No touching. Do you understand?"

"Yes. Help with food is welcome. Children are welcome."

The Sarturn's answers were more than adequate. I almost enjoyed having a new alien in our midst. Almost. However, what was I going to do about Sarturn secretions throughout the hotel?

Chapter Eighteen

The Sarturn's secretions were a problem with humans operating within the Sath-Ooby Golden Hotel.

My mind churned, and then an image of a garden plot popped into my mind.

One summer, Mom had arranged for me to spend time in a Martian garden. Curious about what my major interests might turn out to be, she provided numerous activities during my childhood for experience and exploration.

The garden plot grew numerous items and had corresponding wet and dry areas. After I complained about mud on my shoes and legs, she found me a pair of bright red galoshes. They were pretty ugly, but I loved them.

So I decided the Sarturn needed boots to contain his secretions.

"Would you mind waiting a moment? I need to talk to my assistant about a hotel issue."

"Agreed, agreed."

I motioned Cara outside and explained my solution for the Sarturn's secretions.

"Possible, back shortly," she replied.

So I went inside and sat across from the Sarturn.

"What else do you require?"

"Escorted tours through Ooby. Tourist requirements."

A topic I had yet to pursue, so my interest was piqued.

Before I had a chance to explain to the Sarturn I needed to consult with Cara again, she popped back into my office.

"Matters shortly arranged."

I took her words to mean the required item would soon appear, so I went ahead with my question. "Cara, do we offer guest tours around the city?"

"Two hotel helicopters. Used for tours. Reception staff accompanies."

So our reception staff had been trained for guest tours. What a great bonus for me. "Do we have a list of available tours and their schedules? Or do tours happen after a request is made?"

"Both ways available. Let me find. Most recent schedule."

Cara hurried out and returned within moments. She handed both me and the Sarturn a printed pamphlet.

I ran my reader over the pamphlet's printing. The Sarturn watched my actions, and I knew what he thought. So I handed him the reader and said, "I hope this translates into your language. Please try the machine."

The Sarturn ran my reader over his brochure. He didn't appear frustrated, so I waited for his response.

"Tour of cultural buildings; tour of cultural buildings." The Sarturn peered at my face. "Wish your presence for tour; wish your presence for tour."

He wanted me to accompany him. What would everyone say? "I'm very busy. However, let me see if I can arrange the time. I'll let you know. Please choose one of the other tours for the rest of your day, and Cara will make the arrangements. By the way, what is your name? We haven't been introduced. I'm Sylvestine Amera from Mars. You may call me Syl."

The Sarturn made a croaking noise. Laughter, I suspected. "Testarn, Testarn. You may call me Testarn. A likeable Sarturn name."

I grinned. Laughing at my words, laughing at the Sarturn's words, was a terrific way to hold a conversation.

Cara and Testarn studied the brochure and came to a decision. She motioned him outside my office, and they disappeared.

A few moments later, Cara returned. "Sarturn tour arranged."

"Thank you. That's wonderful. Dealing with new aliens can be disconcerting. Did you find me and the other aliens, humans and Irion, difficult to understand at first?"

"Difficulty not unusual. Particlans from outskirts. Behave very differently."

To find out Particlans were not a uniform race, but one with societal differences, fascinated me. "Cara, we need to talk to Hart and make sure every hotel employee has a translator and a reader. The way we're going, we'll probably have a new alien every week."

We both laughed. "Call to Hart."

"Yes, please do. If he has any questions, he can contact me." I took a deep breath. "Now, I need to sit at my desk and organize."

My life had a habit of getting out of control.

I worked for a couple of hours updating my projects and arranging them in order of importance. An unknown priority might appear and screw up my schedule, but I couldn't plan for that contingency.

Sounds of construction penetrated my consciousness. I peeked out and saw Sain watching Particlan workers putting up finished walls. At this rate, the new office would be completed in no time.

"Sain, where did you find these pre-finished parts?" I asked.

"Talked to Cara. She knew company from previous renovations. Worked out well. Office will complete in a couple of hours."

"Nice and efficient. Do you want lunch? I'm hungry, and I want to close my office door to ignore the construction noise, so perhaps you would join me."

Sain agreed, so I asked Cara to arrange lunch for the three of us, and we then retreated to my office to wait.

Before our food arrived, Tarin walked into my office. We hadn't made plans to meet so I suspected this was an unannounced inspection.

"Sylvestine, what happens?"

The time to be diplomatic had arrived. "If you mean the construction outside, my new assistant, Cara, needs an office nearby for consultations with me. The hotel is running smoothly right now, however, we need constant contact for efficiency. Cara knew of a construction company with pre-finished walls and such, so the office could be constructed in record time to minimize distraction to our guests."

Tarin studied Cara and Sain and then looked outside to the construction, and I gathered he didn't know quite what to say.

I took advantage of his confusion. "The restaurant is in its final planning stages. When planning is complete, the restaurant should be constructed in record time, and with minimal interference to our guests." I laughed. "In fact, I think the construction will interest current guests who'll help pass the word about the Sath-Ooby Golden Hotel having an attached restaurant." I smiled at Tarin.

Again, he had a lack of words. Finally, Tarin turned to Cara. "All permits required?"

My goodness. I hadn't thought about what this world, or the city of Ooby, might want in the way of construction permissions.

"Discussions with Sain. Applications with city. Required permits purchased."

I tried not to show relief.

Without another word, Tarin left my office. He had uttered no complaints or criticisms, so I decided all was well.

After Tarin left, our food arrived, so we ate at the conference table and discussed a few topics one of which Sain brought up.

"No mention of Gift Shop?"

I laughed. "I'd hoped neither of you would mention the Amenities Shop. If he'd asked, my answer to Tarin would have been *it's part of the restaurant.*"

We all smiled.

Eventually my thoughts turned to Particlan social aspects. "Cara, I'm still confused about your religions." Actually, I knew almost nothing. "I'd like to visit at least one church this afternoon. Can that be arranged?"

She agreed and went outside. After Cara returned and announced she'd arranged a visit to a church via helicopter, we finished our food.

"I will accompany. Moveable partitions inserted this afternoon. Much confusion for all. No work done in this area."

I'd forgotten about the partitions Sain had suggested. When installed, my conference table and area could be either linked with my office or Cara's depending on our needs. And Sain was correct—neither Cara nor I would get much work done with the construction noise and interruptions. So I grabbed my bag for our afternoon excursion.

Once we were on our way I asked, "Is the church close by, Cara?"

"Quick air ride."

Our landing area was a huge field for air vehicles. The helicopter first settled close to the church buildings allowing us to disembark, and then it took off for a far part of the field to await being summoned for departure, Cara explained. With this procedure, passengers had little distance to walk to the facilities.

This church consisted of three structures connected by walkways. The outside two were three-story enclosed buildings over an open ground floor. The middle building appeared to have only one floor built over the usual open area. A soaring roof and numerous windows letting in light completed the majestic structure. The outside color schemes of the three buildings focused on blues and greens.

We walked to the first building on the left side of the pathway. After we climbed the stairs to the immediate above ground floor we entered into a small reception area where a security guard hovered.

"Individual residence areas. Permanent or casual. Church employees reside," Cara informed us.

"Are there joint kitchens, social rooms, and such?" I asked. "Can we see one of the residences? Though we wouldn't want to bother anyone." Seemed like a typical scheme for in-house employees.

The security guard led us to an unoccupied residence. Although small, it contained a bed, bathroom, and sitting area. The color schemes were again blues and greens. Kitchen facilities were not attached.

"Are all the residences in the same color scheme?" I asked.

"Individual preferences allowed. Rooms refurbished upon occupancy. Comfort to residents," the guard answered.

The kind security guard then led us to a communal living area with a large attached kitchen. I snooped in the kitchen as Sweety'd probably have numerous questions for me.

"Cara, I noticed a dumb waiter. What's that used for?" As I waited for Cara's response, I wondered what the translator would do with the words *dumb waiter*.

"Elevator for food. Main kitchen top. Orders arrive here."

"So the residents don't have to cook if they don't want to." I nodded. "That makes sense. And they have a communal kitchen if they have the desire." Information to pass along to Sweety.

Cara didn't argue with my conclusion but simply waited for my next question. She knew numerous ideas always ran through my mind.

"What're we going to see next?" I really didn't have a handle on religious institutions—especially alien ones.

"Building on right. Back to elevator. Short walk now."

Cara was obviously leaving the middle, biggest building for last.

The building on the right was of the same structure as the one on the left. Again we took an elevator to the first floor.

There I found a much different layout from the residence building. The first upper floor of this building had one spacious room filled with displays, much like a retail shop. We wandered through, and I found the items to be particularly interesting. The colors were gorgeous, but I didn't understand the purpose of most of the objects.

"Cara, this is a store, right? Can we purchase items?" My shopping urge kicked in. So far, I'd been denied satisfaction on Particle.

"Open to public."

"Would you walk around with us so you can explain more about the product? Some are obvious, but most of the ones I can see are not."

I glanced at Sain. I'd clued in he wasn`t a shopper, but for our safety he was on alert. I hadn't noticed anything or anyone to worry about, but his security presence reassured me.

Included in the familiar objects category I discovered a table of scarves and also one of necklaces.

Although predominantly black in color, the scarves and necklaces were also infused with strands of color.

"Cara, these are scarves, right?" I asked, pointing to a table. "What're they used for? When are they worn? Do you call them by another name?" I continued my questions, before she had a chance to even answer my first one.

She picked up a scarf and tied it around her waist.

"Worn in church. Symbol of devotion. Colors match church."

I took a closer glance at the scarves on the table. "Do you mean the imbedded colors are for different religions?"

"Items different religions. Scarves are for. Redeemed Water Tower."

I thought she'd said scarves were for only one religion. My head hurt. "Is *Redeemed Water Tower* a religion?"

Cara pointed to a wall. The displayed painting depicted a priest with a scarf tied around his waist.

"Here home base. Formal *Church of. Redeemed Water Tower.*"

"So this is the parent church, with many subsidiary churches, ah, ah branches, belonging to the *Church of Redeemed Water Tower*?"

A little complicated, but I hoped I understood this part of their alien culture.

In response, Cara beckoned us over to a window and pointed outside. A tall, black obelisk glistened in the sunlight. The tower's sparkling gold streaks reminded me of the scarves we'd recently seen.

"Parent church, yes."

"Cara, is that the *Redeemed Water Tower*?" I pointed to the obelisk. Since we were at the church's home base, the *Redeemed Water Tower* must be somewhere around here.

"So how's everyone, today?"

Shocked to hear my mother's voice, I asked, "Mom, what're you doing here?"

Chapter Nineteen

"Mom, what're you doing here?"

With hands on hips, she glowered. What angered her?

"Since I was supposed to investigate churches for my history of Particle, I decided to join you. I learned from one of the sweet employees in Reception where you'd all gone—without me."

Oops. I'd forgotten about her research. "Sorry, Mom. This was a last-minute idea in my overwhelmed brain. I'm so glad you took the initiative. How did you get here?"

"Oh, I sweet talked the Particlan in Reception into arranging one of the helicopters used for tours. Since it was idle, I didn't think my commandeering would cause a problem. Once I saw your helicopter parked and waiting, I sent mine back to the hotel."

"Smart thinking. Now, let me give you an update." I scratched my head. I wasn't quite sure where to begin.

"Cara, correct me when I'm wrong as I explain to Mama A what we've found out so far today." I gathered my thoughts. "Mom, this set of three buildings is the home base of the *Church of the Redeemed Water Tower*. That's the tower out there," I said, pointing at the black obelisk. "We first went into the building on our left. It's a residence building for the church's permanent staff. Quite nice. Now we're in this building where they have items for sale to support the church." I glanced at Cara. "So far, so good?"

She smiled, and made a motion with her hand that indicated, at least to me, to continue.

"Mom, this floor is the church's retail outlet. We've just started looking at the items for sale, so you're in time. Oh, and scarves are a way to indicate you belong to the *Church of the Redeemed Water Tower*. Because the obelisk is black, the scarves are mostly black, with some having strands of color woven in. The scarves are worn about your waist." I turned to Cara. "Are you allowed to wear the scarves around your neck?"

Cara gave me a questioning look, so I picked up one of the scarves and tied it around my neck. "Is this allowed?"

"Not mean church," Cara said.

"That's fine. I love scarves and like to wear them. Is that allowed?"

"Acceptable to everyone."

Okay, so far no faux pas from me today. "I might pick up a couple of scarves. They're delightful. However, I want to see the rest of the retail inventory before I make any decisions."

Mom laughed. She and I were the shoppers in today's group. Sain didn't seem particularly interested, which didn't surprise me. He hadn't expressed interest on Irion, either.

"Cara, why's the church called *Redeemed Water Tower*? What, or who, was redeemed?" I hoped my question made sense.

"Wars over water. Much history involved. Water tower stolen."

"Did countries fight over the water tower? Or did churches?" I didn't understand how water towers were important on Particle when there existed so much water here.

"Desalination water tower. Important in past. Obtaining water difficult."

So in the past clean water had been hard to obtain. Didn't surprise me. Primitive cultures had all sorts of problems. Actually, clean water had always been a problem. Wars over water would be similar to wars over land, coins, or other objects crucial at that moment in time.

Cara hadn't really answered my question about who rescued the water tower, so I took a wild guess. "Did a group of Particlans take back the water tower and then start a church?"

"Water tower rescued. End to wars. Beginning of church."

I thought Cara agreed with my analysis, but I decided to leave her vague details alone. I could always spend time in the hotel library and update my incomplete information.

Next our group came upon a table covered with necklaces whose main components were pieces of stone.

I studied them briefly. "Cara, these necklaces, are they significant in any way?" I pointed at the table. Their colors were outstanding, but I didn't particularly like how the stones were linked together. The jewelry seemed to lack a certain elegance, but perhaps that was a human-centric vision of how jewelry should be made.

"Sister church emblem. Necklaces also black. Link to here."

A sister church should have a link of course. However, the necklaces triggered another question.

"Cara, do the sister churches also wear scarves, not just necklaces?"

"Scarves and necklaces."

Then it dawned on me what my real question was. "Sain, Cara, do any of these necklaces remind you of the one around the neck of Teeka's second assailant?"

They both turned their complete attention to the necklaces.

"Yes, the same," said Cara after a moment.

"So Teeka's assailant with the knife belongs to one of the branches?" I asked.

"Branch near here," said Cara, answering my next question before I had a chance to verbalize it.

"Sain, let's go there and find out what we can about this church and its members."

"No. Call to Vara." He walked away as he talked into his brooch.

A much more practical and appropriate idea, so I tried not to argue. I had an urge to run to the helicopter and travel to this church branch, but I only sighed and said, "Okay, let's continue our research into what's for sale in this room. Mom, have you found anything intriguing?"

"Lots." She turned to Cara. "Why does this table have lengths of beautiful cloth stuffed in pots?"

"Blessing of material. By religious elders. Suitable for church."

"You mean you can't wear anything you want to a church service?" I asked.

"Most clothing appropriate. Addition of scarf. Overrides material requirement."

Cara glanced at our faces and decided to continue her explanation.

"Church open everyone. Some standards apply. Only scarf necessary."

"But the church still sells blessed clothing?" I asked.

Mom stopped me in my tracks. "Syl, don't worry about it. Every church has its idiosyncrasies, and they all need revenue to survive."

I shook my head. As always, Mama A was wise. So I changed the subject. "Cara, what's on the upper two floors?"

"Items being made." Cara pointed around the room.

"Oh, so the upper two floors provide stock for this store," I said.

Cara waved her hand with a motion I considered as agreement.

"Are we allowed to see the processes?"

"Approved for off-worlders."

So we found ourselves upstairs in a large open room. Various areas had Particlans working on producing individual items. I assumed the top floor had a similar layout. We spread out, and I found the table where the stone necklaces were assembled. "Cara, are these black stones made from the *Redeemed Water Tower*?"

She laughed. "Little tower remains."

"Oops. Silly question. You're right. After a short time, the tower would be a stub. So where does the church get stones for these necklaces?"

"Received from quarries. Owners to provide. Small polished stones."

Okay, so quarries existed on Particle. What else did these quarries produce? Then I noticed another area. "Cara, why are knives being made? Are they for sale downstairs?"

"Outlet sells knives." Cara agreed.

"Why would a church sell knives?" I asked. On Earth, we'd had religious wars. Had they also happened on Particle?

Cara gathered her thoughts.

"History of church. Confrontation with others. Now only ceremonial."

So humans weren't the only ones with a history of church conflicts. "Mom, maybe you could research this confrontation." I glanced at my watch. "I should get back to the hotel fairly soon, so let's finish our tour."

We made our way down to the retail floor. In addition to scarves, blessed material, and necklaces, I acquired two knives. I wanted to study how well they were made or if they were only decorative. The knives fit into an outside pocket of my backpack.

I also found piles of small stones, flat on one side, for sale. "I'd like to purchase a few buckets of these. Could everyone carry a bucket to the helicopter for me?"

"Syl, what're you up to?" asked my mother at the same time Sain asked, "Why?"

"You're a couple of suspicious people, aren't you?" I pointed at the buckets of stones. "Come here. Look at all the lovely colors. I'm told these are leftovers they don't use in any of their own various projects. I want to turn a painting or two into a kind of mosaic. With their flat surface and small size, they'd be perfect for gluing to the surface of a painting. And they cost practically nothing."

"Syl, if you keep this up you're going to run out of room in your suite." Mom laughed. "But I'll help the hoarder in you. And besides, your idea is interesting."

Sain and Cara also agreed to carry the heavy buckets. So we called the helicopter, loaded our purchases, and then trooped over to the main church building—the middle building—unburdened.

The church had the usual open area underneath. The outside of the main floor was wreathed in decorative rectangular stonework—mostly black with gold flecks.

After we went through the automatic doors, water engulfed us from above. Apparently, a *water cleansing* wall was necessary to cleanse the heathens. Ah, I meant church goers. No one had worn waterproof clothing today, so a bedraggled group emerged from the waterfall.

"Syl, we're going to have to get the hotel seamstress to work up more waterproof clothing. Being soaked to the skin is not comfortable or healthy for humans."

"You're absolutely right, Mom. Let's make our visit short and then return to the hotel and clean up," I said.

After we shook the water off our bodies, we were greeted by three priests. Glancing around the interior, I noticed the church empty of other Particlans, so I suspected we were between services.

"Greetings to off-worlders. Please join me. In church tour."

The presence of the priests was serendipitous. Or was it? A handy guide or two would help us find out a lot more about the church and its history. However, I hadn't expected one of our greeters to be the chief priest Saska et Tong. He seemed to turn up everywhere.

Saska led us around the inside walls of the church service area. Like every other church I'd been in, I'd found myself in a large area.

The décor fit a water world. Numerous windows in the upper half of the walls let in brilliant light. I suspected the window glass was tinted blue as the light coming through had a blue sparkle. The lower halves of the walls contained large aquariums. Even at a distance, I noticed unusual fish swam in the glass containers. I took a guess of the inside height of the soaring room and estimated two and a half human normal stories.

The chief priest's title had been translated to Chief Motivator. "Chief Motivator, are these all Particlan fish, or are some from other worlds?" My way of digging into how many worlds they knew about.

Saska et Tong appeared taken aback.

"Particlan church ours. Water is life. No other similar."

There went my idea of offering to import human and Irion fish.

I returned to studying the gorgeous Particlan fish. Only a few were similar to the ones we'd seen in the fish farm pyramids. Perhaps these fish weren't edible by Particlans, but could they be sustenance for either humans or Irions? I'd keep an eye out on future menus.

We arrived at the front of the church where a large, raised dais occupied the center of the floor. On the right side, the space was occupied by three rows containing three drums each, with each drum accompanied by a stool. On the left side, I found a three-level area again, with stools for singers I suspected. I'd dearly love to enjoy a service to confirm my suppositions.

"May we return to experience a church service? When would be an appropriate time?" I asked.

"Arrangements be made," said Saska et Tong.

Then Saska gave me a glance I couldn't decipher.

"Schedule not made. Study of religion. Church classes ongoing."

Oh, that's right. I'd agreed to church education.

"Sorry, Chief Motivator. I've been so busy; I haven't had time." I pointed at Cara. "I will have my new assistant, Cara, make the arrangements." I glanced around the church. "Saska et Tong, it is time for us to return. We must change out of our wet clothes."

"Wet clothes hazardous?" asked Saska.

"Somewhat. We have some clothes made from Particlan waterproof materials, but we need more for everyday wear. That should solve these problems. However, we must change because we could contract an illness if we wear wet garments too long. Being on a new planet, we need to be careful. Thank you for your time, Saska et Tong. We'll be back soon."

Farewells were said, and then we traipsed out to the helicopter and returned to the hotel. I'd told Cara I didn't think we had time to visit an additional church today.

Upon our return, we found Sweety and Hart lounging in my office. "About time you guys returned. We wondered where you'd gone," said Sweety. "A shopping trip I wasn't invited to, I see."

"Not exactly. We scouted the main church of one of the Particlan religions. Be patient. All the information you need will be revealed at dinner. We all got soaked again and need to shower and change. Would you arrange dinner, Sweety? I'm starving."

"When aren't you?" Sweety smiled. "Of course, I will. Cara, want to give me a hand? You don't look very wet."

Laughter abounded, and then the others went their ways after dropping off my buckets of stones.

"I have a copy of my first cooking show for your viewing pleasure and subsequent critiques," said Sweety after we'd spent a companionable time eating and talking. "Hart, would you load it up, please?"

I suspected Sweety didn't know how to access my machine any more than I did.

Watching her cook Martian dishes amused me. Sweety made an excellent host and chef and explained the dishes and procedures well. At the end of her presentation, Sweety asked for a volunteer Particlan host to co-cook a Martian dinner.

"Well done, Sweety. The pacing is appropriate, and you kept me interested until the end, which makes me believe the Particlans should be fascinated. The techs did a wonderful job of following you around. Where did you do your cooking? Doesn't appear to be the media lab." I'd quite enjoyed her presentation.

Sweety laughed. "Chef cleared out a corner of his kitchen. And whenever I want to do another episode, the space will be available. I just have to coordinate the time. Chef's a sweety."

"Have you sent this video out?" I asked.

"No, not yet. The techs know all possible sites, so I'm leaving it all up to them to promote the cooking show. They're quite excited about the publicity it'll bring the hotel. However, I wanted to run it by everyone before I gave the techs the go-ahead. I need your opinions, guys."

The general consensus was enthusiastic approval, so Sweety beamed and said she'd give the techs the word for its release.

"Have you worked with the Sarturn yet?" I asked. So many questions for poor, pregnant Sweety.

"Actually, I helped with his first meal. I happened to be in the kitchen at the time of his call, so I eased the staff along. Right now, there are too many aliens for the Particlans to easily cope with, Syl. You need to ease their anxiety somehow."

I needed to ease every employee's anxiety somehow.

"How did you know what he likes?" Mom asked.

"It turns out Sarturns can eat what Irions eat, so that simplified everything. Hart discovered that detail." Sweety blew him a kiss. "Of course, the Sarturn wants some of his own particular dishes, but they won't be hard to reproduce. I'll spend time in the kitchen again. This time will be for the Sarturn."

"Thank goodness you're here, Sweety. I don't know what the hotel would do without you. And not just the hotel—I'm totally indebted." Sweety and I became teary-eyed.

"By the way, the kitchen staff need translators. If I hadn't been there, no one would've known what the Sarturn wanted," Sweety remarked after taking a moment to collect herself.

"Agreed. That topic's been in my thoughts all day. Hart, we need to equip everyone in the hotel with translators and most likely readers. It's absolutely necessary," I added.

"No protest. In fact, I've had the spaceship replicating both items. They should soon have enough to cover every employee."

"Good thinking. Speaking of the spaceship, Dedare's last letter said he should be here soon," I remarked. "I'm so looking forward to seeing him."

Smiles lit up my living room, and then Sain said, "Teeka walked from our suite."

I glanced at Teeka and saw no wheelchair. "Teeka, show us how you walk," I demanded.

He stood and said, "Cane or arm necessary." Teeka took Cara's arm and walked a short distance around my living room. "Running soon." While we laughed, Cara settled Teeka back on his stool.

"Sylvestine, I have an update on the Olympics," said Dad, interrupting my elation on Teeka's progress.

"Good news, I hope." My Olympic training would do or die on what he managed to arrange.

"The official Olympic committee has tentatively agreed that non-Particlans can be part of an Olympic team sent to the trials. In other words, you and Reena can be part of the first stage if you qualify for the Sath-Ooby Golden Hotel's Olympic team. One stipulation, however, is that there must be more Particlans than aliens on each team."

"The best words I've heard all day, Dad. How did you manage to accomplish this?" I asked after I gave him a hug.

"I have no idea. Their initial reluctance disappeared, for no apparent reason. Don't forget, Sylvestine, this is a tentative agreement. Politics may interfere and change everything. For now, you and Reena need to continue your practicing."

"Don't worry, we will. And I need to continue my research on the judging rules," I added. "Another project for tonight. Any other updates?"

Reena sported a huge grin throughout our exchange. The thought of trying out for the Particlan Olympics had inspired her.

She stood. "Time for homework. Busy day tomorrow." She said goodnight to everyone, and I gave her a hug.

After she left the living room, Sweety commented, "Such a nice, mature child. You're lucky to have a wonderful almost-stepdaughter, Syl."

"Indeed I am." I reflected on Reena for a moment.

"Cara's office finished," said Sain. "Occupancy tomorrow."

I turned to Cara. Her flushed face revealed her feelings.

"Glanced at tonight. Moving in tomorrow. Thanks to everyone."

Her obvious pleasure was an inspiration. "Cara, you and I'll be more efficient. I can't wait until tomorrow, either."

Cara gave me a big smile.

Then I remembered one of my purchases today. I pulled my backpack toward me and fished out one of the knives I'd bought. "Teeka, do you think this looks like the knife used in your attack? Sain?" I sent an apologetic glance toward Teeka.

Sain and Teeka studied the knife I gave them. I'd left the second one in my backpack since I suspected I wouldn't get the first one back any time soon.

Teeka sent me a questioning look.

"I got this at the *Church of the Redeemed Water Tower*'s retail outlet. It reminded me of the knife in the attack video," I said.

"Give to Vara," said Sain. "Possible link."

That was the reason I picked up the knives. Harrumph. "Okay but tell him I want it back. I like the colors in the stone."

Teeka's expression gave the impression I'd uttered foreign, alien words.

During our interchange, Hart had taken a call. He'd walked away to have quiet to continue the exchange.

"Syl, everyone, I have news." His ashen face made me stop breathing. "Dedare's spaceship is out of communication. No one knows where it is.

Chapter Twenty

"How do you know Dedare's missing?" My breath quickened, and I shivered.

"The captain of the ship Dedare's traveling in didn't give his regular report to the ship currently orbiting Particle," said Hart. "So our ship captain, here in orbit, tried to reach Dedare's spaceship but had no luck."

"What're they going to do? What are we going to do?" I asked Hart. My foggy mind attempted to think.

"I've arranged to go up to the spaceship orbiting Particle. Then we're going to travel to Dedare's last known position." Hart shook his head. "No, that's not right. First we're going to where they should have reported in. Our captain suspects their space radio is having problems, so he thinks that'll be the best place to begin looking. Makes sense to me, at least as a starting position."

"Okay, then I'm going too." I needed to help find the love of my life.

"And I'm going," said Sweety. "Someone needs to look after both of you."

Hart shook his head. "Syl, you need to give the Sarturn his tour tomorrow, and you need to run the hotel and keep this motley crew in line. Without you, who knows what would happen." Then he turned to his bride. "Sweety, I'd love to have you along, but I'm going to be taking up too much space on the ship as it is since I will be staying awake. I want you to stay here and keep our babies calm. You know that's necessary."

Sweety and I exchanged glances. Hart was doubly correct, so we didn't argue.

"When do you leave?" Sweety asked.

"Ah, right now. The captain wants to be on his way. The sooner the better, in case there's something wrong with their ship." Hart glanced my way after he uttered his words.

"Hart, let's get you packed. You'll need clothes and amenities, at least," said Sweety, grabbing him and starting toward the door. "Syl, get some sleep tonight. I'll talk to you tomorrow."

"Hart, call often," I said. "I need to know the status of your search." Especially since they didn't want me along.

"I will also search," said Sain.

"What do you mean?" Hart asked.

"I have computer programs to help in access."

Again, the terse Irion words confused me.

Hart said, "That'd be wonderful. I'll keep in touch. We may need your expertise to widen the search parameters."

As Sweety and Hart moved out, I heard Sweety ask, "Do you need to take food along?" I didn't hear Hart's reply, but I knew they would both think of everything.

I glanced at Dedare's daughter. And the look on Reena's face told me everything. "Mom, I think Reena and I are going to spend the rest of the evening together. Want to join us? Reena, what do you think? I'm going to read you parts of the letters your father sent me. They're quite amusing. What about your letters?"

"He told jokes." Typically terse words from this teenager.

Mom interjected. "Okay, everyone, Syl, Reena, and I are going to have a girls' night. We haven't had one in the longest time."

Mom's message to clear my living room succeeded.

I noticed Cara and Teeka left together. Possibly a coincidence, but I didn't think so.

Reena and I settled on a couch, with Mom sitting a couple of feet away.

"Why don't you tell us a little about the letters Dedare sent you, Reena?" I certainly wanted to hear about the details, but mostly I wanted Reena to talk about her father.

We regaled ourselves with Dedare's humor for a couple of hours, and then I was exhausted, and I wasn't the only one.

Reena retired to her room. Mom gave me a hug and left for the suite she shared with Dad.

I toyed with writing a letter to Dedare but decided against it after I remembered there was no longer a ship in orbit to forward my mail. So I picked up my paints and worked for an hour. The painting rejuvenated me for a short time, and then I fell on my bed, exhausted.

****

For the most part, sleep eluded me. I might've had a few hours, but they weren't restful. "Sweety, have you heard from Hart?" I asked after I woke up.

"Not a word," she replied. "You?"

"Nothing. I don't expect we'll be able to reach the spaceship, either. Someone better call soon, or there'll be hell to pay."

"Don't you and Reena go swimming in the mornings?" asked Sweety.

"Yes. It's close to time," I replied.

"Then go. You should stick to your routines. As much as you'll worry, you need to keep up your regular procedures and run the hotel. There are a lot of Particlans depending on you," said Sweety.

Such wise words. "Reena's just arrived, so I'll take your reminder to heart. I'll call you if I receive any updates."

Sweety hung up, and I turned to Reena. "No one has heard from Dedare or Hart. So, ready to swim?" I asked. "The exercise will do us good you know. And we need to practice our diving."

Reena waved her hand in acceptance, so we proceeded to the employee swimming area and ran into a confrontation.

Several hotel employees were having a loud discussion with Cara, so I approached the group. Reena faded away to the swimming area, I suspected.

"What's going on Cara?"

"Concerns regarding Takka. Not on team. No future employment."

I mentally sighed. I'd suspected I'd be explaining the situation many more times, and this was proof. "Takka is in your Particlan jail for attacking my friend, my alien friend. Takka must go through the Particlan justice system. I hope you all understand what I'm saying."

I received a foot stomp from many, so I glanced at Cara.

"Foot stomp means. Agreement with words. Understanding words, also."

Okay, so far, so good. "When Takka has gone through your legal system and completed his punishment, if any, then he is welcome to return to the hotel and the Olympic team. Unless your legal system forbids it, of course. I have no idea how your system works. Does everyone understand what I'm saying? Are there any questions?"

No one spoke. "Okay, let's get back to practicing. We want a great hotel team this year."

I pulled Cara aside after most of the group had walked away. "Do you think the employees are happy with what I said? Are you?" Unfair questions, but I needed to ask.

"Many differing opinions. Majority word agreement. Approval of decisions."

My interpretation of her words sounded good to me, so I dropped the subject. I did a little swimming and then some diving, but my heart wasn't in it.

I watched Reena for a while, but her performance was also lackluster and unenthusiastic, and I knew Dedare's absence contributed to both our feelings. So I called her over.

"Reena, I have an idea. I'm not feeling the love for swimming today, so I have a surprise for you. Let's go home, shower, and change, and then I'll take you to the surprise."

Cara overheard our conversation and disappeared.

After Reena and I had cleaned up, I took her to the surprise. "Reena, this is Baria tas Confit. Baria, this is

Reena Sath, Dedare Sath's daughter. Reena, Baria is the tailor for the hotel." I grinned at Reena. "I think we need new waterproof clothing, and I also think we need new bathing suits. Let me show you the back room where we can pick out fabrics."

While Reena exclaimed over the selection and tried to choose, I spoke with Baria at her desk. I had a special request with which I wanted to surprise Reena.

Eventually, Reena chose her final cloth selections, as did I. In happy moods, we took our leave of Baria.

Reena took off for her school classes, and I wandered back to my office to find out Cara's plans for my day.

And I returned just in time—although I suspected Cara would have found me if I'd been much longer with my errand—the great tour started in approximately fifteen minutes. We were just waiting on Richard Branson to join.

I received details from Cara. The tour members included Sain for security, Richard Branson, Thaddeus Trent, Mom, Testarn, a Reception employee familiar with tours named Villa est Tenka, and me. Cara would stay behind to oversee the running of the hotel, and Teeka wasn't quite up to a tour yet. Sweety remained at the hotel to continue cooking lessons with Chef and not overstress her physical wellbeing.

Testarn, the Sarturn, had chosen the tour stops as the tour was of his instigation. I found out we were going to the Library, the Botanical History Museum, our favourite restaurant for lunch, and a fish farm.

Not bad choices, and they'd fill the day nicely. After Richard arrived, we started.

Villa turned out to be a knowledgeable tour guide, and perfect for our situation. Everyone in our tour group appeared comfortable with him and his explanations.

The helicopter set down in front of the library's front door. After we'd gathered, Villa led us through the doorway. Of course, we were immediately hit by a wall of water.

By this time, we all knew about the ritual cleansing in various facilities. Everyone had prevailed upon our hotel tailor to create new waterproof clothing. However, I wondered about the Sarturn.

"Testarn, are your clothes waterproof?" They appeared to be, as a growing puddle surrounded him as his clothes shed the water he'd recently encountered. Actually we all had the same situation, but the floor accommodated our predicament as we stood on an open grid that allowed the water to flow away.

"Water, water. No affect; no harm."

"That's good to know. Anything else we should look out for that could have an adverse effect for you?"

"No problems, no problems."

I suspected the Sarturn was being optimistic, but I wouldn't mutter any contradictions. Happy guests were always my goal, and I noticed he wore gloves to lessen contact with humans and other species.

The library staff guide started our tour on the top floor. I wanted to jump out of line and read shelf labels, posters, and the like, but I would've held up our tour. Another day, another visit.

The top floor had the most magnificent view. The majority of Ooby was visible, and this time I took more notice of the distant mountains.

The new library being built rose before us, and I noticed it was now framed in. Much progress had been made since the last time I'd been here.

The full tour of the library took about ninety minutes. By the time we'd reached the ground floor I was antsy. The others were in favor of going to the gift shop, but I wanted something different.

I asked Villa if it would be possible to go to the new library, the one under construction. I particularly wanted to take the elevator to the top of the building and receive another unobstructed view of the entire city of Ooby.

He consulted with various library officials and reached an agreement. Villa brought a Particlan over to our group.

"Meeta tas Eldon. Part of security. Escort to building."

"That's perfect. Could we go right away? I don't want to keep the others waiting for too long after they get their fill of the gift shop."

Mom grinned—she loved shopping.

"Join, join," said the Sarturn.

"You want to join me on my trip to the other library, Testarn?" I asked.

"Engineer, engineer."

Ah. An alien engineer wanted to study foreign, for want of a better word, structures. His request made a lot of sense.

I noticed Sain getting antsy. "Sain, would you stay and keep an eye on the others while I'm gone? Testarn and I won't be long. I know we have a tight itinerary today."

Sain didn't argue.

So Testarn and I followed Meeta outside. Only a short walk led to the construction zone. Meeta talked to the guards, and then we were let inside the security fence.

"Meeta, I just want to go to the top of the tower in the elevator. That way I can see all of Ooby. Testarn, is that alright with you? We're kind of in a hurry. However, you should be able to see how the building is constructed."

"Agreed, agreed."

The elevator, located on the outside of the building, had clear walls on all four sides. The Sarturn was fascinated by what he could see of the inside of the building as I watched him study the images through the clear elevator doors. And I had an excellent view of Ooby as we rose.

At the top floor, we exited the elevator. The top library floor had windows on all sides so my city view was unobstructed. And the inside was unfinished so Testarn could study the engineering as much as he desired.

Before I had a chance to start my study of the view, Meeta spoke.

"Leave tour now. When required return. Use automatic elevator."

An unexpected development. "So you're leaving us?"

Meeta made a hand motion to indicate assent. His black stone necklace bounced up and down.

"Send elevator back."

"Thank you for your help." I thought a tour guide would have stayed with his tour group to answer questions, but every race had different ideas.

Testarn and I continued our separate studies for a short time, and then I heard the elevator. The doors stood open, waiting for our return to the lowest floor.

I found so much to see in my perusal of the capital city that I decided to make a list of questions to ask of Villa, our Reception tour guide.

Finally, Testarn said, "Return, return?"

"Yes, you're correct. It's time."

We got in the elevator. After the doors closed, I pressed the button as I'd seen our guide do, but nothing happened. In disgust, I touched all the buttons I could find. We went nowhere. In dismay, I turned to Testarn, "Apparently, I don't know how to run the elevator. Can you help?"

Dedare's missing and presumed dead—I had read Hart's face easily—and now I'm stuck on the top floor of a very tall building. My life had issues I knew not how to handle. My mood plummeted.

Testarn studied the control panel and then retrieved a tiny box from one of his pockets. His box turned out to contain miniature tools. For a few moments, he worked on the control panel. The doors opened and closed, and then we started to move downward. The fast pace worried me, so I found a strap to hold onto, but we soon slowed down to a more normal rate.

I didn't speak until we stopped and Testarn opened the doors. "Thank you. You are my savior, and so is your handy tool kit."

"Prepared, prepared."

"Well, I'm glad you were with me, Testarn, I didn't know what to do." And I really hadn't.

After the Sarturn and I exited the elevator, Mom came stomping over. "What took you guys so long? We need to get on to the next stop as soon as possible."

"We were stuck. Our guide went away and left us to return on our own. After we got in the elevator, it wouldn't move. Luckily Testarn had his handy toolkit, and he took care of the problem. I was kind of worried, though."

"I bet you were. Thanks, Testarn, for helping. I'm going to talk to Villa about the security guide leaving you alone in a new, empty building."

"Don't bother, Mom. Just get us on our way. I know we need to stick to schedule. If we decide to, we can look into the situation later." And I thought we needed to.

Our next stop was the Botanical History museum. At first I wasn't quite sure what the museum was all about, but I soon discovered it contained a visual history of Particle's vegetation. And then I remembered six holes in the ground named *The Botanical History Museum*. They were either replacing this museum or adding a museum with further exhibits to their collection. And considering the six holes in the ground, I suspected the latter.

I noticed a good portion of the vegetation in the museum had been found in their numerous oceans, but not all, so I was curious and became focused on their land-based vegetation. Apparently, somewhere near the base of a group of mountains there were giant tree-like growths. The branches formed a table at the top, and there were a few branches on the lower parts of the trunks. Could Particlans jump from one tree to the next? Was the canopy sturdy and able to hold their weight?

I turned around to find Villa since he was our tour guide for the museum. He was nowhere to be found, and neither was Mom. Walking to the door of the current exhibit, I marveled at the expansive area the Particlans had used. These exhibits appeared full sized and, I assumed, painted to match real life colors.

The door is locked! I'm stuck!

Chapter Twenty-One

Frantically, I studied the room for any little details I'd missed that might help me get out.

I noticed a window set high. It had an attached handle so the Particlans had a way to open the window from floor level. The window opening looked large enough for me to pass through. However, my problem was how to reach the window.

Pacing around the large room, the only idea I came up with was to climb the canopy exhibit. The canopy appeared high enough and near enough to the window to allow me to get close and crawl through.

My main adventure would be the canopy. It appeared made of a paper product like papier-mâché, which is none too strong. A logical choice for a display but not one appropriate for climbing adventures. However, I had little choice—I needed to get out of this exhibit room.

Since the canopy display contained treetops, each slightly higher than the previous one, I found a natural staircase to climb. After I started my climb, I soon discovered the problem. I found the surface very slippery, so standing was not an option because I felt like I was going to slide off the display, and handholds were few and far between. By the time I'd managed three of the levels, sweat dripped off me.

"Syl, what're you doing up there? I don't think our hosts would look kindly if you destroyed one of their exhibits," said my mother.

I turned around so quickly, I started to slide off the canopy. Luckily, Testarn was there to help. He held out both hands so I had a stirrup for my feet, and then he lowered me gently to the ground while I held on tightly.

"Mom, the door was locked. I couldn't get out that way, so I devised another. The climb was tough, but I was on my way to the window exit."

"Well, the door wasn't locked when we came looking for you. Perhaps you didn't try hard enough to turn the handle."

I decided not to argue. However, I knew I'd been frantic when I tried the door so my efforts reflected this.

"Mom, what's next on our itinerary?" I thought I knew, but the way my day had been going my memory might have been cloudy. And I needed to distract my mother. She worried too much about her one and only child, adult that I might be.

"It's lunch time," she replied with a huge grin on her face. We all loved to eat.

"Where are we going?"

"To your favorite restaurant. I saw the menu, and they have lots of food for everyone. Every species, I mean. If we give them more practice, before long they should be excellent, not that they aren't good already."

"You know, we really should patronage more than one restaurant. I don't want to be seen to be playing favorites." Our guide gathered everyone up, and we flew to the restaurant we'd previously visited.

Even though I'd espoused trying different restaurants, I was happy to be in a familiar location. I didn't have to worry about the restaurant not understanding the various alien dietary requirements. Too many new things had been flung at me, and I needed assimilation time. And feeling like I was being harassed by various incidents didn't help my mental well-being.

Oh well, food cures all.

Thankfully my favorite meal, spaghetti and meat balls, was still on the menu so my order was easy. I glanced at Richard Branson and wondered what he was thinking of ordering.

"Richard, does the menu interest you?"

"Oh, yes. Especially some of these foreign, ah alien, items. There are so many interesting choices, I don't know how to decide."

"Alien ones? How do you know if the food is compatible with humans? We don't need anyone getting food poisoning. I remember an incident on Irion." Somebody was after me there, and the poisoning had been deliberate.

"Look at the menu. Every item has an indicator for each compatible race. I'd like to try a few dishes, but I need to share. Are you up to it?"

I hesitated. How brave was I? Then Richard said, "You're a curious person, Syl, otherwise you wouldn't be traipsing all over the universe. So let's be adventurous. I'll let you choose items also so you don't have to rely on what I might personally like."

I grinned at Richard. He was teasing me, but I happily went along with his food ideas and inserted a few of my own.

To help, I went around the table and explained how to choose compatible food items. Most of the group were relieved by my explanations. They'd been struggling with their choices and hadn't understood the menu.

Soon food covered our table, and the crowd started sampling. Menus were close by to help us understand the choices.

There were a couple of items I chose not to sample since they were still moving. I preferred my food dead and not resembling their original shapes. However, I had lots of other dishes to choose from, and they were quite enjoyable.

And, my goodness, the colors! A vibrant yellow predominated, but all sorts of hues prevailed. Purple, bright red, and a slimy black stood out in my mind.

As for the smells, nothing stood out.

I glanced over at Testarn's plate and saw mostly food Irions could also tolerate. That made sense as we'd already determined the Sarturn's tastes were compatible with Irion food.

"How's the food, Testarn?" I asked, getting his attention. He certainly had a wide range on his plate.

"Wonderful, wonderful." He smiled and kept eating.

"That's good. You'll have to come back another day." We did have helicopters for guest use.

"Every day; every day." Testarn grinned.

At least one of our guests was happy.

I spoke with our guide, Villa, and found out we were to visit a fish farm in the afternoon. The farms within the vertical pyramids fascinated me, and the process for moving the fish around was so unique, in my opinion.

Only a few moments passed while we traveled along the coastline to the Ooby Golden Harvest Fish Farm. Much to my surprise the fish in this particular farm were all yellow. They didn't look like the goldfish on Earth, but they were very attractive. It suddenly dawned on me why the fish farm had the word *golden* in its name.

After promising to meet back at the bottom in one hour, we took off in various directions on the same pyramid.

I wandered alone to the top of the pyramid and took a good look around. Peaceful water lapped against the bottom layer. Close by, islands vibrated with commerce as ships sped between the islands and the mainland. I would've loved to see what commodities were being exchanged. A faint breeze carried Particle's distinctive hint of lime water scent.

One of the see-through metal mesh troughs covers propped open caught my attention. The fish were trying to escape, which seemed life-threatening, so I tried to close the cover.

Suddenly, I found myself in the water with the fish with the trough cover thumped shut over me. Someone had given me a hard push and locked me in.

I tried to lift the cover, but the latch was securely fastened, so I started yelling. I also swam slowly in the trough hoping I'd find a place that had a loose cover.

Gross smelling water assaulted me. Between fish smell and fish food, I hoped I'd survive this adventure without any medical side effects like an infection. Worse thoughts popped into my mind.

Then I heard "Sylvestine, Sylvestine." Testarn was trying to get my attention. I turned around and gouged my right leg on an item poking out from the sidewall. Pain assaulted me, and the water turned red. The trough fish attempted to get away from the polluted area.

"Patience, patience," said Testarn while he proceeded to open the cover above me. Then he lifted me out of the water but as he did my right leg got a second scrape. And then I started freaking out—I was going to die from blood loss.

****

Testarn laid me on the wooden walkway and glanced at Mama A.

"Okay, Syl, you have a couple of gashes on your leg. I don't think they're life-threatening, but you need to go to the hospital. If nothing else, the Particlans will get more experience in treating aliens."

"I'll arrange the helicopter," said Branson. "Let them know what's going on so they can alert the hospital that you're coming in." Branson disappeared from sight.

"And I'll get a gurney. You're not walking right now, Syl," said Thaddeus. My brother ran off. Apparently, he'd noticed an item he decided could be used as a stretcher.

"What about the blood loss?" I asked my mother.

"There's been little that I can see. It's all relative, you know. Let's let the Particlan medical system deal with you. Hart's been training them quite a lot."

With so many people looking after me, I relaxed a bit while lying on the boardwalk. After Thad came back with his stretcher, I cheered up. He'd also found a pile of blankets, and he and Mom covered me up—I really was cold.

Then they trundled me off to the helicopter, and we traveled to the hospital.

The Particlan medical personnel seemed a little nervous without Hart's presence, but perhaps that was only me missing Hart's expertise. Naturally, being in an ER, blood tests were organized and physical examinations to determine the depth of the gashes in my leg were arranged. They sewed me up, and then the arguments about whether I'd be allowed to leave the hospital began.

"Syl is fine with me," said my mother. "I have medical training, and she just needs to rest her leg. So we'll make her keep still for a few days. Not an easy task, by the way."

Everyone laughed—except me. Apparently, the Particlans knew me too well. So my friends trundled me into the helicopter, and we returned to the hotel.

On the way, Sain received a call from Vara.

From what I overheard, Vara quizzed Sain about what had happened on our tour, but the only item Sain emphasized was finding cameras at the fish farm so we could discover who had pushed me in the trough and locked the cover.

After we arrived back at the hotel, we found Reena upset, as was Cara. I picked up on Reena's motivation. However, it turned out Cara had other reasons for her concern.

While we were away, she had arranged for religious classes for me commencing this evening.

"Oh, Cara, I can't go to any class. My leg is in a great deal of pain, and I need to rest. I can't really walk very well."

The anxiety on her face was obvious.

"Chief Motivator unhappy."

"Have you talked to him?" Better Cara than me.

"Discussion already occurred."

"He can reschedule. Being not able to walk is a good excuse. I really need to lie down. Our day was full of exercise, and now I'm full of pain." I studied Cara's face. I saw a few emotions flit across and interpreted most of them. They included confusion.

"Cara, I know it's difficult dealing with aliens. We're new and strange. And you haven't had any time off. I want you to take tomorrow off away from the hotel and relax at home. Relax anywhere you want to. I'll take care of things at the hotel, and then the next day you can take care of the hotel and I'll relax. I'm sure I'll be tired again as I heal. What do you say to my idea?"

"Agreed."

I didn't know how to take her one-word answer. Was one word an emphasis, or did it mean something else? However, one thing I was certain of she wasn't happy. I'd given her a day off, what more did she want?

And I wasn't happy with Cara arranging church classes for me. I guessed she thought that was part of her job and we had discussed doing it, but I would have liked a heads-up. Surprises weren't one of my happy places. Perhaps I could blame the situation on the Chief Motivator—that would work for me. Then I admonished myself for giving Cara mixed signals.

Relaxing in my living room, I chanced a call to Hart. "Hart, how's everything?" Which wasn't the question I wanted to ask.

"There's no trace of Dedare or his ship. We've been trying all sorts of options," said Hart. "How's my lovely wife?"

"As pregnant as ever. Have you heard from her?"

On my little screen, Hart shook his head.

"You might want to call. We've been confused as to whether we had access to you or not."

"Ah, so that's why the lack of messages. Thanks, Syl, will do. Hopefully we'll hear from Dedare very soon. Have you been writing letters to him?"

"No. I thought access was cut off after his spaceship became lost."

"Yes. There's still a satellite in orbit, so messages can be forwarded."

What Hart wasn't saying was whether there would be anyone to receive our missives or to respond.

Mom and Charles joined me in my suite. Mom fussed over tea and me while we chatted about various topics. Finally, I suggested Charles take Mom home as we were all tired from our day's activities. I wanted peace and quiet. We'd had a long day, and I wanted to rest my leg. At least that was the excuse I used.

I found a high stool that would allow me to paint a picture sitting down, and the process calmed me. A pretty strange abstract painting emerged. The predominant colors were purple and orange—not ones I usually used. I decided to hang it in my office and contemplate my art in a different setting. Perhaps I was in a new phase of my artistry.

Calm after my painting session, I decided to write a letter to Dedare. At the moment, letter writing was our only mode of personal conduct. The letter became long, but the process relaxed me a trifle.

****

The next morning, I dragged last night's painting into my office. I needed to find someone to frame and hang my art, but in the meantime I leaned the painting against a wall.

I'd barely settled at my desk before one of the Reception staff showed up.

"Manager Syl, help. Scheduling in confusion. Lack of staff."

His concern was clear. "Who normally does the scheduling or fixes problems?"

"Cara does all," my nervous employee replied.

Well, that put a wrinkle in my day. Since I'd given Cara the day off, I needed to handle the problem. "Who's Cara's assistant? Does she have one?"

The Particlan pointed at himself, so I asked, "Do you know where the scheduling problems are? And do you know how to fill in the gaps?"

"Yes. Able, willing." He grinned while he studied my face. Particlans and humans alike strived to understand other species.

Thank goodness his answer had been yes. "Okay, let's make you my assistant for the day. Please fix the scheduling problems. I'll discuss compensation with Cara tomorrow. Is that okay, Jesto las Habbo?"

At least I'd remembered his name.

Jesto left with a purposeful stride, and I realized I'd accomplished something early in the morning. Life was good.

Then reality hit.

Before I had a chance to deal with Dedare's absence, Richard Branson, Testarn, and Thad, my brand-new brother, filled my office.

"What can I do for you fellows?" I asked. They gave the impression of a team.

"We'd like another tour. Aside from your mishap, yesterday's tour was quite informative. We'd like another one just like it but with new locations. Can you arrange this?" asked Richard.

"Of course. When would you like to go?"

"Tomorrow would be nice, and we'd like you to join us. You're quite amusing and relaxing."

I didn't know about relaxing, but amusing delighted me. Hotel managers should be entertaining.

"Well, tomorrow is a busy day for me. However, we could plan for after then." I really needed my day off.

"Can we get a small tour today? We're all very excited about seeing parts of Particle."

"I tell you what. Talk to our tour guide of yesterday, Villa, and see what he can plan. You can also talk to him about you want for the tour involving me. Will that work?" I hoped so. I had no idea which cultural aspects and other highlights were available for touring.

Richard agreeably turned away to find Villa. However, before he'd moved more than one step the Sarturn spoke.

Testarn pointed at my painting leaning against the wall. "Yours, yours?"

"Yes, I painted that picture. Do you like it?"

"Acquisition, acquisition."

His words seemed clear—Testarn wanted to buy my painting. However, to my mind the idea was bizarre. This would be the first ever. "Do you like my painting?" I asked. "What do you like about it?" I had no idea what to ask, and apparently Testarn didn't know how to answer my questions. No one had ever expressed any interest in my paintings before. Of course, my canvases really hadn't seen the light of day.

Reena had popped into my office during Testarn's comments about my painting. "Manager Syl, let me help. Experiences with gift shop." She glanced at the Sarturn as she whispered.

What could I lose? So I replied *yes* in a quiet voice.

Reena and Testarn huddled in a corner while Richard Branson and Thad went outside to start arranging tours.

"Manager Syl, Testarn and I are going to find an empty desk in Reservations to conclude our negotiations. May we take the painting with us?"

"Of course, Reena. Whatever you wish." I did not want to inhibit her resourcefulness.

Finally, I was alone. And it was time to settle my mind. While contemplating meditating, I received a call from Hart.

"Syl, you'd better sit down; I have news." I didn't know how to interpret his voice, but I heard a lot of sadness.

"Hart, just tell me. I need the details." Dragging it out just magnified the distress, in my opinion, and *sitting down* were trigger words.

"Okay. We've found Dedare's ship."

"That's good, right?" I interrupted.

"Yes, it's good. We've found the ship. However, it's in pieces and no life forms are evident, just debris."

Chapter Twenty-Two

No life forms. "Hart, what're you telling me? I don't understand." My mind had frozen. Was Dedare dead? Is that what Hart tried to say?

"There's no evidence Dedare and the crew died in the accident. There are no life pods in the vicinity of the broken ship, so we're going to look for them. The life pods have transponders that we can lock onto if they haven't been destroyed. And we've already grabbed onto two, so the others may also be close by. Syl, the news is actually quite good since we haven't found any bodies."

Hart got a look on his face that said he knew he'd mishandled our exchange. I did appreciate his availability.

"Go do your thing. And please keep me updated. Now call your wife. She needs to hear your voice."

My mind floundered as I tried to process his words.

Then Mom arrived. "Syl, I talked to Richard and Thad, and they have a tour arranged for tomorrow. And they are in the middle of arranging something for the next day where you'll be involved. Is that correct?"

"Ah, ah, yes. That's what we talked about. Good, everything's under control." It sure didn't feel like it, but my mother was here.

"Syl, let's go back to your rooms. I need a cup of tea."

My buzzy brain didn't argue, so she quietly led me there. The haze in my mind had overwhelmed me. I managed to sit down, but I really wasn't quite sure what I was doing.

"Mom, Dedare's in trouble?" I asked.

"Yes, dear. However, Hart's taking care of the situation. We should hear from him very soon as to Dedare's status."

"I love him, you know." I shook my head. "I mean Dedare, not Hart. Actually, I love Hart too. He's a longtime friend of mine."

"And also mine. You guys are always bugging me. Then Sweety came along, and the harassment is continuous."

I glanced up. Mom's face sported a large grin. I had an excellent group of friends and family. "Where's Sweety?"

"She'll be over after she finishes talking to Hart. They haven't talked for a while and they need to catch up. She misses him."

"I miss Dedare," I said. And I desperately did.

The look on Mom's face told me she thought she'd said something wrong, but I couldn't pick up on what it could be. I sighed. All I wanted was to see Dedare again.

Sweety popped in, and we sat and cuddled while Mom poured fresh tea. "Sweety, Hart is being very helpful in keeping me updated. I don't know what I'd do without him," I said.

"Hart's the best," said Sweety. "Of course, I wouldn't have married him otherwise."

We hugged again, but emptiness coated me.

"I must get back to work. Cara is off today, and I need to handle her duties."

Sweety and Mom exchanged very obvious glances. "Sounds like a good idea, Syl. If you need any help let me know," said Sweety.

I thought for sure they would've protested my proclamation, but I was glad they hadn't. I wanted to continue running the hotel smoothly for Dedare's sake.

My office felt comfy—my home away from home. I suspected I'd begun to settle into this new world, and I wondered whatever had become of Reena's and Testarn's negotiations, but Reena would soon let me know.

My new assistant stood in my doorway trying to attract my attention. "Yes, Jesto, how may I help you?"

"Tarin et Tong. Wishes to speak. With you, now," he responded.

Of course, Dedare's co-owner would show up at an inconvenient time and start snooping.

"How are you, Tarin? How may I help you?" I asked. Pleasantness seemed to throw him off.

"Dedare not here?" he asked in typical Particlan speech patterns.

"No. He's on his spaceship traveling to other worlds to visit his other holdings." I wanted to give him the impression Dedare was a powerful person.

"Wish to speak."

"Well, Dedare is difficult to contact right now. If you give me a letter, I'll forward it to him. Will that work?" Would that get Tarin off my back?

Tarin wasn't happy with my response I suspected as he turned away and left without speaking.

That was alright—I didn't want to talk to him either. Although I did wonder if Tarin would eventually show up with a letter for Dedare. Oh well, I'd keep the option in the back of my mind.

Now I needed to settle down and focus on seeing if any part of Reception needed reorganizing and then work on the rest of the hotel. Reception seemed to be under control, but I really needed to understand the management structure of the whole hotel.

I started looking at all the hotel notes I'd taken since we'd arrived. I found huge gaps in the management structure, and I certainly had huge gaps in my knowledge about the actual departments that existed. However, my most important chore was an in-depth analysis of the spreadsheet Mom and Cara had created. I needed to see if their data matched mine and where conflicts arose.

The next thing I knew, the head priest of the Church of the Redeemed Water Tower stood in front of me. "Come to class," he demanded.

"Now?" Nothing like giving me a few hours' notice.

"Introductory classes begin. Wait for you. New group starts."

I didn't know why they'd waited for me, but the priest gave me a quandary, and I didn't particularly want to upset him.

"Okay. Let me gather up a few things and I'll join you momentarily." I grabbed a notebook and writing instruments and my survival backpack and followed Saska et Tong out the door.

Apparently, I'd missed the first lecture regarding *Introduction to Faith* but the students were more than happy to go through it again with me.

No one criticized my inclusion in the group, and I actually gained a great deal of knowledge of Particlan society from the simple lessons I'd received today.

Afterward, we mingled and snacked. A little difficult for me since the church had yet to adjust to alien members, but they'd tried.

However, I needed to return so I made my excuses. "This was truly informative, Saska et Tong. I look forward to the next class. Please arrange the time with Cara." I tried to shake his hand, but he ignored our human process.

"Dedare must study."

"As soon as he's back in town, I'll give him an update," I said. "Dedare's quite interested in other cultures or he wouldn't be acquiring hotels on many planets."

The helicopter had been called, so I had a convenient excuse to retire.

No shouting greeted me, and no lineup of guests were waiting outside my office area as I sneaked into my home away from home. Reception saw I was back, but no one else had noticed. I required a few moments, probably more, to regroup.

Of course, my life couldn't be quite so simple. Reena worked at my conference table—on her homework, I hoped.

"Reena, how has your day been?" I dumped my belongings on my desk and walked over to the worktable.

"Excellent school day."

"How did your negotiations with Testarn go?" Selling a painting quite excited me. It had never happened before. In fact I'd never even envisioned offering one for sale.

"Negotiations complete. Adequate remuneration acquired. Testarn happy Sarturn."

Reena handed me a pile of Particlan paper currency. "How much is this?" I asked.

After Reena named a sum, I calculated ten percent and gave her that share.

"This is for you, Reena, for selling my painting. It's called commission. Do you have commissions on Irion?" There was so much I didn't know about Irion, and now we were on another new planet.

"Irion commissions available but not as high. Thanks from Reena."

Reena gave me a hug. For a stepdaughter, she was the sweetest, and we got along quite well. Did she know about Dedare's status? Had anyone told her? Before I sprung any news I needed research, and that meant talking to Hart and the others.

"Reena, why did Testarn want my painting? It was abstract art—I don't actually try to faithfully reproduce any image."

She smiled. "Each Sarturn paints. Each Sarturn collects paintings from acquaintances."

"So he wanted one from me to remind him of our meeting?"

Reena agreed. "Testarn wishes paintings. Family arrives soon, and they will also acquire."

So Testarn would have his family joining him and holidaying on Particle after he'd determined its safety. I hoped I'd helped him make his decision. Apparently,

Sarturn were all painters, of some level or other, and Testarn's family would eventually be introduced to me, so they'd each need one of my paintings.

"Reena, this is quite exciting. I need to get painting, and then you'll have lots of product with which to negotiate. In the meantime, perhaps you could look at the paintings in my room and decide which are salable. Then we can display them on my office walls. What do you think?"

She grinned. Receiving income and negotiating—something she loved— cheered her.

I needed to find all the paintings I'd done so far so Reena could take a look. Most importantly, I needed to get busy producing new paintings. My evenings would be busy.

Then reality thumped my brain. What's going to happen if Dedare dies during his current trip? Would I own all his holdings, or had he set things up differently? Would I understand any of the Irion legal system? Would anyone help me? Would I even be eligible—being an alien? I really, really didn't want to think about our situation. However, I couldn't bury my thoughts.

I had so many questions with no answers. My day seemed dark—my life *was* dark.

Wandering outside my office I ran into Sain. "How're things? Have renovations been completed?"

"Renovations under control. Much pleasure in solutions. You will be happy with results. Restaurant beginning serving."

"That's wonderful, Sain. I'll take a look." The restaurant has already started serving!

My brain slowly chewed through information, but I eventually found a question. "Sain, have you heard from Hart today?" I needed any information I could pull out of anyone.

"No response."

The typical Irion terseness drove me crazy at the best of times.

"Where's Teeka?" I thought I would have seen him hobbling around trying to keep an eye on hotel security.

"Day off." A flicker of a grin appeared.

Day off? When Cara was off? Actually, the situation made sense and added to my data collection. Ahem. Of course, I might possibly be indulging in gossip.

Then the lights went out.

Chapter Twenty-Three

Enough light came through our Reception windows to allow me to see quite well.

Jesto, my assistant today, ran up. "Crisis in Engineering. Help wanted now. Suggestions from manager."

This was a situation I hadn't imagined. "Sain, what do you know about power systems? Have you met whoever is in charge within our hotel?"

"Know of employee. Wish me to join?"

"Yes. Please find him and see if you can give any assistance. In the meantime, I'll keep our guests calm."

Sain spoke with Jesto las Habbo to find the engineer's current location.

After Sain took off, I turned to Jesto. "What do you think we should do to keep our guests calm."

"Gather guests pool. Have Olympic display. Offer guests refreshments."

His ideas interested me. "Excellent. Please arrange for our employees to move the guests to the pool area. Will there be enough room for everyone?"

"Seating increased immediately."

"And then we need…" Then the signals came through. "Have you already started?"

Jesto pointed to his brooch. "Employees notified tasks. Gather soon pool. Refreshments being delivered."

I glanced around and recognized employees fulfilling these duties. "Wonderful, Jesto. You're very well organized. I'll make my own way to the pool. If there's anything I need to do, please let me know. I'm very happy with your organizational skills."

Jesto beamed and then took off to continue organizing the Particlans, I assumed.

I noticed Reena hovering, so I explained the situation and she left to gather up her swimsuit and accessories and also grab my swim bag.

Walking over to the main level pool, I was joined by hotel employees. They carried chairs and small and long tables. I assumed the tables were destined for food, drink, and guests to sit at.

The employees quickly set up the sitting and eating areas and put the long tables against the outer level of the pool area against the shrubs.

Guests soon occupied the chairs and watched the Olympic hopefuls practice their routines.

The long tables soon emptied of food and drink, and my employees rushed to refill the empty spots.

I heard nothing besides happy conversations so our guests coped with the power outage.

"Manager Syl, should I try diving now?" asked Reena.

I pulled my mind back from Dedare's plight. "Have you loosened up with some easy dives?" I remembered she had been doing laps.

"Yes. I want to try your dives."

"If you're comfortable, please do so. Don't overexert yourself though. You need to gradually build up your muscles and your diving skills."

Reena grinned and bounced away to the diving platform.

The hotel guests took a keen interest in Reena's diving. Of course, her movements were different being not Particlan, so curiosity was high.

Then Reena convinced me to join her. I decided her idea wasn't bad and would make our guests even more curious. Of course, from what I noticed food and drink were their primary interests.

I did a quick change and then did a couple of laps to warm up. Even my limbering up activities were of interest to the hotel guests.

I performed quite a number of different dives and then it was time to retire. My audience had been receptive, but my body could only handle a certain amount of physical activity.

After covering up, Reena and I talked to the other Olympic hopefuls. I'd have to talk to Reena about what she learned, but I heard positive vibes from the Particlans I talked to. And I conversed with a number of guests. Their questions mostly concerned the Particlan Olympics. They were not particularly upset about the power outage. I think Jesto's plan of gathering everyone around the pool and offering entertainment and refreshments minimized their inconvenience.

Shortly the power hummed back on, and the guests gradually gathered up their belongings and headed off for their planned activities.

The hotel patrons smiled as they left the public pool area.

"Reena, let's go home and shower. I don't know what the hotel uses to keep the pool water clean, but my skin tends to get slightly irritated. Are you okay?" I hadn't thought about what it might do to an Irion or our other alien guests come to think of it.

"Skin fine. Shower good." Reena grinned at me as we walked home.

After my shower, I headed back to Reception. I had a lot of work to do to understand this world, but I also had personal matters to deal with.

Sain worked on the new office so I called him into mine. "What did you find out about the power outage? Was the hotel engineer cooperative?"

"Hotel *Power Supply Manager* helpful. Excellent explanations."

So Sain was happy with my manager. However, I had a concern or two. "Was this power outage normal or an act of sabotage?"

Sain shook his head. "Concerns about sabotage lead list of questions. This method of shutdown difficult to perform unless upheaval desired."

His words confused me, so I decided to be blunt. "So the shutdown seemed deliberate?"

"Agreement with *Power Supply Manager*."

Whether deliberate or not, what could I do about the situation? Perhaps ask one of the few security experts I knew. "Sain, what should we do?"

"Need to monitor security weak areas. Manager in agreement. Source checks being implemented. No current concern."

Okay, Sain's information all sounded good. He and my in-house manager had the situation under control. "Do we know why this happened? Assuming sabotage, of course. Why would anyone want to sabotage the Sath-Ooby Golden Hotel?"

"*Aliens go Home*," commented Sain, laughing up a storm. He remembered the *Martians go Home* incident on Irion.

In a serious voice, I asked, "Perhaps we should increase security in and around the hotel. What do you think?"

"Security at adequate level. Particlans need to adjust to aliens. Your antics in the pool and in the hotel are helping immensely." Sain grinned.

My antics? "Okay, Sain, that's very funny, but I have a serious matter to discuss. You and I both know that Dedare is possibly…" I couldn't continue. My fiancé was probably dead, and I hadn't yet dealt with the outcome.

Sain patiently waited.

"You and I both know Dedare is, is,…is probably dead. The life pods have not been recovered, and his ship is in pieces. Have you talked to Reena about the possibility her father will not return? Do you know if anyone has? I haven't, and I've seen no sign she knows about the situation."

"No discussion," said Sain.

I didn't know whether he meant he hadn't discussed Dedare with Reena or anyone else had. "Well, I think someone should talk to her now since the odds of finding Dedare and the others alive are slim."

"Syl as mother, not Sain as uncle."

The answer I'd expected. "Okay, I'll talk to Reena." Although I had no idea how to talk to a teenager about her father possibly being dead I needed to try.

"Manager Syl, I need talk," said Reena, standing in my office doorway. Tears ran down her face. Humans and Irions were alike reacting to stress.

Sain helped Reena to a chair at the conference table and then scooted out of my office and closed the door as he did so.

I grabbed a chair next to her and asked, "Reena, what's the problem?" I had a good guess, but perhaps something else had come up.

"Mama A told me about my father's ship. Is he dead?" The tears flowed quicker. At least Mom had broached the subject, so she'd made it a little easier for me to talk about Dedare.

I leaned over and put my arms around her. "I don't know, Reena. I know Dedare's your father, but he's also my life-mate. Perhaps we'll grieve together, but not yet. I have a feeling he's alive. And Hart's out there looking for the life pods, so we still have a very good chance that Dedare and the others will be found. Don't give up hope."

Reena turned into my shoulder and cried, and I joined her. After a few moments I found tissues and passed them to her. I used a few myself.

"Syl, what do you really think?" Reena's face had swollen, and she had a tough time talking to me.

So many words from an Irion. "I think tomorrow will come with news. We need to wait and be patient. Your father is a strong man. I'm sure we'll hear from Hart with good news very soon."

Reena sniffed against my shirt and then said, "Time for rest. Emotional upheaval tiring."

I gave her another hug and helped her to her room. I really hoped a rest would bring her a modicum of calm.

After I got back to my living room, I found that Sweety and the others had gathered. Efficient Sweety had ordered dinner. And thank goodness since I'd possibly missed a meal today, and my stomach growled when I thought about sustenance.

As we ate, we discussed Dedare's absence. Of course, Sweety's concerns focused on Hart looking for the missing personnel, but her updates from him had helped alleviate some of her distress. Sweety also had concerns about Reena. We'd all grown to know and love Reena. Being Dedare's daughter brought his absence closer to all of us, and particularly me.

"What's going to happen if Dedare is really dead?" asked Sweety.

"There are many legal issues to pursue," said Charles. "Obviously, the diplomatic concerns are many. We must be patient and hope for a positive outcome."

"Dad, that's putting off reality. If Dedare is dead, are we obligated to go back to Mars? Perhaps we should go back to Irion to take care of his hotels there."

"It's too soon for you to worry about the legal consequences. Think positively," said my father.

Easy for him to say—it wasn't his spouse he spoke about. If Mom were missing, how would he react?

Then I scolded myself. We were all under considerable stress considering we were on a foreign world and our alien relationships tended to grab on and hold us ransom.

Laughing inside at my extravagant words, I talked everyone into a sugar fix. Sweety had ordered lots of sweet desserts so we dug in. I contemplated getting Reena out of her room but decided to let her be. She could always eat leftovers or order a meal later.

As our mealtime began to end, I heard a noise at my door. I glanced at Sain, so he got up and answered it. The chief priest asked to come in, so I nodded agreement.

"Yes, Chief Motivator, how may I help you?" Strange that he was in my home during my off time. Maybe I shouldn't have let him in.

"Now instruction time. Return to church. Continue with education."

I locked eyes with Sain. His expression matched my feelings. I knew neither one of us thought I should go off with the chief priest.

"I will accompany Syl. I need to learn about the church system," said Sain.

Sain and Saska et Tong argued for a bit, but Sain exhibited more effective reasoning. Actually Sain's final argument was that Dedare wanted him to learn all he could about Particle, and those words stopped the priest in his tracks. So Sain and I said goodbye to the others and accompanied the head priest.

I joined the Particlans of my previous instruction group. We were on our next lesson. I think Sain was a little lost, but he sat beside me and took in what he could. After all I'd brought him along mainly for protection.

On our way back to the hotel, I said, "Well, nothing went wrong. I thought perhaps I'd be abducted or something."

"Concern from everyone," said Sain.

Well, he had that right. I had looked at the faces of my dinner companions before we left, and I knew everyone had been unsettled. So I called Mom and let her know all was well and Sain and I were on our way back.

After I'd thanked Sain for his security help he disappeared. I continued to my suite, and there I found Reena crying.

I sat beside her and held her tight. "Reena, talk to me. What's this all about?" I thought I knew, but I needed her words.

"My father might be dead. Mother is dead." Her tears didn't cease; in fact, they may have increased with me sitting beside her.

"Reena, I'll always be here for you. In fact I consider you my daughter. Stepdaughter is probably more accurate, but to me you're my daughter. I'll look after you as best I can, no matter what happens."

I hugged her tightly. "And of course you have Mama A as your grandmother and Charles as a grandfather. Where are your Irion grandparents?"

Reena gave me a confused look. "Retirement planet."

Two words, and I was supposed to understand everything. I mentally sighed but gave it a shot. "Do you mean everyone who retires moves to another planet?"

"Yes. New information for Syl?"

"Very new, but I never asked before so no one told me."

I wondered what happened if someone wanted to retire but not move. Oh well, a question for another day when my head wasn't filled with anxiety.

"Now I don't know about you, but I'm tired. I think it's time for bed for both of us. Keep your brooch close, but I don't expect any information at this time of day. Let's have a good sleep, and then we can figure out what to do tomorrow. What do you think?"

"Tired I am," said Reena. "Time to rest. Thank you for help."

"You're my daughter. I'll help you any time. Now let's go."

I first put Reena to bed and then myself. It only took one glass of wine and two pages of my current novel, and then I was out for the night.

Chapter Twenty-Four

The next morning, I talked Reena into going on our tour. Somehow, I'd arranged a day off—a little optimistic I knew. However I didn't plan to worry about anything—except Dedare—so it would be like a holiday—a delusion perhaps. As for Reena, a distraction from the plight of her father was necessary, so she readily agreed to the tour.

I talked her into a brisk walk around our building a couple of times before we joined the tour as I'd stiffened up as a result of my leg gashes. The short walk certainly helped my mobility. I hadn't realized how deeply my stiffness had penetrated.

Reena and I arrived at Reception, and I talked to Cara while the others gathered. I gave her specific instructions on many topics until I realized I bumped my head against my personal problem—trying to do everything. "Cara, you know how to take care of these items, so just ignore what I said. If you need advice, give me a call."

Cara wasn't the only one trying to hide a smile. They all knew my proclivity for micro-managing, and I needed to recognize my action a little sooner.

Richard Branson stepped up. "Manager Syl, I wish to pay for this tour for everyone. I've quite enjoyed my stay and activities on Particle, especially with these worthy companions."

I glanced at Cara, and she made a hand movement so I knew she'd take care of the billing. "Richard, thank you for your kind gesture. We'll make sure to give you a great discount. Now let's get on with our wonderful tour." So we took off for the first stop.

The Ooby zoo fascinated me. The native animals near me had two-toned fur coverings—not graduations in coloring, but very distinct colored patterns in their fur. Think swirls, dots, stripes, and others I couldn't describe.

The trend also continued in skin surfaces, beaks, shells, and such. I couldn't see the patterns being used for camouflage, but what did I know of this planet yet.

"Wrong, wrong," Testarn spouted in a loud voice.

We turned his way, and I wondered what had upset him.

"Cage, cage. Bad, bad. Hurtful, hurtful." Testarn pointed at the caged animals. Most of the animals in the zoo had large areas for roaming but a few which I assumed were dangerous were locked in large cages. Mentally I agreed with Testarn after he'd pointed out the situation.

"We need to do something about this, Syl," added Richard.

"That's tricky. Diplomacy is needed since we don't want to upset our hosts. Of course, they may just need the hurtful situation pointed out."

"Because of the diplomatic overtones I believe Charles and I can introduce the issue. I suggest, Richard, that you, Testarn, and I join in the discussions. Would you do that?" asked Thad.

Richard spoke with Testarn and then turned back to Thad. "We have agreed to pursue the matter. Let's discuss this after we return to the hotel."

With understanding in place, we resumed our tour, thank goodness. The diplomatic issues concerned me, but with Charles involved perhaps we could make headway. And I didn't want anything to stop the efficient running of the hotel.

Our next tour stop was the highest point in Ooby. The helicopter landed on a beautiful, large, circular flat area with low surrounding walls. The majority of us decided to walk along the perimeter.

A beautiful 360-degree view of Ooby enlightened me. Many built-up urban areas were revealed, but I was glad to see large green areas interspersed amongst the groups of dwellings.

The most astonishing vision was fields of orange. Blossoms or perhaps fruit on low-lying bushes greeted us.

"Orange, orange," said Testarn.

"It's quite beautiful, isn't it?" Perhaps one of the most beautiful vistas I'd seen on Particle.

"Paint, paint."

"Do you paint, Testarn?" I knew art interested him, and I knew Sarturns painted, but I didn't know how often he found time to paint.

"Paint, paint. Hotel, hotel."

What did he mean? Surely, he didn't want to paint a picture of our hotel. "Do you want to return to the hotel and start painting pictures?"

"Relax, relax."

I suspected Testarn had stressed out over the animals in cages and wanted to do the one thing he could do on Particle to relax—sit down and paint.

How was I supposed to make this happen? Being in the middle of a tour raised some interesting logistics questions. One of which was—what did the rest of our tour involve?

After receiving the information, I formulated a plan. I talked to our guide, and we changed things around a bit. We decided to have lunch next, and while we did the helicopter would take Testarn back to the hotel. The rearrangement worked so one scheduling crisis was avoided and one guest made happy.

After we'd settled at our table in the restaurant, I received a call from Cara. We were in the middle of giving our orders, so I told her I'd call her back. Too many things on my mind, and I wanted to keep my guests happy.

"Cara, what's the problem?" I eventually asked.

"Two tours tomorrow. Manager Syl requested. On each trip."

How could I manage two tours in one day? One in the morning, one in the afternoon? I should never have started going on tours; I needed to focus on the hotel.

"Cara, I can't go on any more tours—I need time for the hotel." Then I had a possible solution. "I'll call you back; I have an idea how to keep everyone happy."

A moment later, I asked, "Sweety, how're you feeling?" I hoped her pregnancy continued to proceed normally.

"I feel great. The babies aren't causing any problems, and the Particlan doctors say everything is normal, although I'd like a human doctor to give me that conclusion. And sorry, but I don't have any news from Hart. I haven't heard from him recently. Have you?"

I shook my head. I kept telling myself no news is good news.

"I have a question, Sweety. What do you think about going on some of our tours? Apparently the guests want me to go on two tours tomorrow, but I need to focus on running the hotel. Anyway, I think you'd be the perfect alien to be sociable with the guests. You could sit down a lot, and no one would complain. You don't have to explain the tour stops; you'll have a guide with you. What do you think?"

"Boy, that's a big project, but I'd love to do it. Hopefully requests for tours involving us don't happen too often. I still need to focus on my tv station, my cooking, and helping out in the kitchen. And of course my babies." Sweety laughed. "I know I've forgotten a bunch of other things I'm doing. I have to admit my life is full and fascinating."

"Thanks for doing this, Sweety. If it gets to be too much—and I mean all your projects—then let me know, and we'll adjust your activities. In the meantime, I'll call Cara and tell her about our decision. Then I expect you'll soon get a call from Cara. Thanks again for helping me out."

"What are friends for," said Sweety before she hung up.

I explained the situation to Cara and she didn't seem particularly upset. I suspected one alien was as good as another.

My next call came from Sain. "Restaurant is completed and ready to use."

"Wow, that was fast. Thank you for being so efficient, Sain."

"Good workers from Cara. And excellent paperwork arranged by Cara."

"I think Cara needs a raise," I commented.

Sain didn't respond to my observation but merely said, "Test dinner this evening?"

"An excellent idea. Would you get hold of everyone and let them know? Let's keep it to our regulars for this first meal. By the way, what did we finally decide the restaurant's name would be?"

"Sath-Ooby Golden Restaurant."

"Excellent. Quite appropriate for the Sath-Ooby Golden Hotel."

The rest of the afternoon went off as planned, and the tour returned to the hotel at our expected time. I spoke with Cara for a few moments, and then I escaped to my suite for a little rest before dinner. Reena and I walked over together to the new restaurant.

Sain and Cara had done a marvelous job on the outside of the new facility. Signage with golden letters clearly announced the Sath-Ooby Golden Restaurant. Since the hotel entrance stood only a few feet from the restaurant, the association of hotel and restaurant was clear.

The outside wall of the restaurant sported shiny black tiles with gold swirls. The gold designs made me take a second glance as my mind tried to read significance into the markings.

The spacious interior included windows along three walls. The fourth wall hid the kitchen from view.

Large and small tables were scattered about the interior with stools nestled around them. Booths were attached to the walls. Of course, stools in a booth seemed odd from my human-centric point of view.

Sain manned the door. He let us in but not the general public.

We met the staff that would run the restaurant. Tonight was the equivalent of a test session, so we decided to order a lot of items from the menu in order to pretend the restaurant was full of patrons. Sweety explained our actions to Chef, and he understood. The leftovers would go home with us and the restaurant staff to be saved in our personal kitchens.

Thad spoke to Charles. "Dad, Syl and I were wondering. Do you have any other offspring—half-siblings to us, of course, we should know about?"

Chapter Twenty-Five

All conversation at our dinner table ceased, and the focus turned to Dad. I took a quick peek at my mother. She stared at Charles and obviously waited for his answer.

"Not that I know of. We'll discuss this at a later, ah private time," my father mumbled.

Not that I know of seemed flippant, but the words were probably for my mother's benefit since she hadn't told him about me in a timely manner.

No one argued with his response, but I and I suspected everyone else wanted to know about his life on Earth and as an ambassador to and on other planets. I knew my mother's curiosity was greater than ours, though.

However, Thad and I had a deep interest concerning other brothers and sisters. I know I certainly did since I'd grown up without one. On another day Thad and I would probably have a major discussion so I could understand his history.

Our main server for the evening approached and had a quiet conversation with Sweety. Sweety patted her on the shoulder and then turned to us.

"This is probably your domain, Syl." Sweety grinned. "We've begun to receive requests from hotel guests to have their evening meal here. What can we do? What do you suggest? And I mean tonight's evening meal."

I asked the main server, Noora pic Petane, "Should we allow other guests for dinner? This would be a good practice run for your staff. What do you think? If your staff's not ready, that's fine with me."

"Continue trial run." An excited Particlan wanted to continue with the evening's activities.

"Does Chef agree?"

"Excited to produce." Noora grinned.

I glanced around the restaurant and saw a lot of hotel staff with big smiles.

So that's what we did. Sweety, of course, acted as Hostess and explained to our guests we really weren't open yet, so the guests had to excuse any inconvenience, but they were welcome to try the food and the restaurant and let us know what they thought.

The restaurant soon filled, and I spent my time watching. I heard no complaints nor saw any disgruntled patrons.

With the restaurant full—the word must have somehow gotten out—the staff hopped to fulfill their demands. I wandered around and spoke to a few of the guests. Apparently the idea of eating outside their rooms but close by delighted them. So far our notion had passed muster.

My brooch rang with a call from Hart. I didn't expect news, but I asked anyway. "Any word about Dedare?"

"Yes. All the life pods have been found, and everyone is okay," replied Hart. The screen showed a grinning Hart.

"Put him on. Put him on. Let me talk to Dedare," I demanded. My arms started flailing, and tears dripped down my cheeks.

"Can't do that, Syl."

I opened my mouth to protest, but Hart interrupted. "Sorry, but there wasn't enough space for everyone on the ship to stay awake, and the stasis pods also double as medical pods. So all the travelers rescued, including Dedare, are in stasis until we get home. I did a quick exam before they went in the pods, and they all seem fine."

"How soon will that be?" Good news, bad news. Why does that happen so often?

"Probably a couple of days. I'll get a better estimate from the captain after we're on our way. As you can imagine, the crew is busy right now. They've been getting everyone settled in the pods, and now they're computing our way home. I'll give you an update as soon as I can."

"I know, I know. I'm just a little anxious and a whole lot happy," I answered. So happy I couldn't stand still.

"Would you give your brooch to Sweety, please? I'd like to talk to her."

After I did so, I relayed to the rest of our group the good news, and then the room suddenly got bright, and then almost immediately dark.

My next vision included me lying on a couch in a corner of the restaurant being fussed over. "Mom, what happened?"

"Oh, you fainted from excitement. We're flying in a Particlan doctor from the clinic, and he took a look at you from afar, but he thinks nothing's wrong with you.

The news was too much to comprehend, and your brain collapsed. Seems a strange comment, but I can understand your excitement being too much. However, we're all so happy everyone on the spaceship is alive and well. The doctor will be here in a moment. Just rest until he arrives."

So I slouched on the couch while Mom sat beside me. Such good news but assimilation proved difficult especially since I'd been trying to grasp the idea of a negative outcome.

The Particlan doctor checked me over and said I was fine and to take it easy. So I thanked him and then partied with my friends after he left.

****

While I waited for Dedare to return, I needed more than ever to keep the hotel running efficiently. However, I realized I needed to understand how other Particlan hotels ran, how Particlans like things done. I had up to now made far too many assumptions based on only one hotel combined with my human beliefs. Field trips popped into my mind.

"Accompany," said Sain. "Chance to investigate non-hotel eating facilities."

Sain uttered a logical argument—one I couldn't argue with—to give himself the chance to keep an eye on me during my wanderings. With our restaurant completed, he had time on his hands. And Sain considered me a troublemaker. Although troublemaker wasn't quite the right word. More like someone interested in everything, which could lead to trouble. I had to laugh; I'd take Sain along for the ride.

We checked out one hotel before we realized we needed a Particlan from the Sath-Ooby Golden Hotel to vouch for us. Dumping aliens who wanted to know how a hotel was run on an unsuspecting Reception clerk or manager pushed the bounds, and I should have known. If we had a Particlan that knew us and could explain things quickly, I was convinced our investigation would proceed smoothly.

So Sain and I gave up after the first hotel and journeyed back to ours. I called Cara into my office and explained what Sain and I had experienced. "So I think we need to take a Particlan from the hotel along with us to explain the situation to other hotels. What do you think, Cara?"

Cara studied Sain and me. "Unreasonable to expect. Competitors to welcome. Manager competing hotel."

Hah. I'd been pretty naïve to even embark on this activity, and Cara had just agreed.

Seeing the disappointment on my face, Cara added, "Cara to find. Hotels that welcome. Innovative alien ideas."

Particlan speech had become much easier for me to parse. "Thanks, Cara. Hopefully you'll be successful. In the meantime, are there any problems we need to discuss?"

Cara didn't speak, but Thad interrupted from his position in my doorway. "Forgive me for overhearing your conversation, Syl. I've been standing outside waiting for my turn at an audience."

Thad and I had a good laugh, but I wasn't sure Cara understood our historical reference. No never mind.

"What's up, Thad?" Having a half-brother still struck me as strange.

"I've been dealing with Reception for tours, additions to my room, and such. And I've been interacting with different Particlans." Thad laughed. "Some of your staff have no problem talking to me, but some do. Not that they don't try, but they haven't had any education regarding alien races. Syl, I think each of your Reception staff should be trained in at least one new race. Then any guest would have someone to help them. Of course, ideally each staff member should understand all alien races."

I smiled at Thad. "Are you offering to teach a few Particlans about humans? And human idiosyncrasies, of course. And human history, and human…I don't know where you would start, let alone finish. Sounds like a clever idea, though."

Thad had the look of someone who'd been thumped on the head. "Thad, I'm just kidding. However, I would like to discuss where you think my staff need training. They are our first line of welcome, and appropriate knowledge would help. I haven't been watching the interactions, so your advice would be invaluable. When you have a few moments, perhaps we can discuss this topic," I said, pointing at my conference table.

"Of course, Syl. Tomorrow?" said Thad. "Do you have a specific time that would suit you?"

After we arranged our meeting, Thad said, "I'll see you at dinner."

I lifted a quizzical eyebrow.

"Apparently, all aliens, ah non-Particlans, are meeting in the restaurant for dinner. To promote the venue, of course."

"And I'm sure Sweety will have new recipes available. All chefs love her." I laughed. "I'll see you then. Have a nice afternoon, Thad."

I watched Thad leave my office. How many traits did we have in common because we had the same father?

"Cara, did any of our babbling confuse you? My conversation with Thaddeus involved having Reception staff understand the requirements of various alien races." I really wondered what she'd taken from listening to our conversation.

"Excellent idea proposed," said Cara.

"Oh, good. Do you have any ideas on how we should implement this?" I asked.

"Planning and schedules. Interests with understanding. Training and motivation."

I wasn't sure what Cara had just articulated, but I knew she'd help out.

The next couple of days proceeded in a slow manner. Dedare still hadn't arrived, and now he wasn't expected until the third day.

I think we made progress with the Reception staff, and the restaurant was catching the eyes of the Particlan public in Ooby.

Early the next morning, I had the surprise of my life. I awoke, to find a body dug in beside me.

"You're back! I can't believe it." I grinned. "I've been waiting forever for you," I said.

"Cuddle time," replied a grinning Dedare, who proceeded to use his hands.

I agreed with his sentiment, and time passed pleasantly.

****

Sometime later, I asked Dedare, "Do you want breakfast here in our rooms, or do you want to see the new restaurant?" So we wandered over to the Sath-Ooby Golden Restaurant. Dedare spent time studying the room, the servers, decorations, and whatever else caught his eye while I ordered breakfast for us. He'd been away so long, and we had many topics to catch up on.

After he expressed his approval of the restaurant, I said, "Dedare, I think you spend too much time away. Away from me, of course, but also away from your current project that I'm involved in. It's nice to be given the authority to make decisions, but I really need your input on some of the items. Obviously, Irions have many points of view different from humans.

"However, I don't want to change you, Dedare. You have so many delightful qualities, not the least of which is your affinity for business. So if trying to run many worlds makes you happy and makes you who you are, I will accept your absences. I love all of you."

For once, Dedare didn't offer a look that implied *impossible*. "Changing method of work under consideration. Syl, first to offer opinions. Quality of life paramount. Quality of life with Syl most important. Life together is *tissile*."

Tissile took the translator a moment to figure out, but *non-negotiable* was the result. What a sweet thing for Dedare to say.

Before I had a chance to quiz Dedare regarding his delightful words, our breakfast table expanded. I had to laugh because Sweety, Hart, Mom, Charles, and Reena all had a million questions for Dedare. As he tried to answer them, others joined us. Thaddeus, Richard

Branson, and Testarn also had questions they needed answered.

"Let's give Dedare a chance to eat," I said. "I'm sure his energy was depleted during his ordeal. In fact, I want to talk to his doctor. By the way, who is your doctor, Dedare?"

"Personal doctor on Irion. Consider Hart doctor during trips," answered Dedare.

Hart had a stunned look. Apparently Dedare's decision was news to him, although it seemed logical to me. However, before Hart could talk to his new patient Sweety interrupted.

"Hart, I'm having pain in my abdomen. I'm not sure what it's from, but a trip to the clinic might be in order."

Sweety suggesting a medical checkup immediately interrupted our conversation. Resting at home would have been her usual response.

"Hart, take the helicopter," I said. "If there are any problems, let me know, and we'll pop over." I had no idea who *we* referred to, but I knew I wanted to be by Sweety's side if she was at risk.

"There are always numerous pains with a pregnancy, especially twins, and a checkup is routine," said Hart.

Hart didn't want to upset any of us, least of all Sweety. As he reassured us, Sweety said, "Hart, I need to go now. The pain has increased." Hart grabbed Sweety and hoofed it to the roof elevator. Cara ran to the Reception front desk and then continued to Sweety to give her a backpack before they entered the elevator.

After Cara rejoined us, I asked, "What was in that backpack you gave Sweety?"

"Necessities for patient. Hospitals can neglect. Alien, foreign, patients," she replied.

"Cara, you're the best," I said. "If you need anything for your backpacks, let me know. I'll round up supplies."

We eventually settled down to our meals, but I hoped to hear from Hart before very long.

A topic occurred to me. "Cara, I know we're finding Reception staff to help with each alien type, so do you have backpacks already designed for each species?"

"Backpacks under consideration. Contents not finalized. Practice models available."

I wouldn't argue with her methods since they were proactive and efficient. I certainly didn't know what should be placed in a backpack for a Sarturn, for example.

After Dedare noticed I'd finished breakfast, he held out a hand and we left the table and began walking.

"Dedare, did any of our decisions upset you?" I asked. "We've had numerous opportunities where we've needed to make decisions while you were gone."

"Decisions appropriate. However, ideas exist. More meetings appropriate. Your office, of course." Dedare grinned. He knew I loved my office.

"Okay. Why don't we go now? We have lots of things to discuss. And since you're the boss I'd dearly love your input."

"Invite other boss?" questioned Dedare.

Oh dear. I'd forgotten Dedare's co-owner. Do I lie? "No, I haven't yet. I was so excited about you being back. I'll invite him right now. In the meantime, we can discuss some of your other interests."

Dedare and I didn't get very far in our discussion before Tarin et Tong and his brother, the chief priest, appeared. I didn't like the looks of this gathering. Probably nagging about church instruction for both Dedare and me.

Well, we'd have time together.

However, I turned out to be wrong. Since I'd had a few lessons and Dedare had not, we'd be in different classes. I didn't voice my concerns in front of the priest, but Dedare would hear about them later. Thankfully, our lessons wouldn't start, or continue, until the following day, so Dedare would have an additional day to acclimatize and rest from his ordeal.

Saska et Tong only spent a few moments with us. However, Dedare's co-owner sat down and joined our discussion. After I asked him if he'd sampled the food in the restaurant, Tarin replied he hadn't realized it was open for business. I explained we were having a *soft* opening so we could work out the kinks in our plans and procedures so we hadn't really advertised the fact that the restaurant was available for service. However, word of mouth appeared to be working, and the restaurant was becoming busy. So far we'd found the in-house guests outnumbered the walk-ins.

I explained to Dedare and Tarin I thought alien visitors and a chance for guests to get out of their hotel rooms were the two biggest draws for the restaurant. And I hoped we'd start getting more walk-ins and even introduce the concept of reservations.

Restaurant reservations took a few moments of explanation for Tarin.

I received a welcome call from Hart. "Sweety's fine. I examined her, and she's healthy. Pains are normal, but they should be checked out, nonetheless."

"Excellent. Are you on your way back?" I asked.

"Yes. Even though Sweety is fine, she wants to rest at home, and I need to get back to work. Is Dedare there?"

"Right beside me."

"I'm going to call him right now."

Dedare's brooch rang before I'd uttered anything more than "Hart." I gleaned little from Dedare's side of the conversation.

Then my brooch rang again. "Syl, can you get Dedare back to your suite. Since he thinks I'm his doctor, I need to examine him. I want to determine how healthy he is and what effect the life pod had on his body. This will be excellent experience for me in regard to an Irion male."

"Any objections?" I asked. Hart wouldn't have called me unless he thought he had a problem.

"Some resistance, so it's all up to you to maneuver Dedare to your bedroom. Ha, ha." Hart added a laugh. "I'll be there in a couple of minutes. So if you don't manage to move him, it doesn't matter."

I had no idea how to get Dedare back to our rooms. We'd already had our romantic interlude. What else could I come up with?"

Before I had a chance to motivate Dedare, Cara interrupted my thoughts.

"Wish to discuss. Group alien assistants. Management some concern."

After I deciphered her words, I believed Cara had concerns with the Reception assistants assigned to each alien race.

"Cara, your alien backpacks proved an excellent idea. The aliens would have no idea what to expect on a tour, but they will now have adequate fluid and backup snacks. I assume you added a lightweight jacket of some sort to help preserve their heat. So what are your concerns?"

Cara laughed—at my ignorance, I assumed.

"Control of assistants. Grouped by species. Need overall management."

"Can you manage the control yourself, Cara? Do you want to? Or should we appoint another person to help out?" Her comments confused me.

"Assistant will help."

"Do you mean a new assistant or the one you already have?" I asked.

"Current assistant wonderful. Excellent work ethic. Compensation needs improvement."

Damn. I'd forgotten about Jesto's salary. "Excellent idea. We need to discuss his salary and also have it start when he filled in for you on your day off. And I suspect we should take a good look at yours. You do so much."

Cara gave me a wide smile.

Her assistant must be working out well. I also needed to keep my office door open more often so I could perhaps overhear what Cara and her assistant discussed concerning the day to day running of the hotel.

Then a thought occurred. "Cara, does the hotel have a medical room? One we can take a guest to if they're not feeling well and before the medical services arrive?"

"Second floor space."

"Good. Can we go there as soon as Hart arrives from the hospital? He should be here any moment."

Almost before I'd finished uttering my words, Hart popped into view. "Just in time, Hart. We're off to visit the hotel medical room on the second floor. Perhaps you'd like to join us."

Hart grinned at my deviousness. I knew Dedare suspected something, but he didn't ask. He followed us, as I knew he wanted to learn everything about his hotel.

Cara showed us the medical room and then received a call on her brooch. She left to return to Reception, and as I followed her I heard Hart say, "Dedare, wait a moment; I need a word with you."

Dedare would get his much-needed detailed medical checkup from Hart after Dedare's disastrous space adventure.

Chapter Twenty-Six

Dedare and Hart returned to my office, and Hart declared Dedare's medical exam had proceeded smoothly. He declared Dedare in good health, just needing rest after his stressful time.

Hart disappeared and left me with an annoyed Dedare.

"Don't look at me like that," I said. "You know Hart needed to examine you after your ordeal. After all, you said he was your doctor." I hoped my logic would calm him.

Dedare laughed. "Good reasoning. However, sadness. Ship destroyed, so no presents for you."

"Well thank you for thinking of me anyway, Dedare. The gesture is appreciated." I wondered what he had brought for me that I'd never see.

"Except for one." He dug in one of his pockets and produced a necklace.

I examined the arrangement. "This is gorgeous, Dedare. I really like the combination of black stones with silver ribbons on them and shiny blue stones with silver dots. Where did you find this? Thank you so much. This is absolutely wonderful" I reached up and rubbed his cheek.

Dedare responded by kissing me and giving me a tug. I knew what he wanted.

"Do you think we can sneak away without anyone noticing?"

"No problem. Owner," he said, pointing to himself and laughing.

I joined in his laughter. "Okay, just let me call Cara and let her know that we'll, um, um, be taking a walk around your property discussing possible improvements. Will that work?"

"Too much discussion," said Dedare, rubbing my cheek.

"Smartass. Let me call Cara."

I didn't know if my explanation to Cara rang true, but I really didn't care. We, ahem, we had a pleasurable time at home and then managed to walk around the Sath-Ooby Golden Hotel property and discuss possible changes.

At lunch, we again partook of food in our new hotel restaurant.

"Sain, Dedare and I had a walk around the hotel. And guess what, we have ideas about updates. We'll need to get together for a discussion."

"Changes? Really? Changes? Hard to believe. Hard to handle," Sain replied, laughing up a storm.

I knew too many smartasses. "Perhaps you have suggestions of your own?" I asked sweetly.

"Yes." Sain continued his laughing.

"Well, then our meeting might go a little long." The rest of our company had a good laugh at my comment.

"If anyone else has ideas for change, please pipe up. I like to hear new perspectives. Let me know, and I'll add them to my list." I sincerely believed more views were good.

Cara caught my eye. "Yes, Cara? Do you have anything to add to our discussion about hotel changes?"

"Not hotel changes. Rest needed everyone. Water Wonderland appropriate."

"Everyone has been working hard with no time off. I agree. What is this Water Wonderland?"

"Water sports abound. Simple and athletic. Types for everyone." After her last comment, she glanced at Sweety.

"This is a wonderful idea," said my mother. "I don't know about the rest of you, but I definitely need a change of pace. Days off would be nice, but *a change is as good as a rest*, goes the saying. So your idea sounds heavenly, Cara."

General enthusiastic agreement was heard, and Cara appeared pleased.

"Dedare, please declare an afternoon of research at the Water Wonderland," I said.

He grinned and proceeded to do so.

"Swimming clothes?" I asked Cara.

"Swimming and comfortable. Weather is warm. As is water."

So a bunch of us—actually all except Dedare, who stayed behind to work to catch up on his work—gathered day packs and proceeded to the roof. Everyone chatted cheerfully and anticipated a relaxing afternoon. Cara also had cases loaded onto the helicopter. I didn't know what they were for, but I knew we'd find out this afternoon. She had everything under control.

The Water Wonderland turned out to be a water park. Not surprising at all but with a couple of unique twists.

They had an area dedicated to pregnant Particlans. Being humanoid their pregnancies ran similar to humans, so Sweety was gathered right in after Cara's discussion with the leaders.

Then Cara organized the rest of us. There were a dozen or so activities we could engage in. Since Cara knew us quite well by now, she found suitable activities. Actually she offered a few to each of us, and we chose our first one. Apparently we had enough time this afternoon to engage in more than one.

My first activity was just lying on their beach relaxing, and I was joined by Hart. Neither of us had had much time to ourselves since coming to Particle, and we both needed to unwind.

"Hart, what do you think about Particle?" I asked.

He sighed. "Not a bad place. And obviously the conception place of our twins, so it must have good vibes." He grinned. "This is a place Sweety and I'll never forget no matter how many planets we end up visiting." Hart took a deep breath and then sat back. "We've all been quite busy, so this is a well needed break. Forgive me if I don't talk to you a lot."

I laughed. "I just want peace and quiet, too. You won't hear much from me either."

And that's what we did. Hart and I had the loveliest time—with no interaction. I read a book, and Hart just closed his eyes and relaxed. I didn't know how he could relax that completely so quickly. I'd need to learn the trick from him some day.

An hour or so went by, and then our peace was shattered. "Manager Syl, problem," said Cara.

I opened my eyes—so much for my actually reading—and became aware of Cara, as did Hart.

"Is there a problem?" Obviously I had been asleep as I just repeated her words.

"Sweety in distress."

Hart jumped up and said, "Where is she?"

"I take you. Emergency services called. Here in moments."

Cara grabbed both our hands and started jogging. In moments, we were at Sweety's location.

Many Particlans clustered about, and Hart dropped to Sweety's side. "What's the problem?"

"I seem to have contractions. Well, maybe only pain, but I think we need to have my symptoms looked at. A little early for the twins, but you never know."

Hart didn't respond to her words because the emergency services personnel had just arrived. Sweety chatted with them so they could record her details. Apparently most of them were the same staff from her previous visit to the hospital.

"Syl, don't let anyone know about this," said Hart. "It's probably normal for twins. However I'm a little concerned about two incidents in one day. I'm sure we'll be back in no time. I might call and ask you to send your helicopter. Is that okay?"

"Of course, Hart. Just keep me posted."

I watched the two of them retreat, and then I said, "Cara, please take me back to my resting place." I laughed and so did Cara. She knew what I'd asked.

A little while later I had a visit from Teeka and Cara.

"Syl, confusion with Cara and relationship. Would you help?" asked Teeka.

This was not what I wanted on a relaxing afternoon. "Okay, Teeka, perhaps you could expand on *confusing relationship*?" I asked.

"Threesome required for mature relationship," said Teeka.

Threesome. Hmm. I took a deep breath. "So who is the third person in your relationship with Cara?" I took a big leap with my conclusion about him being in a relationship with Cara, but neither one of them contradicted my statement.

"Cara's mother offers options," said Sain.

What did the hell did that mean? So I was here on Particle offering words on Particlan relationships? Actually, ever since our arrival Particlan relationships had confused me. Who had the information I needed?

An older female joined us.

"My mother happy. To make acquaintance. Hotel manager, Syl." Cara seemed to think she'd given a clear explanation.

"Of course, Cara. I'm happy to meet your mother." I rose and offered a hand to shake. Then Cara's mother and I settled down beside each other in chairs on the beach.

"Hello, I'm Sylvestine Amera. I manage the Sath-Ooby Golden Hotel. What's your name?"

A stricken look appeared on Cara's face. She hadn't actually introduced her mother.

"Chera ast Hembole. Is given name. Happy to meet."

"Subjects of interest. Discussion to have. Teeka and Cara," she added.

I laughed. "Yes, those two are a subject of interest. Shall we throw them in the water, and let the fish try to eat them?"

All movement ceased, and then they realized I'd made a joke. Laughter sprouted from the people around me, and I was thankful I hadn't uttered a faux pas.

"Okay, so we have a problem—well, Teeka and Cara do." I glanced at the parties involved. "Chera—may I call you Chera?" I really didn't understand Particlan societal niceties yet.

"Honor is mine." Chera's rounded face went well with her slightly curly brown hair and her infectious smile. Then she gave me a pat on my head.

Oh my, I really had a lot to learn. "So, we have the party of two—Teeka and Cara. Now we need a third to join them?"

"Advice required, new. Relationships are difficult. Wisdom helps all," said Chera.

New relationships certainly could be difficult. "So, an experienced elder helps those involved in a new relationship?"

"Agree with Syl," said Chera. "Syl to join?" added Chera.

Now I was stumped, but I plowed on through the language barrier. "Chera, do you want me to help you advise Teeka and Cara? Is this possible on Particle?" Did I understand the situation and her suggestion?

Chera laughed. "Couple needs help."

"I have to agree with you—this couple does need help. So this threesome is actually a foursome. Or, Chera, do you and I actually count for one half each?"

She caught my eye, and we burst out laughing.

Glancing at Teeka and Cara, I didn't think they were particularly amused—in fact, the opposite.

"A perfect solution, Chera. Please keep me updated on what I need to do." I laughed. "Shall we let these two go off and splash in the water? I just want to sit here and relax. Would you like to join me?"

Chera agreed, and we had a pleasant couple of hours relaxing and uttering few words.

In the middle of our relaxation, Hart and Sweety reappeared, and I jumped up and grabbed her in a hug. "Sweety, are you okay?"

"Another false alarm. One for each baby. Although this time the medical staff were more concerned. Perhaps *third time lucky* and I'll have the babies." Sweety grabbed onto Hart.

"Hart, tell me what's going on?"

"The general consensus was that Sweety is going through perfectly normal reactions. She does have a modicum of stress in her life, but everything seems fine. Don't worry, Syl, the medical staff have everything under control."

I grabbed a look at him, but I wasn't convinced. Then I looked at Chera and made a motion for her to speak.

"Pregnant women uncomfortable. Love to join. Group of others."

I glanced at Sweety. "Are you suggesting Sweety rejoin the Particlan pregnant women and share their experiences?"

"Start down beach." Chera beamed, stood, and then grabbed Sweety's hand. The two of them wandered down the beach. Waddled on the sand, in Sweety's case.

Hart bounced on his feet.

"Hart, that is Cara's mother who took Sweety away. Everything's under control."

"Seriously?" A sheen of sweat covered his face, and I didn't think it was the humidity.

I laughed. "Hart, Cara's mother will take care of Sweety. Just sit back down in your chair and relax. We don't have all day here, so enjoy your precious moments. And goodness knows you've been stressed enough recently."

Hart slumped in a chair and closed his eyes. I didn't hear a word from him for a long time, and that made me happy because I needed silence to settle my mind.

Apparently a couple of social problems including Teeka and Cara and Sweety's pregnancy had been taken care of. Should I pat myself on the back? Probably not. I suspected new problems would soon appear.

"Syl, you're awfully red. Did you apply any sunscreen?" asked Hart.

"I didn't know I had any. My fault for not thinking about it. Do you have any ointments I could use?"

"Yes. And I think it's time we returned to the hotel. It's almost dinner time, and we need to gather in the restaurant and regale each other with today's exploits. What do you think?"

"Good idea. I want to have a shower and use one of your creams. Let's find everyone and be on our way."

Hart and I had difficulty arranging our leaving. Apparently the Water Wonderland had become a favorite spot for all manner of species. This pleased me since we needed to assimilate on every world we interacted with.

Dedare joined us in the restaurant.

After a wonderful day a great dinner was welcome. Dedare ordered a selection of dishes unknown to me. Apparently he'd researched while we were away.

The tales of our afternoon exploits took up most of our conversations. Sweety exuded a positive aura, even though she'd had a couple of incidents.

"I am so even with the universe," Sweety said. "My vibes are calm, and my reasoning is excellent. Does anyone have any questions?"

Her words flustered me. I didn't really know what she meant, but I couldn't ignore her. "Sweety, is there anything you need for your babies? Another visit to the Water Wonderland? Or perhaps a visit to one of the cultural wonders of Particle? Or a shopping trip? What do you think? What do you need?"

"I think I just need time to adjust to the notion of two little offspring. Two little offspring arriving at the same time. Can you imagine, Syl? Well, I guess you can't. However, I know you are doing everything you can to help me. And don't stop!"

Sweety appeared quite excitable, but I'd probably also be if I were in her circumstances.

"Syl, what're you wearing? Let me see that necklace." Sweety held out her hand.

I removed the necklace and handed it to her.

"Where did you get this? It's gorgeous," she said, flashing it around, and then putting it on.

"Dedare brought it from Irion for me, so give it back." I wiggled my fingers at her.

"Oh, if you insist." Sweety handed me the necklace. I put it on and then gave Dedare a big smile.

"Reminds me a bit of the church necklaces but much more gorgeous," added my best friend, Sweety.

I needed to think about all the church events we'd been involved with. A pattern was starting to develop, and I thought Dedare's co-owner was deeply involved.

"How're your church lessons going?" asked Charles, interrupting my thoughts.

I laughed. "I'm certainly gathering lots of information about Particlan religions. Actually only one religion, though. Whether the data helps me run the hotel remains to be seen. I suspect it will make a world of a difference. So I may have to delve into others."

I turned to Cara. "You know the shower at the entrance to our chapel?"

She waved her hand in agreement.

"Well, I'd like the shower changed so anyone entering can choose whether to have a shower or not. This way, aliens or non-religious types can be spared an unnecessary drenching. What do you think, Sain? Can you hook up something like that?"

"Easily. Button to push for shower."

That certainly would help. "Cara, would there be any problem installing a button like that? We want our chapel to be available for all guests. Of course, we may have to install other items as religious needs are revealed. And that goes for the rest of the hotel as issues arise."

"Appropriate to me. Check with priest. For final answer."

"By the way, everyone, I think dinner has already become an appropriate time to discuss any innovations we've thought about during the day. This is an intelligent group, and we may come up with ways to improve on any of our suggestions. Of course, some ideas may be dismissed in a rude manner, but that's just the rest of you being silly."

I suspected some of my tablemates wanted to throw something, but the majority roared with laughter. And I also recognized Cara began to understand the level of our teasing and fond regards for each other. As for Cara and Teeka, who knows what they understood about each other.

When Cara and Teeka weren't around, I needed a long discussion with Chera about Particlan society and how it affected inter-racial relationships.

As our mealtime wound down I said, "I don't know about the rest of you, but I've had a tiring day. Time to rest and recover. Dedare?" I held out my hand to him, and he took it. "We'll see everyone in the morning."

Reena stayed behind to chat while Dedare and I settled in our living room. I grabbed a glass of wine, and Dedare obtained a drink with which I was unfamiliar. We sat together on the couch, and I tried to find words to bring up the subject foremost in my mind.

"Dedare, this current episode of you being missing and presumed dead has brought many thoughts to my mind. The most important of which, other than me missing you desperately, is the situation with Reena. Okay, now I have tears in my eyes."

Dedare handed me a cloth.

"Sorry about that." I wiped my eyes and face.

Dedare leaned over and kissed me before I could utter another word.

"If you keep kissing me I'll never finish this conversation," I said. "Now, what I want to say is that if you really die…" I stopped and did a lot of deep breathing. Dedare continued to hold my hand and tried not to kiss me.

"I'll start again. If you die, then I need to tell you I'm willing to look after Reena. I love Reena, and I think she feels the same about me."

Reena popped through the doorway. "I do, I do. I want you as mother. Now I will go cry good tears." Before anyone had a chance to respond, she popped out. On her way to her bedroom, I assumed.

"All good decisions," said Dedare, giving me another kiss or two.

I hugged and held on to him for the longest time. "Dedare, this is a difficult time for all of us. I think Reena and I have an understanding. However, my next question concerns where you want us to live. Should we stay on Irion?"

"Perhaps Irion. Perhaps Mars. Decision of two— Reena and Syl. Perhaps Sain have input."

"You're right. Sain is level-headed and might know what's best. You'd better not die because I don't want to make these decisions." I sighed. "So, that's Reena sort of taken care of. Now, here's a serious question which is none of my business."

Before I had a chance to articulate, Dedare leaned over and kissed me. "Your business as fiancée. Business holdings and such taken care of. Sain has documents."

"Oh, good. So I don't have to worry about any of that?"

Dedare gestured a *no*.

"And Sain will tell me what to do?"

Dedare laughed. "Will you listen to Sain?"

"Maybe. Well, just don't die or get me upset again." We kissed and rubbed cheeks. At least Dedare had arranged contingencies. So much worrying about nothing on my part.

Then my brooch rang. The message I received was broken up, garbled, but the substance was that Sweety was experiencing pains and would like us to join her in the hotel's medical office.

Dedare and I had listened to the message together, so after it finished we ran out our door.

Outside we were grabbed by two people, and I was injected with a substance. The next thing I recognized was waking up on a bare floor.

After I'd regained consciousness, I looked around and realized I was on the top floor of the new library. I spent a few moments looking for Dedare. I found him slouched behind one of the supporting pillars.

"Dedare, are you okay?"

"Headache. Extreme headache. Want to throw up." He moaned, which was quite unlike him.

What could I do about an extreme headache? "Let me help you sit up slowly." I worked with Dedare, and he finally moved into a sitting position.

"I have my pack here. Do you want some water?" I didn't know what else to ask.

"Water welcome."

So I rummaged in my pack. I was sure Dedare's pack also had water, but now wasn't the time to search. Dedare sipped from my water bottle and gradually regained his composure. I suspected his headache had begun to pass.

"Dedare, why have we been brought here?" Then I smelled smoke.

We grabbed each other, and I moved him toward the elevator. I pushed him inside and followed, and then the elevator door closed.

"Dedare, see if you can send our elevator down to the bottom floor," I suggested.

He shook his head. Apparently he was still befuddled from the drugs we'd been given.

"Dedare, I'm not an engineer. Can you get this elevator moving?" I laughed. "When Testarn and I were in here and facing problems, he pulled out his handy toolkit. It was a miniature one. Do you have one of those?" Dedare laughed. He put his hand in his pocket and came out with a toolkit similar to Testarn's. What was it with guys and toolkits?

Dedare hunkered down at the control board and began working. I loved to watch him work but not so much at the moment.

"Ah, Dedare. The smoke's getting strong. Is there anything you want me to do?"

"Quiet is good. Part owner information," said Dedare.

Perhaps insulting, but I understood where he came from. Although I wasn't entirely sure about the *part owner* comment.

I started to huff a little from the smoke and eventually lay down on the elevator floor. Lower is better when smoke was involved, I decided.

The elevator started to move. I started to lift myself from the floor. "Lie down. Smoke still strong," said Dedare.

Arguing seemed silly.

Eventually the elevator doors opened and we were pulled out.

Dedare had called his security staff. They loaded the two of us on stretchers and proceeded to my helicopter, and we returned to the hotel. Dedare thanked his staff, and we shuffled to our rooms.

"Dedare, I'm tired and stressed. Can we just go to bed and sleep for about twelve hours? Do you know what I'm saying?"

"Want to spend twelve hours alone with me?" asked Dedare.

"The most wonderful thing in the world," I replied, grinning.

Chapter Twenty-Seven

The next morning after our breakfast companions noticed Dedare and me having a coughing deluge, they demanded an explanation. Everyone wanted to know why we hadn't called for help. I tried to explain the situation we'd escaped from and the injection and that these occurrences had sucked the energy out of us both. All we had wanted at the time was twelve hours sleep.

"You both do look pale this morning. Perhaps you should have an easy day," said Hart, the doctor amongst us. "I can examine you if you wish, but I'm sure I'll only find the effects of a sedative and smoke."

"The easy day sounds wonderful," I commented. "Vara should probably be updated."

"Will do that," said Sain. "Teeka and I talk to him today."

"That's a relief. Just tell him to add the details to my file."

Laughter rang around the table. We all seemed to like Vara.

Sweety said, "Ah, Syl, I don't think I can go on those two tours today. I too need to have an easy day and give the babies much needed rest. Sorry. I'm going to record a cooking video. That'll take up my time."

"Considering the false alarms you had yesterday a reasonable decision," I commented. "And I want to see your cooking video this evening. In the meantime I'll do the tours. My presence had been requested, anyway. So I'll go and let the tour guide answer all the questions—even mine. A holiday for me." I laughed.

I didn't think anyone actually agreed with my holiday comment. I sure didn't. However, I knew my day needed to be lighter than normal.

"Extra security needed. I will accompany Syl," said Sain.

"I have meetings. Cannot go," said Dedare.

"I will go," said Teeka.

"My presence sufficient." Sain sounded slightly frustrated.

No one argued with Sain whether they agreed or not. And a silence descended. So Dedare defused the situation by saying, "Teeka required for hotel security." Dedare could be tactful with his employees, and I loved him dearly for that.

Reena jumped in. "Father, Syl, everyone, two new friends from school."

Mom said, "Reena, making friends is wonderful. What are their names?"

"Binti and Boota et Tong," replied Reena.

Those names rang several bells in my mind, so I gave Mom the signal to dig out more information.

"Are they brothers?" Mom asked.

"Yes, and twins," answered Reena. "One class same. Friendly to me."

Not too friendly I hoped.

"You'll have to bring them around to meet us," said Mama A.

"This afternoon to see hotel library," said Reena.

I wasn't going to be here, so I sent glances to Sweety and Mama A.

"What time will they arrive?" said Mom. "I'd like to meet them."

They agreed upon a time, and Reena appeared pleased to have been the subject of interest even though I knew the interest was actually concern for her well-being.

I glanced at Dedare and recognized a pleased facial expression with the interest we took in Reena—trying to keep her out of trouble.

"Well, I need to get together with today's tour guide, so please excuse me. I'll catch up with everyone this evening." I hoped to have a relaxing day after last night.

"I'll accompany you, Sylvestine. I'd like to find out if there's room for me on today's tours," said my father.

What's going on? I thought Dad would have to deal with the Particlan ambassadors every day. Although I guessed it would be natural for a diplomat to learn about the world of his assignment, I wished I could read his mind.

So Dad, Sain, and I walked over to Reception and found the tour guide of the day. The guide turned out to be Villa, who ran our last tour, so we were comfortable with his presence. While we waited for the tour participants to arrive, Sain pulled an item out of a pocket and said, "Gift from Dedare. Tool kit to keep Syl out of danger." He laughed uproariously.

"Very funny, Sain, but not a bad idea. Do you know how to use it?"

Sain took a moment to realize I teased him in retaliation for his previous comment.

I did get along well with the Sath brothers.

"I also received a tool kit," said my father. "I'm not quite sure why."

After I returned this evening, Dedare would die a slow death. "Dad, why don't you give it to me? You know I'm more mechanically inclined than you are." He readily gave up the toolkit, and I now had an item with which to harass my fiancé.

"I'm glad you could accompany us, Syl," said Richard Branson. "I'd been disappointed with your previous prior commitments."

"Now, what do we have? I'm out of touch with today's schedule. Sweety was actually going to join the tour in my place."

"First off we're going to see what's essentially a farmer's market for hotels. The hotels send representatives to buy product for their restaurants and other necessities," said Richard Branson. "It's actually quite interesting how the purchase and distribution of foodstuffs, toiletries, and other items are handled. I imagine it's different in numerous respects on each world."

"Why are you interested in these procedures, Richard?" He didn't act like a procurement officer to me.

"A little weird, right? Well, my father wants me to run more of our properties. So he added a ski resort to my responsibilities. Of course, the resort has a hotel and restaurant attached. So they both need products to sustain their guests. And there are probably other items for the resort I need worry about. This trip is all about learning what's necessary for a ski resort. Of course I haven't seen one on Particle, but my questions remain the same."

I laughed. "You really haven't bothered me with questions, Richard. When is that about to change?"

"Very soon, Syl," answered Richard. "I've been trying to be discreet and not annoy you." We both had a good laugh.

"Well, you've done a fine job." We grinned. "However, please do ask questions. They'll help me run my own hotel. And I don't think there's too much competition between Particle and Earth, at least at the moment."

We laughed, and I put the situation aside.

Richard had an accurate description of the farmer's market for hotels. I wandered by so many booths I lost count. I knew someone at the Sath-Ooby Golden Hotel looked after procurement, but I'd have to dig to find out who was in charge. On the other hand, I could ask Cara. However, today's trip did let me recognize there were products I wanted to use to sparkle up the hotel, and this would be an excellent way to meet more employees.

I saw many items that would be appropriate for an Amenities room, so I needed to bring Reena here— actually, Reena and the hotel representative in charge of procurement.

"Manager Syl, time. Next stop close. Time to proceed," said Villa. Our guide needed to keep us moving. I'd find a future time to return to this fascinating market.

I turned around to survey our tour participants and found one in distress. "Dad, do you have a problem?"

"Sorry, Syl, but some of the perfumes I've come across today are too strong for my liking. I do have a minor ailment, or allergy I guess you could call it. My doctor's not concerned, but right now my body is reacting."

"As am I, but to a lesser degree than you are." I turned to Villa. "Would you arrange for the helicopter to return Charles to the hotel? His allergies are causing a problem."

I studied Dad. "Make sure you report to Hart. I'll be notifying him of the problem, and since he's spending today at the hotel that's serendipitous for you."

Villa sweetly helped Dad to the helicopter and relayed our instructions. I waved goodbye and immediately notified Hart of the situation.

I wasn't particularly worried about my father. His reaction was perfectly normal in the situation, but alien scents were involved, so I wanted to be careful. I decided my new hotel label should become *first contact specialist*. I laughed internally. Anyway, I needed to talk to Cara and the tour guides to watch out for unusual or overpowering scents in the future.

Scents should be added to our General First Contact Guide when we had one. Perhaps required reading before traveling to a new planet. I imagined Dad had a diplomatic First Contact Guide. Would he let me take a look?

Villa announced, "Ooby Theme Park. Next on agenda. Experiences for everyone."

Innumerable experiences were certainly available. Villa tried to keep us together for one ride or situation at a time so he didn't lose track of any of us. Although a bit of an unruly bunch, he tried to pick experiences he thought we'd all enjoy. Villa mostly accomplished his goal at the theme park.

Our first activity was a ride taking us through ancient Particlan history—could you say dinosaurs? Of course dinosaurs weren't part of the exhibit but large Particlan animals were. Actually this was a wonderful ride and would especially be for children. You could either ride in an open-air tram or be strapped onto an animal. Villa made us stay in a tram for safety, and Sain agreed with his reasoning. I needed to come back one day and try riding the animals when I wasn't inhibited. Harrumph.

However, I learned a great deal about Particlan pre-history. My mind fixated on the fact that numerous ancient Particlan large animals continued to exist to this day—unlike on Earth.

Our next experience consisted of a ride where we strapped in and experienced various water activities. Most of our tour had waterproof clothing—we'd learned by this time. I'd brought my swimsuit along as well, so I changed and rejoined the group.

This was my favorite experience of the theme park. We dipped through the bottoms of waterfalls and then went down rapids. The ride climbed up high rivers and then meandered through a series of lakes.

At the end of our boat's wandering, we drifted to shore and found lunch waiting. Perfect timing.

"Villa, what's happening next?" I asked after I'd had my fill of food.

"Return to beginning. Gather more participants. On to next activity."

"Will it be wet during our return to our starting location?" I asked.

"No water anticipated."

"Good. Then I'm going to change back into my regular clothes." Swimsuits were fine for a while, but only a short time.

At our starting location, we were joined by new tour participants.

"Villa, where are these people from?" They weren't from the hotel. I would've recognized their garments.

"*High Enlightenment* outliers. Members of religion. Respect for height."

Villa's words made no sense. Perhaps our afternoon experiences would enlighten me.

Our group rode via gondola to the highest museum on Particle. The location hosted a museum purporting to contain the highest items on Particle. Before we had time to investigate the museum, verify the claims, and actually understand what the statement meant, we took another gondola even higher. Our final destination contained a swimming pool and a diving board, and I had no idea why. A viewing platform ran around the entire top of the mountain.

Since there was a diving board, I knew the Particlans present would love a display from an alien. I warmed up with a few laps and then performed a number of my comfortable dives.

The *High Enlightenment* members of our tour were astounded by my antics. According to Villa, they'd practiced their entire lives to be long limbed and fast. They were speed sprinters and long-distance runners. Recently they'd added diving to their repertoire. My display had astounded them. They asked me to reproduce the dives I'd just done so they could study them closely and make their own attempts.

If I understood Particlan electronics, recording devices were everywhere, but I didn't care. I loved to perform.

My dives were mostly perfect, but I knew the Particlans would improvise anyway. Then I realized the rest of our tour group were also astounded by my antics.

"Richard, did you mind me showing the Particlans my dives?" I asked. I hadn't really wanted to take over our tour group. Richard and Thad, I believed, had previously coordinated with Villa regarding the contents of our tour.

"Syl, your diving is unbelievable. Do whatever you want. I'll be here for you. Of course, adding Martian antics to bedevil the Particlans is not a bad thing from the General Manager of the Sath-Ooby Golden Hotel."

"Thanks, Richard. It's hard to know where to intersperse alien ideas and actions. Thankfully the Particlans were receptive and actually suggested a repeat of my dives so they could study them."

Villa interrupted our musings.

"Time to change. Time to experience. Particlan sports game."

Really? I needed to watch a basketball game, or something similar? Okay, not an interesting activity, but I'd be polite.

The Particlan game of running and throwing balls to attempt goals reminded me of a human game. Of course, the Particlans added the idea of water balls and sticks to puncture them. What a surprise and what a mess your attempt could turn out to be.

Villa organized a game for our group and stood by the sidelines and laughed. I imagined we made a pretty comical group, but I enjoyed the endeavor.

Eventually the end of the tour and dinner time arrived. I cleaned up and wandered down to the new restaurant. I found a chair beside Dedare and gave him a hug. Then I noticed others at our table.

"Welcome, Vara. How do you like our new multi-species restaurant? Something you have never experienced, I imagine."

Ignoring my teasing, he said, "Investigating incident involved. Library last night. Dedare and Syl."

"Very efficient. I imagine Teeka called you." I didn't really want to talk about last night's mess, but Vara wanted to do his job. And I imagined his superiors were putting pressure on him to solve the aliens' problems.

"Dedare made call. Concerned about Syl. And friends, guests."

Vara quizzed me about what I remembered from last night. Comparing viewpoints was an excellent way to test our fallible short-term memory. In that respect I assumed Irions were similar to humans from the nature of his questioning.

"Syl has situations. More than normal. Particlans, Irions, humans."

I ignored Vara's insinuation I got into a lot of trouble. "Do you have any answers as to who is doing this, Vara? I'd really like the situation to stop. I want to have some quiet time to learn how to run the hotel and be with Dedare."

I gave Dedare a big smile and then gave my dinner order to the hovering waiter. Our long day had made me hungry.

Vara stood and then said, "Must run office. Clear remaining work. Always something left."

He studied me. "Dinner sometime soon."

"Just give me a call, Vara, and I'll see if I'm free and whether Dedare is also." I knew Dedare wanted to discuss our comments about dinner, but the timing wasn't right.

Mom, Reena, and two young male Particlans showed up before Vara had a chance to leave. Introductions made us realize the boys were Binti and Boota et Tong, brothers. They were also the sons of the high school principal I'd met when we thought Reena was lost during our early days on Particle.

While we were being introduced and finding room at the dinner table for four new participants, Vara received a call from the boys' mother, Samilt et Tong. Apparently she'd lost track of her boys and decided they were missing, and she needed to talk to the police about the situation.

Vara reassured her they were fine and sitting with him in the new restaurant. He handed his brooch to one of the boys to talk to his mother.

After that conversation, the boy handed Vara's brooch to me.

"Wish meeting tomorrow. Both Reena, Sylvestine. Mutual interests discussion," said Samilt.

I mumbled to Dedare that the principal wanted to meet with Reena and me. After I saw the look in Dedare's eyes, I asked, "Do you wish Reena's father to be present?"

"Father not necessary."

So, after more eye contact with Dedare, I agreed to go to school tomorrow morning with Reena.

"Why don't you come along with Reena and me, Dedare?" I tried to study his facial emotions. "I'm sure you'd be welcome even though she said you weren't necessary." I tried not to laugh at Samilt's words.

"Unnecessary. Syl and Reena have control. Come to me with problems, though." Dedare started laughing.

I wasn't impressed with his attitude. "We'll have control, don't worry. We won't have any problems." Since I was for some reason miffed at his remarks I didn't reply to his laughter with my own.

Oh well, we were from different worlds and had different interpretations of words. I needed to stay flexible with my dealings with aliens—especially ones I loved dearly.

I glanced around the dinner table. "I have a suggestion for after dinner. Perhaps we could go to the hotel's game room and try some of the board games and other items there. Cara, do you have time this evening to teach us a game or two?"

"Games learning experience. Happy to help. Many games available."

I laughed. "Probably more games than we can possibly learn in one sitting. So, if anyone is interested let's retire to the game room, which is next to the library."

Most of group hopped up—Sweety, perhaps a little slowly—and joined me in the game room. The room had a pleasant and relaxed atmosphere. A few guests were already indulging in games.

Cara grabbed a table and searched for a game from the shelving. While she interested some of the aliens in playing, I took a look at the other games being played in the games room.

"Manager Syl, welcome. Wish to try. Game of chance?" asked a guest I recognized being at the hotel for a couple of weeks.

"Will I lose all my money?" I asked.

They pointed at the tokens piled up.

"Fake money, lose," replied the guest I recognized. We all laughed.

"Okay, deal me in. I want to learn this game and lose money, of course," I said. I loved games of all sorts but particularly board games. And we hadn't played any since we'd gotten to Particle.

I had a great time with the Particlans playing with me. They taught me the basics, and then I taught them a little strategy. At first, they were taken aback at my antics, but then they started adding their own. We had a fun time.

Glancing over at Dedare, I knew he'd reached his limit. "Guys, this was great. If you are ever looking for a player and I'm not in a crisis with the hotel, please come to my office and invite me. I very much enjoyed our game."

I walked over to Dedare and whispered in his ear. Then he said, "Tiredness this evening. Wish to resume game another time." His team members understood his words, so we left and went to our suite.

We relaxed in our living room with a couple of drinks. "Dedare, is everything okay? I mean okay with your businesses. I want to learn about them although I don't seem to have much time right now."

Dedare laughed and cuddled up to me. It was late and time for bed.

However, Dedare wanted a bit of exercise before we retired, so I suggested a walk along a canal. He hadn't seen one yet, so the walk would increase his knowledge of Ooby.

A faint breeze stirred the pleasant evening air. A whiff of a floral scent caught my attention, and then I noticed the flowering trees lining our path. I pointed them out to Dedare, and he gave me a squeeze.

We found an accessible area on the side of the canal containing a bench giving a lovely unobstructed view up and down the canal. Dedare and I walked closer to the edge.

The next thing I knew something had been thrown over my head, tightened around my body, and I landed in the water. I heard a second splash and assumed Dedare had fallen to the same fate.

I struggled with my bindings and although I was a strong swimmer I had a hard time keeping my head above water, and the bag over my face made breathing difficult.

Dedare! I couldn't remember whether he could swim. So he was in the same predicament as I was, or even worse.

Then a miracle happened. I felt myself being lifted up and towed. Toward the bank of the canal, I assumed. Set down on land, someone pulled off the cover that had confined me, and I started to breathe easier. I glanced around and discovered the same thing happening to Dedare.

Starting to come back to Earth—okay, wrong expression—with my body starting to calm, I noticed our rescuers were members of High Enlightenment, the group I'd been introduced to on our recent tour.

"Dedare, are you okay?"

"Wet and annoyed. Want to find culprits."

Okay, Dedare was returning to normal.

"Who shall I thank for our rescue? I know you are members of High Enlightenment, whom I met earlier today."

"No thanks necessary. Honored to meet. Diving routines delightful."

"Did you just happen by and notice our distress?"

"Out brisk walk. Attempt for limbering. Exercise most important."

"Well, I'm most grateful you came along when you did. I manage the Sath-Ooby Golden Hotel, so if you ever wish a free stay, please let me know. I wish to thank you for rescuing us."

"Show more diving?"

Before we had a chance to continue our conversation, Hart and Sweety appeared. Then I heard a helicopter landing.

"What's going on?"

"What's going on? You two are going on—right to the hospital. One of these lovely people called the ambulance, who then called me because an alien or two were involved in an incident. Surprise, surprise, it turned out to be Syl and Dedare."

I tried to interrupt.

"Yes, yes, I know it wasn't your faults. In fact, this young lady has kept the coverings you were wrapped up in so I can give them to Vara. Thank you very much, dear," Hart said to the High Enlightenment member I had been conversing with previously.

Hart laughed. "Anyway, Syl, you are both going to the hospital to be checked out. Probably nothing wrong with either of you, but I don't want any random bacteria or virus to suddenly show up in your lungs." He shook his head. "I'm your doctor, so you have no say in the matter."

I glanced at Dedare, and he shrugged. Such a human response.

The medics wanted to strap us down on gurneys and Hart agreed. "Syl, this is their job. Let them do it."

So Dedare and I relaxed enough to lie down and be administered to. And then we took a ride in a helicopter ambulance.

At the hospital we were familiar with we landed in ER and were subjected to numerous tests.

"Syl, just relax. These guys are great, and they want more experience with aliens. They know what they're doing, so just let them do it," said Sweety. "Trust me. I have experience in this hospital."

We both laughed.

Having my best friends, Sweety and Hart, along to help us improved my mood. So Dedare and I allowed the professionals to do their jobs. And spending a bit of time in the local ER gave me a better understanding of local dynamics.

Then Vara arrived. "Causing problems again? Police other activities. Aliens want attention."

Of course, Vara had a challenging time containing his laughter after uttering those words.

Annoyed, I asked, "Do you have any questions? We would be happy to answer them. However, we'd also be happy to go home."

Dedare and Vara exchanged glances.

"Any information available? Source of attackers? Reason for happening?"

I sighed. "Why don't you ask our rescuers? Perhaps they saw something. The whole incident was a surprise to me. Dedare and I were just out for a walk along the canal. In fact, I didn't even see or hear our attackers. The first thing I noticed was the bag being put over my head."

Wordlessly, Vara left to walk over to the High Enlightenment group. For some reason, they had followed us to the ER.

Hart appeared, so I asked, "Can we get out of here?"

"Soon. Just waiting for results of your blood tests to see if you picked up any bug in the canal. Otherwise, everything looks good."

We talked about the possibility of catching something from the canal water. Our conversation seemed inconclusive to me.

Vara returned, so I demanded information.

"Little information available. Two culprits seen. Same height, build."

"But what about their faces? Can any of the High Enlightenment group describe them?"

"Both faces covered. Ran from scene. Left no evidence."

"Sure they did. They left the coverings," I protested.

"Investigation under control. Syl recover tonight. Discussion in morning."

Okay, I received Vara's message to leave the sleuthing to him.

So Dedare and I took a second attempt at relaxing

on the couch. Apparently, I fell asleep in his arms because my next conscious thought was of the covers being pulled up around me.

Chapter Twenty-Eight

The next morning, Reena and I skipped our usual practice with the hotel swim team. We wanted to meet Samilt et Tong in a relaxed mood, both mentally and physically.

Our meeting took place in the principal's office.

"Reena, Sylvestine, thanks," said Samilt et Tong.

"We're happy to be here. What do you wish to discuss?" I was curious as to our meeting's purpose. "Is Reena doing well in school?"

Reena gave me a disgruntled look, but I ignored her.

"Reena good student. Accomplishing work well. Discussion related others."

The principal's words appeared positive towards Reena. Apparently our discussion was related to other topics.

"Reena try out. For school team. Join Olympic hopefuls."

"Reena, congratulations, your principal wants you to try out for the school team. What do you think?"

If my interpretation was incorrect, the principal would let me know I imagined.

"Wonderful chance to meet other students and learn," said Reena, with a huge grin on her face.

"Your presence mentioned. By other students. Witnessed your diving," replied the principal.

I wondered when they had seen Reena diving. At the hotel's employee pool? I'd have to study my memories. Maybe she'd performed for the principal's sons.

"Request for Sylvestine," continued Samilt et Tong.

"What do you require?" She'd made me curious.

"Diving demonstration students," said the principal.

That I couldn't refuse. "I'd love to show your students some dives. Reena could also."

"Diving instruction possible?" she asked.

Teaching had always interested me. "Possibly. I'm busy running the hotel. I'll let you know when I have time available," I said.

Her face didn't reflect happiness, but I needed to manage my time properly, and the hotel was foremost.

On that note, I left Reena to enjoy her classes and I returned to the hotel.

I found Dedare in my office. "Meeting okay?" he asked.

"Oh, fine. The principal wants Reena to try out for the school's Olympic team. And she wants me to give a diving demonstration and perhaps tutor students. Reena said yes to trying out for the team, and I said yes to a diving demonstration. As for instructing the students, I told her I'd just have to see what time I had. The hotel takes up a lot."

Dedare smiled.

"I do want to focus on our hotel. It's important to me."

"And to me," said Dedare, moving closer and giving me a kiss or three.

"Okay, okay, no more fooling around this morning. I have work to do." Of course, I added a big grin, and Dedare understood my reluctance to discontinue our amorous moves.

Just in the nick of time, or perhaps not, my father arrived.

"Hey Dad, how're things?" I asked.

"Very well. Understanding with other diplomats continues to develop, and we're all learning about the various alien races. In that regard, after pushing from numerous sources, the Particlan Olympic Committee decided to allow aliens in the Olympics as a test sport. However, in swimming and diving only. The participants will be able to vie for awards. Depending on the outcome, the committee will perhaps allow these and other sports in the future."

"That's wonderful. I don't think we could've expected more. You've done a fabulous job." I gave him a hug and laughed. "Now that you've accomplished this major hurdle, what's next on your plate?"

"Quite a few things, actually. However, I cannot yet talk about them. Particle and its history make this an interesting world. Now I must leave—I have meetings."

We hugged, and Dad waved to Dedare as he headed out the door.

"Father fits position of ambassador," said Dedare.

"I agree with you. He's quite happy meeting new people and in particular aliens. And the history and practices of a new world will keep him fascinated for a very long time."

"Work for me?" asked Dedare.

"Well, you'd have to ask him, but I don't think so. I suspect he wants to be an envoy for humans and work for the Earth government. However, go ahead and ask. I haven't known him very long." And I certainly hadn't.

"Oh well, I must get some paperwork done," I said, adding a sigh.

"Occupy conference table?" asked Dedare.

"Of course, any time." I hadn't thought of that occurring on a regular basis. Dedare did have an office in our suite, but perhaps he wanted to gauge the hotel's ebb and flow. Or even keep an eye on me. Harrumph. Perhaps an overreaction on my part.

"I'd quite enjoy your company. We'll have lunch together." He smiled and went to work. My day had perked up. Of course, my office didn't turn out to be tranquil today. Next up was my mother.

"Syl, I need to talk to you." Mama A glanced at my conference table. "Oh, Dedare, how nice to see you."

"Want me depart?" Dedare didn't understand Mom's problem and neither did I.

"Oh no, not at all. This affects you, too." A distressed look occupied Mom's face. "Dedare, I'm trying to write a history of Particle, as we discussed. And then as you put a bigger toehold on Particle how this Particlan history affects Sath Enterprises."

I caught Dedare looking at his naked toes. Apparently, toehold hadn't translated well. Of course, I really wanted to know how it *had* translated. So many pictures fluttered through my consciousness.

"Yes," said Dedare, in typical Irion terseness.

I had no idea what his *yes* referred to.

"Well, I have a lack of source material. The main library is restricting me to certain sections which don't really answer my research questions. So I don't know what to do."

"Charles," responded Dedare.

I laughed. "Of course. Mom, get Dad involved. This really is partially a diplomatic situation, and he just solved one problem, so he probably has a bit of time on his hands." Or maybe not.

"Excellent. Dedare, thank you for suggesting Charles." Mom laughed. "Now, how shall I do my research in the meantime?"

I laughed. "Why don't you use the hotel library? You're sure to find history books applicable to your needs. What little I've seen of the library, it's quite well stocked. And if there aren't any or there are gaps we need to add them, oh librarian."

"I am so glad I came here today to whine, Syl. And Dedare was a bonus. Now you guys have solved all, well today's, problems, and I can get on to my work. See you later."

Mom sailed out the door in a fine mood.

"Not a quiet day, Dedare." Actually even busier than normal.

Dedare smiled. Then his smile disappeared after he glanced at the two humans entering my office. Sweety was obviously in a hormonally induced depression, and Hart didn't know what to do.

Being an intelligent male, Dedare said, "Hart, need discussion," and pointed outside.

So Hart and Dedare escaped, and I eased Sweety toward my conference table. "Sweety, what's wrong?"

"The babies are going to be here any day now. I want to go home to Mars." She patted her belly. "I think of my family all the time. Not Hart, of course, but my mom and dad. They would so love to be at the birth. I can't even send them mail to let them know about their grandbabies as Dedare doesn't have a ship orbiting Mars. By the way, Dedare needs to do something about communications for us."

Sweety had a valid point. I'd bring this up with Dedare at a more convenient time.

"Sweety, have you and Hart got everything ready for the babies? I mean cribs, clothing, and such."

"There are still a dozen or so specific items we need. And lots of clothing and diapers, of course. Babies are so messy," said Sweety with a laugh.

"Well, I have a plan for the rest of the day until dinner time. You and I need to go shopping. The babies should not want for anything, and I need to buy them lots of toys."

An idiotic grin grew on Sweety's face. Crisis passed, hormones under control I suspected. And I got to go shopping.

I called Hart and Dedare into my office from where they'd been hiding—cowards that they were.

"Sweety and I are going shopping. Hart, can you give instructions to the helicopter pilot about where the shopping areas are? And Dedare, do we have enough money on our credit cards to shop for the babies?"

"Adequate," he replied.

"Okay, we'll be back later. I'm not sure when but for dinner of course. If you need to talk to us, call. Hart, you owe me one. And Dedare, think about finding a way for us to communicate with Mars. Sweety needs to talk to her parents."

Dedare nodded. He understood my underlying messages.

Solving crises had a happy ending when I had a shopping trip.

Sweety and I had an enjoyable lunch at a new restaurant. Their menu reflected what we could eat, so the idea of aliens residing in Ooby had caught on. Of course, Sweety, being pregnant with twins, wanted more food than she normally would. The restaurant was solicitous and made Sweety feel special. Of course, her status was obvious at this point in her pregnancy.

For no particular reason I'd been slightly anxious all day. I had no idea where the mood came from, but my feelings didn't go away, even when we shopped. Although come to think of it being thrown in the canal last night contributed to my irritability.

I helped Sweety carry her purchases. Actually, our pilot noticed us struggling and ferried our parcels back to my plane. He asked me to call him the next time we were similarly burdened.

Sweety sat quietly while I examined canvases and paints in the hobby shop. I had an enjoyable twenty minutes before Sweety needed to be on the move.

"I think it's time to return to the hotel. I have some work to do, and you probably need a rest, Sweety."

"You're right. I'm tired."

"And I think our transport has reached its limit of shopping bags."

We laughed and took off back to our ride and our ever-patient pilot. Sweety fell asleep during our trip home. Thankfully, she was strapped in. I phoned Hart and asked him to meet us and bring Dedare along to carry packages. I think my statement shocked Hart. He had little idea about what Sweety had been up to. Hart would have the surprise of his life.

The four of us took the mound of packages to my office so I could find mine within the pile. Of course, I had only a half dozen. A few clothes and canvases, paints, and brushes. I'd remembered I needed to produce numerous paintings for Reena. We were both getting a kick out of selling my paintings—she got a commission, and I got recognition and remuneration—at least enough to pay for supplies. I thought Reena would turn out to be quite the entrepreneur, much like her father.

As I'd predicted, Hart was shocked at the pile of Sweety's purchases. Dedare quietly helped him take the shopping bags to their rooms and then bowed out. Hart and Sweety were in for a discussion, I imagined.

"Only few purchases," said Dedare after he'd returned to my office.

"I only needed a bit of clothing and a pile of painting supplies. I didn't even ask if you needed anything. Are you short?"

"Height not changed."

The laughter gave Dedare and me a moment's relief. Thinking back, we hadn't laughed enough recently.

"Perhaps you and I should go shopping one afternoon. I think we'd enjoy the experience of being together."

"Lots of presents," Dedare said.

"That's not what I meant. Maybe I could pick out some underwear for you."

The shock on his face amused me. "Okay, maybe not underwear. Is there anything you need?" I asked.

"Time alone." Dedare smiled.

"Well, then, we could have lunch together in the marketplace and pick up a few items for you afterward in the market. What do you think? Is there something else you need to purchase?"

Dedare didn't answer.

"Anyway, we could spend a few hours together and away from the hotel."

"Excellent plan. Details to be arranged."

I wouldn't argue with his agreeableness. However, we'd leave Sweety at home. Whew, what a shopper.

Although dinner time neared I decided to try and accomplish a modicum of office work. My afternoon had been a write off in that respect. Then Thad popped into my office.

"Syl, we're going on a tour tomorrow." I saw Richard and Testarn standing behind him. "Is there any chance you can join? You're so much fun. Interesting things always seem to happen when you're around."

Before I had a chance to answer, Cara crashed into my office. "Important note arrive." She held up a piece of paper and then thrust it at me.

Cara's body shook and I had no clue why. Then I realized the note was open, had no envelope, so she'd probably read it to figure out who it was for.

I turned to Dedare and pushed the note at him. "Do you have your reader? Can you read this? Cara, do you know what it says?"

"Yes, to knowledge," Cara answered.

"Quiet. Let me read. Addressed to me and Syl," said Dedare. His color blanched as he continued to read.

"Dedare, talk to me." I didn't like the look on his face.

"Reena abducted. Must find the Five Keys of Enlightenment in a timely manner to have her released."

Chapter Twenty-Nine

Reena abducted! I couldn't think clearly, so Dedare must be in deep despair.

The Five Keys of Enlightenment sounded religious. I wondered if my old buddy, the Chief Motivator, was involved in this crime. Or perhaps our new friends the High Enlightenment group.

"Syl and Dedare, we're here for you. We'll help you find Reena," said Richard Branson. "Just tell us what to do."

I took a deep breath. "Let's all sit around the conference table. I want to call in a few more people. Okay, Dedare?" After all, his daughter was our concern.

"Yes. Organize."

So I rounded up Sain, Teeka, Mom, Charles, Sweety, and Hart. They added to my previous collection of Cara, Richard, Thad, and Testarn.

"Okay, here's the deal. Reena's been abducted. We're not sure why—the note didn't really specify— but we need to find the Five Keys of Enlightenment to free her."

"Let me see the note, Syl," demanded Hart.

"Let me read it to everyone first," I responded. "You must find the Five Keys to Enlightenment to free Reena Sath. The first clue is contained in the enclosed bag." I handed the note to Hart but showed the contents of the bag to everyone else.

"From what I can determine, we have a small bag that contains a vial of something that looks like water, an emblem, and a tiny key. So we have to figure out what they all mean and how they relate to each other." I passed the bag around the table.

After the bag got to Mom, she wiped her eyes— after all her step-granddaughter was involved— studied the contents, and then took out the emblem. "Syl, this metal symbol is the emblem for the Heeght-Ooby Pre-school, the one Reena goes to. Cara, do you agree?" Mom passed the emblem.

"Heeght-Ooby Pre-school correct." Cara's eyes were also full of tears.

I took a few deep breaths. "Sain, Teeka, has anyone called Vara? He should know about Reena's abduction."

"Knowledge is good," Vara responded, standing in my doorway.

"How did you get here so fast?" I'd barely finished explaining the situation to everyone, and Vara showed up.

"Going by, close. Sain informed news. Help with abduction."

"Help wonderful for my daughter," said a solemn Dedare.

"Vara, what should we do? Tell us what to do, please," I implored. The room full of people needed to be organized since they wanted to help.

Vara took the small bag we'd been passing around the table. "Medal for what?" he asked.

Cara answered. "Heeght-Ooby Pre-school emblem."

"Reena Sath's school?" Vara wondered.

"Yes. In fact, Reena and I were there this morning talking to the principal. I came back to the hotel, and Reena stayed to go to class," I said. "At the time, she was happy. The principal had asked her to try out for the school's Olympic team, and the principal had also asked me to do a diving demonstration and teach diving if I had time."

"Whoever abducted her has taken her brooch, otherwise she'd try to contact us," I pointed out.

"Hart, vial contents?" asked Vara after a moment of silence and thought.

"I'll take it to the lab and get a priority analysis." Hart grabbed the vial and put it in one of his sample bags.

"I think we need two helicopters. Hart can have one to run to the lab, and we need one to get to Reena's school. Hart, join us as soon as you receive the results from the vial. Everyone agree?" I asked.

Total agreement quickly appeared.

"Analysis needed," said Vara. "Key to understanding."

Nobody argued with Vara. Was the vial one of the five keys? Or is what we find after we figure out the puzzle the first key? Or perhaps the key in the little bag was the key? My mind boggled. Our current puzzle had too many variables.

"Okay, everyone. Grab a backpack from Reception. We may need the sustenance during our investigation. Add anything else you need, of course. Let's meet back here in fifteen minutes."

With purpose in mind, our crew scattered.

"Nice organization, Syl," said Vara, after everyone had gathered with backpacks and supplies. I'd taken a short side trip to my rooms and picked up a couple of things and also gotten a pack for Vara.

"If you mean the backpacks, thank Cara. She's very organized. I don't know what I'd do without her."

Hart had gone directly to his helicopter, so Sweety picked up a backpack for him. We were all soon ready, so we traipsed up to the roof for the short ride to Reena's school. Dedare had called ahead, so the principal met us and led us to her office.

"What is problem?" asked Samilt et Tong.

I thought Dedare had explained everything during his first call, but he repeated the situation and showed her the note, the school emblem, and the little key. The vial was with Hart, of course.

"Do you know what the Five Keys of Enlightenment are?" I asked the principal.

Samilt professed ignorance.

Before we had a chance to decide on a plan of action, Hart called. "The substance in the vial is just plain water, Syl. Does that help?"

"I have to think about your news. Come over here to the school. I'm sure we'll need your help."

I explained the situation to everyone. "Does this mean the Key to Enlightenment is found in water somewhere in the school?" I asked Vara.

"Logical thinking, Syl," said Vara. "My top choice."

"Principal Samilt et Tong, where do you have water in the school? Where can we look for the key?" I assumed we were looking for a physical key.

The principal led us all over the school in search of water. We checked out large water bottles used in dispensers for the students; water tanks in the science labs full of fish; water containers outside collecting rainwater; and outside tubs like hot tubs for students to clean up in after sports activities.

Finally, the principal said, "Out of ideas."

I had no argument—I was out of energy. Then I had a thought. "We haven't checked the inside swimming pool where Reena has been swimming and diving." Why hadn't the Principal thought of that location? Probably as tired as I was.

Those of us with swimsuits checked out the bottom of the pool while the rest searched the remainder of the room.

Time passed, and the urgency in finding Reena pressed heavily. Eventually I found a bag in the bottom of the pool. I swam up, and I raised the package over my head so everyone noticed. Relief flooded the pool room. However the relief may have been premature.

I climbed out of the swimming pool and handed the bag to Dedare. The rest of us gathered round to see what I'd discovered.

Dedare pulled out a tiny key and an even smaller spoon.

"Okay, so another key and now a spoon. What does the spoon mean? Anyone?" I asked. A clue too vague for my taste and my stress level.

"It might point to any of the restaurants we've been to," said Sweety. "It could also indicate the room where I made my cooking videos."

"Also the hotel restaurant," said Richard. "Although that may be too obvious." He sighed. "I'm also thinking about food markets and bazaars. The possibilities are endless." He shook his head. "What do you think, Syl?"

"I think we need to go back to the hotel and grab some food. I know my brain is starved and needs fuel. Dedare?"

"Hotel restaurant for a brief time," he replied. Dedare's color had faded, and I worried.

"Okay, quickly to the helicopter. Let's fuel up." I certainly needed to. My stomach growled, and I wanted to get away from the school. Even though we'd found the key, I didn't like the atmosphere at the Heeght-Ooby Pre-School today.

Back at the hotel restaurant we ordered up a storm. Thad, Richard, and Testarn were still with us and continued to be concerned about Reena. Actually they'd formed a trio, which delighted me—aliens and humans bonding. Actually humans were also aliens, which I had to frequently remind myself.

Sweety walked around the Sath-Ooby Golden Restaurant, talking to guests. If she weren't pregnant, I suspected she'd lobby for a hostess job. She loved to meet people and had been quite the hostess on Irion.

"Dedare, Syl, I've found it!" she yelled. Sweety held up a small bag. I'd watched her pull an item out of the live fish tank, but I hadn't paid much attention. Sweety ran over to us—well, waddled.

"Here, Dedare. It's all yours." She thrust the bag at Dedare and then abruptly sat on the chair next to him. "The babies are cooking up a storm," she announced.

"Sweety?" I had no idea what she meant.

"Oh, they're kicking me everywhere. It's not labor, but it's not comfortable. I just need to sit and relax, and then so will they."

Now that made sense. The babies would mimic their mother in my ignorant fantasy world. So we needed to keep Sweety calm and quiet as much as possible. Even though Sweety thought her children would be here tomorrow, she still had months to go.

I pushed the babies to the back of my mind. "Dedare, what's in the bag? What clues do we have?"

He held up the bag and said, "Small key, small fish."

"Let me see the bag," I demanded. I was sure I'd come up with better descriptions. "I do see a small key and a similarly sized fish. The key is an exact copy of the others. The fish is a small golden metal fish."

"Does it remind you of your favorite fish farm?" asked Richard.

A lot of laughter resulted from Richard's question. My swimming with the fishes had been memorable apparently.

"Actually, it does. So that's one place to look. Any other ideas?" I asked. The answer couldn't be so simple.

"I bet there are a lot of fish farms with goldfish," said Thad. "This clue is vague. Probably deliberately so."

"Agreed. Anything else, anyone? We're getting desperate here." I sighed. "Finish your food and we'll go check out the oldest fish farm first, my favorite one apparently. If we don't find anything, we'll have to start on the other fish farms and also brainstorm new possibilities."

Depression about Reena's status began to take hold of me. We were being proactive, but the clues we'd just received were too generalized to convince me we were on the right track.

Nonetheless we finished our meal and took off again. We talked ourselves into positive attitudes on the helicopter, and by the time we reached our destination of my original fish farm my mood had lifted.

Everyone spread out because there were numerous pyramids to investigate. A pretty difficult task confronted us actually.

"Syl, the three of us, Thad, Testarn, and I, are going to investigate your infamous pyramid. You know, the one where you decided to swim with the fishes." Richard laughed. "Do you want to join us? Or did a different pyramid catch your eye for swimming?"

Everyone thought they were humorous. "I'll go along with you guys. The more eyes, the merrier." I laughed. "Why don't you start at the top of the pyramid? I'm going to try and find my old watering hole."

My comment brought much needed laughter.

So we went our separate ways. I had a vague remembrance of the level where I'd been stuffed into the smelly water, so I headed that way. The openings along the troughs were now secured with padlocks. I sure hoped it wasn't because of me. Although more security wouldn't be a bad idea.

I eventually came upon a small building housing the controls for the water shutoff. I turned the doorknob, and found the door unlocked. I stepped into the small shack and discovered another small bag. My heart leapt into my throat with excitement. However, before I could exit the shack and start yelling about my newfound discovery the door closed. Not only closed, but I heard the lock click. I had to assume I was now a prisoner.

My adversaries weren't too bright, I decided, because I still had my brooch. I called Cara but received no answer. I called Mom and then various others, and I still couldn't get through.

Okay, maybe I wasn't the one so bright. Why couldn't I get through? Had Hart ever told me about anything that could interfere with my brooch's signal?

I started banging on the door. Electronic signals wouldn't work, so perhaps physical ones could.

A pattern might catch someone's attention, so I had an enjoyable time—well, maybe not good—making up rhythms. Eventually, I heard a voice. "Syl, are you there? Give us a hint. This is Thad."

"Oh, thank goodness you're here, Thad. I'm locked in this shack, and I don't know how it happened. Can you get the door open?"

"Give me a minute."

I heard scrabbling and decided Thad had a plan. "There we go." The door swung open, and I escaped. I laughed and took a deep breath then gave Thad a hug—my brother and my savior.

"How did you open the door?" I glanced at my surroundings to find a knob or a keyhole.

"There was a latch holding the door closed. Sure looks like someone locked you in," commented Thaddeus.

"So I haven't been imagining my misfortunes?" I knew I hadn't.

"I don't think so and don't imagine anyone else thought that," Richard added. "Once we get to the bottom of these Five Keys of Enlightenment, we might ourselves be enlightened. What a strange but interesting planet."

"I did find the small bag with our clues, though," I said. I wondered what reaction I'd receive.

Either Thad or Richard immediately tore it out of hands after I waved it around. Testarn stood back with what I thought was an amused look on his face. I was learning to read these aliens.

I immediately called Dedare. He needed news about his daughter. And I spoke to Cara and asked her to call everyone and have them meet us at the bottom of the pyramid to examine the bag.

After we gathered at the bottom, Thad handed Dedare the bag I'd found.

Dedare studied the contents and announced, "One tiny key and one tiny stone, flat on one side. Where does the stone come from?"

That's right, he wouldn't know. Dedare had been on his ill-fated trip when I'd found the stones at the Church of the Redeemed Water Tower.

I explained my discovery and what I'd brought home for my artistic supplies. "So I think we should go to the church. There may be other places that have these stones, but that was the first place I noticed them." I paused for a moment. "Cara, are there other places we should look?"

"Obvious first place," she replied.

Cara really didn't answer my question, so off we went.

The Church of the Redeemed Water Tower was new to Dedare, so while we traveled on the helicopter I explained the history of the tower and what we'd discovered on our first trip to the church. Dedare was amused about our finding a place to shop. He listened closely to everyone's experiences.

"Cara, I know we can find stones in the church's marketplace, but are there other places we should investigate?" I asked.

"Perhaps stone sources," she replied.

Hmm, indeed a good possibility. "How many quarries provide these stones?" I asked.

"Great number offer."

Oh. So I hoped we wouldn't have to go that route. There were probably too many suppliers to make our search feasible. We entered the church market, which happened to still be open.

Most of us wandered about looking for a little bag, but Dedare gravitated toward the window and studied the Redeemed Water Tower.

I glanced over every pile or source of stones I could find, but no little bag revealed itself. Perhaps we really did need to go to one of the sources of the stones. Or maybe all of them.

"Syl, Redeemed Water Tower is possible location. Please join me." Dedare turned to Cara. "Please lead to Redeemed Water Tower."

We followed Cara out of the room. We'd been watched by the others so the whole group began the trek.

Okay, it wasn't much of a trek, and I noticed my friends from High Enlightenment had joined us. I didn't know where they had come from, but meeting them in a church didn't seem unrealistic.

We wandered around the base of the Redeemed Water Tower. After only a few moments, one of the High Enlightenment crew yelled. Dedare ran over to them and then shouted and held up a bag similar to the others. The rest of us rushed over and examined his prize.

I saw another small key and an even smaller item that looked like a painting. I shook my head because I decided I must be seeing things. Both items were miniscule.

"Syl, that second item looks like one of your paintings," said Sweety. "It's small and hard to make out, though."

Sweety's comment became the general agreement. "Okay, if this token is a painting, what's it trying to tell us?" I asked.

"Where do we find paintings in Ooby?" asked Richard. "I think we have to start with that question."

"No. Wrong question," said Sweety. "Where do Dedare and Syl have paintings? After all, they're Reena's parents."

The glances coming my way reinforced my sudden obsession. "Dedare, we need to get to our rooms. I have lots of paintings there. And, Testarn, go check out the painting you bought from me via Reena. Maybe there's a clue there. Cara, check out the paintings in my office. Someone may have broken in and left a clue."

I babbled, but I still thought my logic worked. "Everyone, keep thinking and looking."

After we returned to the hotel, we ran off in various directions. Dedare and I scurried home.

My paintings were piled in our bedroom and also in the living room in a corner.

Dedare and I hastily studied the pertinent areas, and then I had a thought. "Dedare, Reena had taken a few of my paintings so she could try and sell them to Testarn and other guests. May I enter her room?"

He didn't answer but simply grabbed my hand and led me to Reena's room. We dispersed to study her room's contents.

"Small bag," said Dedare after a few moments. He stood in front of one of my favorite paintings and pointed at the bottom.

Behold, another little bag. I picked up the bag and saw nothing—the bag was empty. What kind of clue was this?

My brain worked overtime. "Dedare, we need to …"

Suddenly, we were grabbed by a couple of black clad humanoids. Not an unusual occurrence for us, it seemed to me. Dedare and I broke free and ran into our spare room.

I'd become tired of their antics—whoever they were—so I tipped over one of my buckets of flat sided stones. The beads went everywhere, and Dedare followed suit with two more buckets. The Particlans went down, thank goodness.

"Dedare!" I yelled. He pushed the beads out of his way and went toward the Particlans. The beads were easy to get rid of if you knew what they were and weren't surprised by them.

Then Vara showed up.

I pulled out my knife, and Vara made a gun I'd never seen before appear. However, the attackers apparently had since they immediately stopped their antics. With Dedare's help, Vara tied them up. I pulled off their head coverings, and lo and behold Binti and Boonta appeared.

Vara and Dedare sat the attackers down in our living room, and Vara began his interrogation. In the meantime, our compatriots began arriving and calling. I managed to convince everyone to wait in the restaurant until we had news. Of course, I filled them in with our antics and my useful flat stones.

I anxiously awaited the result of Vara's interview. Reena was still missing.

Binti and Boonta's hands were tied behind their backs, and their feet were also bound. The twins appeared sad and scared. However, I didn't care since someone they most likely knew still imprisoned Reena.

"Anything tell me?" asked Vara of the boys.

I assumed he meant *do you have anything to tell me?*

Silence from the twins.

As a result, Vara turned to two of his officers who'd appeared.

"Take to cells. Separate from each. No contact allowed."

The twins understood they were being taken to the police station and put in separate cells since I recognized understanding in their eyes.

"Wish to talk," said one of them. I couldn't tell Binta and Boonta apart.

Vara studied them, and then asked, "Why five keys?"

"Do not know."

"Who in charge?" Vara perused their faces for any telltale signal I assumed.

No answer from the et Tong boys.

"Probably their mother," I commented to Vara.

The twins glanced at each other.

"What actions perform?" asked Vara.

"Attack alien parents. Abduct alien parents. Bring to leader."

"Who is leader?" asked Vara for a second time.

No answer.

"Where is Reena?" Vara continued. Dedare had been remarkably quiet.

No answer again, and I recognized Vara's annoyance.

"We're not getting very far." I glanced at Dedare to gauge the level of his anxiety.

"Off to jail," said Vara, gesturing to his two officers. "Put separate cells."

Vara's officers patted down the boys, searching for knives and such I assumed. I thought they would've done it earlier, but what did I know. One of the policemen handed a small package to Vara.

"Give to you. When to jail. Leader told us."

Vara waved at his officers to continue on their way with the prisoners and then bemusedly stared at the package in his hand.

"Perhaps we should join the others in the restaurant so we can analyze this package together. We'll have lots of crazy ideas." I caught Vara's eye and smiled.

He didn't argue, so off the three of us went.

Dedare and I explained the situation to the beings around our big table, and then Vara opened the bag we'd been given by the et Tong brothers. Vara pulled out a snack, a water bottle, a timer, and a piece of cloth.

After the items got to me, I said, "This looks like Reena's timer for timing her swimming laps and also a piece of her swimsuit. Anybody else recognize them?"

Sweety agreed with me regarding the swimsuit. She always knew what everyone wore. Clothes were her thing. And heaven help her children's wardrobe, which increased by the day.

"Well, that gives us a big clue. I think we need to go up to the Employee Training Facility," I said. "That's where Reena and I swim and dive and Reena times her laps. And she always had a snack and a bottle of water in her backpack. The items must mean our employee facility." A glimmer of hope cheered me. "Vara, what do you think?"

"Show me facility," he announced. "Everyone stay here."

I laughed. "That's not going to happen. At the minimum, Dedare and I will come with you. The kidnapper's probably expecting the two of us anyway."

"Everyone else stay," commanded Vara.

As Dedare and I stood up to follow Vara, I gave a glance at Richard and Thad. I hoped they understood my nonverbal suggestion.

I explained to Vara where the Employee Training Facility was and then I asked, "Should we be careful entering the room?"

"I go first," he responded.

Since Vara had some version of a gun and I didn't I'd let him lead the way. I had taken along my knife and my backpack, but my infamous beads were impossible to carry.

Dedare and I stood aside as Vara opened the door to the training facility.

"Come in police," said Samilt et Tong, the principal of Reena's school. "Bring along parents."

Samilt knew her boys were off to jail, otherwise we wouldn't have been given the final clue that led us to the Employee Training Center.

Dedare and I walked into the facility behind Vara and found Reena on the diving board. Samilt stood below.

"Where are sons?" asked Reena's principal in the typical Particlan three-word sentence.

"Going to jail. Attack Reena's parents. Justice from courts," said Vara.

Samilt et Tong took a moment to digest Vara's words. I assumed she realized we wouldn't be here without the clues from her sons, so Samilt needed to decide what to do to advance the situation for herself and also her family.

While Samilt digested Vara's words, I studied Reena and the Employee Training Center.

My first impression was that Reena sat comfortably on the diving board. Then I realized weights had been attached to her legs. If Samilt pushed her off, she'd sink to the bottom of the pool and drown. After I glanced at Dedare, I knew he'd also come to the same conclusion.

"Bring sons now. I release Reena. All be well."

I hoped Vara wouldn't agree to Samilt's terms. Of course, I knew little about the Particlan justice system and how Particlans would react in this instance, so I had no idea how Vara would respond to Samilt's words.

"Cannot allow sons. To be released. Must face justice," said Vara.

Samilt's face became deeper blue. Was this similar to when humans turned red as a result of stress?

Before she had the equivalent of a stroke or heart attack, Vara added, "Tarin and Saska. Do brothers agree. With your actions?"

Interesting question regarding her brothers Vara brought up.

Samilt studied Vara. I really wondered what her thought processes currently were.

Then she said, "Brothers will help. Release sons, jail. Bring siblings here."

Vara pointed at me, so I ran outside to find a quiet spot to call Tarin and Saska, Samilt's brothers. Their common emotional reaction was resignation. Perhaps Samilt really was a Particlan weirdo.

After I returned to the employee training room, I noticed the conversation had turned to why Samilt had abducted Reena.

"Reena's parents mixed. Alien parentage disallowed. Council and government."

"Are you sure? And why not?" I asked. "We've been welcomed everywhere we went. I have heard no questions or criticisms. And by the way I'm Reena's stepmother, not her genetic mother. Her Irion mother died when she was young."

I was going to make a comment about how aliens were *not* mixing romantically with Particlans, but then I remembered Teeka and Cara and kept my mouth shut.

At the front of the room, Samilt walked to have a conversation with Reena. Dedare and I hadn't been able to get close to Reena, but she appeared well. Although Samilt had tied Reena to the diving platform, she sat on a stool, and her demeanor indicated she hadn't apparently had to stand for any length of time.

However, she must be freaking out about the weights tied to her body. Poor girl.

"I hear the elevator, Samilt. I'm going to find out if your brothers are here. Is that okay?" I asked.

"Quickly return all."

"Sure. No problem." I raced outside and whispered to Tarin, the part owner of the hotel, and Saska, the Chief Motivator. And I gave an okay signal to Richard and Thad loitering with Sain and Teeka. I knew they had contingency plans, but I wanted to let them know the situation seemed under control.

I walked inside the Employee Training Center with Samilt's brothers and wondered what had possibly changed during my short absence.

Vara said to Tarin and Saska, "Samilt says you. Agree with her. Notions against aliens."

I watched Tarin think about Vara's statement and prepare words. I had no idea what he really thought about Samilt's ideas. They were siblings, though.

"Interesting ideas offered. With much weight. Being agreed upon," said Tarin.

I had no clue what Tarin meant, but Samilt smiled, so she at least understood Tarin's words in her bizarre way.

Saska added, "Join Samilt discuss. Agreement on principles. Moving forward today."

Samilt motioned her brothers toward her. The trio stood together and spoke for a few moments and then, all of a sudden, Samilt had been tied to the diving platform.

An unexpected happening. Tarin gestured us forward.

Tarin and Saska undid Reena's ties and weights, and Reena climbed down the diving platform and over to meet Dedare and me as we ran to her. Lots of hugs ensued. "Reena, are you okay?" I asked. "Are you hurt anywhere?"

"Not hurt. Thirsty and hungry. Long day."

Reena's spirits seemed positive. "Okay, let's go to the restaurant. Lots of food there," I added. Reena and I laughed. Yes, we'd be able to get anything we wanted. A wordless Dedare simply kept his arm wrapped around Reena. He needed nothing else at the moment. With such relief in my mind, I could only imagine what Dedare currently felt.

"Vara?" I asked.

"Questions for Reena. But sustenance first. Arrangements to make."

Vara made a call, and I assumed he'd contacted the police station to get a couple of officers to assist him in Samilt's arrest. As we left the hotel employee facility, I noticed he'd finished his call and now spoke with Samilt.

Reena, Dedare, and I settled at our big table. The other aliens were there, including the tourist trio and Cara unabashedly sitting beside Teeka.

"So, who's running the store?" I asked Cara. Cara had no idea what my words meant, so I explained.

"Assistant to Cara," she replied.

Her assistant had worked out well the other day, so she'd made an excellent choice. "Reena, remember to order lots of food, and you need fluid to rehydrate," I added.

"Yes, Mom," she replied with a smirk on her face.

I eventually realized my mouth hung open. I needed to get used to her calling me mother. I turned my head toward Dedare, and I found him gazing fondly on both of us. I decided we'd made much progress on this trip to Particle.

Just then the High Enlightenment group wanted my attention. "Join for meal?"

"Of course. You helped us out today in our search for Reena." So we added a table to ours, and the six of them joined us.

While Reena took care of ordering food for her health and well-being, I turned to Sweety. "How are you and the twins feeling?"

"Right now, quite calm. They were a little upset earlier, but everything is currently good." Sweety turned to Dedare. "Is there any way Hart and I can get a trip to Mars? Maybe holidays since we haven't taken any yet?"

Sweety had a point. We hadn't stayed long enough in one place to get into a routine. Would that change in the near future?

Vara created a distraction by joining us at our large table. "Did Samilt say why a small key was included in each bag?" I asked.

"Keys of group. High Enlightenment members. Samilt wishes recruits."

For a moment, I didn't understand any of Vara's comments, but then I remembered the High Enlightenment group entranced with my diving at the highest place in Ooby—or was it the highest place on the planet? I'd ask Cara later. Anyway, they were now at our table.

"Well, I think Samilt's plan failed. The High Enlightenment members loved me when they joined us on a tour, and they especially loved my diving. And they helped us out today to find the last key, and now they're at our table."

Vara glanced around and decided my words had some truth.

"Samilt under care. Psychiatric healing awaits. Her brothers organizing," Vara added.

Yeah, I didn't think the future would hold any problems for the off-worlders regarding Samilt. Of course, Reena's school needed to replace their principal.

"Reason for Mars trip understood," announced Dedare, glancing at Sweety and her swollen tummy. "Another reason..."

Dedare took hold of my left hand and rubbed my engagement ring. "Marriage on Mars?" he asked me.

To clarify his Irion terseness, I asked, "You want to get married on Mars? You want to take a trip to Mars soon?"

Dedare reached out and rubbed my cheek in front of my friends and relatives. How embarrassing. "Ah, Dedare..."

My mother interrupted, so Dedare stopped rubbing. "That's an excellent idea, Dedare. It's about time you two got married. However, before you guys leave and get married on Mars and Sweety has her babies there, Charles and I want to marry here on Particle. This place is special to us, and not only because I've discovered a stepson." Mom beamed at Thad.

"Mom and Dad, how excellent!" I said. I ran over and gave them a hug. Thad wasn't far behind. So we had a foursome hug or two.

Sweety raised herself from her chair. "Pictures are needed." So the four of us obliged Sweety as she took numerous potentially embarrassing pictures.

"Mama A, I hope you'll let me help you plan your wedding to Charles. I have so many ideas," exclaimed Sweety. "And we did such a fantastic job on my wedding to Hart."

"Of course, of course. We did design a spectacular Irion wedding, didn't we," said my mother.

"Thanks to you," said Sweety. "You and I make the best planners. We'll start tomorrow." Sweety grinned as she glanced around the table. "Mama A, maybe we should start a business designing alien weddings."

Conversation stopped as the concept was examined, so I jumped in.

"Now that you guys are organized for your future, it's my turn," I said. "Dedare and I *were* discussing our wedding."

"Oops, sorry about that," said my mother. She grinned and gave me a hug from where she sat in the chair beside me.

I shook my head. I held the hand with my engagement ring out to Dedare, and he grabbed on.

"Dedare, do you wish to marry me?" I asked.

He rubbed my cheek as he responded, "Yes, yes, yes." Quite wordy for an Irion.

"Would you like to be married on Mars?"

"Yes, yes, yes." He pulled me close and rubbed my hair.

"Would you like a second ceremony on Irion? We could invite your parents and Reena's other grandparents to attend, and your friends, of course. The grandparents will be pleased, I imagine." Since I'd made a wild guess, I watched Dedare closely. "I'm sure you can get them away from their retirement planet."

Everyone laughed, and Dedare seemed to agree with my suggestion since he said, "Second wedding with family and friends on Irion. Agreeable."

"Ah, Dedare. Stay on Particle and do hotel security," said Teeka, interrupting our moment. His Irion terseness was understandable, for once.

"And keep close to Cara, I imagine," I added. "Well, her mother is here to keep an eye on the two of you. I'll have a little chat with her before I leave, though." Laughter abounded.

And then Vara added a question. "Join Dedare, friends?"

"Someone to replace Teeka," suggested Dedare.

An excellent idea, from my point of view—as long as he didn't want to go out for dinner.

So we continued to make plans long into the evening. Reena was home, and our world was on an even keel again.

****

Apparently our first action would be to plan Mom and Dad's wedding on Particle. While Teeka and Cara learned about becoming co-general managers of this hotel, I'd advise them and also manage the hotel's Olympic team. Then it was off to Mars, where Dedare and I would get married and Hart and Sweety would have babies.

Then Dedare had suggested a return to Irion to check up on the hotel and have our second wedding with Irion guests and his family and friends. And of course I would be able to once again communicate with hotel employees and help run the Sath-Satre Golden Hotel.

Then it was a tossup as to whether we would return to Particle or to Mars. Apparently, Dedare had his eye on buying the Mars Best-Tycho Basin hotel—my old stomping grounds.

Of course, alien plans are always subject to change.

GLOSSARY

CHARACTERS

Humans – Homeworld: Mars
Sylvestine Amera
- Aka Syl
- On Mars, hotel Manager of the Mars Best-Tycho Basin Hotel; on Irion, hotel manager of the Sath-Satre Golden Hotel; and on Particle, general manager of the Sath-Ooby Golden Hotel.
- Engaged to Dedare Sath.
- Daughter of Sylvia Amera and Charles Clarke.
Sylvia Amera
- Aka Mama A to Syl's friends
- Mother to Sylvestine Amera
- Author, Historian for Sath Enterprises
Charles Clarke
- Ambassador; representing human interests on newly found alien home worlds
- Father to Sylvestine Amera (recently revealed)
- Engaged to Sylvia Amera
Hart Adair
- BFF to Sylvestine Amera
- Worked at Mars U (University of Mars); scientist and medical doctor
- Married Sweety Finn on Irion
- Works for Dedare Sath
Sweety Finn
- BFF to Sylvestine Amera
- Socialite on Mars
- Married Hart Adair on Irion
- Works for Dedare Sath

Thaddeus Trent
- Half-brother of Sylvestine Amera
- Son of Charles Clarke

Irions – Homeworld: Irion
Dedare Sath
- Irion businessman; in particular, owner of Sath-Satre Golden Hotel on Irion, and Sath-Ooby Golden Hotel on Particle
- Hired Sylvestine Amera to run his flagship hotel on Irion (Sath-Satre Golden Hotel), and now on Particle (Sath-Ooby Golden Hotel)
- Engaged to Sylvestine Amera
- Father of Reena Sath
- Brother of Sain Sath
Reena Sath
- Daughter of Dedare Sath and Gyra Sath (deceased)
- Niece of Sain Sath
- Irion teenager
Sain Sath
- Brother to Dedare Sath
- Uncle to Reena Sath
- Involved in Sath Enterprises (security and construction)
Teeka Cole
- Irion homicide detective
- Friend of Dedare Sath

Particlans – Homeworld: Particle
Cara ast Hembole
- Reception Manager of the Sath-Ooby Golden Hotel

Tarin et Tong

- Co-owner of Sath-Ooby Golden Hotel (with Dedare Sath)
- Brother of Saska et Tong
- Brother of Samilt et Tong

Slia est Parcet

- Head botanist of Sath-Ooby Golden Hotel

Axert al Tiste

- Head of Particlan Planetary Council

Saska et Tong

- High priest of a religion
- Brother of Tarin et Tong
- Brother of Samilt et Tong

Baria tas Confit

- Sath-Ooby Golden Hotel seamstress

Vara il Vast

- Particlan police officer in charge of investigation into attacks on aliens

Sara ild Tamark

- Housekeeping and cleaning at Sath-Ooby Golden Hotel
- Swimmer wishing to be on hotel's Olympic team
- New friend to Reena Sath

Tamars ata Vilue

- Reception clerk at Sath-Ooby Golden Hotel

Chef Petra

-Restaurant chef at Sath-Ooby Golden Hotel

Chef Mastis tel Ramand

- Restaurant chef at Ooby City Restaurant

Villa est Tenka

- Reception tour guide at Sath-Ooby Golden Hotel

Meeta tas Eldon

- Security, Library at Sath-Ooby Golden Hotel
Jesto las Habbo
- Assistant to Cara ast Hembole (Reception Manager of Sath-Ooby Golden Hotel)
Noora pic Petane
- Chief Server at Sath-Ooby Golden Restaurant
Chera ast Hembole
- Mother of Cara ast Hembole
Samilt et Tong
- Principal of Reena's high school on Particle: Heeght-Ooby Pre-School
- Sister to Tarin et Tong
- Sister to Saska et Tong
- Mother of Binti and Boota et Tong
Binti and Boota et Tong
- Twin brothers
- School acquaintances of Reena
- Sons of Samilt et Tong
- Nephews of Tarin and Saska et Tong

Sarturn: Homeworld: Sarturn
Testarn
- Tourist on holiday on Particle

Hotels
- Mars: Mars Best-Tycho Basin Hotel
- Irion: Sath-Satre Golden Hotel
- Particle: Sath-Ooby Golden Hotel

A word about the author...

After accumulating books on writing for many years, Roxanne kicked 30 years of procrastination out the door in 2011 and started writing. In addition to novels, numerous minimalistic science fiction poems were also published in many magazines. Roxanne can be contacted at hyperlight@hyperwarp.com.

Publications (novels)
    Revolutions
    Sacred Trust
    Alien Innkeeper
    Alien Innkeeper on Particle
    Kaiku
    An Alien Collective / An Alien Perspective
    An Alien Confluence

Thank you for purchasing
this publication of The Wild Rose Press, Inc.

For questions or more information
contact us at
info@thewildrosepress.com.

The Wild Rose Press, Inc.
www.thewildrosepress.com